Out *of* TIME

A Novel

M. Jacqueline Murray

COLE JACOBS BOOKS LLC

Out of Time. Copyright © 2022 by M. Jacqueline Murray
All rights reserved. No part of this book may be scanned, reproduced, or distributed without permission. If you would like to use material from this book, please contact: Cole Jacobs Books, LLC
www.colejacobsbooks.com

ISBN: 978-0-9991493-3-1 (Hardcover)
ISBN: 978-0-9991493-6-2 (Jacketed hardcover)
ISBN: 978-0-9991493-4-8 (Paperback)
ISBN: 978-0-9991493-5-5 (eBook)

DEDICATION

For Mike

CHAPTER 1

It was a glorious June afternoon and the sun spotlighted us through the car's open sunroof. We sang along with *The Temptations*.

"I've got sunshine… on a cloudy day…."

My daughter Anne always prepares a soundtrack for road trips. She was in high school when we started our mother-daughter travels and she crowned herself the 'Travel Mixtape Queen'. Of course, it's not a cassette tape anymore, it's a playlist on her iPhone. The technology may have changed but certain songs are always in the mix. *My Girl* is one of our songs.

I'd been looking forward to this trip for months. Being retired, I had plenty of time and flexibility for us to travel together. Unfortunately, Anne didn't. Her work had become more demanding and hectic. We'd not been on a trip together since last fall, breaking our decades-old pact to do something "away" at least once a quarter. As a single parent, I'd promised her, and myself, that I'd make time for us to see the world, and we had.

As soon as I stepped out of the car, I knew she'd been right. I'd wanted to book at one of the small hotels in town, but she'd insisted on this B&B for our stay in Bar Harbor, Maine. The picture-perfect lighthouse, the expanse of ocean, the sound of the waves crashing on rocks, the smell of the sea, and the sun on my face – I breathed it all in. It felt right to be here.

I looked over at her as she opened the trunk to pull out our bags. Seeing my face, she broke out into her version of the 'I told you so' dance from the *Will and Grace* show. I gave her my best eye-roll as she continued her silly stir the pot, washing machine gyrations, singing, "I told you so, I told you so, I told you, told you, told you so." I couldn't deny it; this place looked amazing.

It had already been a long day, but I felt a burst of energy as we crunched up the gravel path to the open front door of the two-story, red and white house beside the lighthouse. Anne abandoned our bags with me at the door and hurried over to the group gathered in the large room just off the foyer. She scooped up baby Jake.

"Come here you little monkey." Jake let out a little cry. She jiggled and rocked him and cooed, "I'm your Godmother, so you better get used to me."

Anne was delighted to be Jake's Godmother. His mother Emily had worked for Anne for several years, first as an intern, then full-time after graduation. Anne started as her mentor, but over the years, they'd become good friends. When Emily heard I'd be visiting Anne the same weekend as the baptism, she extended an invitation to me and insisted I join them for the celebrations. Anne decided to take a couple of days off work so we'd have time to explore Bar Harbor instead of heading back to Boston immediately afterward.

Emily's mother's name was also Ann, spelled without the "e". I'm glad Anne's namesake grandmother spelled it with an "e". It feels more complete somehow. Watching Anne fuss over Jake in his white lace outfit, I couldn't help but think back to her baptism day. It didn't seem possible that it was 45 years ago.

Lost in my reverie, I was startled by a soft voice saying, "You must be Mrs. Tobias?"

"No, I'm Ms. Cole. Maddie Cole."

It wasn't unusual for people to assume I had the same last name as my daughter. However, my correction came out sounding harsh. I turned to the voice and looked into the dark and slightly puzzled eyes of a handsome gray-haired gentleman. He was a little taller than me, maybe six feet, broad-shouldered, not thin, but fit-looking. I recognized him from earlier at the church for the Baptism. He'd been wearing a sport coat, but now, was dressed simply in a white dress shirt and blue dress pants. I admired how his clothing was completely free of wrinkles because I can never seem to stay unwrinkled.

"Pleased to meet you, Ms. Maddie Cole, I'm Nate Jacobs, Jake's great-grandfather. Welcome to the Hope Point Inn."

I was so preoccupied contemplating the crispness of his shirt that I didn't realize he'd extended his hand. He withdrew it before I could return his handshake.

I was embarrassed to be caught gawking at his clothing. "I'm sorry."

Nate smiled and chuckled. "It really is true. You Canadians say 'sorry' even when you've done nothing to be sorry for."

I extended my hand and smiled. "Nice to meet you, Mr. Jacobs. It seems you know a little too much about me already."

Nate continued to smile as he shook my hand. "Emily might have shared a few details in advance of your arrival. You can leave your bags here. Come, join the party." He ushered me towards the other guests. "Can I get you something to drink?"

"That would be lovely. I'm parched."

"We have beer, wine, soda, iced tea, water..."

"I should start with some water, but I'd love a glass of wine."

"Red or white?"

"Red, please."

Nate left me standing by Anne and the baby. Anne was still cooing at Jake. I looked around the room and spotted a stack of gifts on a small table. I moved towards it, rummaging in my purse for the card I'd brought so I could put it with the other gifts. As I did, Nate reappeared with water and wine for me.

"I brought both. I guessed you'd like sparkling water. Is that OK?"

"Perfect! It's like you read my mind."

He beamed and seemed delighted he'd guessed correctly. He turned and pointed across the room. "If you need the facilities, there's a powder room down the hall past that window. I need to go check on the kitchen. Do you need anything else?"

"Nothing. Thank you. Please don't let me keep you."

Thirsty, I downed the glass of water. I felt silly holding both glasses and my purse. I looked around, but saw no obvious place to set my empty glass.

The room we'd gathered in was spacious and bright with several large windows facing the ocean. There was a small counter in a closet-sized nook next to the foyer where we'd entered. Behind the counter, on the wall, there were what appeared to be antique wooden message boxes with a key hanging below each one. The room itself was furnished with a variety of small sofas and chairs arranged in small groupings. One cluster was centred on a large stone fireplace that had wood set in place ready to light.

The décor was nautical, but not in a predictable way. Many of the furnishings were dark wood and leather. There was a steamer trunk as the base of a glass-topped coffee table and a ship's bell reading lamp on the reception counter. But what gave the room its real character, were the numerous models of ships and boats, ranging from a well-used antique child's toy to a delicate pulled glass sailboat that looked like Murano glass.

"It's time for lunch," announced Nate, taking the empty glass from my hand and ushering us all toward a double door that led to a sunny patio with a long table shaded by big umbrellas. Anne relinquished Jake to Emily and came to stand by me.

"I saw you met Nate, Emily's grandfather." She leaned in and whispered, "He doesn't look like a great-grandfather, does he?"

As we watched him directing people, seating the ladies, overseeing, like a maître d', the two white-shirted young women who were carrying platters of sandwiches and bowls of salad. He did seem too young to be a great-grandfather.

"He must have started young," I mused. "Unlike me. Having you at the ancient age of 32. You'd be at least 10 years older had I been a more conventional woman of my time."

Anne gave me a playful elbow jab. "I guess unconventional women run in the family."

After lunch, cake, and gift opening, the family and friends who had come to celebrate little Jake's Baptism began to leave. Anne gave Jake one last big kiss and hugged Emily goodbye. Anne and I were left by ourselves on the patio while Nate went to see his family off.

Nate returned a little while later. "I suppose it's about time I showed you ladies to your rooms."

"We're enjoying the view," said Anne, "but, that would be great."

Nate held open the patio door for us. "Ladies, please come this way."

Anne went to the foyer and grabbed our bags. We followed him down a hallway off the main room and up a steep wooden staircase to the second floor.

"Anne, this will be your room." He opened the door to the first room at the top of the stairs and handed her the key. "And this room is for you, Ms. Cole," he announced emphasizing my name; clearly teasing me.

"You may call me Maddie, Mr. Jacobs," I replied echoing his formality as I passed him to enter my room.

"Well then Maddie," he said winking, "you may call me Nate."

The room was quite large with plenty of room to move even though it was furnished with a queen-size four-poster bed with bright white linens, a dresser, a small upholstered armless chair, and an antique desk under the window facing the water. It struck me as odd that the room had one wall painted white while the others were a deep sea-green colour.

"This is our 'Dover' room," said Nate.

"Ahhh, the White Cliffs of Dover," I said, clueing in to the one white wall.

"Yes," said Nate, handing me the room key. "Each of our rooms is named for a place. My late wife Betsy loved to come up with interesting ways to decorate each room after its namesake."

"How creative."

"If you'd like to see the rest of the inn and grounds after you've settled in, please come find me in the kitchen and I'll give you a tour," he said before leaving us and heading downstairs.

"That sounds lovely," I called after him.

Anne was in my room seconds later. "Isn't this place great?" she bubbled. "My room is called 'Tokyo'. You've got to come see it."

Anne's room had pale pink walls and a large painting of cherry trees in full bloom. The bedding was again white, but the decorative pillows had a red band around them with black katakana script. I recognized it as Japanese but had no idea what it said. Like mine, the room had a dresser, a small desk under the window, and an upholstered chair. But the furnishings in her room were more delicate, Asian-looking black lacquer, and quite different from the old-world antique pieces in my room.

Anne was unloading her bag onto the bed.

"I'm going to unpack a bit myself," I said, "Then I'm going to take Nate up on his offer to show me the rest of the place. Are you going to join me?"

"I need a nap first."

"Naps are evil, but I can wait for you."

"You go ahead when you're ready. I'll catch up."

I left Anne in 'Tokyo' and went back to 'Dover'. My first priority was finding a plug to charge my camera battery, phone, and iPad. For a woman, 78 years young, I'm still a technology-loving engineer at heart. I found a plug beside the desk but as I stood up from plugging in my adaptors, my elbow struck the large model of a ferry boat perched on a wooden stand on the desk. The boat listed perilously. I picked it up to set it right and took a closer look.

It was an intricate model, about 18 inches long, of a blue and white P&O ferry. As I carefully balanced it back in its cradle, I noticed the name, it was the MS Pride of Dover. I wondered if all the rooms had boats in them, as I'd noticed a model of a Japanese-looking boat in Anne's room as well.

I had, as usual, over-packed. I'd made a list of possible things for us to see and do, but, as was our travel custom, we decided to play it by ear based on the weather and our mood. So, I'd added a few extra things 'just in case'.

I smiled to myself as I arranged my toiletries on the small shelf over the vanity of the ensuite bath. Having travelled the world together for decades, Anne knew having to make sure I was 'decent' first thing in the morning to use a shared bath just irritated me. She'd assured me I'd have a private bath, and to my delight, Dover had an enchanting full bath; complete with a toy boat perched on the rim of the tub and a view of the lighthouse from a high round window that made me think of a ship's portal.

Once I'd unpacked and arranged things, I checked out my appearance in the full-length standing mirror. It had been warm on the patio for lunch, so I'd removed the jacket of my suit and rolled up the sleeves of my blouse. My blouse still looked pretty good, but my dress pants were unacceptably wrinkled. I changed into a pair of jeans and swapped my heels for a pair of sneakers, so I'd be more comfortable.

I considered waiting for Anne, but I was restless and I was looking forward to exploring the grounds and lighthouse. I headed downstairs along the hallway past the main sitting room where we had first gathered and to the far end of the building. I passed the doorway to the patio and walked through a dining area until I found the doorway to a spacious kitchen. Despite the large professional appliances, the room was homey and welcoming.

Nate had his back to me and looked busy. I paused, debating if I should interrupt his work. I felt a wave of self-consciousness and I almost turned to slip away. But remembering how sincerely he'd offered to show me around, I took a deep breath and walked into the kitchen.

CHAPTER 2

Running a B&B doesn't feel like work. I'm still surprised how much pleasure I get from simple things like doing the prep work for the next day's breakfast. Before buying this place, I'd been tempted to invest in a restaurant one of my golf buddies was opening with a chef friend. I'd decided against it because I'd been underwhelmed by the chef's first restaurant. But it got me thinking about how much I'd enjoyed working in kitchens as a younger man. From my college days working the graveyard shift at the local diner in St. Petersburg Florida to now making breakfast for my B&B guests; working in a kitchen, feeding people, has always been gratifying.

As I went about my daily prep routine, I found myself thinking of Ms. Maddie Cole and how much I was looking forward to showing her around. Just as that thought crossed my mind, she appeared at the door of my kitchen. She was strikingly lovely. Her blonde and gray shoulder-length hair framed her oval face, her hazel eyes were bright and friendly, and she held her head high. I couldn't help but notice, and admire, her pleasantly curvy figure.

She stopped just inside the kitchen door. "I hope I'm not interrupting you."

"Of course not," I said, wiping my hands and moving around the large island in the center of the kitchen to greet her. "Let me just tidy this up." I pointed to the vegetables I was chopping. "Then I can show you around my humble inn. In the meantime, can I get you a glass of wine?"

She looked at my prep area with concern. "I don't want to impose…"

"No problem. Please sit. I'll pour you some wine. Red, right?"

"Yes, please." Her face was lit up by her lovely smile as she settled on one of the stools along the backside of the kitchen island.

I'd already set out glasses and opened a Barbera d'Asti, one of my favorites, in anticipation of offering her a glass. I poured the wine, placing one glass in front of her and one for myself near my cutting board.

"I won't be too long," I explained. "I'm prepping for your breakfast tomorrow. Do you like frittata or are you more of a sweet breakfast eater?"

"I'm not a big breakfast eater, but coffee is a necessity," she said apologetically. "It's a lifelong addiction of mine. As for what to eat, I'm not picky. Whatever you make will certainly be fine with me."

"I can do almost any kind of coffee for you; espresso, cappuccino, latte, or good old American coffee," I said, sounding a bit like a human menu. "I'm a coffee man myself. I got hooked on great espresso when in Italy and sometimes nothing else will do."

She grinned. "Sounds like you're a man after my own heart, Mr. Jacobs. Can I put in my order for a cappuccino right now?"

Her eyes were bright, and I couldn't help grinning. "As you wish, My Lady."

I noticed she'd not reached for her wine, so I picked up my glass and raised it to her with a "Cheers". She raised her glass in return and took a sip of wine.

"This wine is very nice," she said, after a few seconds of sniffing, savoring, and holding the glass to the light to examine it.

"I'm glad you like it. It's one of my favorites, Italian, a Barbera from Piedmonte."

"I'm a fan of all things Italian. Food, wine ... shoes". She had a cute mischievous look. "One can never have too many pairs of Italian shoes."

I shook my head. "I've never understood women and their need for so many pairs of shoes. I think I could get by with a pair of black dress shoes and a pair of sneakers and be fine for the rest of my life."

She chuckled and shook her head. "You don't want to know how many pairs I brought for our three-night stay."

Her laugh made her seem much younger than I knew she must be. I guessed she was close to my age because her Anne was of similar age to my Ann. I was curious, but I knew better than to make assumptions or ask a lady about her age. I focused on finishing my prep work while she chatted to me about her shoes.

When I had cleaned up and put everything away, I asked if we should wait for Anne to start our tour.

Maddie hopped off her stool. "She's napping. We can start without her."

"Well, this is the kitchen," I made an exaggerated arm gesture. "It's been renovated and expanded from the original as we needed more space when we turned this house, which was originally a private home, into a B&B."

Maddie nodded. "It's a very cook-friendly kitchen. I bet you could prepare enough food to feed a small army in here."

"Thankfully, I don't have to. We have four double rooms. A couple of them, like yours, have space for a cot. But most of our guests are couples looking for a romantic getaway. So, when we're full, it's usually eight guests and me."

"How long have you had the B&B?"

"We bought it almost 20 years ago, in 1997, and immediately began renovations to turn it into a B&B."

"Have you always been in the hospitality business?"

"No, I was a lawyer, corporate law."

"Whatever possessed you to buy a B&B?"

"I've always enjoyed cooking and entertaining and had this dream of one day running a restaurant. Then walking through Heathrow Airport in 1996, I saw an exhibit of photographs and there was this picture of a red and white house beside a lighthouse overlooking a rocky shore. I thought to myself that it would make a great B&B. Shortly after I returned home from that trip, I saw a real estate listing for a similar-looking place in the paper. And the rest, as they say, is history."

"You said a photography exhibit at Heathrow in 1996? A lighthouse photo?"

"Yes. Why?"

"You're not going to believe this coincidence, but that could have been my photograph!"

"What? How is that possible?"

"Heathrow was celebrating its 50th birthday and there was an open photography contest. One of the categories was 'all the places you can fly from Heathrow' and my photo of a Newfoundland lighthouse was chosen for their 'New World' section."

"Are you a professional photographer?"

"No, an engineer," she said holding up her right hand and pointing to a dull ring on her pinky. "I think I just got lucky with that one. But I've loved taking pictures since I got my first Leica M3 camera for my 16th birthday. My grandfather bought it for me. He said 'Maddie, you look at the world in your own way. I'd like to see what you see. Take pictures.' And I did. I'm sorry I'm babbling on about me…"

"My tour will seem dull compared to learning about you, I'm sure."

As she looked at me, I thought I detected a slight blush on her face. There was something about looking into her eyes that drew me in. I momentarily lost my train of thought.

"I doubt that," said Maddie.

"It's lovely out," I said recovering, "Warmer than usual for this time in June. How about we start outside and see the grounds and the lighthouse first?"

"Would it be OK if I took some pictures?"

"Of course."

"I'll just run and grab my camera; I forgot it in my room."

"Take your time. I'll meet you in the foyer."

Maddie left me and headed towards her room. I couldn't help thinking about the remarkable coincidence she had a photograph in the same exhibition that gave me the idea for this place. It was bitter-sweet thinking about traveling with Betsy; particularly that trip.

Although there were many opportunities for Betsy to travel with me on my business trips, she rarely did until Ann moved to England. Only then did she agree to accompany me if my trip was to the UK, or somewhere in Europe, where I could arrange a stopover to spend time with Ann.

When I retired, I had hoped Betsy and I would travel more. We wouldn't be limited to my few weeks of vacation or the few days I could extend my business trips. I hoped we would take long trips where we could thoroughly explore great cities or maybe cruise around the world. That plan was not to be.

Betsy insisted our first trip once I retired would be to see Ann. They were still living in London at the time and Emily was a toddler. Their flat was too small to accommodate us, so we stayed at a hotel nearby. We spent a couple of weeks doing toddler-friendly activities like going to the park or to the Natural History Museum to see the dinosaurs. I suggested we take a train trip to the seaside, but Betsy didn't want to 'waste time' being away from Ann and Emily.

We returned to England a couple of years later when Ann and Lane moved to Oxford. They wanted to be closer to Lane's family and have Emily attend the same elementary school Lane had attended without having her board there. Other than the trips to see Ann and an extended winter stay in Florida each year, Betsy had no interest in traveling.

About five years after I retired, Betsy was diagnosed with breast cancer. Betsy didn't want to tell Ann about her diagnosis over the phone or in a letter. We had a couple of months before Betsy was scheduled for her surgery. So, before she started her treatment, we decided to go see Ann. She was delighted when we told her we were coming for an extended visit, but she didn't know the underlying motivation for the trip.

Telling Ann about her mother's diagnosis had been the hardest part. She'd burst into tears. Lane, her husband, had hugged her and then went to put the kettle on to make tea. 'Time to make tea' became Betsy's code phrase for when things were getting too stressful, or sad, and it was time to change the subject. We drank a lot of tea.

Betsy had wanted to use the trip to make happy memories. We took trips by train or car with Ann, Lane, and Emily, who was only 7 or 8 at the time. Using Oxford as our home base, we went to London several times with Ann during the week, but each weekend we crammed into Lane's car and headed in a different direction: northwest to Liverpool and Manchester, southwest to Southampton, and southeast to Dover.

I'd insisted we be at the airport the suggested two hours in advance of our return flight. As it turned out, we had quite a bit of time to kill. We had walked past a series of photographs on the way to our gate. At the end of the corridor, there was a sign about the photo exhibition and a map of the terminal showing where the other groupings were displayed. Betsy was happy to sit at our gate and wait for our flight to depart, but I was restless. So, I went for a walk to explore the other exhibition areas.

I distinctly remember seeing the photograph of a house and lighthouse with a stormy sea in the background. I recall thinking living by the sea was something that had always called to me, and perhaps it was the reason I felt compelled to surround myself with boats. I realized I wanted to have a place where I could entertain guests, like the house pictured with the lighthouse.

Over the years, I accumulated many boats for my collection on business trips and on trips to see Ann. Betsy had tolerated my boat obsession as long as they stayed confined to my office at work and my den at home. Because I'd accumulated so many on that trip, including the ferry boat that is on the desk in the Dover room, I had to have them packaged up and shipped home. In the weeks waiting for them to arrive, I found and purchased the Hope Point lighthouse property.

Instead of traveling myself, I focused my energy on remodeling the house as a B&B to entertain travelers. Within a year we relocated to Bar Harbor from Boston. There was no need to downsize as we were moving to a much larger house that accommodated everything we owned, including my boat collection. Because we'd decided on a nautical theme for the B&B, Betsy had agreed to let my boats populate the rooms – within reason.

CHAPTER 3

As I climbed the stairs to get my camera, I marveled at the coincidence; my photograph in the same exhibit that inspired Nate. I remembered the rush of excitement and pride I'd felt when I received the invitation and airline ticket to attend the exhibit opening. It was a black-tie affair. Even though I hate dress shopping, that was one of the few times in my life I was motivated to get the perfect outfit. I went to the most fashionable shop I knew in downtown Toronto where the designer herself helped me pick just the right outfit. As I stood by my photo in the exhibit area with a glass of champagne in hand, I felt like a celebrity. For one night I was a professional photographer, an artist, and it felt like a dream. I haven't thought about that trip in years. Looking back, I could have taken more time to savor the moment. I believed I couldn't leave my business in anyone's hands for too long. So, I flew to London for the event and home the next day.

I took my camera from my purse, checked the battery. It was low so I switched it with the one that was charging. Over the last 10 years, I've made the switch to digital. I had my Nikon 35mm SLR for so long it was like I was abandoning an old friend the first time I left it at home and took my digital camera instead. The instant gratification of seeing my picture on the spot, without having to wait to develop the film, was addicting. Anne teases me about how many pictures I take of the same subject because I no longer have the limitation of running out of film. Looking out the window to the water, the lighthouse, and the late afternoon light, I was glad I'd brought my better camera.

I headed back downstairs to meet Nate and he was waiting for me in the foyer. "Do you want to climb the lighthouse?"

"Absolutely!"

"Then we'll start our tour there." He opened the front door and gestured me to go ahead. "After you."

Even though it was late afternoon, the sun was still high, and it was very warm. Nate started his tour commentary as we walked along the path leading from the door towards the lighthouse.

"The house was formerly the lighthouse keeper's home, so this path has likely been here as long as the lighthouse, which dates back to the early 1800s. Now the light is automated and electric, but originally the light source was an oil lamp that needed to be tended multiple times a day. This is one of the few privately-owned and still operating lighthouses in Maine."

I got the impression he was quite proud of that last fact because he stood a little straighter and held his head a little higher as he unlocked the red door and swung it inward.

It was dim inside the lighthouse. As my eyes adjusted, I looked up into the brick conical tower about 20 feet across at the bottom. The interior of the tower was dominated by an iron staircase spiraling up the perimeter of the inside. The only light came from 3 windows, spaced at about 1/3 intervals up the staircase, and from an opening at the top of the tower.

"It's 88 steps to the top. Are you OK with a climb?" asked Nate.

"Yes, I might be slow, but I take every chance I get to have a bird's eye view."

"We're not in any hurry. My knees aren't what they once were, so I take my time climbing." He gestured for me to go ahead of him. "After you."

I began climbing, but resisted the urge to count the stairs, deciding it was better to just move towards the light at a steady pace. In my mind, I'm the same adventurous gal who always said yes to any challenge put in front of her. The reality, that I'm not as young as I think I am, is sometimes made clear to me when it's a physical challenge I've undertaken.

The stairs ended on a platform that ran around the lighthouse lantern. The lantern room was about 10 feet across. In the center were large, thick, cut-glass panes with the light source behind them.

"When does the light come on?" I asked.

"It's on from sunset to sunrise each day. In the old days, the lighthouse keeper had to come light and extinguish the lamp each day, but now it's automatic. The keepers also used to have to clean the Fresnel, which is this glass part that focuses the light into a characteristic pattern that can be recognized from far away. The keepers used to have to clean them every day when the lamps were oil-burning because they got sooty and clouded over. Now it only needs to be checked and cleaned each month because it has an electric bulb, and the windows are modern, so they don't let in birds or rain. I'm told there was also a fog bell at one time, but it isn't here anymore."

"How interesting. I've never been inside a lighthouse, just photographed them from a distance." I genuinely found it all fascinating. I took out my camera and took close-up photographs of the multi-faceted Fresnel lens.

"Would you like to go outside?"

"Can we?" I asked, surprised.

"Yes, but you must go out the window." He opened one of the large windows and swung it inward. "Watch your step."

I hadn't noticed the upper catwalk from the ground since it was painted white and, from below, blended into the lighthouse. I clambered out the window and walked around, eager to take in the view from all directions. If I wasn't already breathless from the climb, the stunning view would have taken my breath away. I looked down at the house and garden and out to sea. The sun was reflecting off the water. There was a bright white cruise ship moving out to sea, and numerous seagulls soaring and squawking. As I came back around to the open window, I saw Nate had not followed me out but was standing half in and half out of the window holding on to the large glass pane.

He must have sensed my curiosity. "The catwalk is very safe, I'm just not fond of heights."

"I've always loved heights." I started another slow walk around. I took several pictures from each side and even one of Nate straddling the window when he wasn't looking. Seeing his expression as he looked out to sea, I imagined the lighthouse keepers of old looking for ships on the horizon.

Nate swung his leg back inside the window. "Ready to head back down?"

I nodded and Nate held out his hand to help me back through the window. "Thank you for bringing me up here. The view is amazing."

Going down the stairs was considerably easier. When we emerged from the lighthouse, we continued in the direction away from the house and around to the ocean side of the lighthouse. As we did, I could see its foundation sat on a large pink granite outcrop that ended in a steep cliff. On the far side, there was a low stone building Nate said was the boat shed, but it wasn't in great shape, so we'd skip going inside. Between the two were stone steps leading down to the water. At the base of the stairs, there was a narrow strip of pebbled beach that infilled a tiny cove sheltered by the rock face below the lighthouse.

Like a good tour guide, he continued to offer information. "Not much of a beach. We have a couple of kayaks, and this is the best spot to launch them. Even at high tide, it's easy to pop them in the water from the base of the steps, as long as it's not too rough. If you and Anne would like to use them. Just let me know. I'll have them brought out for you."

We didn't go down the steps to the water but continued past the lighthouse. In the space between the lighthouse and the cliff, there was a small garden with numerous small bushes including at least a dozen rose bushes with buds that were just starting to open. At the far end of the garden, there was a heavy stone bench facing out to sea and a large flawless fir tree.

"This is my attempt at a formal garden," said Nate. "One must always have some shrubbery."

"A shrubbery? One that looks nice, and not too expensive," I said in a silly voice.

Nate laughed. "Yes, a shrubbery to appease the *Knights Who Say Ni.*"

"I can't hear the word shrubbery without thinking of '*The Holy Grail*'."

"I'm a Python fan myself, silly walks, lumberjacks, and the Spanish Inquisition."

"No one expects the Spanish Inquisition!"

We both chuckled.

I shook my head in shame. "It's terrible watching Monty Python with me. I laugh before the funny parts. Doesn't matter how many times I see their sketches; they make me laugh."

"You're an interesting woman Ms. Maddie Cole. Photographer, engineer, Python fan…"

"Interesting? A kind way of saying 'odd'."

He looked directly into my eyes and said, with much sincerity, "I didn't mean that at all."

His expression was as if he was admiring something fascinating. It was unnerving, so I was relieved that, just then, Anne came around the lighthouse and called out, "Hey there, I was wondering where you were!"

"I was just showing your mother around. Would you like to join us?"

"Sounds great," said Anne with an enthusiastic smile.

"We already went up the lighthouse before you arrived. Do you want to climb up?"

"Did you take pictures?" Anne asked me.

"Of course. The view is incredible."

"Then I'll see the pictures." Anne looked at Nate and shrugged. "Not a fan of heights."

"Neither am I. Shall we head inside and see the rest of the house?"

"OK," Anne and I replied in unison.

Anne took my arm and we followed Nate back to the house. We crossed the patio where we'd had lunch and entered through the door facing the water. Nate led us through the dining area and back to the main living room.

"Let me just grab the other guest room keys." Nate hurried over to the counter and took the two remaining keys hanging from the wooden message boxes. He then led the way up the stairs to the guest room floor and opened the first door on the right, across the hall from Anne's room.

"Venice?" I guessed, seeing the model gondola on the desk complete with a miniature gondolier.

"Precisely," said Nate.

The room was painted an antique-looking yellow-gold color. Two elaborate masks were hanging on the wall above the bed. One was mostly black and masculine and the other feminine, painted regal purple and gold and embellished with feathers and sparkling crystals. The bed had all-white linens, like our rooms, but the throw pillows had scenes of the Grand Canal and Piazza San Marco. The bedside lamp was metal and glass and looked like a bunch of tulips. I presumed it was Murano glass or at least it looked like it could be.

"It's a charming room," I said, "Have you spent a lot of time in Venice?"

Nate closed the door to Venice and locked it. "I've been to Italy a few times. As you might have noticed, all the rooms have some connection to water. Venice was the obvious choice for our Italian room." Nate opened the door to the room across the hall from mine. "And this is our Bar Harbor room. It has the best view of the lighthouse."

The room had a window on the side of the building facing the lighthouse. There was again a small model on the desk, this time it was a detailed lobster fishing boat complete with a pile of miniature traps, painted buoys, and coils of rope.

"It's remarkable how you have a perfect model boat for every room. Were the boats what inspired the design, or did you look for a boat for each one?" asked Anne.

"I've been collecting boats for many years. Betsy tolerated my collecting, but she never had much use for them until she decided to use one in each of the rooms."

"I noticed you had several in the living room downstairs," I said.

"There are more in my office as well. Betsy didn't want my collection to overrun the place, so I don't have them all out on display." Nate relocked the door and turned to us. "There's not much more to show you, the only other rooms are my private quarters which are located over the kitchen on the other side of the house. I have an office, two bedrooms, and a sitting room."

"You needn't show us your private space," I replied.

Anne's stomach grumbled. "Sorry. Hungry. We should figure out what we're going to do for dinner."

"I can make some suggestions if you'd like," offered Nate as we started back downstairs. "Maddie, you still have some wine in the kitchen waiting for you." Then nodding to Anne, he added, "I can fix you both a snack, so you don't starve while you decide."

Anne grinned. "A snack would be great."

We followed Nate to the kitchen, and he handed me a binder labeled Restaurants and gestured for us to take a seat on the stools at the kitchen island. "I'm happy to help with a reservation and give you directions."

I sipped my wine and flipped through the binder. Nate went to the fridge and pulled out a cheese plate.

"I thought we might need a snack," he said, winking at Anne as he passed her the plate.

"Perfect!" Anne helped herself to a slice of cheese and then leaned in to peek over my shoulder. "Anything look good to you? We don't need anything fancy, do we?"

I skimmed the menus. "Something casual and local …."

"In that case, I would suggest The Chart Room." Nate reached over and flipped the pages to their menu. "It's on the water. If it's nice, you can eat on the patio with a view of the bay. It's casual, but the food is good, and they always have a good selection of local seafood."

Anne nodded enthusiastically. "Sounds perfect, eh?"

I memorized the address before closing the binder. "It's settled then."

"I know the owners. I'll call ahead for you," offered Nate.

"How do we get there?" asked Anne. `

"565 Eden Street," I replied, fishing my phone from my pocket. "I'm making a note. We can put it in the GPS."

"You won't need your GPS. It's easy to find. Just follow State Road 3, through Bar Harbor. It will be on your right, just past the entrance to Acadia National Park," explained Nate.

I finished my wine and excused myself to go upstairs and freshen up. I left Anne chatting with Nate. I decided against changing my clothes but switched from my sneakers to a more evening-appropriate pair of flats. I brushed my hair and, after a quick inspection in the mirror, decided against bothering with lipstick. Purse in hand, I headed back to the kitchen and found Anne and Nate looking at pictures of Jake that were pinned to a bulletin board on the kitchen wall.

"He's adorable," Anne gushed. "I promise I'll be a great godmother. If you think about it, since I'm the godmother, and you're the great-grandfather… that would make Mom the real great-godmother, right?"

"I suppose it would," mused Nate, "I never thought of it that way… and here she is now, the great-godmother herself."

I joined them in front of the photo gallery. "Isn't great for the generation after grand? So I'm the grand-godmother? Either way - I'll take it because he is a cutie."

"Are you ready to go?" asked Anne.

"I'll give the restaurant a call and let them know you're on your way," said Nate.

Anne was already headed for the door, but I stopped and turned back. "Thank you for your hospitality. Please add the wine and cheese to my bill."

"That's not necessary. You're Jake's grand-godmother after all. Practically family."

"That's very kind. Thanks again for taking time to give us a tour. I especially enjoyed going up the lighthouse. That view. Amazing."

"It was my pleasure," said Nate, waving goodbye to me as he picked up the phone on the kitchen wall.

Anne was already in the car, scrolling through her GPS menu. "It should take us about 20 minutes to get there." She waited for me to buckle in before putting the car in gear and maneuvering so she didn't have to back out the long driveway to the road.

The evening was still bright and warm, so we drove with the windows down. Driving through Bar Harbor, we chatted about the town sights. There were lots of interesting shops selling everything from cheap souvenirs to antiques and quite a few artisan shops and galleries. And restaurants, lots of restaurants. We speculated that some of them survived by catering to the cruise ship traffic while others would be popular with locals and tourists alike.

As we headed out of town, the road wound through heavily forested areas and around large rock outcrops. I can't help wondering about the geology of a new area when I see its rocks. I made a career out of figuring out the ground beneath my feet. Although my father and grandfather were thrilled when I'd chosen to study at their alma mater Queen's University, my mother thought I had rocks in my head when I also chose to study mining engineering as they had. Being asked why I didn't become a nurse, secretary or bank teller was a typical reaction from my family. The consensus being, nice girls shouldn't have a job where they need to dress like a construction worker.

Anne interrupted my thoughts. "What are you thinking?"

"Just wondering about the local geology. It looks like granite but hard to say for sure at twilight and 40 mph."

"Shall I stop?" Even though she was looking straight ahead I could tell from her tone that she was rolling her eyes at me.

"No, I'm more hungry than curious."

"That's a relief. I'm too hungry to wait for you to go exploring. You're thinking about rocks. I'm thinking about lobster."

"It's a bit early in the season. Hopefully, this place will have some."

We pulled into the parking lot of a white building with blue awnings, and a sign with a big red lobster on it.

I pointed to the supersized crustacean overhead. "I think if there's lobster to be had, they will have it."

Anne grabbed her purse from the backseat and hopped out. "Looks busy. That's a good sign."

Once inside we were greeted by Terri (according to her name badge). Anne let her know Nate Jacobs had called for us, Anne Tobias for two.

"I've a table all set for you." She led us to a table by the window with a view of the water. "Here are some menus and a wine list. Can I start you off with something to drink?"

"Some sparkling water and I'll look at the wine list." I looked over at Anne to see if she approved and she nodded.

"I'll be right back with your water. Jane will be your waitress and she'll be right with you." Terri left us to greet another party that had come into the restaurant.

Anne dove into analyzing the menu, as I looked over the wine list.

"Anything look good by the glass?" asked Anne from behind her menu. "I know you usually stick to red, but I feel like this menu is begging to be accompanied by a white."

"I was thinking you'd prefer white. There's a sauvignon blanc?"

Anne nodded in approval and closed her menu. "Steamers and a lobster roll will go nicely with that."

"Then I don't need to look at the menu, we'll make it two of each." I slid my menu on top of hers. Our waitress Jane appeared with our water, and we placed our order for food and wine.

"I discovered an interesting coincidence today," I began. "It turns out Nate got the idea for the lighthouse B&B from a photo exhibit he saw at Heathrow airport, the same photo exhibit where one of my lighthouse photos was on display."

"Wow! I remember that. It was your photo of Quirpon lighthouse in Newfoundland. My twenty-first birthday trip. The first and only time I've ever seen icebergs in person. I'll never forget it."

"We've taken a lot of good trips together. You've been an excellent adventurer ever since our first big trip together to London for your sixteenth birthday."

"How did you end up in that photo contest?"

"I saw an ad in the Globe and Mail, I figured it was a long-shot, but I sent in an entry anyway."

Jane was back with our wine and informed us our steamers would be just a few minutes. Anne picked up her phone and started reading messages. As I looked across the table at my daughter, I couldn't help but see a lot of myself – poor thing. She wasn't wearing any makeup and she had my mousy blonde hair. She wore her hair shorter than I did, in a stylish feminine cut, but she was dressed rather boyishly in khakis and a golf shirt.

"It's so nice to finally be sitting across from you, being waited on. We have a chance to really catch up," I said, hoping she'd stop checking emails and put down her phone. Other than the drive up from Boston, we hadn't had much time for conversation. She'd worked late and apologized she was too brain dead for anything but a pizza and some mindless TV. She'd promised, after the Baptism, we'd do some proper meals together in Bar Harbor.

I had no right to complain. If I'd still been running my company, I'm sure I'd be tethered to my phone the way she is to hers. She was just like me;

single, independent, and focused on her career. If she couldn't give me her full attention, it's at least partially my own fault. I wasn't a stay-at-home mother like her friends' mothers. I was an anomaly; divorced, climbing the corporate ladder with no intention of ever needing a man to support me. I'd felt the sting of their judgment; I was neglecting my daughter because I was working hard to be successful to secure our financial stability. I would never want to make her feel guilty that she was neglecting me.

She didn't look up from her phone. "There's not much to tell. Other than I'm totally swamped with Emily out on mat leave. The person filling in needs constant supervision."

"You've been working with Emily for a long time. It takes time to get someone new up to speed. Tedious."

Anne glanced up briefly and smiled. "Don't get me wrong. I like being a mentor. I'm so proud of Emily. Sometimes, in private, she calls me her 'work mom' which I take as a compliment."

"It's nice you have close connections with your colleagues. Just don't forget to have a life outside of work."

Anne slapped her phone down on the table and snorted sarcastically. "You're hardly the role model for work-life balance. How to succeed in business, sure … but you're not exactly the poster girl for healthy relationships."

Anne's words made me bristle. "I have plenty of long-term relationships outside of work."

"Claire doesn't count. I mean a soulmate. That person who's your perfect counterpart that balances and completes you."

"Men have never proven to be a reliable source of balance."

"Maybe you've just never found the right person."

"I don't think there's a right man for me."

"Perhaps because you weren't looking?"

I was indignant at the notion my life was incomplete without a man. Anne was spared a rerun of my lecture on why needing a man is for weak women because our steamers arrived. Our conversation turned to our food and plans for the next couple of days.

Anne dipped a chunk of bread into the buttery clam broth and sighed. "This is so good. I need more time for this in my life."

"I could change my flight if you want to stay an extra day."

"I wish I could, but I can't. We just need to squeeze in as much as we can."

"How about after breakfast tomorrow we investigate the galleries we drove past tonight?"

"Then stop for lobster for lunch. To fortify us for an afternoon hike."

I nodded because I'd just taken a big bite of the lobster roll Jane had delivered.

Another attribute I shared with my daughter was that we're both a bit lobster crazy. Planning our sightseeing to fit our eating plans is what we do best. So, it wasn't surprising we were making plans for more lobster tomorrow when we'd not even finished eating today's.

As evidenced by our clean plates, we thoroughly enjoyed our meal. We lingered, sipping our wine, in no hurry to ask for our bill.

Jane appeared with a strawberry shortcake and two forks. "Dessert on the house. Friends of Nate's are friends of ours." She set it down between us. "This is our seasonal dessert. We have our homemade strawberry biscuits with macerated fresh Maine strawberries and orange whipped cream. Enjoy!"

When we arrived back at the B&B, Nate was sitting in the main room reading. He welcomed us and asked if we'd liked the restaurant. Anne recounted our meal selections and added, "Thanks for the use of your good name. It scored us a scrumptious dessert on the house."

"Glad it's good for something. So, ladies, what are your plans for tomorrow? What time would you like to have breakfast?"

"We're going to do some exploring around Bar Harbor in the morning," said Anne. "But we're not exactly early birds. What do you think Mom, eight-ish for breakfast?"

I nodded in approval.

Anne looked at her iPhone and scrolled through her messages with a frown. "I'm sorry, I've got to deal with a few work things tonight so I'm free to play tomorrow."

"Go get things sorted. I'll see you in the morning. Good night, honey." I gave her a hug and a peck on the cheek.

Anne headed towards the stairs and waved at Nate. "Good night, Nate."

CHAPTER 4

Anne left to go take care of her work leaving Maddie and me alone. Usually, I would feel inconvenienced by the obligation to entertain a lone guest but, in Maddie's case, I felt pleased to have some time alone with her.

"Would you like to join me?" I offered.

"I won't bother you," she declined politely.

"No bother at all. Can I get you anything?"

"It's a lovely evening so I think I'll take a little post-dinner walk."

"There's a path that runs from the lighthouse around the point and follows the shoreline for a couple miles. I'd be happy to accompany you."

"That's unnecessary. It's not dark yet and it's a clear night. Do I need to take a key, or will the door be open for a little while longer?"

"If you don't mind, I'd prefer to accompany you. Just in case." I got up from the sofa and retrieved one of the flashlights I kept in the front hallway closet.

"If you insist. But I'm fine on my own. I don't want to interrupt your evening."

I directed us to the back door, and we headed across the brick patio towards the edge of the yard. The path was clearly visible in the twilight. As we stepped onto it, I extended my arm to Maddie but she either didn't notice or ignored it.

"I love walking at night," said Maddie. "Always have."

"Me too," I answered. "Especially when there is a bright moon, so I can see where I'm going without a flashlight."

We walked in silence for a few paces and then Maddie said, "I was telling Anne at dinner about the coincidence of my photo in the same exhibition that inspired you to buy this house and lighthouse."

"How remarkable if it was indeed your photo I saw? I don't recall the title or location, but I do remember a red and white lighthouse and building on a rocky shoreline."

"There could have been other lighthouse pictures in the exhibit, but it sounds like mine. It was of Quirpon Lighthouse in Newfoundland; a red and white building and lighthouse on a rocky cliff with icebergs in the background."

"That sounds like it. Now that you mention it, there might have been icebergs in the background." I looked over at Maddie and she was smiling. "And now, 20 years later I finally get to meet the photographer. Were you in London for the exhibit?"

"Yes, but only briefly. It was quite the thrill. I attended the opening, at the end of May and then returned home the next day. I believe the exhibit ran for several months but I'm not sure when it ended."

"Then we were in England at the same time! I remember we left for our trip around Memorial Day, and we returned home in time for the 4th of July."

"You were in London for quite a while. Were you on vacation?"

"Betsy and I were in Oxford, visiting Ann and her family. Betsy had cancer and she wanted to spend time with Ann and Emily while she could."

"I'm sorry to hear that. I understand wanting to spend time with your daughter."

We'd gone about a half-mile down the path by then and had rounded the point and were climbing slightly uphill. The cliff beside us got higher and steeper and the sound of the waves hitting the shore was louder.

"How are you doing?" I asked Maddie. "Shall we start back?"

"I'm happy to go a little further if that's alright with you," she answered turning her head to look at me. "I can find my way back on my own, no problem, if you'd like to head back."

"I am happy to walk as long as you'd like."

"I hope asking about your trip to London wasn't too personal?" Even in the dim light, I could see she was concerned.

"No not at all," I assured her. "The circumstances were not the best but the time we spent with Ann and Emily was priceless."

"There's another coincidence, our daughters are both named Anne." I suspected she was attempting to move the conversation in a different direction. "Anne was named after her father's grandmother," she continued. "Not after Anne of Green Gables, even though it's spelled with an 'e'. How did you come to pick Ann?"

"We didn't. We adopted Ann when she was nine."

"Nine. Wow. Not a baby then."

"Betsy yearned for a baby. She got pregnant a couple times but miscarried."

"Oh, I'm sorry. I seem to be asking all the wrong questions today."

"It was a long time ago. It was more difficult for Betsy. I had my work and career, and I didn't share her need for a baby."

"Did you try to adopt a baby?"

"No, we didn't. Because we had tried for several years to have our own children, we thought we were too old for a baby. Funny how 35 seemed very old when I was 35." My last comment made us both chuckle.

"If we only knew then what we know now, eh?"

"Hey, that's the first 'eh' I've heard from you!"

"Useful word 'eh'. Turns any statement into a question. You should try it."

"Nice night, eh?"

Maddie laughed with a cute snort. "It's a perfect evening and that's a perfect use of 'eh'."

The breeze off the water picked up and the air was suddenly cooler. Maddie suggested we start to head back. The almost-full moon was quite high, and its light was reflecting off the white lighthouse and house. I pointed out the lighthouse light pattern. "Now that it's dark you can see it's two flashes then a pause."

"Nice view from here. Good spot for pictures, but I'd need a tripod…and I didn't bring mine."

"Maybe next time you visit you can plan it for the full moon and bring your tripod."

"I'm not sure when I'll be this way again. Anne and I don't repeat our vacation destinations as a rule. Unless we have unfinished business."

"Well, I hope photographing my lighthouse at night qualifies as unfinished business and you come stay here again. How long will you be staying with Anne?"

"Just one more night at her house after we leave here. You've heard the saying … family and fish should both be gone in three days."

"You and Anne seem to get along well."

"We're comfortable traveling together. We've been taking mother-daughter trips since she was very young. But I think it's different when you're staying in each other's homes. We're both too used to living alone."

We had arrived at the back door, and I thanked Maddie for the evening stroll.

"It was just what I needed." Maddie stifled a yawn. "Thank you for accompanying me… but now I'll leave you and head up to my room."

"Then I will bid you goodnight, Ms. Maddie Cole. I'll be ready to make you your cappuccino at eight."

"Goodnight, Mr. Jacobs."

CHAPTER 5

Passing Anne's room on my way back to mine I thought back to our dinner conversation. She was right that most of my long-term relationships had been tied to my work life. Seeing the Tokyo sign on Anne's door I couldn't help but think of Dave Bennet, the founder of DB Engineering where I worked for my entire career. Dave and I had a close relationship that would definitely qualify as long-term.

DB Engineering had hired me, right out of graduate school, or more specifically, Dave had selected me over several other candidates. At the time, I was the only female professional in the firm. I'm sure there was some resistance to hiring me from the other partners. But Dave, being the boss, had the final say.

It was 1962, and although women were gradually moving into professional roles, we were frequently marginalized, belittled, and not taken seriously. The only other women in our office were secretaries or clerks and their roles were drastically different from mine. My male colleagues often forgot this and expected me to fetch coffee or do other tasks they typically delegated to their assistants.

Dave was different. I admired the way he treated each person as a professional whether they were male, female, black, white, old, or young. He had the ability to see and draw out people's talents no matter what package they came in. It was one of the reasons why DBE was so successful and had lower staff turnover than similar engineering firms. Dave set a good example for all of us. I tried to emulate him throughout my career. It seems a simple thing to not 'judge a book by its cover', but our biases, often subconscious, influence our decisions and behaviour much more than we'd like to believe.

As my boss, Dave believed his job was to teach me everything I needed to know to be able to take his place. Much to the disapproval of my male counterparts, he selected me, over several other engineers, to assist with a big international proposal even though I'd only been at the firm a few years as a staff engineer. It was an opportunity to show Dave what I was capable of and I jumped at the chance.

The proposal was a success and resulted in a major project in Japan. No one was more surprised than I when Dave asked if I was willing to go to Japan and be part of the team for the duration of the project. Of course, I accepted. I was as excited as I was terrified.

It was my first experience working internationally in a foreign culture. Japanese business culture, rigidly structured with seniority and status dictating a clear hierarchy, was something we all needed to learn about before going so we wouldn't inadvertently offend our client. But what I didn't anticipate was that Japanese men made my worst Canadian colleagues seem enlightened.

I was there in both a technical and supervisory role. Greg and Paul, the other members of our team, reported to me, making me the most senior person behind Dave. This completely confounded the client as their staff had never seen a woman above men in the workplace hierarchy.

I'm grateful I had the chance but sometimes I was quite lonely. It wasn't just the months away from my friends, family, and fiancée, as a woman, I wasn't welcome at much of the socializing that went on between our team and the client. Many evenings I ate alone in the hotel restaurant and then, while my colleagues were out drinking, passed the time in my room typing up the day's reports until my eyes were tired and I was drowsy enough to sleep.

On top of that, Japanese men had a difficult time accepting me as an expert. I often joked afterward that it was only because I was a head taller than most of the men, that they couldn't look down on me all the time. It was Dave who made the work environment tolerable for me. Because he was the most senior, our client, whose name was Takashi, would listen to what he had to say. Dave used his rank to ensure I was heard in meetings where my expertise was valuable.

Beyond the project work, Dave made time to see and experience Tokyo. He told me many times he wanted to experience as much of Japan as we could fit into our schedule. I doubted I'd ever get another chance to be in Japan, so I accompanied him everywhere I could.

We were just wrapping up one afternoon in early April when Dave informed the team that the following day we didn't need to be in the office because it was a local holiday.

"Also, Takashi-san has invited us all to join his family tomorrow for a hanami." We were all surprised by his announcement since it was the middle of the workweek.

"What's a hanami?" I asked.

"It means 'flower viewing'," Dave explained. "Takashi-san told me it's a very old tradition. Family and friends gather in the park with food and drink under the flowering cherry trees, called *sakura* in Japanese. He said we will start around lunchtime, and the party will run into the evening. Apparently, it's a pretty big deal. His family has a spot they have been going to for many years. We will be picked up outside the hotel tomorrow at 11:30. One of his nephews will show us the way to the location."

Being the only female on the project, I couldn't ask my colleagues about what to wear. In fact, the guys were useless, and rarely gave good advice on the subject. As I shuffled through my hotel closet the next morning, I tried to guess what our Japanese hosts would be wearing. I decided to err on the side of being overdressed and to go with something 'garden-party-like'. I selected a cute, navy and white, A-line mini skirt and matching top that together looked like a dress, low-heeled mary-jane shoes, and a sweater, in case it was cool. Fortunately, Japanese women's fashion in the sixties was a few years behind Canada, so even though my outfit wasn't new, I was satisfied I looked fashionable, yet comfortable, as I headed to the lobby to meet the others.

At precisely 11:30 we were approached by a man about my age. "I am Hiro." He bowed as he spoke. "My uncle wishes me to escort you to hanami place." He gestured toward the door.

A multi-coloured Volkswagen bus was waiting at the front entrance. Hiro directed us, bowing and gesturing, to indicate we should get in. He then maneuvered the absurdly large vehicle through the scooter and bicycle-jammed streets of Tokyo. We were all relieved when we came to a stop at the Uneo train station. Hiro jumped out and handed the keys to another young man who was waiting on the curb. They spoke briefly in Japanese.

"My brother take car to parking. Come with me," explained Hiro.

We followed him along the front of the station and then turned right onto a wide path leading into the park. The path was crowded with people of all ages, carrying bags, neatly wrapped and tied boxes and packages, and rolled-up mats. Hiro led us around another corner, and I finally understood what all the fuss was about. Hundreds of cherry trees in bloom lined both sides of the path that curved in a gentle arc around a large pond.

"Wow. This is quite the spectacle," I said to Dave as we followed Hiro, weaving our way through the throng of people.

"Obviously, a lot of people think this is the best hanami spot," said Dave putting his hand on the small of my back, in a gentlemanly way, to steer me through the crowd.

"This is place." Hiro pointed to a large group gathered in an open area under the cherry trees with an excellent view of the pond and the cherry tree lined causeway leading to the islands in the center of the pond.

Takashi approached us and we exchanged the good morning greeting. "Ohayou gozimasu."

"Arigato, Takashi-san for inviting us today," said Dave in a polite and grateful tone.

"Youkoso irasshai machita, douzo," replied Takashi with a welcoming smile, gesturing us to join the group gathered on the large woven straw mats. We removed our shoes, placing them alongside the many pairs that ringed the mat.

"Let me introduce my family. This is my wife Chiyako."

Chiyako bowed to us. "Haji memashite."

"Haji memashite," we echoed, with varying degrees of success pronouncing 'nice to meet you' in Japanese.

"This is Dave-san, Maddie-san, Greg-san, and Paul-san." We each bowed in turn to Chiyako as Takashi introduced us. She gave us a demure smile and another bow and then turned to speak to the children who were rummaging through a large bag, searching for something.

"There's Keiki-san," said Dave, with a visible sigh of relief.

"I requested Keiki-san to join us today," said Takashi.

We were all happy to see Keiki. She was one of the interpreters who helped us at the office and at job sites. We had a second interpreter, Tomio, who also worked with us, but his English wasn't as good as hers. Keiki was about my age and was the daughter of a US serviceman. She was half Japanese and spoke both English and Japanese fluently. She was the person most sympathetic to my situation as she had endured discrimination based on her mixed race and because she was a woman. Like me she was not permitted to attend many of the male-only events, hence the need for the inferior Tomio.

"Ohayou," said Keiki brightly, using the more familiar form of the greeting, which was much easier for us to remember because it sounded just like the state Ohio.

"Keiki-san, can you explain a bit about this hanami event?" I asked.

"Of course, the most important thing is to enjoy yourself and admire the beautiful sakura trees. Takashi-san, as our host, has provided the food and drink. Treat the mat you are standing on as if it is their house – ah – good - you have removed your shoes."

"Can you ask if it's OK for me to take pictures?"

After a brief exchange in Japanese with Chiyako, Keiki answered me. "You are welcome to take pictures, and Chiyako suggests that after lunch you walk through the park, as there are many beautiful areas you might like to photograph. But first, you must sit and eat."

"Arigato," I said bowing my head to Chiyako and venturing "Oishisou," my attempt at "It looks delicious" in Japanese. Chiyako beamed at my effort and gestured Keiki and me to a spot on the mat near her.

Dave, Paul, and Greg had joined the group of men and Keiki and I the women.

Dave looked over at me and mouthed, "Are you OK?" I nodded and smiled in response because I was.

"Please enjoy," said Chiyako, looking to Keiki for approval of her pronunciation as she gestured to the food arranged on small, short-legged tables that were placed at regular intervals on the mat. We both grinned at each other, nonverbally communicating our mutual delight at attempts to speak each other's language. With Keiki interpreting, I learned from Chiyako that she had three children, enjoyed painting, and she would like to go to Paris to the Louvre to see the great masters' works. I shared with her that I had a fiancée at home and dreams of visiting all the great cities of Europe someday.

While we talked, we ate kara-age, bite-sized fried chicken, onigiri, rice balls stuffed with a variety of things like fish, pickled plums, and salted cherry blossoms, and a stunning variety of sushi and sushi rolls. We sipped sake and sakura flavored pop. The food was as beautiful as it was delicious, and I couldn't keep myself from snapping a few pictures of the bento boxes, covered trays, and platters filled with multicoloured miniatures. We sat on the mat by the tables as Chiyako kneeled near the center of the mat rearranging the food so each guest could sample the different items. A young man I didn't know circled the mat constantly refilling our sake cups.

I looked up and Dave was extending his hand to help me up from the mat.

"Shall we take a walk around the park?"

"Yes, I'd love to get some pictures," I answered, ignoring his hand and getting up unassisted. "Anyone else coming?"

No one else budged from the mat. "I guess it's just us." I grabbed my purse with my camera in it and slipped on my shoes as I stepped off the mat.

Dave pointed towards the center of the park. "How about we head this way first, then around the point to the path out to that island?"

"Sounds good to me."

Stepping onto the path was like entering a river of people streaming in a continuous flow below the pink and white blossom-filled cherry trees. Mats lined both sides, filled with people eating, reclining, laughing, talking, and, of course, drinking sake. Dave reached for my elbow so we could stay together in the crowd.

The path gradually widened and the stand of cherry trees on either side was deeper.

I was captivated by the sheer number of trees. "There must be a thousand cherry trees here."

Dave pulled his tattered Tokyo guidebook from his jacket pocket. "The book says 800, so you're pretty close. Did you peek or are you just that good?"

"I'm just that good, and you know it," I said with a wink.

The path dead-ended in a large open square with side paths exiting from all four corners. We consulted the park map in the guidebook, and we identified the buildings on either side of the square as the art museums and the large building to the north of us as the National Museum. We decided to follow the path to the left, towards the zoo, and then make our way in a loop past the pond and back to our party's mats.

I stopped to photograph the five-storied pagoda that, according to Dave's guidebook, was one of the few original Kanejii Temple structures that survived destruction during the Boshin War. I focused my camera on the pink blossoms, the people, the curious circle-shaped pine tree, and architectural details like the carved edge of the roof. I snapped away, taking extra shots, varying my aperture and exposure, to give me the best chance at getting a perfect shot.

"I've already blown through another roll of film," I said stopping and digging in my purse for another roll. As I changed the film in the shade of the shrine, Dave read from the guidebook.

"This pond is called Shinobazu Pond, and Bentendo is the temple in the center of the pond on what was an island but is now accessed by a stone causeway."

"That must be it." I pointed to an octagonal two-story building. When I finished reloading my camera, we headed towards Bentendo Temple.

Crossing the causeway, we found a lively area, crammed with food stalls.

"Are you hungry," Dave asked.

"No, but I wish I was because there are a lot of interesting looking things."

"Interesting isn't always good."

"Where's your sense of adventure?" I teased.

Dave pointed to something that looked like a webbed duck foot. "I haven't had enough sake to think that's a good idea."

"I would agree."

"See... I knew you were clever. Or is it this place? It says here this temple is dedicated to Benten, the goddess of good fortune, wealth, music, and knowledge." Dave looked up from his guidebook and into my eyes. "You should feel right at home here. You are my Benten."

I was thrown by the unexpected compliment. Before I could come up with any reply Dave continued, "I know that sounded corny, but I've been wanting to find a way to tell you how important you've been to making this project a success, and how much I've enjoyed the time we've spent together both in and out of the office."

"I've enjoyed working with you too," I said trying to sound professional, "and the opportunity to see Japan has been incredible. I'm grateful you've taken me with you sightseeing."

Dave was quiet, looking at me, listening. I filled the awkward silence by suggesting, "Shall we go inside the temple?"

"Definitely."

We walked through the door and were struck by the contrast between the festival atmosphere outside and the tranquility of the temple. The scent of incense and flowers was sweet and calming. A monk was seated at a small table, just inside the door, selling charms and amulets including miniature temples. Dave picked up one of the tiny wooden temples and paid the monk for it.

He handed it to me. "A temple for my goddess Benten."

I admired how detailed it was and thanked him for it. "I love miniature things and this little temple will remind me of today."

"I won't need a souvenir to remind me of today," he said in almost a whisper.

I saw the potential for this to become an awkward moment. "I'd like to walk around the rest of the island before it gets too dark for pictures."

"Then we shall." Dave extended his arm with an exaggerated gallant gesture complete with a little bow. I laughed and took his arm.

The sun had set, and the sky was a pale grey. The dark bark of the cherry trees stood out starkly against the sky, but the blossoms shimmered. In the bright sun, I hadn't noticed the small lanterns strung through the branches. Now that they were lit, their light reflected off the pink and white blossoms bathing the entire area in a soft pink glow. I took a lot of pictures because the scene was mesmerizing and I wanted to capture it.

We worked our way around the perimeter of the island so we could look back towards the causeway lined with cherry trees. The reflection of the lighted trees in the still surface of the pond was magical. Focusing more through my camera lens than on where I was standing, I stumbled as I stepped backward. I literally fell into Dave's arms as he was standing close behind me. I was embarrassed at my clumsiness, but his arms felt good. Instead of pushing away, I turned to face him. He looked into my eyes and said, "You're so beautiful."

I scoffed at the compliment. "It's just the light, it's soft and flattering."

He lifted his hand and his fingers brushed a strand of my hair from my face. "It's not just the light. You have it all my dear, beauty and brains. It's a dangerous combination."

I looked at my watch. "We should get back before the boys think we're lost."

Dave drew a deep breath and stepped back. "We should. Time flies when you're having fun."

We made our way back to our group and settled in on the mat to sip more sake under the illuminated blossoms. I was keenly aware of Dave's closeness. It was obvious to me he was finding me attractive in a way he'd never let on before. I was enjoying the feeling of having him want something that I was in complete control of.

"Chiyako-san would like to know if you enjoyed the park," interpreted Keiki.

"Absolutely. It's a beautiful park. The temple we visited was so peaceful."

"Did you take pictures?"

"So many I've used up all the film I brought with me today."

"Well then, you must make memories," Keiki interpreted as Chiyako gestured overhead to the illuminated blossom canopy.

"Today will be a very special memory." As I answered Chiyako, I could feel Dave's hand on the small of my back.

He tilted his head close to my ear and whispered, "For me too."

We spent the next several hours sitting under the lit trees, drinking too much sake, eating, and listening to music played by Takashi's nephews. When the evening ended, Hiro brought the van to return us to our hotel which was about 20 minutes away near the Imperial Palace. Dave and I took the rear bench. Greg and Paul, under the influence of much sake, were sitting in front of us singing. Dave watched their antics but moved his hand slowly and placed it on my knee. It might have been the sake, but it caused a wave of excitement to run through me. Dave then looked at me mischievously while sliding his hand up my thigh to the edge of my mini-skirt. I felt a pleasant warm tingle between my legs, but I brushed his hand away and mouthed "you're bad" just as we pulled up to our hotel.

"Shall we have a nightcap?" asked Paul.

"I'm all for that," Greg slurred.

I headed for the elevator. "Count me out. I've had more than enough. I'm going to call it a day."

Greg and Paul headed for the bar, but Dave followed me towards the elevator.

We got in the elevator, and I pressed the button for my floor. Dave didn't press his floor.

"It would only be right that I escort the lady to her room."

I pressed the button for his floor just as the door opened at mine. "Funny how on workdays, when I'm loaded down with maps and reports I manage just fine, but tonight you think I need accompanying?" I stepped out and held up my hand to stop him from following me. "Go to your room. You've already been a bad boy tonight."

Alone in my room, I considered the unspoken offer Dave had made when he'd touched my leg in the car. I picked up the phone and asked the operator to connect me to Dave's room.

"I know I sent you to your room, but I like bad boys," I purred into the phone when he answered.

"Sometimes bad can be very very good."

Emboldened by the sake, I purred, "If you want to screw just for the fun of it, we can you know."

"I would like that very much." Dave hung up the phone without saying goodbye and knocked on my door a few minutes later.

"Are you sure about this?" he asked once I'd locked the door behind him.

"It's 1966, not the dark ages. This doesn't have to be complicated."

Dave grinned and stepped forward putting his arms around me. His lips met mine and he pressed against me. His hands moved up my back and he slipped my cardigan from my shoulders. Setting it aside he ran his hands down my bare arms. I turned away from him, lifted my hair, and looked back at him over my shoulder. "Un-zip me?"

Dave slowly unzipped my top and as he did, he leaned in and kissed the back of my neck. While continuing to kiss my neck and behind my ear, he slipped off my top. I leaned back into him, and luxuriated in his hands moving over me, around my waist, up my belly, skimming the lower band of my bra, and then around to my back where he unhooked it. Still standing behind me he slowly slipped off one strap, kissing from my neck across my now bare shoulder. Then moved to the other side, slipping the strap down my arms, and kissing the other shoulder.

I pulled my bra from my arms, tossed it aside, and leaned back into his arms that now wrapped around me. His hands cupped my breasts. His thumbs stroked the outer curves while he continued to kiss my neck and behind my ear. I allowed myself to melt back into him, and I moaned a little as his fingers lightly skimmed over my now hard nipples. I turned to face him. Looking at him, I began to unzip my skirt. He watched me as I let it fall to the floor, and I stepped out of it. Never taking his eyes off me, he removed his dress shirt and pants, and, as he stood there in his t-shirt and boxers, I could see how aroused he was from the tell-tale bulge and hungry look in his eyes.

"You're so beautiful," he said somewhat breathlessly. He moved closer and ran his hands from my face down and over my chest. I was surprised that instead of backing me onto the bed, he dropped to his knees in front of me. His fingers traced the waistband of my pantyhose. He began to slowly, carefully, roll them down off my hips. As he did, he kissed the newly exposed skin, my hips, my thighs down the inside of thighs to my knees, my calves, my ankles. I steadied myself by placing my hands on his shoulders as he slipped the hose from my feet. He then traced the edge of my panties with his fingertips. My skin prickled with excitement as his fingers followed each edge, tracing the band between my legs. He slipped a cool finger under the band and brushed a finger over my softest skin. He smiled and sucked in a deep breath as he realized how wet I already was. He moved his finger, caressing me under my panty. I closed my eyes, enjoying the waves of warmth rippling through me as his fingers explored.

"I want to taste you," he breathed, pulling my panties down to my ankles.

I stepped backward and sat down on the edge of the bed.

"Lie back," he directed, and I scooted back onto the bed.

Dave stood at the foot of the bed. He caressed my legs, and then grasped my ankle, easing my legs apart. Leaning in, he kissed one ankle, then the other, then crawling forward, kissed the inside of my knees, and my inner thighs. He seemed to move slower with each kiss. I could feel myself drip with anticipation. As he slowly inched himself up between my legs, I could feel his breath warm on my skin. When his tongue traced up and down and then made slow circles, I was lost in the pleasure of the moment.

"Mmmmm, yes," I moaned.

"The pleasure is all mine," he replied as he buried his face between my legs and hungrily licked, sucked, and kissed until I was shivering in a lovely orgasm. He then crawled up beside me. I reached out and tugged at his boxers.

"We don't have to go any further, I'm happy just to satisfy you," he said.

"Oh no you don't. I'm not satisfied yet," I growled and pulled down his boxers and rolled him onto his back.

He looked up at me, directly into my eyes as I climbed onto him and lowered myself, slowly taking him inside me. His eyes closed, and he moaned as he slid deeper. He reached out and put his hands on my hips, guiding my tempo up and down. I leaned forward over his chest and as I did, Dave sat up and rolled me over, so he was on top. He began pressing into me harder, and faster. I could feel his urgency.

He let out a little yelp as he came. "You excite me so. I couldn't … stop it," he said breathlessly and apologetically as he rolled to one side, still holding me close cradling my head with one arm and the other wrapped around me.

I looked into his eyes and scolded, "Well you better do better next time."

"I like the idea of a next time," he said with a wink.

We continued to hook up during the rest of the project in Japan. We were discreet. Although we were together many nights, we were never anything but professional in public. We even booked separate hotel rooms when we took a weekend trip together to Kyoto.

While we were in Japan, the only communication with home was by letter or phone calls; and phone calls were infrequent because they were very expensive. My letters to my fiancé Will and my parents were filled with details of the project, my observations of the culture, descriptions of the sights, sounds, and food, but I barely mentioned Dave. When we returned home at the end of the project, we went back to being strictly colleagues but closer friends. We vowed to not speak of our physical relationship, and no one ever suspected I was anything more than his highly respected protégée.

It's hard to believe something as simple as the word "Tokyo" could bring up 50-year-old memories. I'm not ashamed of what we did, but I've never told anyone because of the promise I made to Dave. As I crawled into bed, I thought about how young I was. I chuckled to myself; the sexual revolution didn't work out the way we thought it would. Today our encounters would be sexual harassment and possibly even more scandalous than it would have been in 1966. I guess it was Dave that made the difference. I never felt powerless or taken advantage of. I felt desired, which was flattering, but also empowered and free to be and do anything I wanted. He was one of the few people who encouraged me to take charge and not curb my ambitions. Ultimately, when he retired, I purchased the firm which turned out to be a sound investment that has afforded me a very comfortable retirement.

"Thanks, Dave," I whispered to myself, "I've not forgotten you. Hope you're in a good place."

CHAPTER 6

I woke up before my 6 am alarm. I was glad neither Anne nor Maddie had asked for an early breakfast because I'd stayed up later than usual on account of going for a walk with Maddie. I like to have at least a couple hours to myself before starting to serve guests.

I showered, dressed, and headed down to the kitchen. I listened to the news on the radio, while I worked through my morning routine to prepare for my guests. The espresso machine was my first priority. As soon as it warmed up, I made one for myself and left it on so it would be ready when it was time to make Maddie's cappuccino.

Italy had ruined me when it came to coffee. An Italian colleague once told me, "Life is too short to drink bad coffee." Since coffee is essential to breakfast, I vowed when we opened this place we'd never serve bad coffee. The wisdom of the adage extends well beyond coffee. Life is too short to settle for bad anything. Bad food, bad wine, bad service … but it's a little more complex when it comes to bad relationships. One often tolerates them because they're not as easy to dump as a mediocre cup of coffee. It's only in hindsight you realize how much precious time you wasted that could have been invested in building something better and stronger.

Anne was the first to appear. "Good morning, Nate."

"Good morning. Sleep well?"

"Yes, great. It's normal for me to wake up a few times during the night, but something about the sound of the waves lulled me back to sleep."

"I often sleep with the windows open so I can hear them. Can I get you a coffee? Cappuccino? Tea?"

Anne stifled a yawn. "Plain, ordinary coffee. Please."

"You're welcome to pull up a stool here or I can bring it to you in the dining area if you prefer."

"Will I be in the way if I stay here?"

"Not at all. Coffee coming right up. How do you take it?"

"Black with sugar."

I poured Anne's coffee and set it down in front of her. "Are you hungry?"

"No, not yet. I'll wait for Mom."

"Since you two are the only guests this morning I didn't prepare a buffet. I thought instead I'd just make you whatever you'd like, whenever you'd like it. Here's the list of options. When you're ready just let me know." I handed her a little menu I'd typed up the night before while they'd been out for dinner.

"That sounds like special treatment."

I leaned in as if to share a secret. "Don't tell anyone or all my guests will expect it. I'm going to go get the paper. I'll be right back."

When I got back, I found Anne hunched over, typing on her phone. Her face was crinkled in an annoyed frown.

"Everything OK?"

"No. We've got a lot of stuff going on at work. I'm afraid I'm going to have to break it to Mom that we're going to have to cut our trip short. I need to get back."

My heart sank at the thought of Maddie leaving so soon. "That's a shame. Your mother mentioned she doesn't fly back for a few days. Perhaps she'd like to stay longer?"

"It's a long bus ride to Boston."

"I could drive her back. It would give me an excuse to see Jake and Emily. I didn't get to spend much time with them because I was so busy getting everything ready for the Baptism party."

"That's a lot of driving."

"I don't have any guests coming until Saturday, so it wouldn't be a problem. I still like to drive. I just don't drive at night as much anymore."

"I'm not sure Mom will go for it."

"Go for what?" asked Maddie as she came into the kitchen.

I turned to start making Maddie's cappuccino as Anne explained, "I've got to go into the office tomorrow, so I need to leave this afternoon. But Nate was just offering to drive you back to Boston if you wanted to stay as we planned."

"That sounds like a lot of trouble," said Maddie.

"Not at all," I said putting her cappuccino in front of her. "And to sweeten the offer – you would stay as my guest – no charge."

"That sounds like an offer too good to refuse," said Anne looking at Maddie.

"But I came down here to spend time with you…"

"I'm not going to be any fun. I'll be tied up at work."

"I don't know. I suppose I could look into renting a car…maybe from the airport and I could book a flight back to Boston?" said Maddie looking at Anne and then at me with those beautiful eyes.

"I was just telling Anne I don't have any guests until Saturday. I can drive you down on Wednesday and then drive back here on Thursday at my leisure."

"You don't want to just hang around, alone, all day at my house," said Anne.

"I'm perfectly capable of entertaining myself or I can change my flight and head home early if I'm underfoot."

"But you've been looking forward to this trip. It would be a shame…"

"You're taking the car, so I'll need a way to get around," said Maddie. "So, before I decide, I'll need to make some calls and see if I can find a rental car."

"I would be happy to take you anywhere you'd like to go."

"I couldn't…"

"It would be my pleasure to be your chauffeur and guide to the area," I reassured her.

"I would enjoy seeing more of the area…," said Maddie.

"Then it's settled. I'll let Emily know Grandpa is staying over on Wednesday night."

"Thank you. You're too kind." Maddie lifted her cup as if to toast. "And the cappuccino is perfect."

"I'm thinking we should have a bite to eat and get going since I'll be taking off after lunch," said Anne.

That was my cue to get breakfast going for them. "What can I get you both?"

"I'd like toast and peanut butter if you have it," said Anne.

"Would you like banana with that?"

"Even better."

"And you Maddie, what would you like?" Anne passed Maddie the list I'd given her.

"I'll have toast, no peanut butter, no banana, but jam."

"Aren't you going to ask for some cheese with that?" said Anne. Maddie scowled at her.

"Cheese?" I asked.

Anne didn't let Maddie answer. "Yes, cheese. She has a thing for toast with jam and cheese."

"What kind of cheese?"

"If you have strawberry jam and cheddar cheese, you'll make her very happy."

Maddie grumbled. "Must you tell all my secrets?"

"And I thought I'd heard every possible breakfast request. First time for everything. Fortunately, I have everything on hand. Wheat or white toast?"

"Wheat," said Anne and Maddie in unison.

"Coming right up."

Maddie and Anne chatted and drank their coffee while I pulled together the ingredients to fill their breakfast orders. I had to interrupt them to ask about the cheese.

"Excuse me Maddie, but how do you want the cheese? Sliced? Grated?"

"Thin slices please."

"And for you, how do you want your banana?"

"Any way you slice it is fine by me."

"I can slice the cheese and bananas if you like?" offered Maddie.

"You two just relax and let me serve you. If you'd like to go sit in the dining area near the window the view will be more interesting than watching me make toast."

Anne picked up both of their coffee cups. "Come on, let's get out of Nate's way."

It made me happy to fill Anne and Maddie's requests. I smiled to myself as I scooped out peanut butter and jam into small serving bowls and arranged banana and cheddar cheese on side plates. The cheese was a surprise. I put a little strawberry jam on a broken piece of cheddar and popped it in my mouth. It was a surprisingly good combination. I thought to myself that I might just add this to the regular menu, perhaps on a warm flaky biscuit.

I arranged plates, linen napkins, silverware, and the toppings on a large tray. Once it was ready, I put the warm toast in a lined basket and added it to the tray, and carried it over to the table by the window.

"Here you go, ladies. Wheat toast for each of you with peanut butter and sliced banana for Anne, strawberry jam and cheddar for Maddie. Buon appetito. Would either of you like more coffee?"

"I'll have another cup, please," said Anne.

"Your cappuccino was excellent. I'd love another, but just a regular coffee would be fine if that's less trouble," said Maddie.

"No trouble at all. I'll be right back," I answered as I headed back to the kitchen to get the coffees, returning with them a few minutes later.

"Can I get you anything else?"

"Not for me," said Anne.

"Nor I. You're spoiling us," said Maddie.

"It's my pleasure. Just let me know if you need anything. I'll be in the kitchen."

Back in the kitchen I switched off the radio and turned on the small TV to listen to the Monday morning news shows while I tidied up the kitchen. I was in a very good mood. In fact, I was feeling elated and excited Maddie would be staying on. Which reminded me, to call Emily and ask if it was OK for me to drop in and stay Wednesday night. I checked my watch, 9:15, too early but I made a note to call her, so I wouldn't forget.

"Thanks for breakfast," said Anne coming into the kitchen with the tray filled with their breakfast dishes. "Where should I put this?"

"Just put it anywhere. You didn't have to bus your own table."

"The least we could do in return for our made-to-order breakfast. My bananas were perfectly sliced." Anne had an impish grin and winked at me.

"Oh Anne, you're terrible. Come on, let's go before Nate regrets inviting our type to stay longer."

"Have a good time. Take this key in case I'm out when you get back." I handed them a key on a lighthouse keychain. "I'm going to the farmer's market to pick up some things for dinner, but it closes at noon, so I should be back around lunchtime."

Maddie took the key. "Thanks. We'll probably be back early afternoon, eh?"

Anne nodded. "We gotta be because I'd like to get on the road early this afternoon."

After they left, I took stock of the refrigerator and pantry. It's unusual for me to offer to make dinner for my guests, but I was looking forward to the prospect of spending the evening with Maddie. I wondered what she would like and regretted not asking her before they left.

I debated with myself over what to make. I didn't want to make something elaborate and come across as ostentatious, but, on the other hand, I wanted to do something nice. I decided to go with crab cakes. Everyone seems to like my crab cakes. I opted to wait to see what looked good at the market before settling on what else to make.

There was a lot of great local produce to choose from at the Eden Farmer's Market. We'd had an early spring and there were excellent asparagus that would pair nicely with the crab cakes and some irresistible strawberries.

I couldn't help thinking of Maddie and her breakfast choice as I passed the Fuzzy Udder Creamery stall. They make excellent cheese. I picked out several that would pair nicely with red wine. I was pretty sure Maddie would enjoy a little cheese plate – either before as an appetizer or later in the evening. If not, having a little extra cheese on hand is never a problem. I could always set it out next weekend for my guests.

After putting the groceries away, I went up to my office and got out the file box where I kept my local guidebooks and maps. I wanted to be prepared to show Maddie around and to have a plan in case she didn't already have a list of things she'd like to do. I was determined she wouldn't regret her decision to stay.

CHAPTER 7

We drove into Bar Harbor and along Main Street until we found a parking lot near the harbor. "The sign says we can park here for three hours," said Anne looking at her phone for the time. "We're good until 12:45."

"Which way do you want to go first?"

"How about we work our way up this side first," she said pointing back the way we'd come into town. "As enticing as that pub across the street looks, it's too early for that."

Both sides of the street were lined with old and irregularly shaped buildings. Most were two stories and made of wood or wood and brick. Many had bright-colored awnings extending out over the sidewalk. Gaslamp-looking lampposts added to the old world feel of the street. The first shop we came to had a sign claiming it was the oldest bookshop in Maine.

Anne held the door open for me. "We should at least see what the oldest bookstore looks like on the inside."

The shop had an eclectic collection of books with many selections from local writers or set in the northeast.

"I read mostly on my Kindle these days," said Anne "but I love a good bookstore."

"I still prefer a book. Turning pages is more satisfying than swiping. Old fashioned I guess."

"But you can carry lots of ebooks at once without taking up any room in your suitcase."

I picked up Before the Fall by Noah Hawley. "This looks interesting. I left my book-club book at your house. It would be good to have something to read this evening, since I'll be on my own."

Anne raised her eyebrows and gave me a suggestive nudge. "You won't be entirely alone."

"I can't expect Nate to entertain me all evening and all day tomorrow."

"Maybe he's looking forward to it?"

"Maybe he'll be sick of me in an hour."

"I doubt that."

"Just in case, I'll have a book to read if things get awkward." I cut off further conversation by taking the book to the counter to pay for it.

"I enjoyed this one a lot," said the librarian-looking woman behind the desk. "The author was here for a book signing last summer on a cruise ship day. We sold out in an hour."

We left the bookstore and continued up the street. We decided to skip the Chocolate Emporium but wandered through the Christmas Spirit store next to it. Then, we visited a gallery that had some beautiful watercolor sunrises and seascapes. We wandered through several more of the shops. There was the Bar Harbor Hemporium that had more tie-dye than the sixties, a shop specializing in all things moose, another Christmas store, and a unique pet supply store called Bark Harbor. Anne bought a birthday gift for her friend Linda who liked to have matching outfits for her and her Maltese, a matching bracelet and dog collar beaded with rose quartz and amethyst.

We continued along the main street until the shops gave way to a residential area. Then we crossed the street and worked our way back down the other side, window shopping and going into any that struck our fancy. Many of the stores were quite busy.

"It seems like the streets have a lot more people walking around since we got here," observed Anne.

"I'm guessing it's because the tenders from the cruise ships we saw offshore have been steadily dropping off passengers."

"I'm glad we have a car, so we can escape if it gets too crowded."

"Are we hungry for lobster yet?"

"When am I not hungry for lobster? Shall we go for a drive and look for a roadside stand for lunch?"

"I think we passed one on our way into town."

"Shouldn't take us long to devour a couple of crustaceans, and then I'd better get on the road home," said Anne checking the time on her phone. "Are you sure you're OK staying on your own and coming back to Boston with Nate?"

"Of course I am! Worst case I read my new book." I patted the bag with the book in it.

Along the highway, on the way back towards the B&B, we found Rose Eden Lobster. It wasn't fancy, not much more than a shed and a couple of picnic tables on the edge of a small parking lot.

"It's a good sign that the lot's full," said Anne as she parked the car just barely off the road.

"Hopefully the wait isn't too long – I know you're anxious to get going."

"Not anxious enough to miss out on fresh lobster. You'd think after a decade of living in Boston I'd be sick of it. But I'm not, I still can't pass up a chance for a fresh one."

We walked up to the window and placed our orders.

"You're number thirty," said the young woman with dark hair behind the counter. "There's a $5 deposit for the crackers. You'll get it back when you return them."

"Not a problem. We'll bring 'em back," said Anne.

We stood off to the side holding our crackers, drinks and numbered receipt until a pair of spots opened up at one of the tables. Just as we sat down, they called our number.

Anne went to the counter and came back carrying a blue plastic tote. In it were our steamed lobsters on blue-flowered paper plates, two containers of melted butter, plastic forks I was sure would be useless, and several wet wipes and napkins that I was sure we would use.

"Time to get messy," said Anne, grinning as she put the tote down between us on the table.

"At least they were generous with the wet wipes for when we're buttery and lobstery."

"Lobstery? That's a new word." Anne tore off a claw splattering herself. "Yup. We're gettin' 'lobstery'," she continued with a giggle.

We tried to eat carefully but, like the other diners at our table, we couldn't help the odd splatter as we cracked and pulled apart the lobsters to get at the goodness inside.

"Did you know lobster was once considered poor man food; fed to servants and prisoners? There was even a court case where a judge ruled it illegal to feed servants lobster more than three times a week?"

Anne raised her eyebrows and looked at me incredulously. "I might consider adding that to my next employment contract... except it will be you must feed me lobster at least three times a week."

"You have butter on your arm."

"So do you. They are sorta ugly. The first guy to eat one was pretty brave."

"Technically they are closer relatives to bugs than fish."

"No matter how many times you remind me of that, it doesn't deter me."

"Me neither," I said frowning at my shirtsleeve that had soaked up the butter from my arm. "I'm going to have to change my shirt when I get back so I'm not spotted and smelling of lobster."

"I'm sure Nate's had messy, lobster-eating guests before – I doubt your appearance will shock him."

"I suppose not, but I don't want him to think your mother is a mess."

We finished up our lobsters, returned our blue tote and crackers, and collected our deposit.

Nate was home when we got back.

"How was the morning in Bar Harbor?" he asked as he opened the door for us.

I held up my bag. "Successful. We did some window shopping and shopping-shopping."

"Have you had lunch?"

"Can't you tell?" said Anne grinning. "We're wearing our lobster and butter."

He sniffed the air near her. "I thought I smelled Eau du Lobster."

"I'm going to tell Emily her grandpa gave me a hard time if you don't behave, Mr. Jacobs," she teased back.

I gave Anne my best scolding glare. "Mind your manners! I'm sorry Mr. Jacobs. My daughter can be quite impertinent."

Nate chuckled, good-naturedly, at our exchange, and I couldn't help but smile. I actually forgot to be self-conscious that I too was speckled with lobster-butter spots.

"I'm glad you ladies had a nice time. I took the liberty of shopping for dinner for us tonight. Are you OK with eating in, Maddie?"

"I don't want you to go to too much trouble."

"No trouble at all, as long as you like crab cakes because that's what I planned to make."

"I love crab cakes."

Anne came back into the main room with her suitcase and briefcase. "I'm ready to head out."

Nate turned to her and gave her a big hug. "Jake is really lucky to have you for his godmother. I hope you'll be back soon. You're family now."

"Thank you, Nate, I will. And thanks in advance for bringing Mom back to Boston."

I stepped in for my turn to hug her. "Drive safe, Honey."

"Behave yourself, now that I'm leaving you unchaperoned." She gave me an exaggerated wink.

"I'm a little old to need a chaperone. Go on, get going."

"Don't worry," chimed in Nate. "I'll keep an eye on her and make sure she doesn't sneak out with any of the young boys from town."

"That makes me feel ever so much better."

Nate held the door open, and I followed Anne outside. "Text me when you get home. Drive safe."

"Yes Mom. Bye Mom."

Nate joined me on the front porch. Together, we watched Anne get into her car and waved to her as she drove away.

"Is there anything, in particular, you'd like to do while you're here?" he asked as we went back inside.

"I was hoping to see some of Acadia National Park, and I'd like to see the sand bar of Bar Harbor at low tide."

"We could take a drive up to Cadillac Mountain this afternoon and then catch low tide in the harbor afterward. I can check the time for low tide. I have this month's tide table printed out. It's on the bulletin board in the dining room."

I followed Nate to the dining room and he checked the tide table. "Low tide is at 5:03 pm today. If we time it right, we could take a walk across to Bar Island."

"That sounds great, but I don't want to take you away from your work."

He ignored my concerns. "Then tomorrow we could go for a little hike if you'd like."

"I would like that. Anne and I had planned on it. We read there were lots of trails. I didn't bring hiking boots, but I did bring my walking shoes so if you could recommend a trail that is 'sneaker friendly' that would be best."

"Most of the hikes I take now are 'sneaker friendly'. The Great Head Trail is considered a moderate hike but it's short, only about 2 miles and it's been dry. It's a bit of a climb but you get good views."

"You don't have to go with me. You could just drop me off and we'll set a time to meet up."

"It will do me good to take in some of the sights I recommend to my guests. A reconnaissance mission of sorts. You'll be doing me a favor by giving me a reason to do it."

"All right then. We have a mission. What time should we head out today?"

"As soon as you like but at least a couple of hours ahead of low tide so that we have time to visit both Cadillac Mountain and Bar Island."

"2:15? If that works for you?"

Nate checked his watch. "Perfect. I'll meet you here in… about an hour."

CHAPTER 8

Leaving Maddie in the main room, I headed up to my private quarters. Betsy had overseen the renovation of our private space that includes an office for me, a laundry room, two bedrooms, one with a small walkout balcony, and a sitting room with a TV and a large window facing the sea. My office faces the front yard and driveway. Betsy's logic was that if I had work to do and guests were arriving, I would see and hear them pull up. At the time, I didn't imagine I'd be running this place alone, but, as it turns out, Betsy's suggestion had been a good one.

In my office, I got my small worn rucksack from the closet. I put the Acadia National Park guidebook I'd consulted earlier, my binoculars and pocketknife in the pack. Taking it with me, I went to change into my hiking pants. I'd gotten into the habit of wearing the kind with long deep pockets when Emily was a toddler. She loved to pick up treasures when we went for walks and have grandpa carry them home. I doubted Maddie would be collecting anything for me to carry, but just in case, I was ready.

I carried the pack and my hiking shoes down to the kitchen. I filled two thermoses with ice and water, picked out a couple of granola bars and a small bag of cashews, and packed them all in my rucksack. Setting it aside, I went through a mental checklist for dinner to make sure I had everything organized for when Maddie and I returned. I wanted everything to be just right this evening. Even though I'd only just met her, what she thought of me, and my hospitality, mattered more than it usually did with my guests.

Even after double-checking that everything was ready, both for dinner and our walk, it was only 1:45. So I went and sat on the sofa in the main room. I pulled out the guidebook to refresh my memory on a few facts about Acadia National Park and to look at the park map. I mentally planned our route for the afternoon.

Maddie appeared, camera in hand. "I'm ready early, so, whenever you'd like to head out is fine with me."

"I'm ready too. I packed some water for us." I patted my rucksack.

"Thank you! I was just going to ask if we could stop somewhere to pick some up."

"Shall we head out now then?"

"Yes. Let's."

I locked the front door behind us, and we got into the Jeep. "It'll be about 15 minutes to get to the entrance to the park."

"I remember passing it on our way to dinner last night."

"I thought we'd stop at the visitor center first. They have an exhibit explaining the history and geology of the park. Then we'll drive up to the top of Cadillac Mountain."

"Sounds like a good plan."

Maddie looked out the window as I drove, not in a rude, ignoring me way, but in a curious, enjoying the scenery way. It was a comfortable quiet, but I was searching my brain for something to say when she blurted out "That was a strange outcrop," twisting in her seat to look behind us.

"Do you want me to stop?"

"No, No. I just can't help looking at the rocks when I'm not driving. Anne gives me a hard time about it and teases me about how many rock pictures are in our vacation photos."

"We'll see a bunch more rocks today, but if there are any you want me to stop for, just let me know."

We pulled into the park entrance and stopped at the gatehouse.

"Good afternoon, sir," said the ranger in the booth.

"Good afternoon. I have a pass, but I'd like to get one for my guest."

Maddie opened her wallet. "Let me pay for my entrance."

"I'd like to gift you a pass," I said, and then, turning back to the ranger. "Can I please get an annual pass – senior rate?"

"I don't think I need an annual pass," protested Maddie.

"It's only $20, Ma'am," said the ranger. "Less than the day pass and it's good for a year for entrance to any national park."

"I suppose it makes sense then," conceded Maddie.

"Here's your pass, Ma'am, enjoy your visit," said the ranger waving us forward.

We parked in front of the visitor center and climbed the 52 steps to the entrance and made our way through the exhibits.

Maddie pointed to the date the park was founded. "The park is celebrating its 100th birthday this year."

"I wonder if Rockefeller understood how much of a difference giving away some rocky bushland to the government would make to future generations?"

"It does seem that era's ultra-rich were more altruistic and motivated to make a difference. One that would not just benefit their families, but the whole country."

"You think we're all getting more selfish, us Yanks?"

"Maybe not all of you," she said sincerely turning and looking me in the eyes as she did. She had such pretty eyes. They sparkled when she teased or laughed.

I think I stared into them too long because she turned and headed for the door.

"Shall we take the drive up to the top now?"

We followed Park Loop Road and then turned on to the winding Cadillac Summit Road for the three-and-a-half-mile drive to the top.

"You don't get car sick, do you?" I asked Maddie.

"Rarely. Only if I read on a winding road. As long as I'm watching where we're going, I'm fine."

"Looking only ahead, you might miss the rocks," I teased, making her chuckle.

"Don't worry. I'm keeping an eagle eye out for those striations we saw in the visitor center pictures."

We took our time, stopping at several of the scenic pullovers before arriving at the parking lot at the top. We walked up the paved path from the parking area to the top and we took in the expansive view. Then we followed the path around the summit and walked across the rounded rocks towards the edge.

"I thought you didn't like heights?" said Maddie. "This is pretty high."

"I've been here several times, but this is close enough for me." I stopped well short of the area where the rocks began to slope steeply downhill.

Maddie continued closer to the edge, taking pictures. "Those cruise ships look pretty small from here. Kinda like your toy boats."

"I prefer not to think about how far down they are."

"According to the visitor center, about 1500 feet."

"Thanks. That's not helping."

I watched Maddie take pictures of the boats in Frenchman's Bay and of the rocks and tiny sub-alpine plants growing out of the cracks. I did notice how the afternoon sun, still high but slightly behind us, sparkled on the water and reflected off the white cruise ships. But mostly I found myself watching Maddie. She moved confidently over the smooth rock outcrops. She looked very at home, but she made my stomach churn, and my knees feel weak when she moved closer to the edge and peered down. I felt a wave of nausea just thinking about looking over the edge let alone actually looking. I looked out to sea, or at Maddie, never down. Down was very bad.

Obviously, Maddie was unaffected by heights. She had walked the outside ledge of the lighthouse and was now casually strolling around at the edge of a cliff.

She looked back at me smiling. "The light is really nice. I'll just take a few more pictures. OK?"

"Take your time, just please be careful. Don't go too close to the edge."

"Don't worry. It's not as perilous as it looks from there."

I took out my binoculars and studied the markings on the cruise ships. The tenders were ferrying people back from the dock in the harbor which meant they'd be moving on soon and the town would be back to its normal tranquility.

Thankfully, Maddie started walking back up the rocks towards me. I felt a rush of relief when she was safely on the path beside me. I could finally stop imagining terrible scenarios where she slipped and disappeared over the edge.

"Are you ready to head down and get a close-up view of the land bridge and Bar Island?" I asked. Both were visible because we'd walked around the summit and were now facing northeast, although the gravel bar was still quite narrow.

I handed her my binoculars and she trained them on the harbor below. "There are people walking across already."

I checked my watch. "We should have plenty of time to walk across. It's not quite low tide. The bar should still be getting wider when we get there."

"So we'll keep our feet dry then?"

"Hopefully, but if we need to dry our shoes, I can always light a fire this evening and they'll be ready by morning."

"I so appreciate you taking time to show me around."

"It's my pleasure. Really. Since retiring I've kept busy with the B&B, but I still have lots of free time. It's not often I get the pleasure of escorting a lovely young lady around town."

Maddie laughed off the compliment. "Lady, perhaps. Young. Not so much."

"Age is only a number. You seem young to me." I felt a warm rush when I detected a slight blush on her face.

"I'm no spring chicken."

"Now that sounds like something an old lady would say. Does anyone actually know what a spring chicken is anymore?"

Thankfully, Maddie wasn't insulted but snorted in laughter. "Guess that makes you an old man for knowing."

She had a lovely honest laugh. Not fake. When she laughed, I couldn't help but laugh too.

After driving back into town, we parked near the end of Bridge Street.

I pointed to the sloping path leading to the beach and the gravel bar. "It's almost low tide, we should have plenty of time to make it over and back."

Maddie scooped up her camera and hopped out of the car. "No time to waste."

We picked our way across the gravel and sand bar, avoiding the pools of water that were swirling and draining as the tide pulled the sea away. Maddie stopped several times to photograph little sea creatures in the pools. She also picked up stray pieces of trash.

"I can take that from you. I have big, empty, pockets."

She handed me the bits of plastic and paper. "I can't leave it. I don't understand why people can't use trash cans."

"The willingness to clean up other peoples' messes. Admirable quality."

"I made a career of it."

"I thought you were an engineer."

"I am. But in the late seventies, our firm transitioned from purely structural into environmental engineering. Once we started investigating groundwater, we discovered it needed to be cleaned up."

"Other peoples' messes?"

"Exactly."

"In my 35 years with Bond Technologies, we had to pay to clean up a few messes. We didn't realize in the fifties and sixties how expensive it would be. It wasn't even on our radar. Back then environmental audits weren't even a part of our acquisition due diligence. If we'd realized the future liability of some of the sites, I bet we'd have passed on some of the deals."

"It's expensive either way. Pay more upfront, or possibly pay much much more when it's a disaster. Unfortunately, it can't always be avoided – shit happens – excuse the swearing."

"Do you miss your job?"

"Yes and no. It was interesting to see the field change and the science evolve, but by the late 90's it was already becoming a commodity. The industry was viewed as an expense. Jobs went to the lowest bidder, not the most technically competent. I think my timing was good to sell the business when I did."

"When was that?"

"January 2006. When did you retire?"

"91. Got my 35-year gold watch. I thought Betsy and I would travel and relax but within 5 years I needed something to challenge me and, voila, your picture inspired the Hope Point Lighthouse B&B. 19 years later, I'm still at it."

"Look. We've made it to Bar Island without getting our feet wet."

I'd been so lost in our conversation I hadn't noticed we'd crossed the half-mile land bridge and were standing on the cobble beach on the edge of Bar Island.

"What would you like to do now, Ma'am?"

Maddie pointed to the many rock pile sculptures that looked like little people standing guard on the slope leading up from the beach. "I'd like to make an inuksuk."

"What's an 'eenookshook'?"

"They were an Arctic communication device marking trails or a location. The Innuit people would build them on the tundra for things like marking a migration route to follow and hunt caribou."

"You mean like Eskimos?"

"Yes, but I don't think Eskimo is politically or culturally correct anymore -although I'm not really sure."

"If I ever meet an Eskimo, I'll ask him what I should call him."

"Or her," corrected Maddie grinning. "One must be gender-sensitive as well these days."

"Well if we're going to make an inooka-whatever, we need to gather up some rocks. First day with you and you already have me picking up rocks."

"Pick flat, square ones. It will make it easier to build."

"Yes Boss-Ma'am."

We found a nice flat spot facing town and we constructed our little man. He even had stubby arms sticking out and a roundish stone for a head. He fell over several times during construction, but with four hands working together to balance the stones, we eventually got him standing proudly – all twelve inches of him.

"We definitely need a picture with 'Inny'," said Maddie.

I thought it was cute that she'd named him. "Want me to take one of you with the little guy?"

"No. We can both be in it. Sit beside Inny and hold out your arm."

Maddie put the camera in my outstretched hand with the lens facing me. She moved it slightly up and down and pushed several buttons.

"I'll set the timer and hop into the picture. Now, hold still."

She pushed the button on top and the camera started beeping and blinking. She scrambled in beside me and said "Smile!" Just then, the camera clicked and stopped beeping. "Stay put," she ordered before I could say anything or move.

Maddie took the camera from me and shaded the screen with her hand. "Not bad, but we should try one more. Give me your hand."

I obediently stretched out my arm and took hold of the camera as Maddie aimed it and pushed buttons. She scrambled back to her spot beside me while the camera beeped. Just as she scooted into position, she hit Inny with her elbow. Inny crumbled, Maddie fell back laughing and I dutifully held the camera steady.

I couldn't help but laugh. "I guess we won't win any awards with that shot."

Maddie squinted at the camera screen. "It just might. It's actually pretty funny."

She tilted the camera towards me and shaded the screen with her hand so I could look. The picture was a definite keeper. Maddie falling backward, laughing, and me looking at her with a shocked expression, all perfectly framed and in focus.

I pointed to the land bridge. "The tide's starting to come in. We should start heading back."

Maddie saluted our fallen rock pile. "Bye Inny. Sorry we don't have time to fix ya."

"Poor Inny. Such a short life."

Before we got to the mid-point of the channel the waves were starting to lap over the gravel bar.

I could tell we were going to have to wade the last bit. "We probably should take off our shoes."

We rolled up our pant legs and carried our shoes and socks the rest of the way.

Once on dry land, Maddie wrung the water out of the bottom of her pant legs as best she could. "It's all Inny's fault that I'm going to drip in your car."

"Whose idea was Inny?"

"You may have a point … but if you'd been quicker with the stones…"

"I don't mind a little water in the Jeep. Ready to head home?"

"Yes. Thank you. It's been a lovely afternoon."

"My pleasure. I hope you'll show me the rest of the pictures you took."

"I'd be happy to send you any you like. It's easy with digital. Not like the old days with film, waiting to get them developed, and then making reprints of the ones you wanted to share."

"Not to mention the postage to mail them, keeping your fingers crossed that they wouldn't arrive bent or damaged."

Maddie looked at the screen on the back of her camera as we drove home. "There are a few promising ones. If you give me your email address, I can send them."

"I definitely want the picture of poor Inny's demise." What I didn't say was that I hoped that picture would remind me of her laugh, hearty and genuine. I couldn't help smiling thinking of it.

We pulled into the driveway a few minutes later and I hurried around and opened Maddie's car door while she was gathering up her camera and purse.

"Thanks again for being such a great tour guide."

"As the kids say…no problem! Shall I open some wine for us ?"

"Sure, but I'll just run up and change out of these damp pants."

"If you want, I can pop them in the dryer for you."

"No need. They'll dry in my room. I'll be right back."

"Take your time. I'll be in the kitchen. I presume a red wine would be ok?"

"Yes. Thank you."

Maddie headed upstairs to her room, and I headed for the kitchen. I started to wonder if I'd made a mistake with the menu, given Maddie's preference for red wine. I scolded myself for not asking if she'd prefer white, given we were having crab cakes. I selected both a white and a red that would be good with dinner and set them on the counter. It was not like me to be second-guessing and nervous about hosting. It's not like I never entertained dinner guests. I'm usually very relaxed. I was, however, out of practice 'courting' a lady. And that was the moment that I realized that I wanted to 'court' Ms. Maddie Cole.

CHAPTER 9

When I walked into the kitchen, Nate had his back to me. He was dicing a red pepper and humming to himself.

"Can I help?" I asked.

Nate turned around, washed his hands in the sink and dried them on the bar towel he had draped over his shoulder. "You can by keeping me company. Pull up a stool. Can I pour you a glass of wine?"

I took a seat at the kitchen island. "Only if you're having one as well."

"I have a Sauvignon Blanc and a Beaujolais Nouveau that I think will both work with the crab cakes we're having for dinner. Which would you prefer?"

"I'm not strict with the 'white with fish' rule so, if it's OK with you, I'll have the Beaujolais."

Nate opened and poured the wine deftly as a sommelier. As if he read my thoughts he said, "I waited tables and tended bar all through college and law school."

"Did you and Betsy do a lot of entertaining before starting the B&B?"

"I've always enjoyed entertaining. Betsy didn't particularly enjoy cooking or hosting. It was stressful for her because she worried about making a good impression. So, we usually hired caterers for the food, but I liked to bartend for our guests."

Nate moved the cutting board he was working on to the kitchen island so that he was facing me as he worked.

"Just let me know if you want any help," I offered. "I enjoy cooking and I'm pretty good in the kitchen. I can be your sous-chef and work for my supper."

Nate ignored my offer. "Are you hungry? I picked up some local cheeses at the farmers market today that I thought we could have either before or after dinner."

"Either is fine with me," I answered, then added with a wink, "or both."

"I did notice that you and Anne are big fans of cheese."

"I don't think I've met one I haven't liked."

"I hope the ones I picked aren't the first."

"I can't imagine it."

Nate opened the fridge and took out a wooden tray covered in plastic wrap. On it were three different cheeses. All very yummy looking.

"These are all from the Fuzzy Udder Creamery," he said, setting the tray down in front of me.

"What a great name!" I couldn't help grinning with happy anticipation of trying the cheeses from the curiously named dairy.

Nate described the cheeses while placing a knife by each one. "This is 'Whirlwind' which is a mix of sheep and goat and has a layer of ash. This is 'Frost Heave' made from goat milk. This is 'Cyclone' which is strong and a mixture of sheep, goat and cow's milk. It's a bit like taleggio."

"Yum."

"Here are some crackers and bread. Please, help yourself."

To my embarrassment, my stomach growled, probably because I was hungrily eyeing the cheese. "Excuse me."

"Huh?" said Nate looking at me with a puzzled expression.

"My stomach growled."

He smiled and waved towards the cheese. "You better give it what it wants."

"I'll try the Whirlwind first."

It was soft, and I spread it on a cracker. A few small crumbles fell to the plate Nate had set out for me. I cleaned my plate of any remnants of the first cheese before slicing a piece of the Frost Heave and putting it on a thin slice of bread. I didn't eat it immediately, although, I wanted to. I set it down on my plate and took a sip of wine. I let the wine linger on my palate.

I appreciated that I was getting VIP service from Nate. He was very attentive and was scoring high marks for the red wine and cheese. I hoped he wasn't finding entertaining me a bother. He'd said I was here as his guest, so I wasn't sure how I'd broach the subject of payment for all the extras that he was giving me.

"Is the wine ok?" asked Nate picking up his glass and taking a sip.

"Yes. Lovely. Perfect with the cheese."

"You haven't tried the Cyclone yet. Do you like aged cheeses?"

"I'm just trying them from mildest to boldest. I love aged, stinky cheeses." I smiled at him to show my appreciation.

"Good, then we should get along perfectly."

"You like blue cheeses, too?"

"Not my favourites, but I am rather aged myself," he said with a playful grin.

I couldn't help laughing. I pretended to sniff the air. "I hadn't noticed any stink."

"Ahh, but you didn't dismiss the 'aged' part. I'm crushed." He clutched his heart and feigned pain. "You wound me, Madam."

"Tis only a flesh wound."

It was Nate's turn to giggle. "That should be my line. But here's to getting in today's Python quote within the first cocktail." He raised his glass to me and took a sip.

I lifted my glass, toasting in return. "Here's to being a little silly every day."

"Is that your secret for looking and staying so young?"

Nate said it sincerely, and I was surprised by the compliment. "You're too kind. I wish I knew the secret. What's yours?"

"Keep waking up every morning."

"That's an important first step. The experts say having a 'purpose' is key, but I think that's just a polite way of saying 'busy'. I feel better when I have a full schedule, but I've always been that way. It's not a 'now I'm old I need to keep busy' thing."

"What keeps you busy?"

"Lots of different things. Some I enjoy, others, I feel I should do."

"What kind of things 'should' you do?"

"I get asked to mentor and speak at Women in Science events at both my alma mater Queen's and U of T. I'm known for being a bit of a pioneer. In my day very few women were engineers, let alone have careers that didn't end when they got married or had a baby."

"Times have changed."

"Not as much as I would have liked. The numbers of male and female students are equal, but women are still under-represented in senior positions or as owners."

"There were a few women at Bond, but in my day, the only women on the executive floor were the receptionist and secretaries. Sorry, executive assistants."

"I don't recall the exact statistic but only a very small percent of Fortune 500 companies are led by women. In the sixties and seventies, when we were fighting for equality, if you'd told me that in 50 years we'd not have at least fifty percent women in positions of power, I wouldn't have believed it. It's a bit discouraging."

"We might get a female president this time," Nate offered hopefully.

"That would be a major event, but over 50 other countries have beaten the US to that milestone. Canada, Germany, England, even countries you wouldn't expect like South Korea, have had female leaders. So, it's about time."

"The Republican party hasn't given me much to vote for this time around. As much as it pains me to support a Democrat, it's looking like Hilary might be the most reasonable choice."

"I guess we'll see in November if your fellow countrymen agree."

"They usually recommend avoiding controversial topics like religion or politics on a first date," said Nate.

"Good thing we aren't on a date then. I was just thinking of asking you if God is your Lord and Saviour."

Nate laughed, reached for the wine bottle, and topped up our wine glasses. "I hope that doesn't prevent us from going on a date someday."

"I think I'm a little old for dating."

"I'm a great-grandpa and I think dating a lovely younger woman would be just, well, great."

My mind skipped around wondering how to respond. He didn't seem to be much older than me. I wanted to ask how old he was but resisted, to avoid being inappropriately personal.

Nate seemingly read my thoughts. "You're too polite to ask, so I'll tell you. I'm 83."

"How'd you know that's what I was thinking?"

"Well, I know I should never ask a lady her age, so I figured this was a way to trick you into sharing."

"I admire your strategic thinking. I'm 78."

"I'd have guessed much younger. Now you must tell me your secret."

"I don't have a secret. I just try to never say no to a new experience and to laugh some every day, even if it's at myself. And, most importantly, never think about my age."

"Wow."

"Wow?"

"Yes. Wow. The more you talk, the more you amaze me."

"I'm not that interesting. But I have been told I talk a lot."

"You do talk a lot."

I made a pouting face and grumbled, even though I knew he was teasing.

"I mean that in the best of ways." Nate was back-peddling, which made me smile.

I helped myself to more of the Cyclone. "I forgive you. But only because you're bribing me with good wine and cheese."

"I hope you like my crab cakes and asparagus just as much."

"I'm sure I will."

"I decided on asparagus because that's what was fresh and local at the farmers' market."

"That's the best way to decide what's for dinner."

"I've practiced eating what's local and seasonal much more since going to a cooking school in Italy."

"When did you go?"

"In 2006, after the Olympics. I combined a family trip with Ann, Lane, and Emily to the games with some wine and food education. The school was just outside Turin, The Italian Culinary Institute for Foreigners."

"That's a remarkable coincidence. Anne and I went to Torino for the Olympics as well. I also stayed on to take a cooking class, but at il Melograno in central

Torino."

I'm not exactly sure what Nate was thinking, but I was stunned that in the past twenty-four hours we'd discovered two significant coincidences where we crossed paths. My photo in London and now the Olympics.

"I suppose a lot of people went to the Olympics, so that alone isn't much of a coincidence but also staying for a stint at a cooking school... that's ... astonishing," mused Nate.

"Did you go with a group or a friend?"

"No, just me. I met several nice people in my class. Two Aussies and a couple from New York. How about you?"

"I attended alone as well. I was in a class with a family from England, a retired couple and their daughter and son and their spouses."

"I kept in touch with some of my classmates, the Aussies actually came and stayed here. They were a lot of fun and one of the few guests that were allowed to mess up my kitchen. We made polenta and tajarin that we learned to make together in Torino."

"So you're not letting me help because you don't want me messing up your kitchen?"

"If you'd like to help..."

I hopped off my stool and moved towards the sink to wash my hands. "Put me to work, Chef."

"I picked up some strawberries at the farmers' market."

"Local and seasonal. Chef Bosco would approve."

Nate pulled a heaping quart of berries from the fridge. "If you could wash and slice these. Here's a bowl. The knives are in the first drawer to the left of the sink and the colander and cutting boards are in the cupboard under the knife drawer."

"These are beautiful. How would you like them sliced? Thin? Thick?"

"As you like. I was thinking I would serve them over a scoop of vanilla ice cream."

Working side by side in the kitchen felt surprisingly natural. We chatted about our cooking school experiences, marvelling several more times at the coincidences. Nate started assembling the crab cakes just as I finished with the berries.

"Did you learn your crab cake recipe in Italy?"

"No, this is my recipe. I started making crab cakes when I moved to Boston for my first job. I think I've perfected the recipe for my taste. It's heavy on the crab, light on the filler. They pretty much always fall apart, but I prefer my cakes to be crab cakes not 'filler cakes'. I also bake them in the oven rather than frying."

"Unconventional recipe and technique."

"I hope you'll like them."

"I'm sure I will. What else are you putting in there?"

"The usual ingredients, just very light on the mayo and breadcrumbs."

"So, you're not going to share your secret recipe, eh?"

"If I told you, it wouldn't be a secret and you wouldn't need me around to make them," he said with an impish twinkle in his eyes.

"I should have paid closer attention to what you were doing earlier. I'll take notes next time."

Nate made four nice-sized crab cakes and put them on a cookie sheet and then moved on to the asparagus.

"Do you want your asparagus steamed or roasted?"

"Chef's choice."

"I think roasted is best." Nate put the asparagus on another sheet pan, drizzled them with olive oil and sprinkled them with coarse salt. "Are you hungry now?"

"Not starving. I've been nibbling cheese. You?"

"I'm a bit hungry so if you don't mind, I'll keep things moving and serve us as soon as everything is ready."

"Can I do anything else to help? Set the table?"

"That would be nice. I thought we'd eat in the guest dining room. Pick any table. In the sideboard, you'll find everything you need. Don't worry about plates I'll bring them from the kitchen. While you do that, I'll get these in the oven and make the tartar sauce."

"Is that because you're keeping that recipe a secret too?"

"As a matter of fact, I am! A guy's got to have a few secrets."

I went into the dining room and chose the same table by the window that Anne and I had used because it had a lovely view. So close to the summer solstice, even though it was almost 8 pm, it was still very bright outside, and the sun was reflecting off the water.

I set out napkins, silverware, and water glasses. I looked around for something to use for a centrepiece. Nate had gone to the trouble of making dinner, the least I could do is put a little effort into the table setting. I remembered seeing some candles in the living room. So, I helped myself to a candle in a small glass holder and set it in the center of the table. The glass holder was colourful, even if the tea light inside wasn't lit.

Satisfied with the table setting, I went back to the kitchen. I chatted with Nate while our dinner was in the oven and then watched him expertly plate our dinners, arranging the asparagus in neat lines beside two crab cakes and two wedges of lemon.

He nodded at our wine glasses and the bottle. "If you could take our wine through, I'll bring the rest."

Nate followed me into the dining room carrying two dinner plates in one hand and a small tray with condiments in the other. He handled them like an experienced waiter, setting them on the table with a little flourish and a big smile. "Dinner is served, Madam."

He bowed and pulled out my chair for me to be seated.

"Thank you, Sir."

"The table looks lovely. As is the company."

I felt a little embarrassed by the compliment, so I picked up my fork and said, "Buon Appetito."

Nate watched me as I took a bite of the crab cake. "I recommend a squeeze of lemon and, of course, some of my very secret tartar sauce."

"It's very good. But I always give due consideration to the chef's recommendations."

I helped myself to a spoonful of the sauce. "You said you perfected this recipe after moving to Boston?"

"I did. I moved to Boston just after finishing law school."

"Why Boston?"

"I got a job working as a patent attorney with Bond Technologies."

"What sort of technology were you patenting? Is patenting a word?"

"It is. Chemical formulations and coating processes. At the time, we were developing layering technologies to make glass shatterproof."

"Interesting."

"Learning from the scientists, mostly chemists, was. Their inventions, the processes and properties... fascinating. But much of my work was tedious. Investigating prior art in the days before computers meant hours and hours in the basement of the Boston Public Library, searching card catalogues, printed volumes of Gazettes and microfilm."

"How did you find the time to perfect your crab cake recipe? Did you patent it?" Just as I finished speaking, the forkful of crab I was holding disintegrated and fell to my plate. "You could have called it 'Delicious Self-destructing Crab Cake'."

"There's not much holding it together, but a claim of self-destructing would never hold up," he said in a very lawyer like way.

"Perhaps you should serve them in little pots, or maybe a cup. You could call them crab cupcakes? There might not be any prior art for that."

"I do make a delicious hot crab dip, which is essentially crab in a cup."

"Whatever you call these, crab crumble cakes, they are excellent."

"Crumble cakes? I should feel insulted. But the guest is always right, I shall call them Crab Crumble Cakes from now on."

I was a bit worried that I'd come across as critical. "I'm sorry. I didn't mean to imply anything negative about your crab cakes. Dinner is excellent and I'm enjoying it, and the company, very much."

"No offence taken. Since you've eaten all your crab cakes, they are clearly not that bad." He smiled amiably and reached for the bottle of wine to refill our glasses.

I looked out the open window beside us. There was a cool breeze blowing in. "Nice evening, eh?"

"We don't see the sunset, but the evening light on the ocean can be very pretty."

"I saw a bit of a lovely sunrise this morning. I was awake, briefly, around five, but I fell back to sleep and didn't get out of bed to investigate in detail."

"I see the sunrise most days. I'm usually up early."

"Maybe I'll try to catch a bit more of it tomorrow. Speaking of tomorrow. I hope I'm not putting you out. I bought a book this morning, so I can always go for a walk on my own along the path you showed me last night and then curl up with my book. I can entertain myself if you've got other things to do."

"I'm looking forward to entertaining you. I was thinking we'd do our little hike in the morning."

"Do you know what the weather is supposed to be like?"

"The forecast is for low 60s all day. No rain but it could be overcast."

"Sounds like a good day for a hike."

"After our hike, I thought we'd go to lunch."

"A roadside lobster perhaps?"

"That can be arranged. Since you and Anne explored Bar Harbor today, I thought we'd take a drive to Seal Harbor."

"Sounds like a great plan. I hope you'll let me take you to dinner tomorrow evening."

"That's not necessary. You're my guest."

"Either you let me cook for you – or you let me take you to dinner. I insist."

"I have a feeling that you'll not take 'no' for an answer."

"You are correct."

"Then I suggest we go to Paddy's Grill, one of the pubs in Bar Harbor. If that works for you?"

"Sounds like we have the perfect day planned."

"Would you like any more asparagus? We've eaten all the crab cakes."

"No thank you. I'm saving room for dessert. I didn't clean all those lovely strawberries for nothing."

Nate began clearing the dishes from the table and I started to get up to help.

Nate shook his head. "Sit. I'll be right back with dessert."

I settled back into my chair to enjoy the view and the sound of the waves breaking against the shore. The air was humid and cool, and I could smell the sea. A 'briny breeze' I thought to myself. The words sounded funny. I must have been grinning because Nate looked at me inquiringly.

"What's so funny?"

"I was just enjoying the sights, sounds and smells."

"Not laughing at me, then?"

"No. Not at all. I was thinking the sea air was a 'briny breeze' and was amusing myself with the alliteration."

"It is a 'briny breeze' which is much better than 'fishy funk', which we also get sometimes."

"That doesn't sound good."

Nate had brought bowls of vanilla ice cream with strawberries and whipped cream, topped with a crunchy cookie straw.

"Very fancy." I took a moment to admire it before digging in.

"Nothing but the best for my VIP guest."

"I hardly qualify as a VIP guest. Have you had any real VIP guests?"

"I've had a few, but they usually want me to keep it quiet so they can have privacy."

"Then I'm definitely not a VIP. No paparazzi following me."

"I think they like that the old man won't be posting instatweets or whatever it is the kids do."

"Instagram posts or tweets. They are two different things."

"Not my thing. You youngins can keep it."

"I don't do much myself, but I follow Anne and I post the occasional photo."

"Email and Skype is pretty much the limit for me."

"So which VIP guests can you tell me about?" I knew I was being nosey, but I was curious.

Nate looked at me and had a few silent spoonfuls of dessert before answering.

"I can't tell you, but there was one particular guest who was my biggest thrill. If you guess who she is, then it's not like I told you."

"At least you've given me a clue, it's a she. Is she a movie star?"

"Not going to tell you that. She came several years ago and bought out the whole place. All four rooms although she only used two of them. One for her and her husband and one for her personal chef."

"Did you let the chef use your kitchen?"

"Yes. He was very respectful. It was normal for him to cook on the road. He told me that he'd cooked all over the world on everything from a camp stove to the kitchens of five-star hotels. He was really down to earth, and I even learned a few tricks from him."

"You're not giving me many clues about your VIP. Just female and travels a lot."

"I did tell her that I was a huge fan, and I had all her records."

"Now we're getting somewhere. She's a singer. What kind of music?"

"The good kind."

"That's very subjective and not very helpful."

"I can tell you she was very appreciative. She sent me a thank you gift you walked right by yesterday."

"Where? When?"

"When we were touring outside?"

"We saw the lighthouse, but that can't be it."

"After the lighthouse."

"The garden on the hill?"

"You're getting closer."

"The bench?"

"That was one part of the gift..."

"What was the other part?"

"The evergreen tree."

"An evergreen?"

"Well, I did tell her it was one of my favourite songs..."

"Get out! You hosted Barbra Streisand?"

Nate grinned mischievously. "I'll never tell. But if it was her, I'd have hosted my all-time favourite entertainer that I've had a crush on forever."

"That's a real VIP."

"She was so gracious. Unfortunately, most VIPs aren't. I enjoy non-VIPs more."

"VIPs too high maintenance?"

"VIPs and brides. Which is why I don't do weddings anymore. With wedding parties come tears or screaming or both." Nate shivered like he was reliving a nightmare.

"That sounds bad."

"Worse than bad. Honeymoons I can handle. But I've had one too many Bridezillas. I'm too old for that kind of drama."

"There it is. I can see your grumpy old man showing."

"We better change the subject. No more wedding talk."

"Fine with me. I don't see myself planning any weddings any time soon."

"What about Anne? Any chance she'll find Mr. Right?"

"I'm not sure she's ever looked for him, or her."

"You two seem close. I'd think you'd share everything?"

"We are close. But I'm not her 'go to' person for relationship advice. To be fair, I've been a single parent since she was young, so I didn't have much credibility from the get-go."

"Ann went to Betsy with relationship or boyfriend questions. I never gave the answers she wanted. I tried to solve the problem, which is, apparently, exactly the wrong thing to do."

"I think parenting is mostly guesswork, getting it wrong sometimes, getting it right sometimes and sometimes just not getting it at all."

Nate laughed. "Yes. That's what it feels like! Grand-parenting is easier. You don't have to worry about doing the right thing all the time."

"And now you're a great-granddad. One more degree of separation from responsibility."

"I may never know if I mess up with Jake."

"I can't imagine you'll mess up. Emily obviously adores you."

"Maybe because when she was little, we always came bearing lots of presents. And, for her alone, I broke my no weddings rule."

Nate stood and picked up our dessert bowls. "Would you like anything else? More wine?"

"Is there any left?"

"Just a splash." Nate poured the last of the bottle into my glass. "I'll just put these in the dishwasher. Do you want to move our conversation to the living room?"

While Nate went to the kitchen, I wandered over to the main room. Setting my wine glass on the coffee table, I picked up the guest book that was open on the reception desk and began reading the entries from previous guests. Some were just names and their hometown while others were long entries with descriptions of their stay or very sweet thank-you notes.

"I hope you'll sign my guest book before you leave," said Nate coming back from the kitchen with a pair of water glasses on a tray with what was left of the cheese plate. "I thought you might want a little water, sparkling of course."

"Thank you. With this kind of service, you'll definitely get a glowing review."

"The fog has rolled in so it's too dark and damp for a post-dinner stroll. Shall I light the fire?"

"A fire would keep the dark and foggy at bay."

"Make yourself comfy."

I settled on the sofa facing the fireplace. Nate lit the fire, that was already set in the fireplace, with a long wooden match, even though he had one of those long butane firelighters alongside the matchbox.

"Are you using a match to impress me with your fire-making prowess?"

Nate chuckled. "It's my new mission in life to impress you. Is it working?"

"You've already impressed me with your skills as host, tour guide and chef."

"This old dog is running out of tricks," he said with a sigh.

"I doubt that."

Nate closed the fire screen and settled into the wing chair next to the fireplace. "Tell me more about your trip to the Olympics and cooking school. I'd like to know how close I came to meeting you in 2006."

"Have you been to other Olympic games?"

"No, only Torino. You?"

"It's the only one for me too. Anne and I have talked about going again. She got the bug after we visited the Olympic Park in Calgary and took a ride in a bobsleigh. We both prefer winter sports to summer."

"Being a spectator outdoors, in winter, can be rather uncomfortable."

"You can dress for cold; you can't undress enough for hot."

"You have a point. But why Torino?"

"We started off thinking we'd go to Salt Lake City. But my mother was living with me at the time and her health was failing. There was too much uncertainty for me to commit to buying tickets months in advance. Four years later, my mother had passed and I was in the process of selling the firm and would finish my transitional time in January 2006. There was no reason not to say yes to going to Torino with Anne. How about you?"

"Like you, it was my daughter who was the driving force behind me being there. She wanted me to join them for a family holiday. I agreed but asked for it to be in the winter when the B&B is closed."

"I bet you thought you'd be going somewhere tropical, or Disneyland?"

"I was surprised when she suggested Torino. But, as it turned out, I enjoyed it much more than I thought I would."

CHAPTER 10

Maddie agreed that going to the Olympics had been a surprisingly positive experience. As she started to talk, she became quite animated. I noticed how her eyes sparkled when she talked about something that excited her.

"What impressed you most?" I asked.

"I'd heard of 'The Olympic Spirit' but it took being there in person to truly understand what it is. I remember I felt it at the first event we attended."

"What event was it?"

"It was luge. We'd watched several runs from trackside and then we decided to sit for a while. We made our way to our grandstand seats at the finish line. There was a large video screen in front of us where we could watch the run and see the times. We could also watch each sled arrive at the finish line. I don't recall the exact countries, but it was the two-man luge. The top two rival countries had runs one after the other. The first team down had a phenomenal run. Their large crowd of fans went wild cheering as they pulled up from their run in front of the grandstand. Their rival team started their run brilliantly and their fans were screaming and cheering. Then they crashed. You could feel the air get sucked out of the whole crowd. Everyone watched the screen, holding their breath until the two men arrived at the bottom and stood up and waved to the crowd that they were all right. The crowd went wild cheering. Not only their fans but everyone. In that moment of their failure and disappointment, the whole community supported them. And, when their next run was the fastest of all the teams, even their rivals were on their feet cheering for them. The emotion of that moment was overwhelming. Remembering it, I still feel it." Maddie subtly swept a tear away from her eyes. "As you can see, it still gets me."

I pulled out my handkerchief. "Here."

She took it with a self-effacing chuckle. "Thanks. I seem to get leakier with age. You don't want to see what happens during National Anthems."

I wasn't sure what to say. I could see she was feeling uncomfortable, so I changed the subject.

"What time would you like to get started tomorrow?"

"As you may have gathered, I'm not naturally an early riser, would 9 am work for you?"

"You're my only guest, so your schedule is the only one that matters. Breakfast requests?"

"A cappuccino like this morning and something light."

"Cheese and jam on toast then?"

"Perfect." She drained the last of her wine and looked up at the clock on the mantle. "Wow, 10:30 already. I'm probably keeping you up since you're an early riser."

"Don't worry about me. I can adjust to any schedule or time zone."

"I'm impressed. I always struggle to change time zones. Thank goodness Bar Harbor and Toronto are in the same one."

"I just set my watch to the new time, and I'm adjusted."

"How fortunate. I'm awake when I should be sleeping, and sleepy when it's bedtime at home. It takes me days before I get back to my usual 7 to 8 hours of solid sleep."

"I can't recall the last time I slept eight hours straight."

"I should get out of your hair. Shall I put this glass in the kitchen?"

"Just leave it. I'll put it in the dishwasher on my way through."

"Thanks, and thank you for a lovely day, and dinner."

"Good night, Ms. Cole."

"Good night, Mr. Jacobs."

From the smirk on her face, as she bid me goodnight, I could tell she was teasing and I grinned back in return. Usually, I'm relieved when my guests finally retire to their rooms, but not tonight. The room felt oddly empty. It's not that I don't make conversation with my guests, but I mostly answer their questions and provide them with information, and they talk amongst themselves.

As I poked at the fire in the fireplace, I kept picturing Maddie perched on the sofa with her wine chatting to me. She did talk a lot, but I liked listening to her. She seemed to have a quick response for everything. She kept me on my toes. Our conversation was easy and rapid-fire. I realized how much I missed having someone to banter with. I'd had my colleagues at Bond and my regular golf buddies at the Country Club, but Betsy had never been that person.

Betsy didn't find any of the projects I was working on interesting and, looking back, I was equally disinterested in hers. It's not that we didn't talk. She would tell me about the art classes she helped to teach at St. Mary's School, update me on the household repairs like what the gardeners had or hadn't done or add items to my honey-do list, or describe what had transpired at bridge club. None of which I found particularly stimulating.

Early in our relationship, I'd tried to find subjects Betsy liked to talk about. She frequently accused me of debating things with her when I thought we were just talking.

"Stop arguing your case," she'd say.

When I reassured her that we were just exploring different points of view, she would look hurt and tell me I was trying to make her look stupid. Over time I stopped making an effort to find topics to discuss with her.

The only subject we shared an interest in was Ann. Betsy and I both wanted the best for our daughter. Because I traveled regularly for my job and worked long hours, I missed a lot of Ann's day-to-day activities. I appreciated that Betsy kept me informed. She relayed every doll crisis, skinned knee, school grade or athletic achievement of our daughter's childhood. But Betsy shared fewer details as the years went on. Apparently, only a mother understands teenage angst and boyfriend drama and Betsy shielded me from it.

Once Ann had left for university, we rarely discussed our day other than to determine what time I'd be home and when dinner should be served. One positive side effect was that we rarely argued. We fell into a comfortable routine. We would watch the evening news together each night. Afterwards, I would often work in my study, and she would read or knit while listening to the radio. We would each retire to our separate bedrooms when we were tired.

As I walked back to the kitchen with the leftover cheese and our empty glasses, I found myself thinking how much I'd enjoyed the back-and-forth with Maddie. It was quite a contrast from what I'd been used to with Betsy. Betsy was a good person, kept our home running well and deserves most of the credit for raising Ann. For 43 years, we had a cordial relationship, but I couldn't say we were ever best friends; we just didn't have enough in common.

I first met Betsy at her parents' Snell Isle home where I was a guest. Her parents hosted a social event that was a meet-and-greet with the local Republican candidates. Betsy's father, Howard Williams, had been a partner in a prominent law firm in St. Petersburg, Florida but had recently been appointed by the governor as a judge. I was 21 years old, and I had just started law school at Stetson University College of Law. Our professor had arranged for a few of us to be invited to the Williams' party. I wasn't keen on going but my classmates insisted we go network. Their logic was that, in a couple of years, we'd be looking for jobs and it would be a good idea to get to know the 'right' people that could open doors for us in the future.

When we arrived at the party our host greeted us and directed us through the main room and screened porch that opened to the yard and pool. The other guests were outside being served drinks and appetizers by white-gloved waiters. It was a cool but sunny Florida afternoon and so I walked around the pool to the end of the yard and stood on the dock to take in the view of Snell Isle Harbor. As I was standing looking at the small fishing boats and sailboats moving in and out of the harbor, a young, very pretty, blonde woman in a yellow dress and a familiar-looking middle-aged man carrying drinks and talking, joined me on the dock.

The young woman turned to me. "Have you been introduced to Congressman Pepper?"

She had lovely blue eyes that caught my attention immediately.

"No, I haven't."

"Congressman Pepper, this is..." She paused and looked at me to give my name.

"Nate Jacobs. Nice to meet you, sir."

He extended his hand. "Call me Claude. I can tell you've not been properly introduced to our hosts' daughter Elizabeth Williams. Miss Williams, Mr. Nate Jacobs. Mr. Jacobs, Miss Williams."

I extended my hand. "Pleased to meet you, Miss Williams."

"Nice to meet you too, Mr. Jacobs. But please, call me Betsy. Everyone does."

"My work is done here," said Congressman Pepper. "If you'll excuse me, Betsy, Nate, my better half, Mildred is speaking with one of my donors and she's signaling me to join her."

I turned to Betsy. "You have a lovely home. It's very generous of your family to host this event."

"This is the third year we've hosted. My parents encouraged me to join the young republicans even before I was old enough to vote. I'd be happy to introduce you to a few people."

"I shouldn't monopolize your time."

"It would be my pleasure. First, we'll get you another drink and then we'll make the rounds," she said with a bright smile, and I think a little wink. "Tell me a bit about yourself, Nate."

"I've just recently moved here from Baltimore to attend Law School at Stetson. I work part-time at the Casa Bonita Hotel on St. Pete's beach as a cook."

"That mustn't leave a lot of spare time to enjoy the beach."

"It doesn't, but I love being near the water. I have a classmate who has a boat, and we sometimes go out fishing."

"Do you like fishing?"

"I like catching, cooking and eating but not a fan of cleaning fish."

She slipped her hand under my arm and guided me towards the bar. "That gives me something to work with."

Fresh drinks in hand, she led me from one cluster of guests to another. Betsy knew everyone. She introduced me to judges, prosecutors, city councilmen, state representatives and even the ex-governor of Alabama.

The afternoon flew by. I looked at my watch and was shocked at the time. "I need to leave for my shift at work."

"That's a shame, we've not had much time to talk just you and I."

"Perhaps I could call on you sometime?"

"I'd like that. My number is Garden 2431."

"Nifty. I'm sorry, but I really need to leave now. Please thank your parents for their hospitality."

"Of course, I wouldn't want to make you late for work." She extended her hand formally. "Nice to have met you, Nate."

I repeated her number to myself as I hurried back to my car. I wrote it on the inside cover of the textbook I'd brought with me to study if it was slow in the restaurant. I wondered to myself how long to wait before calling. I couldn't wait. I called the next day and asked her out to a movie the following Saturday.

She looked so cute when I picked her up for that first date. Her blonde hair rolled away from her face and tied in a low ponytail with a bright blue scarf. She wore a full blue skirt, a white and blue top and she was carrying a white sweater. I remember thinking how the blue was just a shade darker than her eyes.

I opened the door of my 1951 Studebaker for her. "I thought we'd see The Rear Window tonight. That is, if you've not seen it already."

"I haven't. I like Grace Kelly. I saw her in Dial M for Murder last year."

"Did you enjoy it?"

"Yes. Do you go to the movies often?"

"I haven't since starting law school. Do you?"

"Not as often this time of year. But in the summer, when it's hot, there's no better place."

"As kids, the only place with air-conditioning was the movies. We would mow lawns and wash cars just to spend a whole day watching movie after movie to escape the heat."

"Last month I went to see Sabrina with Audrey Hepburn, A Star is Born with Judy Garland, and at Christmas time my whole family went to see White Christmas, which was a lot of fun."

"Is that the Bing Crosby musical?"

"Yes, Bing Crosby and Danny Kaye. Singing, dancing and a good story too."

"I'd probably like it, but I doubt it will be showing anywhere until next Christmas."

"Sometimes they show winter movies in summer as part of the double feature. Maybe you won't have to wait that long."

We arrived at the theatre and I bought our tickets. I offered to buy drinks and popcorn, but Betsy declined.

"I must be the only person alive who doesn't like popcorn."

"Something else then? Candy?"

"No thank you. I don't need anything more than your company." She smiled at me in a way that was utterly charming.

We settled in to watch the show. First the newsreel, then a short cartoon and then finally the feature. When the curtain came down and the lights came on, I stood and extended my hand to Betsy. I remember noticing how light her touch was. Just her fingertips touching my hand. She was delicate, almost fragile and I felt almost instantaneously protective of her.

We left the theatre and made the serpentine walk down Central Avenue, weaving around the peculiar green benches placed perpendicular to the road and jutting into the sidewalk. We watched the people sitting who sat watching the people walking.

"Would you like to go for ice cream? Or is it too cool?"

"It's never too cool for ice cream."

"I know a place near the beach."

"Are you thinking of Peetie's?"

"Is that ok?"

"It's one of my favorites."

"Then Peetie's it is." I opened the car door for her and then hurried around to my side.

On the drive, Betsy sat with her hands folded in her lap, quiet and quite unlike the confident woman who had approached me at the party. I got the feeling she was nervous. I attributed it to the uncertainty of a first date, and I did my best to make her feel safe and at ease.

Peetie's was crowded when we arrived. There were no booths left so I led her to the counter where there were two stools together. Betsy looked at the stools with disappointment

"I'll keep my eye out for anyone leaving. Maybe a booth will open up," I said feeling unsure about what would please her.

She gathered her skirt around her and sat down. "This is fine."

"What would you like?"

"A root beer float, no whipped cream. Peetie's makes them with the only kind of root beer I like."

I ordered Betsy's root beer float and a vanilla milkshake. I swiveled my stool to face her. "What did you think of the movie?"

"I thought Grace Kelly's dresses were great. She is so beautiful."

"As Lisa, she was very brave as well as being well dressed."

"I could never do what she did. Sneaking into that man's apartment like that."

"You have to admire her curiosity and tenacity. She was determined to get to the truth and nothing, or no one was going to stop her."

"They did solve the mystery in the end, which is good, but through the whole movie I had this terrible feeling that something dreadful was going to happen."

"Poor choice of movie on my part. I certainly don't want your recollection of our first date to be a feeling of dread."

Betsy laughed and put her hand on my arm reassuringly. "The best part of the movie was seeing it with you. I felt very safe, even in the scary parts."

Her admission sent a ripple of pride through me. Being needed felt good.

"I'm sure you have lots of people looking out for you. It was impressive how many people you introduced me to..."

"I've known all of them for a long time. Most either belong to the same country club as my family, or they are business associates of my father's."

"Do you work at your father's firm?"

"Oh no! I find anything legal terribly dull. I work in an art gallery."

"Are you an artist?"

"I paint a little but I'm not very good."

"I'm sure that's not true."

"I'm told I have a good eye, and that's important in the gallery business."

"Did you study art in school?"

"Yes. Art history and curating."

"Have you been working there long?"

"Just a few months. My uncle owns it."

"What kind of art do you like?"

"I like all different styles. Currently, we're featuring Cuban artists. It's become our specialty."

"I don't know anything about Cuban art."

"If you'd like to see some, you can visit our gallery. It's just across the street from where we went to the movies. You can't miss it."

Our ice cream drinks were done. I paid our bill, and we headed back to my car. On the drive home, Betsy was very quiet. I was concerned that she hadn't enjoyed the evening. As we approached her house on Cordova Boulevard, I asked her if there was something wrong.

"No, I'm just a little tired. I had a lovely evening."

"I did too. I'd like to see you again."

"I'd like that."

"I'll pick a non-scary movie next time."

"That would be nice."

I stopped the car in the driveway, got out, and escorted her to the door. Just as we approached, it opened, and her father stood there, filling the doorway, looking at his watch.

"At least you've brought her home at a decent hour. Say goodnight Betsy." He stepped aside just enough for her to slip past him.

Betsy waved at me over her father's shoulder. "Good night, Nate. Thank you for a lovely evening."

"Good night, Betsy. Good night Mr. Williams."

I was a little surprised that she agreed to go out with me again when I called the next week. I was flattered that someone of her social status would be interested in me. Looking back, there were clues during that first date that our personalities were a less than ideal match. At the time, I was totally oblivious. I ignored her disinterest and dislike for the legal profession and hints at other attitudes and behaviors that would lead to our clashes in the future. All I saw was the dolly with the bright blue eyes and lovely figure.

As I shut out the light to go to bed, I couldn't help but wonder what Maddie had been like when she was younger. Would she have been as confident and adventurous as she seemed to be now? I fell asleep thinking of her and feeling very happy that I would get a chance to learn more about her tomorrow.

CHAPTER 11

At 7:15 my mobile phone's alarm tore me away from a pleasant dream. I don't recall what it was, but I wasn't happy about leaving it behind. I resisted opening my eyes, shutting off the alarm with a blind swing at the phone. When my eyes finally opened, and I saw the ocean, I felt a little more enthusiastic about getting up. Only a little.

Still lying in bed, I checked my phone for messages. There was an email from Anne from early this morning asking how I was doing and if I was alright on my own with Nate. Instead of replying, I sent her a text.

Having a lovely time. See you tomorrow evening.

Anne replied, almost instantaneously. *R U sure?*

Yes.

I wondered if she was really concerned or just a little jealous that she couldn't stay longer. Her next message came a few seconds later.

What's up for today.

Going for a hike.

Be careful.

Yes dear :)

Wish I was there too.

Knowing she would rather be here with me was consoling because I was still feeling disappointed she had to bail on our vacation plans. I was looking forward to today's hike and sightseeing, but I would have rather been doing it with my best travel partner. Although Nate had been wonderful company yesterday, I worried that multiple days of having to show me around would be tiresome for him, especially since he had the inn to run.

I opened the window and sniffed outside – trusting my face over the weather app on my phone to tell me what I should wear. It was cool, so I dressed in layers. I was glad Anne and I had gone shopping in Boston. I'd resisted, but she'd insisted I needed some new outdoor clothes. We'd bought me a pair of navy convertible cargo pants, the kind that has bottoms that zip off and turn into shorts, a bright red, lightweight t-shirt and a thin navy long-sleeved shirt that zipped like a jacket made of some space-age fast-drying material. Surveying myself in the full-length mirror, I looked much more athletic than I felt. 'Fake it til you make it', I thought to myself. Although, if I haven't made it yet, I'm quickly running out of time.

It was a few minutes after 8 when I joined Nate in the kitchen. He was reading the paper with a coffee and what appeared to be a bacon and egg sandwich.

"Good morning, Nate."

Nate put the paper aside and started pressing buttons on the espresso machine.

"Good morning. I'll have your cappuccino ready in just a minute. Would you like cheese and jam again today or would you prefer something else?"

"Just the cappuccino to start. Don't let me interrupt your breakfast."

"Would you like some of the paper? Or I can put on the TV with the morning news."

"I'd enjoy watching some news…as long as it's not Fox News…"

Nate turned on the small TV mounted high on the kitchen wall across from us. "CBS This Morning ok?"

"Yes, I like Charlie Rose."

Nate went back to eating his breakfast and skimming through the paper. I watched the headlines and sipped my coffee. It was very comfortable. Nate occasionally looked up and watched the TV when a story interested him. He shared tidbits from the paper: a vigil for the victims of the Pulse nightclub shooting in Orlando, record heat in the southwest and the Cleveland Cavaliers winning the NBA final.

"I'm not a basketball fan," he said, "but it's a big deal for Cleveland as they've not won anything in decades."

"I can relate to that being a Leaf fan. 49 years and counting since the last Stanley Cup for Toronto."

The election dominated both the broadcast and newspaper stories as well as the bulk of the commercials that ran between the TV segments. Being Canadian, I didn't have a horse in the race, but I couldn't help but be appalled by the mean-spirited and negative tone of the campaign ads. It didn't matter if the candidates were national or local, negative ads dominated.

"Doesn't anyone advertise about the issues? What they're going to do to make things better? If you believe the advertising, all candidates are evil."

Nate started refolding the paper. "I want to tune out the negative ads, but it's hard to do, so I won't be watching much TV between now and November." I noticed that he checked to make sure all the sections were in order before setting the paper aside.

"We can turn it off if you like."

"It will be over at 9, I can tolerate a little bit more, but then, I'm revoking your TV privileges, young lady," he said with a wink as he opened the refrigerator. "Can I get you some water or juice?"

"Water, please."

"If you want to help yourself to breakfast when you're ready, I've put out a few options. There's bread for toast, English muffins, butter, jam and of course cheese. There are the three cheeses we had last night as well as some cheddar in the fridge. If you'd like something else, I can make you eggs, any way you'd like, and there's bacon and sausage…"

"I can make myself something if you don't mind me messing up your kitchen."

"You proved yourself capable last night."

"Washing and cutting strawberries is hardly a master chef skill."

"But you weren't messy… so I'm confident you won't muck things up too much. I need to go do a few things in my office before we head out. Are you still thinking nine?"

"Yes. I'll be ready. Please go do whatever you need to. I'll fix myself something right now."

Nate left and went upstairs. I made myself breakfast while continuing to watch the morning news. Toasting an English muffin, I couldn't resist topping it with jam and cheese. I couldn't choose between the Frost Heave and Whirlwind, so I had both. Each on one half of the muffin. Both halves were equally yummy.

Just as I was finishing my last bites, Nate returned to the kitchen. He had his backpack with him. He took two water bottles from the fridge and put them into the pack.

I picked up my plate and cup and carried them to the sink. "Perfect breakfast."

"Just leave your dishes. I'll clean up. Do you have anything you need to do before we head out?"

"I just need to grab a couple things from my room and go to the washroom. Why are you grinning?

"Your Canadian-isms… My B&B rooms have bathrooms, not washrooms."

"Fine. I need to use the bathroom and then I'll be back with my things."

"If you want to add your things to my pack, please feel free."

"I brought a small pack, so I can carry my own water. I'll just have my camera and a few small things."

"I'm happy to carry both our waters. I have my pack all ready. I never go hiking without basic survival items, even if it's just a short walk like today."

"You're a good boy scout."

"Never was one, but I do like to be prepared."

"Be prepared is the Girl Guide motto. I should know, I was one."

"When you're ready to go, I'll be here finishing up the paper."

"I won't be long."

"There's no rush. It's going to be cool and clear all day so whenever we hit the trail it will be about the same."

It took me only a few minutes to get ready and in no time, we were in the car and on our way. I was excited and happy to be getting out for a hike. Even if my pace isn't what it used to be, being outdoors invigorates me.

We showed our park passes to the ranger at the park gate. I thanked Nate again for the gift of my annual pass.

He looked over at me and smiled. "It's already been an excellent investment."

Something about his look relieved my apprehension about imposing on him. He seemed to be as happy as I was to be playing tourist today.

We drove along Park Loop Road until we reached Sand Beach. To reach the start of the Great Head Trail, we had to walk along the beach to the far end. The trail began with a set of granite steps leading to an open ledge that gradually sloped upward. At the top of the granite stairs, on the left, there was a large millstone.

"Can you imagine how hard that was to get up here?" Nate remarked.

"I certainly wouldn't want to be the one pushing from behind."

We stopped several times, so I could take pictures. The views of Sand Beach and The Beehive, the majestic peak that overlooks it, were inspiring. The trail curved, following the coastline, providing lots of opportunities to take pictures looking out over the water. Although the sun's position wasn't ideal for the pictures, the views were dramatic and well worth the climb to experience them.

At the highest point, we came across the rubble of a tower. Nate explained that, in the early 1900s, it had been a tea house. We decided to stop and have 'tea', or in our case, the water and nuts that he had packed for us.

"Excellent choice of trail, Mr. Jacobs."

"Thank you, Ms. Cole. I enjoy this one a lot."

"Sitting here on this site, where people have been coming to enjoy the view for over a hundred years... interesting to ponder, eh?"

"Like... Who were they? Who first thought 'Hey this is a great spot for a tearoom'? Did they walk up or come on horseback?"

"I wonder why the building wasn't kept up? It's a spectacular place for a house."

"Except for the lack of a road."

"Well, there is that..."

"And now it's all national park land."

"If it had been my tearoom tower, I'd have wanted to keep it."

"Carrying supplies up on foot might dampen your enthusiasm after a while."

"True."

After our little break, we continued onward. The trail sloped down into the trees away from the shoreline. After about a quarter-mile, the trail rejoined the ledge trail that led back to the granite steps to the beach. Nate stopped mid-way across the beach and picked up a flat rock and skipped it across the water.

I stopped to watch Nate's stone tumble across the water surface. "I've always wondered what makes throwing rocks into water so irresistible. Four skips, not bad."

"Not bad? I'd give it a 'pretty good' rating at least."

"You'll have to do more than 4 skips to impress me, Mr. Jacobs."

I watched, amused, while Nate searched the beach around him for another stone. He selected a good-looking flat one. He wound up to the side and snapped his arm sending the stone skipping.

"I counted 6 that time. Beat that Ms. Cole!" he taunted.

I couldn't resist the challenge. "I'll give it a go."

I searched around me for a suitable flat rock. I wanted one that was the right size, large, but still small enough to fit in my hand and a bit triangular so I could get a good grip on it and put some spin on it when I threw it.

Nate picked up another stone and flipped it around in his hand. "You're being mighty picky."

I made my selection and wound up for my throw. "Ok. Here goes."

I smiled as Nate counted. "One.......Two......Three...Four...Five...Six, Seven, Eight. WOW!!"

"Not bad, I guess." Despite my nonchalance, I felt that surge of satisfaction that beating boys at their games has always given me. "Your turn."

"You some kind of stone-skipping shark?"

"Who me?" I said innocently

"Yes you."

"Want to go another round?"

"Ok, loser buys lobsters for lunch."

"You're on."

We both carefully selected our next rocks. Nate threw first.

"Yes! 8!" He smiled and looked smug while I wound up and threw mine but his brow furrowed as we got to 8 and my stone continued to tumble before disappearing.

"I was going to insist on buying you lunch anyway."

"Are you implying you lost on purpose?"

"I guess you'll never know," he said impishly.

"I'm highly motivated by lobster."

"No problem repeating yesterday's lunch then?"

"You aren't getting out of buying me lobster, Mister. I won fair and square."

"I wouldn't think of it. A deal's a deal. I know a place on the way to Seal Harbor. I'd say I'd race you to the car, but you might agree, and I can only take so much loss in one day."

"Hang around with me long enough and you'll get used to it."

Nate chuckled and shook his head. "Aren't you the cocky one with just one win under your belt?"

"Just you wait and see."

"Sounds like fun to find out."

We'd arrived at the car and Nate opened the door for me and I thanked him as I got in.

"At least you don't seem to mind that I treat you like a lady even if you were the better man at stone skipping."

"I enjoy a gentleman with manners. Although, I've struggled for equality my whole life."

"A few minutes ago you were so confident in your superiority; mere equality would be a step down."

"So you're acting as doorman not gentleman? In deference to my superiority?"

"If that's what it takes to appease your delicate sensitivities... then yes," he said playfully mocking me.

"Delicate? No one's ever accused me of that. Complicated, perhaps."

"You are a mind-bending puzzle. I'll give you that."

"To quote Churchill, a riddle, wrapped in a mystery, inside an enigma?"

"Yes. Precisely."

"I'll take that as a compliment."

"As it was intended."

CHAPTER 12

I suggested we drive through Acadia National Park to our lunch spot. Maddie chatted away to me as we drove. Actually, she did most of the talking during the entire morning. I remember thinking how easily she jumped from subject to subject with a seemingly unbounded ability to find something interesting to talk about.

Maddie looked at me suspiciously. "What are you grinning about."

"You actually."

"Me? Why? Are you laughing at me?

"No. You're fascinating. I was just thinking that for someone who spent their career negotiating and talking – I've barely got a word in for the last 15 minutes."

"I'm sorry. I tend to run on when I'm excited."

"You're excited?"

"Well, nervous excitement."

"Why would you be nervous?"

"I only just met you two days ago."

"But they've been very long days…"

"So you're sick of me already?"

"No of course not. I'm teasing. I don't want you to be nervous around me. I'm just funnin' you."

"Funnin? That sounds like a word my Grandpa would use."

"Now who's teasing who?"

"That wasn't teasing, that was an observation."

I couldn't help but snort a laugh. "You're a rather impossible woman."

"Thank you."

"But really now… Tell me why you're nervous around me."

"Just hoping you're not bored."

I was flustered for a moment. I wasn't sure how to respond to her. I was flattered. This lovely woman was anxious about making a good impression on me. I realized she was silent and wanted to reassure her.

"You needn't worry about boring me."

"That's a relief." She fell silent again.

"You're the most fascinating woman I've met in a very long time."

"Now I'm really nervous. That's a lot to live up to."

"And the most impossible."

"You said that already."

"It bore repeating." I pulled the Jeep into the parking lot of Abel's Lobster Pound. "Come on. We're here. I gotta pay my lobster debt."

As I held the door for Maddie to go ahead of me into Abel's, she looked me in the eye and thanked me. Such a simple gesture, but at that moment, I had a powerful déjà vu feeling. The smell of the sea, the sun on my shoulders, Maddie's eyes; it was like I'd lived that moment before. The queasy feeling of a memory replaying at the same time as reality.

It was only an instant, but it had enough of an effect for Maddie to notice. "Are you ok?"

"Yes, Ma'am. You might think this is odd, but I just had a déjà vu moment."

"That happens to me sometimes, that's not odd."

"Glad you don't think this old man is losing it."

Her eyes narrowed, and she had a mischievous grin. "I would never say so before you buy lunch."

"But you might think it…"

"Not before you pay your lobster debt. Right now, I think you're great."

We both were chuckling as we made our way to the counter. I ordered our lobsters and drinks and I suggested we sit outside with the view. While we waited for our lobsters to steam, Maddie took pictures. First with her camera and then with her phone.

"I want a picture of us with the lobster shack behind us." She took my arm, turned me around and directed me to stand beside her. "I can show Anne you're taking good care of me. Come closer." She put one arm around me and held her phone with the other. "Look at the phone and smile."

I did as I was told. She seemed to take her picture taking seriously. I didn't want to be the reason for a bad photo.

"I'll send this later." She put her phone into her purse and picked up her camera again. "Can I take your picture at the rail over there?" She pointed to the railing that ran along the edge of the patio.

"As long as I can stay on this side of it, sure."

Maddie snapped pictures. I scooted to our table to sit when she finally lowered her camera and peered at the screen.

"You're a very handsome model."

"You know you can stop with the niceties; I've paid for lunch already."

Maddie laughed and smiled at me shaking her head. "Well, you better play nice all afternoon. Remember I'm buying dinner tonight."

"Did I tell you how beautiful you look today?"

Maddie laughed again. "That's a little over the top, but you're on the right track."

I didn't think it was over the top at all. The way her hair blew across her face, her expressive eyes and smile that lit up her face when she laughed; stirred me in a way I hadn't felt in a long while. She was smart, funny, and beautiful. If I'd told her all that, it would have been over the top. Fortunately, I was saved from the subject by our lobsters arriving.

"Two lobsters, two butters, and two cokes," announced our server. "Wet wipes and extra napkins are in the basket. Can I get you anything else?"

"Not for me. These look great!" Maddie's eyes flashed with enthusiasm and desire that gave her an air of youthful exuberance.

I watched her zealously begin to dismantle and devour the steaming red crustacean. "I guess you really like lobster."

"I'm sorry. I should be more lady-like about it."

"Not at all. It's quite ...entertaining... and educational... to watch the way you get every morsel of meat out of that little guy."

Maddie looked up grinning and licking a bit of butter from her lips. "Too good to waste any of it."

She put the large claw into the cracker and squeezed. With a crunching sound, the shell gave way, splattering us both, and sending bits of shell flying.

"Oops," she said with a giggle.

I took off my sunglasses to wipe the lobster-water spots from the lenses. "You're hazardous to dine with."

"Anne should have warned you I'm a bit messy while lobster eating."

"Everyone is messy. That's why they have those plastic bibs. Which, incidentally, you probably should have been wearing." I reached across the table to pull a bit of shell from her hair.

She frowned and squinted at my hand. "What have I got in my hair?"

"Just a bit of shell." My fingers brushed her cheek as I slid it from her hair. She recoiled, and I was afraid I'd been too forward. "I'm sorry. It was a little stuck, I was just trying to get it from your hair." I apologized sincerely while looking into her eyes for her response.

"I'm sorry. I'm such a mess. Spots and shell bits…"

"I think you look adorable, shell bits and spots and all." I was sincere and looked into her lovely eyes and smiled to reassure her. Fortunately, she smiled back and visibly relaxed.

"I'm certainly not making a very good first impression."

"You made your first impression two days ago – you just continue to confirm it."

"That I'm messy and ill-mannered?"

"Hardly. That you're my favorite kind of person. The really interesting kind."

Maddie smiled but looked down at her lobster. She focused on removing the last bits of lobster meat from the shells, perhaps to avoid my gaze. I couldn't tell if she was embarrassed, but she looked uncomfortable.

"You're too kind," she said finally, seeming to regain her composure, taking a deep breath, straightening her shoulders, and looking directly at me. "You should be safe now. I've finished dismantling my lobster, and there's only eating to be done."

"Are you sure it's safe," I said suspiciously. "Butter can be treacherous."

"Only to me. You should be safe. Now stop watching me and eat your lobster. It's really good, eh?"

I did as I was ordered. It was really good. I couldn't help smiling watching Maddie. She was clearly enjoying hers and I resisted the temptation to point out that she had a little butter on her cheek. But it was adorable. She finished hers long before I finished mine and began cleaning her fingers with one of the wet wipes.

Maddie looked at me and frowned. "I don't know how you stay so clean."

"I have a few years on you. Maybe when you get a little older, you'll get the hang of it."

Maddie snorted with laughter. "You think you're a wise old man, but really, you're just a wise ass."

"I resemble that remark." I put my paper plate of empty lobster shells on top of hers and opened a wet wipe for myself. "Are we ready to head out?"

"I'd like to use the washroom first, but after that, I'll be ready."

As we walked out of the restaurant and back to the car, I suggested we head into Seal Harbor and walk around there for a little bit, then drive home along the coast. "Does that sound good to you?"

"Absolutely. Lead on MacDuff."

I drove south and then east on Route Three and into Seal Harbor. We passed the harbor and yacht club and Maddie commented on how picturesque it was.

"I'd really like to walk on the beach and take some pictures."

"We can certainly do that," I pulled into the parking lot across the street from the public beach. "But I have a place I'd like to show you first, that I think you might like."

We walked up Main Street until I stopped us in front of the gray wooden building I wanted to show her. Maddie read the sign on the door of The Naturalists Notebook.

ALERT!!!

This building is flying through space!! And so are you!
You are circling the sun at 67,000 mph.
You are rocketing across the universe at 490,000 mph
as part of the milky way galaxy.
(Yes, you are standing in the Milky Way right now.)
You are spinning around the axis of the earth at 750 mph.

HOLD ON TIGHT!

Step inside to explore the 13-billion-year history of your life.

"We have to go in," she said.

"I thought you'd get a kick out of this place. They call themselves an 'Exploratorium'."

"You already know me so well!"

"I get the feeling I've only just scratched the surface."

"This place is so cool!" Maddie repeated a couple times as she walked up and down the aisles of the shop, smiling and reading aloud the quirky earth facts that were posted over various displays. "There's still so much to learn."

"I could get you these flashcards if you think they'd help?" I winked at her holding up several packets with titles like 'Mushrooms of Maine' and '100 Minerals'.

"I could quiz you on the way home."

I quickly returned them to the display. "Bad idea, flashcards…"

"I do like these ice cube trays." She held up a silicone tray that made ice cubes that spelled out E=MC2, and several other mathematical symbols like the infinity symbol. "I have a friend's dinner party to attend next week. These will be the perfect hostess gift for a fellow geek."

"I'm delighted you're supporting the local economy."

Maddie made her way to the counter to pay, and I stepped outside to wait for her. She joined me a few minutes later. "Where to now, Mr. Jacobs?"

"I thought we'd take a walk along the beach and harbor so you can take some pictures. Then I thought we'd drive through the residential area and see where the rich and famous of Seal Harbor make their nests. From there we can pick up the coastal road for the drive home."

"Sounds great." She pulled her camera out of her backpack and stuffed the small paper bag with her purchases into it. "This is a really pretty little place. I'm glad you suggested it."

"I'm glad we have perfect weather. It would have been uncomfortable had it rained."

"Clear but overcast can be great lighting for pictures."

I led us across the road near where we'd parked the car and we walked out onto the small sandy beach.

"There's a nice view of the boats from here. We can also walk over towards the yacht club."

"I'm surprised we have the whole beach to ourselves," said Maddie.

"It's early in the season, and Tuesday. It will be crowded on the weekend for sure."

I hung back as Maddie walked down the beach towards the surf. She took pictures. I watched her. She would take a few pictures, adjust her camera settings, and then take several more, peer at the screen on the back of her camera, and then take some more. She turned and saw me watching her.

"I'm sorry. I take a lot of pictures, hoping to get a good one."

"We're not in any hurry. Take as many as you like as long as they're not of me."

"It's an interesting little harbor. So many different types of boats. Runabouts, sailboats, yachts and rowboats all mixed up together. It's very interesting to photograph."

"Now what are you taking a picture of," I asked as she pointed her camera downward.

"The sand."

"I don't see anything too exciting about the sand…"

"When I zoom in I can see sand grains, tiny intact seashells, broken shells, bits of seaweed and even some sea glass."

"One of those artsy pictures I'd never think of taking."

"Sometimes looking through the lens I see things I wouldn't notice otherwise."

"But if you're always looking through the lens you might miss something big just outside the frame."

"Valid point." She let her camera hang down and slowly scanned the scene from left to right, turning completely around to face me. "Let's take a selfie here. You have to help again."

I obediently held out my arm as she'd previously taught me, and we documented our presence on Seal Harbor Beach.

She checked the picture. "You're getting good at this."

"See, you can teach an old dog new tricks."

"You're not a dog at all."

I laughed. "I noticed you didn't dispute 'old'."

Maddie giggled and shrugged.

"Let's move along then. If you're done taking pictures and insulting your guide…"

"I'm done." She gave me a playful elbow jab. "At least, done taking pictures."

We drove around the residential streets that overlooked the harbor. Then, we headed home along back roads that followed the coast. Maddie took pictures out the car window. I offered to stop but she declined, she said she enjoyed the challenge of "drive-by shooting". I did insist we stop at the Cooksey Drive Overlook and take the short walk out to the point.

"Wow!" Was Maddie's reaction as we stepped out onto the granite outcrop.

I stayed well back from the edge, but she immediately walked out onto the outcrop towards the edge.

"Be careful, there's no guardrail."

"I will," she called back to me as she took pictures of the rugged coastline.

It made me physically nauseous to watch her so close to the edge, but I couldn't take my eyes off her. I was hugely relieved when she finally walked back towards me.

"Thank you for insisting on this stop."

"I had a feeling you'd like it, even though, watching you perilously close to the edge nearly gave me a heart attack."

"I wasn't that close. I was safe."

"Until the rock gives way, and you plunge to your death."

"That's a terrible thought."

"I can't help it. I'm not good with heights."

"So you've said. Nothing to worry about now. I'm safely back from the edge and on solid ground."

Arriving back at home, Maddie thanked me again for the lovely day and reminded me that she was buying dinner. I told her I was looking forward to it and we agreed to head out at 6.

"If you'd like a glass of wine, or a bite to eat in the meantime…"

"A bottle of water to take to my room would be great."

We walked together to the dining area, and I handed her a bottle from the fridge.

"Thanks. I'm going to do a little packing and organizing. Shall we meet here a little before 6?"

"Sure. If you need anything or you're ready early. Just come find me."

Maddie headed to her room, and I went to mine. I pulled out my worn leather duffel bag and packed it with the few things I'd need for my overnight trip to Boston. Thankfully, the knit polo shirt and khakis for this trip were more forgiving of my folding abilities than my business clothing had been. Betsy used to fold my shirts for me when I packed for business trips, and I've never really gotten the hang of it.

By all appearances, Betsy was a model 1950s wife. She had kept a clean and orderly home, albeit with the help of a cleaning lady. She was particular about the way laundry should be done, starching and ironing my dress shirts with military precision. And she was similarly fastidious about her own appearance. For at least 25 years, she kept her weekly Friday hair appointment with Helen, her long-time friend and stylist and she never went out without doing her hair and makeup and being appropriately dressed for the occasion or activity.

I could be sure that when I came home, everything was as it should be. I found the predictability and order very comfortable, but I knew she wasn't doing it for me. It was Betsy's need to impress others. She insisted on upgrading our furnishings and décor on a regular basis, and she kept up on what was fashionable. I didn't find redecorating or shopping for a new dining room suite stimulating, I just gave Betsy a credit card and let her choose what she wanted.

My travel for work helped satisfy my need for new experiences and excitement. Travel was different then. As an executive, I flew first class. The stewardesses were glamorous and treated us as if we were all VIPs. They took our hats and coats and hung them up. They served drinks in proper glasses and meals on china plates. They were always young and pretty and smiling. Their stylish, but sexy, uniforms frequently encouraged bad behavior, especially when combined with unlimited alcohol. In retrospect, it was shamefully discriminatory and exploitive, but many of them were thrilled to be chosen and relished the adventure of travel to faraway places in the company of rich businessmen and pilots.

I don't miss the smoky air. We used to say having a non-smoking section in a plane is like having a non-peeing section in a pool. The unlimited alcohol, comfortable seats, and the freedom to roam around the plane as if it were a flying bar helped to make the long, boring, noisy, smoky, flights more bearable.

I was one of the few people in our social circle who flew with some regularity. I was the first person in my whole family to fly. I remember how excited I was to tell my parents that I would be flying across the whole country to California. My mother was terrified for me. She cried and said goodbye as if I was facing certain death. In fact, I don't think she ever stopped being terrified for me.

"What's wrong with taking a train?" she'd ask me every time I told her I would be taking a flight.

Betsy suggested I stop telling her, but I wanted them to know. I wanted them to be proud of me. Being able to afford to fly was, for me, a measure of my success, even though the company was footing the bill. I would have saved Ma a lot of worry had I kept it to myself each time. But I was young, a bit full of myself and very proud of how far I'd come from the Baltimore rowhouse of my youth.

Being asked to travel and represent the company made me feel important. Frequently it was expected that my wife would accompany me, particularly when there was a social aspect to the trip. The wives would have lunch and perhaps visit a gallery or museum during the day and then join us for cocktails and dinner. I looked forward to the opportunity to see new places, but Betsy avoided these trips.

When Ann was young, I agreed, the stability of Mom waiting when she came home from school was important. Especially for the first few years after we'd adopted her. We never wanted her to feel like we abandoned her. But even after Ann was away at boarding school, and later, when she had moved away to University, Betsy still only accompanied me when I insisted, even when the destination was one that most people would have been excited to visit.

She'd protested when I told her that we'd be taking a trip to Paris.

"It's such a long trip and what if something happens to us both and Ann is left without anyone?"

"Nothing bad's going to happen. I thought you'd be delighted – the city of romance, famous art and architecture. Don't you want to see it?"

"I imagine it is romantic if you're not spending your day with other men's wives."

"We'll be together every evening and, if you want, I'll extend the trip for a few days, so we can explore the city together."

"Do I have to go?"

"It would reflect badly on me if you didn't. There will be several very important dinner meetings. One will be hosted by the President of the French Chemistry Society, at his home, and they specifically invited you to attend."

"I don't have anything to wear."

"The trip isn't for a month. You have time to shop for whatever you need. Or you could go shopping there. Paris is the fashion capital of the world. I bet you'll be the envy of your bridge club bringing home a little Parisian couture."

"How am I going to buy things when I don't speak French."

"The company has hired a local guide-interpreter to show you and the other wives around during the day. I'm sure she can help you."

"I don't want to go clothes shopping with a bunch of strangers."

"They aren't all strangers. You know Judy and Midge. They'll both be there."

"How long would we be gone?"

"I have three days of meetings, so with travel and perhaps a couple of days for us to explore Paris, maybe a week."

"A week?"

"We could extend it to 10 days or two weeks? I could take a few vacation days if you want to see more of France."

"I'm not sure we should stay away from Ann that long. Why would you want to waste vacation time when she can't be with us?"

I took her hand and kissed it and gave her my best puppy-dog eyes. "I was hoping we could have a little time just for us."

"Oh, alright. You win. But just one week and I'll need new suitcases as well."

I found her reluctance disappointing. I felt so lucky to have the chance to travel the world and I wanted someone to share it with. It was always a negotiation to get her to agree. But once she committed, Betsy made sure she was prepared both with her wardrobe and with as much information as she could gather about the people we would be meeting. She always seemed to know just what to say and do to glide through every social engagement with a sort of easy elegance that I always admired. When she worked a cocktail party or attended a formal dinner, I saw that outgoing and charming girl I'd fallen for by her parents' pool.

She was always perfectly put together. Her white gloves always crisp and white, hat, purse, and shoes always matched, never a hair out of place, and a way of smiling and looking into your eyes that made you feel like the most interesting person she'd ever met. Betsy slipped into character the moment she walked through the door, the perfect lady and supportive wife.

Even in Paris, when she was surrounded by women who spoke little English, she appeared calm and poised.

"Bon swore, mesdam Gattan," she'd attempted in French that even I could tell was awful. But she'd said it so sweetly and genuinely and quickly apologized, "I know that was terrible. I practiced all day with Suzanne, our interpreter, but I just can't get it right."

Our hostess Mrs. Gattan was charmed and replied in her thick accent.

"You say it perfect. Puleese call me Charlotte."

"How lovely to meet you, Charlotte. Please call me Betsy, it's short for Elizabeth."

"Elisabetta, un très joli nom. Viens avec moi." She handed Betsy a glass of champagne and gestured for her to accompany her into the salon.

I was awed by Betsy's ability to win people over so quickly and so disappointed when the spell was broken, usually as soon as we were alone after an event.

Betsy pulled off her gloves as the hotel room door shut behind us. "French women are so indecorous."

"Whatever do you mean? I thought you and Charlotte got along well this evening."

"She smokes cigarettes in a holder three feet long, drinks champagne like it's water, and doesn't seem at all concerned that her husband has a mistress."

"A mistress? How do you know that?"

"She mentioned it, at a dinner party no less. How churlish! She bragged she had Wednesday nights free because her husband always spends Wednesday with his mistress. Crass, don't you think? To air such dirty laundry to a virtual stranger. Has she no self-respect?"

"Perhaps she's OK with him having a mistress?"

"Why would any woman be OK with that?"

"Maybe it gives her free time for her own pursuits?"

"So you think it's OK to be unfaithful?"

"I didn't say that."

"And she insisted on calling me Elisabetta – it was driving me crazy."

"It is your name in French…"

"But my name isn't French and after tonight I would never want to be a French woman if it means putting up with barbaric behavior like cheating husbands."

I took her hand and drew her closer to me. "You don't have anything to worry about."

She wriggled out of my arms. "It's after six at home, Ann should be finished dinner about now. I should give her a call before we go to bed."

"I'm sure she's fine. You just talked to her this morning. You looked really lovely this evening."

I genuinely thought so. I admired her as I watched her remove the red bolero that she had worn over the form-fitting black dress. She turned her back to me and motioned for me to unclasp her necklace. She'd worn the double string of pearls I'd bought for her the previous year on a trip to Japan.

I handed her the pearls. "I thought we might have a nightcap enjoying our view of the 'City of Lights'."

"I think you've had enough to drink. You're trying to seduce me, aren't you?"

"And what's wrong with that? After all we're in the most romantic city in the world."

"You're acting like a teenager."

"Teenagers can't afford a suite at The Ritz."

"You can't either. Your company is paying."

I pushed aside the barb of her words. It was true. The company was paying for the suite. It was a legitimate business expense because we had hosted a private gathering of our international expert advisors and we needed a private location where we could discuss proprietary information regarding our new formulations. But I was the one that was given the suite as my accommodations. I was the most senior executive on this trip, a position I'd worked very hard to earn.

With the jetlag and busy work and social schedule, we'd not had a lot of time for just the two of us. Seeing her this evening, dressed in her evening attire, laughing, and chatting with the other dinner guests, she was hard to resist. I was still hoping to end the evening sharing an intimate time with my beautiful wife.

"Why don't you slip into something comfy, and I'll get us a nightcap."

"I'll need a few minutes." Betsy picked up her gloves and bolero and took them to the bedroom with her.

I removed my jacket and tie and undid my collar. There was a split of champagne on ice on the bar, compliments of the hotel. I opened it, poured a glass for each of us and carried them into the bedroom. Betsy was sitting on the bed in her nightgown and robe and holding the phone.

"I'm just going to check in with Ann."

I held up the glasses and nodded towards the sitting room. "Come through when you're done. Say Hi for me."

I set the glasses on the table, turned down the lights, and opened the large floor-to-ceiling French doors. I moved the chairs closest to the balcony into position to give us a clear view of the Place Vendome. It was a lovely spring night with a light breeze that carried the cool night air into the room. As I waited for Betsy to join me, I stood on the small balcony, leaned on the iron railing, and took in the scene below. The square was quiet at this hour. A small delivery truck and a couple of bicycles were the only vehicles moving. There were a few couples walking and a couple standing near the large column monument in the center who appeared to be locked in a passionate embrace.

Betsy was taking longer than I had anticipated and I started to worry that something was wrong with Ann. I went back to the bedroom to check on her and found the lights out and Betsy in bed breathing softly, asleep, or at least, pretending to be. There was no sense wasting the champagne.

I retrieved my glass and went back out on the balcony to soak up Paris at night; the sound of laughter from the street below, the pattern of the iron lampposts around the square, the flash of stars and moon as clouds drifted across the night sky. I would have liked to share moments like those with someone who delighted in them.

I wondered what Pierre's mistress was like. Did she see magic in the moonlit city? I felt a pang of envy at the thought of his romantic companion. Charlotte didn't seem to mind. Maybe that's what kept the fire alive in their marriage. I'd never strayed from my marriage vows, but this new knowledge made it seem acceptable, healthy even, to be open to the possibility of passion and romance with someone else. What if our puritan ways were the more barbaric? An imprisoning, restricted and small-minded way of thinking. I drank my champagne, and then hers, pondering these things before closing the doors and going to bed.

It's not that our trip to Paris was unpleasant. It was a business success and we had time to explore the major sights. We visited the Eiffel Tower, the Louvre, Notre Dame, Jardin Tuileries, the Arc de Triomphe and walked the Champs

Elysees and the banks of the Seine. But it was not the romantic holiday I'd imagined. There were no passionate kisses on the Pont Saint-Louis in the moonlight. Betsy had said I was being foolish when I suggested it.

"That sounds like something out of a cheap romance novel."

"I thought you liked romance novels?"

"I do, but they aren't real life."

"We could make it real life?"

"Don't be a ninny," she'd said continuing to walk across the bridge.

There was a knocking sound that brought me back to my packing.

Maddie called up the stairs from the kitchen. "Nate? Just letting you know I'm ready when you are."

"I'll be right down."

I hastily moved my partially packed duffel from the bed to the chair by the window and went downstairs.

"I'm sorry if I kept you waiting."

"Not at all. I hope I didn't interrupt you."

"I went up to pack a few things for tomorrow and got distracted."

"That happens to me a lot. Start one thing, see another and then one thing after another and I've spent an hour doing everything but what I started doing..."

"Shall we head to the pub?"

"Sure," she said picking up her coat. "I think you'll want a jacket or umbrella because it's raining pretty hard."

I reached for her jacket and held it up so she could slip into it.

"You're such a gentleman. Thank you."

I grabbed my raincoat from the hook by the side door. "I try. Do you have everything you need? I wouldn't want you to get out of buying me dinner by claiming you forgot your wallet."

"I'm going to take back my gentleman compliment."

"I guess I'm out of practice. Shall we go, m'lady?" I stepped aside and bowed with a broad arm gesture for her to proceed me to the door. Maddie laughed.

"Thank you, kind sir." She batted her eyes dramatically while smiling broadly. I was starting to really like that smile.

CHAPTER 13

Nate started the car and turned the wipers on high. "The sky has opened up on us!"

"We don't have to go out if you don't want to drive in this weather."

"This is nothing. If it were ice and snow, different story. A little rain won't get you out of buying me dinner."

"Alright then. Driver, take us to Paddy's Grill."

It was raining even harder when we pulled into Bar Harbor.

"Would you like me to drop you at the door because the closest parking lot is across the street?"

"No need. I don't melt."

"Ok then. We'll make a run for it."

As I came around the Jeep, Nate extended his hand, and I took it. We hustled across the street, skirting a large puddle at the curb, and bursting, a little breathless, into the pub's entrance. I let go of his hand and began to shake off the water from my coat as we made our way to the hostess. I noticed Nate hadn't done up his jacket and was quite wet.

"Your best table for two please," said Nate in an oddly formal tone for a local pub.

The young woman picked up two menus. "Absolutely, Mr. Jacobs."

She showed us to a table by the window and handed us each a menu. "Emma will be looking after you tonight and will be right with you." She grinned at Nate before returning to her station.

"Mr. Jacobs. I'm impressed."

"Don't be. Darla is one of the gals that comes to help with parties at the inn."

"She obviously likes you."

"She's just being nice to the old man who…"

"Good evening Mr. Jacobs. Ma'am."

"Hello, Emma. How are you this evening?"

Emma nodded towards Nate's soggy shirt front. "Warm and dry which is more than I can say for you lot. What can I start you off with?"

"I'm the chauffeur tonight, so just an iced tea for now."

"Sweet or regular?"

"Sweet."

"Good choice, you can't be too sweet. And for you Miss?"

"I'm the chauffeured so I'll have a small Guinness."

"I'll be right back with those."

"I didn't know you liked beer."

"We're in an Irish pub... When in Rome."

"You could order Irish whiskey?"

"Maybe later."

"You are a complex woman Ms. Maddie Cole."

"Not as complex as this menu. There are so many choices."

"I've tried most of it. You can't go wrong. Just depends on what you fancy."

"I always fancy something with lobster when I'm so close to their native waters."

"Plenty of options."

"Too many."

"Options are good. But too many good options... that poses a challenge."

"Do you like to share, or do you prefer others keep their hands off your food?"

"I've no objection to sharing."

"I'm open to sharing, except my lobster. You might have lost a finger if you'd tried to share my lunch today."

Nate laughed. "You did devour it with a carnivorous gleam in your eye. I could sense danger."

"Have you tried the crab and lobster dip?"

"It's cheesy and good. I think you'll like it, but it has lobster in it. Will you share?"

I glanced up from the menu and across the table. Nate was chuckling and looking at me. His whole face was smiling, and his eyes were focused on me. I noticed how handsome he was. Especially when he looked at me with that teasing boyish grin.

I looked into his eyes and smiled back. "I guess you'll have to be very brave and attempt it. See if you get any, or at least keep all your fingers..."

"I like a challenge. Go for it. Anything else strike your fancy? Something else to share or maybe something just for you?"

"I'm quite drawn to the lobster roll..."

"That doesn't surprise me. Don't worry I won't suggest we share it."

"You can get your own."

"I just might."

Emma returned with our drinks, and we placed our order. When she'd left Nate lifted his glass to toast saying, "As the Irish say... Slainte."

"To new friends."

"Here here."

There was a short pause in the conversation as we both looked towards the small stage area where a band was setting up their gear.

"Are you looking forward to getting home to Toronto?" Nate asked.

"Yes and no. I enjoy travel and I feel sad when a trip comes to an end, especially when I have to leave Anne. But Toronto has always been home, and I always sleep best in my own bed."

"Do you have anyone special waiting there for you?" Nate looked a bit nervous asking the question like he was afraid he'd overstepped.

"Two old men who are probably thinking I've abandoned them forever."

"Really? Two?"

"Not exactly old men. I have two cats at home who will be annoyed I've woken them from their week-long nap."

"Have you always lived in Toronto?"

"Yes. Born, raised, and firmly rooted. How about you? Where did you call home before the inn?"

"Boston. Betsy and I moved there after I finished law school."

"Ah yes, the birthplace of your crab cake recipe. So, you moved there for work and stayed. Were you from that area?"

"No, I was born in Baltimore, then moved to Florida for law school. That's where I met Betsy."

"You met at law school? Was she also a lawyer?"

"Heavens no! She was the debutante daughter of a prominent judge. We met at a party."

"Did Betsy work?"

"Before we were married, she had a job at a gallery. She studied art in college. Later she mostly did volunteer work some of which was teaching art classes."

"So you lived in Boston up until you retired?"

"Yes."

'That must have been a big change."

"I was ready for a change. I needed something to get me out of bed every morning."

"I prefer getting up mid-morning myself."

"I've noticed." Nate's tone suggested disapproval. I would have found it condescending if he hadn't said it with a smirk and a wink that told me he was teasing.

Our food arrived and we chatted while we shared the dip. On the small stage across the room from us, a band started playing Irish folk songs and sea shanties. It was lively and the pub crowd sang along. Although they were very good, they were loud. Conversation was futile. We smiled and used gestures more than talking for the remainder of dinner.

Using sign language that, by some miracle, I understood, Nate asked if I wanted to stay and listen to the music or head home. I suggested going and Nate nodded his agreement and signaled for the check. Although I had to wrestle it away from him, I paid the tab as we'd agreed.

We donned our jackets and prepared to make a dash for the car, but when we got outside it was no longer raining. Nate extended his hand to me as we approached the curb, but I pretended not to notice. I looked the opposite way to check for traffic and then walked ahead of him across the street.

Back at the inn, Nate asked, "Do you want anything? A glass of wine? Another beer?"

"I shouldn't take up any more of your evening."

"So I can't tempt you?"

"I suppose you can try."

"A glass of red then."

"That would be nice."

I followed Nate back to the kitchen and he poured the wine.

"Would you like to watch TV?"

"Sure."

"We could watch in the breakfast room but the more comfortable TV option is my sitting room."

I must have looked wary. Nate stepped back from me and lifted a hand.

"It's quite separate from the bedroom – I'm not suggesting anything... inappropriate."

"I didn't think you were suggesting anything untoward. Wherever you're most comfortable is fine. But first, I need to use the washroom."

Nate suggested the powder room off the breakfast area and picked up my wine glass. "I'll take this up for you. The sitting room is up the stairs, straight ahead, at the end of the hall."

When I joined Nate, he was sitting, feet up, the remote pointed at the TV, and paging through the guide. The room had a large TV on one wall. Facing it was an oversized loveseat and the well-worn recliner that Nate was sitting in. However, I barely noticed the furniture. What struck me as I entered, was the boats. Dozens of boats perched on shelves, in cabinets and on every flat surface of the room. So many that it was impossible to take them all in at once.

I resisted the urge to circle the room and instead sat on the loveseat beside my wine glass.

"You weren't kidding when you said you collected boats."

"My office is where I keep the majority of them." Nate continued to scroll the tv guide.

"Majority!?"

Nate shrugged and looked at me with a sheepish grin. "I've been collecting for a long time. It just sort of happened."

I looked around the room casually, trying not to seem too nosey. "How many do you have?"

"More than I care to admit."

"Ballpark."

"Let's say hundreds."

"Wow." I picked up my wine and sipped it. "Are you still adding to your collection?"

"Yes, but only if I find something really different or special. So, what do you feel like watching?" He brought up the guide and started paging through it again.

"What do you usually watch?"

"Do you always answer a question with a question?"

"Do you?" I kept a straight face as best I could.

"Are you here for an argument?"

"Python reference?"

"No it's not."

I snickered. "Yes, it is."

Nate smiled. "Ms. Cole you're something else."

"No, I'm not." I snapped back and neither of us could keep from giggling.

"Yes you are."

"No, I'm not."

"You know it's not a proper argument if you just disagree with everything I say."

With my final, "Yes, it is," we both burst out laughing.

"This argument is silly. Before you say no it's not, we need to decide what we're going to watch."

"I'm not picky. I watch cooking shows, crime dramas, movies, late-night talk shows and even sitcoms if they are clever. Of course, I also like silly, but I don't suppose there's any Python on tonight."

"How about Chopped?"

I agreed and settled into the loveseat.

We watched the show, then the news and the beginning of the Late Show. After the opening monologue, I got up from the sofa and picked up my wine glass.

"I'm off to bed. Thank you for a lovely day."

Nate clambered from his chair with a sleepy stretch. "Cappuccino? Eight-ish tomorrow morning?"

"Perfect."

"I'll come down and shut off the lights behind you."

Nate followed me downstairs to the kitchen and took my wine glass. "Goodnight. See you in the morning."

"Night."

Back in my room I opened the gift bag from the Naturalist's Notebook and set the small gift and card I'd bought on the desk. I rummaged in my purse and, thankfully, came up with a pen. Sitting at the desk I considered what I should write in the card. I thought back over the last forty-eight hours. How comfortable I was with Nate. It was like I'd known him much longer than a couple of days. I found myself smiling, thinking about how much I'd smiled and laughed these past couple of days. I'm not an unhappy person but rarely do I sit at my desk with a silly grin. But there I was, not focused on the task at hand but staring into space while my mind wandered around the Bar Harbor area with Nate. Forcing myself back to the note, I started writing. I forced myself to write slowly so that my script was legible. I thanked Nate for the company, being a tour guide and lobsters. I closed with a sincere desire to keep in touch and wrote my email and phone number in the bottom corner of the card. I sealed the envelope and wrote his name on it.

I pulled out the piece of ribbon the sales clerk had given me and then placed the card and the small, wrapped package in the bag, tying it with the ribbon. Not the best wrapping job, but, acceptable under the circumstances. The next trick will be to leave it someplace that Nate will find it after he gets back from driving me to Boston. That might require a small diversion and was a job for tomorrow morning.

My phone beeped. It was a text message from Anne.

You still alive?

Just getting ready for bed.

Good day?

(thumbs up emoji)

Eat lobster?

2X

:) Xtra big or twice?

Twice

What time u arriving tomorrow?

Best guess midafternoon

OK Have your key?

Yes. Good night Baby Girl

Night old woman ;)

LOL Smart ass

I plugged in my phone and set it on the desk next to the room's namesake ferry. As I was getting ready for bed, I wondered how they had selected which boats would be used for the guestrooms. After seeing the sitting room full of boats, I wondered how they kept it to just one boat per room with so many to choose from. I was enormously curious to see what Nate had said was 'the majority' of the collection. I might never get to see it now.

If I hinted at wanting to see more of his boats, maybe he'd offer to show me his office. But the office was in his private quarters, and they were off-limits to guests. He might make an exception for me as he'd already invited me upstairs to watch TV. But perhaps that was just because it was more comfortable for him and he'd had a long day of playing host and wanted to relax. I wouldn't want to make him uncomfortable by putting him in the awkward position of having to say no or worse yet feel obligated to show me. The debate between good manners and my curiosity raged in my head until I was under the covers and drifted off to sleep.

The chirping of my alarm from across the room was the next thing I heard.

One long cat-like stretch, before getting up and moving. By the time I'd showered, dressed, packed the rest of my clothes and toiletries, it was almost 8:30. Nate was in the kitchen when I walked in a few minutes later.

"Good morning Ms. Cole. Did you sleep well?"

"Yes, Mr. Jacobs, I did. And you?"

"I woke up during the storm, got up and checked on things, but other than that, very well."

"Storm?"

"You didn't hear it? Thunder and lightning? Wind? Driving Rain?"

"You're kidding, right? I didn't hear a thing."

"You must be a very sound sleeper."

"When I'm asleep, I'm asleep."

"I'm glad it didn't bother you. I was concerned that you might be unsettled by the sounds this old place makes when the storms roll in. It can sound kinda scary, especially at night when it's dark."

"I don't scare easily, even if I had woken up."

"It's my job to make sure my guests are OK. I got up and checked to see if your light was on or you'd gotten up, but everything was dark in the guest wing."

"Do you often go skulking around in the middle of the night?"

"You'd be surprised, or at least I was, how many people get spooked by thunderstorms and come out of their rooms looking for company, and maybe a Scotch."

"Sorry if I disappointed you by sleeping through it."

Nate put a frothy cappuccino in front of me. "Disappoint me? Surprise me, shock me and maybe even scare me a little, but you could never disappoint."

"Other than the storm and you haunting the halls, did I miss anything else?'

"No, that's all the excitement overnight."

"I'm all packed except for my toothbrush. So, whenever you're ready, I'm all set to head out."

"Are you in a hurry to get to Anne's?"

"No, she'll be at work all day. I told her I'd be there by dinner time – so there's no rush. I didn't want to keep you waiting if you were wanting to head out early."

"I was thinking we'd leave around 10. That way I'll get to Emily's before the evening rush hour."

"I'll be ready."

"Can I make you some breakfast?"

"Just coffee this morning. But thanks."

"I need to do a little office work before we go. Help yourself to something if you change your mind about breakfast."

I simply thanked him again, not letting on how curious I was about his office. Nate left and went upstairs. After he'd gone, I mulled over all the things I could have said to lead him towards inviting me up to his office. Usually, I'm not timid about asking for things, but somehow asking Nate to show me his office was just a little too familiar. What if he said no? That would make the five-hour drive to Boston a little more awkward.

Given that we'd be sitting in a car most of the day, I decided to take a walk. I left a note on the counter saying I was going to walk the trail along the coastline, and I'd be back soon. It was a perfect, clear but cool morning. The sun was well above the horizon. I squinted from the sun reflecting off the water, making me wish I'd grabbed my sunglasses. There were puddles along the path, confirming Nate's story about the rain overnight.

I had mixed feelings about leaving. I rationalized that it was because I really enjoyed being close to the sea and it was such a beautiful morning; the waves breaking and pounding the shoreline, the crystals in the pink granite outcrops sparkling, lit up by the oblique morning rays of the sun. But it was more than the environment. I realized that I was also sad to be leaving Nate. Yes, we'd only just met. But there was a comfort and familiarity that made me feel very at home here with him.

I realized I'd already become very fond of Nate. He'd been attentive, funny, and generous with his time. He made me feel special. I felt a tug on my heart as I thought that it was possible that I'd never see him again and I didn't want to leave and break the spell. I wanted to know more about him, like what was in his office. I laughed at myself that I was a little obsessed with being invited to see the rest of his boats. Fortunately, I was alone on the path, so no one thought I was some crazy old lady smiling and laughing to herself.

I stopped and looked back at Nate's place. I could see a resemblance from this angle to the lighthouse I'd photographed in Newfoundland, although the Hope Point Lighthouse had a lot more trees behind it. The morning sun reflecting off the white of the lighthouse was a nice contrast to the green leaves. I took my phone from my pocket and snapped a couple of pictures. I regretted that I'd left my camera in my room. The way the light was this morning, I would have liked to have all my photography gear. I'd not brought my very best camera, my digital SLR, nor my good lenses and all the accessories like my tripod and filters on this trip because it was a pain to pack and carry it all for air travel.

Taking pictures when I'm alone has always been something I enjoyed. I particularly enjoy photographing landscapes with water in them. Before I married Will, I would spend hours scouting a location, checking the light, deciding the time of day to set up and photograph a scene. The expression photographers often say is 'Anyone can take a picture, but a photographer makes a photograph'. Making photographs is something I'm most comfortable doing when I'm alone.

During the time Will and I were married, I didn't make many photographs. It's not that I didn't take pictures. I took pictures to document Anne's childhood, especially milestones like birthdays, family gatherings and during our annual summer vacation. We often went to photogenic locations, but I rarely had time to be artistic. It wasn't that Will overtly prevented me from taking pictures, but he didn't encourage it either. As time went on in our relationship, I took fewer and fewer pictures when he was around.

For one of our summer vacations, we spent a week on Lake Rosseau a couple of hours north of Toronto. Several of our friends, who had children around Anne's age, got together and rented a group of cottages in one of the many bays. It was a great spot. The cottages shared a bonfire pit, a children's playground and a large wooden dock area that extended out into the lake. One of our friends brought his motorboat and several of the cottages had canoes. The dock faced west and there were Muskoka chairs where we could sit and sun or read or just hang out watching our kids swim and play. And it was the perfect spot to enjoy the sunset.

Will had gone on a beer and ice run with a couple of the guys. Several of the ladies were sunning on the dock and Anne was playing with her current best friend Jeannie. I took the opportunity to go back to our cottage and unpack my camera. I'd packed all my photography gear: camera, film, tripod, lenses, filters, light meter, flash, extra batteries in my large camera bag. I took out my camera and loaded it with a fresh roll of film. I got out my light meter and tripod and set everything on the sofa in the cottage's sun porch. The night before the sunset had been splendid. I didn't get any pictures because we were all around the bonfire pit getting it ready for the kids to roast marshmallows. Kids, fire, hot skewers, and molten marshmallows kept my focus rather than the sunset. I hoped I'd get another chance.

It was early summer, so the sun didn't set until about nine o'clock. I reasoned there should be plenty of time to go out and take pictures of the sunset after dinner if it turned out to be a good one. With everything set up and ready, I went back down to the dock to check on Anne.

Jeannie's mom let me know that Anne was invited to eat and sleepover at her house, so Anne and I went back to our cottage to pack her little backpack with her PJs and toothbrush for her overnight stay. I made her wash off the majority of the grime from the day's play before she ran off with a "See ya later alligator" to Will who was just arriving with a case of beer in his hands and more than a few in his belly.

"What's for dinner?" he asked with his head partially in the fridge as he loaded the bottom shelf with beer.

"Anne's eating at Jeannie's tonight. I haven't started cooking yet. Janet told me Carl is lighting the BBQ and said there's enough space and charcoal for everyone to grill. I think it's boys' night to cook."

"You know I don't cook."

"It's not cooking – it's grilling. Man, fire, food – simple."

"But Mads, you're such a good cook…" His tone was sweet but patronizing.

"You want me to go grill with the boys?"

"Only if you want to grill. You could cook right here."

"I have chicken legs that would be good grilled – so I guess it's me and the boys."

"You're used to being one of the boys."

He'd said it in a way that didn't feel complimentary, but he was right. I was one of only a handful of women in my engineering class and I worked in a male-dominated industry. Sometimes the company of men was preferable to women of my age. The girls thought I was weird because I worked when my husband had a successful business and could support me. I found them boring as they prattled about their houses, kids, and husbands. It didn't bother me to hang out with the boys but, because Will refused to cook, I didn't want to let him off the hook. I was all set to go photograph the sunset by the lake and I didn't want to miss it.

"All the other guys will be grilling. What will they think if you let me take over?" I suggested trying to appeal to his male ego.

"Cooking is woman's work."

"Grilling is a man's job. What are you going to do while I do the man's job."

"I'll carry the cooler down to the BBQ – that's a man's job."

In Will's view, there were man's jobs and woman's jobs. He cut grass, shovelled snow and lifted heavy objects. I cooked, cleaned and did laundry. Any variation from this made him uncomfortable.

It was something I never anticipated before we were married. He'd been, or seemed to be, very accepting and actually quite proud that his girlfriend was an engineer and had an interesting job. As the years went on and my career progressed, his discomfort increased. It was as if I was taking something from him the more I contributed financially. I capitulated to his traditional views on male-female roles because it was easier. But I resented it and felt constrained and sometimes, very angry.

"Where's Will?" asked Carl as I approached the BBQ area.

"Right behind me. Coals ready?"

He opened the domed lid of the BBQ to show me the white-hot coals under the grates.

"Yes-sir-ee. I was waiting to spread them out for Will to get here with his meat."

"Here I am with meat and beer." With that broad infectious grin of his, Will opened the cooler and handed Carl a beer and me the chicken.

Carl raised his beer to toast Will. "Beers for the cooks."

I stepped up to the grill with my chicken. "Then you better get me a beer."

Carl looked puzzled and disappointed but was saved from saying something stupid by the arrival of Benny and Don with their chicken and a six-pack of Labatt's 50. Like a well-choreographed dance, they each grabbed one beer as Will opened the ice chest so they could drop in the other four to stay cold.

Benny held up a bowl with a paintbrush sticking out of it. "I brought my special BBQ sauce."

"Don't put any of that stuff on my chicken," said Will. "It's so hot it will make my ass burn tomorrow."

"Thanks anyway, Ben. I rubbed mine with rosemary and garlic, so it doesn't need sauce."

"No sauce?" Will sounded dismayed. "It isn't BBQ chicken without sauce."

"You like my chicken." I kept my voice sweet but was fighting to control my temper to avoid coming across as an overly emotional woman in front of the guys.

"You can always have some of mine," said Benny.

I gave Benny my best scolding look. "Not helping."

"I wouldn't second guess her Will," said Carl. "Hers smells amazing. She might stop feeding you if you complain."

Benny laughed and patted Will's belly. "On second thought, you probably could stand to skip a few meals..."

Will just smiled, opened the cooler, and handed out fresh beers.

It still baffles me how men can just move on; seemingly forgetting the insult or challenge or compliment that was just exchanged. A sort of emotional detachment from every situation just seconds or minutes after it transpires. They seem to have short-term-amnesia-on-demand. They can move on to a joke, a story, sex, or whatever was next with no carry-over from the insults they just hurled at each other.

Ben, Carl, and I grilled our chicken while Don and Will supervised.

"How long until we eat?" asked Don.

Carl poked his chicken legs with his finger. "About 2 beers. 3 at the most."

"Then we'll be needing more."

Will opened the cooler and counted beers. "Got ya covered. Three for me and two for each of you."

"Maddie should get your share," said Carl. "She's the one cooking after all."

"She'll only have one," said Will

He ignored the glare I gave him for speaking for me. "She'll take hers now then, before they're all gone."

Don jumped to his feet. "I can go get more."

"Don't bother. Mine's almost done," said Carl. "Do I know how to make great coals or what?"

Carl, Ben, and I continued to flip and turn our chicken until we were satisfied it was cooked. I put ours on a clean plate and Will and I headed back to our cottage. I set the table and got out the potato and copper pennies salads from the fridge. Will grabbed another beer and sat down at his place while I made him a plate of food.

"Looks good, Mads. I'm starved."

"You're welcome." And then, with a little more sarcasm than I'd intended, I said, "I guess I'll get myself a beer too…"

"I didn't know you wanted one."

"Because you didn't bother to ask. You just assumed you knew what I wanted. Just like you telling the boys I only wanted one beer… Like I wasn't even there or couldn't speak for myself."

"Don't get all emotional. I didn't mean anything by it."

I could feel the familiar wave of hurt and anger welling up inside me. "Don't tell me what I want or what I can feel. It's insulting."

"Don't raise your voice."

Those words were more than I could bear. "Fine. Enjoy your dinner. I'll eat later."

"Don't ruin this vacation. Sit down and eat."

I sat down. I ate but my stomach was in knots, and it took every bit of my resolve to not burst into tears. I knew crying in front of him would just make things worse. The more emotional I got, the more dismissive and cruel Will would get. My defence was to pull back inside myself like the hermit crab that retreats into his shell when poked. I ate silently for several minutes even though on the inside I was crying and screaming.

"Am I getting the silent treatment all night?"

"No."

"Good. Because I told Carl we'd go play cards."

I could see out the cottage window that the sky was turning pink. "I was planning to go take pictures of the sunset. It looks like it's going to be a good one"

"Maybe you could wait until tomorrow? I told them we'd be there after dinner."

"You could have asked me first."

"Janet's making her famous spicy nuts…"

"You don't like spicy nuts."

"I figured Janet already arranged it with you."

"She didn't. Are you sure he meant tonight?"

"Of course I'm sure. Why do you always question everything?"

I knew this was one of those times when any answer I gave would escalate into an even bigger argument. I got up from the table and started doing the dishes.

Will came up behind me, kissed my neck and said, "You know you're my best girl, right?"

"You have a funny way of showing it."

Will didn't answer, instead, he put his arms around me and gently petted my breasts and continued to kiss my neck.

"Now you want to be affectionate?" I was half annoyed, half turned on.

That was our relationship – flailing back and forth from totally irritated and disappointed to playful, fun and sexy. Often my heart couldn't keep up. When I was hurt, I couldn't just bounce back like him. Will could flip from one to the other like he was a different person altogether. His attitude could completely change from one minute to the next. His chameleon-personality made him fit in with almost anyone but in our relationship, it made me feel unsteady and never totally sure of how he would react at any given moment. I was often blindsided. Holding back my tears until I was alone so no one, not even Will, would know how vulnerable I felt.

We ended up going to play cards that night and I never did get to take my sunset pictures because it rained every evening for the rest of our vacation. Proving once again that capitulating for the sake of keeping the peace is a sure-fire path to disappointment.

I'd walked back to the inn and was standing in the garden looking out at the sun on the water and hadn't noticed Nate coming up behind me.

"Did you have a nice walk?"

I jumped at the voice. "I didn't realize you were there."

"I didn't mean to startle you."

"Am I keeping you waiting?"

"No. I just came down and saw you were back. We can leave whenever you're ready."

I started walking back towards the house. "I just need five minutes."

"I'll come get your bag and bring it down."

"No need. It's small. I'll be down in a flash."

I hurried up to my room. Brushed my teeth and used the washroom. I decided to leave the thank you gift for Nate next to the boat on the desk. He would need to change the sheets before the next guests arrived so he would certainly find it soon after I'd left.

I hoisted my bag and carried it into the hallway. Realizing I'd left my key inside, I went back in to find it – but decided to 'accidentally' forget it in the room and tell Nate where to find it once we were on the way to Boston. I put the key beside the gift. I smiled at myself at my impromptu plan to make sure he found my thank you note.

"Did you forget something?" Nate was in the hall picking up my bag and carrying it towards the stairs.

I closed the door quickly so Nate wouldn't see the package on the desk. "No, just a final check that I didn't leave anything behind. Wouldn't want you finding my socks or unmentionables. You needn't carry my bag."

"I must. You are still my guest."

Once out by the car, Nate opened my door and waited until I was in to close it. He went around to the back, put my bag in, and then got in beside me and started the Jeep.

"Ready to go?" he asked, as he activated the navigation system.

"Yes. You don't need to use the GPS; I know the way to Anne's."

"I already put in Anne's address. Best invention ever. This is my first car with it built in. Before that, I used a portable one."

"I like maps."

"I like having a good navigator. Wanda rarely leads me astray."

"Wanda?"

"When we first had one, Betsy figured she needed a name since I talked to her."

"Turn Left on US1 South," directed the GPS voice.

"Thank you, Wanda."

"You know 'she' is just a satellite receiver and a tiny computer doing math?"

"Shhhhh, she might hear you and get offended."

"Continue on US1 South for 18 miles," said Wanda.

"See. She's on top of things."

"I like to plan my drives with a map. Doesn't have to be a paper one, Google maps is good too."

"But what if there's a road closed or you run into bad traffic and you want to 'reroute'."

"If you have a map you can do the same thing – just look for another road going the direction you want to go."

"But Wanda does that for me."

"What if you don't like the way Wanda is taking you?"

"Wanda knows best."

"I think Wanda is taking you the slow way. You should take this ramp onto 395 to I-95."

"So now you're in a hurry?"

"No, but my way is better."

"Ok. We'll take your way but I'm keeping Wanda on as a backup."

"Recalculating route," said Wanda as we turned onto the 395.

"See, the time dropped from 5 hours 32 minutes to 4 hours 33 minutes. That's almost an hour faster."

Nate shook his head and patted the dashboard above the GPS screen. "Wanda, Honey, you've met your match."

CHAPTER 14

Maddie leaned over and started pressing Wanda's buttons. "Perhaps you had it set to avoid toll roads?"

I was both annoyed and impressed by her taking over navigation. "That's possible."

"I'll pay the tolls, and of course your gas for driving me to Boston."

"Not necessary. I get an excuse to visit Emily, Bob and Jake."

"I should at least split it with you."

"Alright. You can pay the tolls. It's your route after all."

"I take full responsibility. Do you make this drive often?"

"Not lately. When we first bought the place, we still had our home in Boston so I drove back and forth a lot. Later on, Betsy liked to go back regularly to visit friends. But, since she passed, I've not done it much."

"How long has it been?"

"Eighteen years."

"And you've been running the B&B alone ever since?"

"I have help for cleaning, yard work, and the occasional special event, but otherwise, by myself."

"You must miss Betsy after so many years together."

"Forty-three years. You get used to having someone around."

"I'm used to being on my own. I have been for the last… ummm… twenty-nine years."

"You must have been very young when you lost your husband."

"Lost is too kind a word for what happened between me and my ex-husband." Maddie's voice had a slightly bitter edge.

"I'm sorry. I shouldn't have assumed…"

"No worries. I'm used to being a divorcé. It was scandalous 30 years ago but these days it's no big deal."

"You never remarried?"

"Husbands are more trouble than they're worth. I managed just fine without."

"But if the perfect one came along…"

"I don't believe he exists."

"Until now of course."

I'm not sure what came over me. It wasn't like me to blurt out something so presumptuous. There was an awkward pause.

Fortunately, Maddie started to laugh. "Well, you took your time showing up.... You're late!"

"Now that hurts. I'm never late."

"You just took the long way? See what happens when you put your faith in Wanda?" Her voice was playful and teasing.

"You hear, Wanda? She's picking on us again."

"On top of that, it's too soon to assess your perfectness. We can put you in the 'possibly perfect man' category for now."

I considered retracting my comment, saying it was a joke. But I didn't. "I guess that'll have to do."

Crazy as it seems, after knowing this woman for only a couple of days, I was thinking I could have been the perfect man for Maddie if I'd met her sooner. I considered telling her she was the 'possibly perfect woman'. She was smart, fun, sophisticated and well educated without being snobby. I'd also noticed how pretty she was.

I kept my eyes on the road and changed the subject. "Do you and Anne have travel plans this summer?"

"Nothing definite. She usually comes home for a visit in July."

"For the fourth of July?"

"No, usually mid-month. She tries to come for my birthday every year."

"When's your birthday?"

"July 14th. But we celebrate it on any convenient day in July."

"So you have a birthday month?"

"Not every day in July – just one day that we're together."

"It's sweet that Anne celebrates it with you every year."

"It's one of our birthday traditions. We're not strict as to the exact day, but there must be a designated birthday celebration day."

"Do you have other birthday traditions?"

"We have three rules. One. You may eat anything you like for breakfast. That was Anne's favorite rule growing up. Two. Singing happy birthday at least once, preferably when it's most embarrassing. And three, you must make a wish for the next year while blowing out your birthday candles – so there must be something with candles in it, but it doesn't have to be a cake."

"Those seem like pretty strict rules. What about presents?"

"All I want from Anne is time with her."

"Time is the best gift."

"The older I get, the more precious it gets."

"And the faster it goes."

"The upside is that birthday celebrations seem to get closer together."

"Downside is you get a year older faster."

"I try not to think about that."

I stretched my arms and shrugged my shoulders behind the wheel. "Can't help feeling it. Not as spry as I once was."

"Do you want to take a break? I can drive for a bit if you'd like." I imagined she was thinking the old guy needed a rest.

"No. I prefer to drive."

"But you drove me around for the last two days, and now to Boston. I assure you I'm a capable driver."

"I have no doubt you are an excellent driver. Do you need a rest stop?"

"Not yet. But probably planning to stop halfway would be good."

As long as I could, I would not be letting anyone else drive; not if I can help it. I've been told I'm a terrible passenger.

Betsy rarely drove. She drove to her hair appointments and the grocery store but when we went places together, I always drove. She would complain that I never stopped, and I was always in a rush to get wherever we were going. When we were young, Betsy needed to stop more often than I did, but later in life, it was me that determined how far we could go in between rest stops.

"Do you want to put on the radio?"

"If you want. You've been keeping me entertained."

Maddie snorted and turned on the radio. There was nothing but static because we were out of range of my local station.

"Do you want me to search for something?" she asked, already pressing the scan button.

"First you take over navigation and now the radio. What next?"

"Probably the driving," she teased. "But for now, just electronics. What would you like to hear."

"I usually listen to news radio, but you're in control now."

After skipping over three country stations, a couple rock stations, an evangelical preacher and some angry-sounding noise that I wouldn't call music, Maddie landed on NPR just as the BBC News was starting. "How's this?"

"Good. We can find out what's going on in the world."

We listened to the news and the programs that followed. Maddie added her commentary at breaks and sometimes during the stories, which was a little distracting. If it had been anyone else, I probably would have been irritated that I missed part of the news because she was talking and listening at the same time.

The drive passed quickly. When I pulled up in front of Anne's house, I felt a bit sad. Maddie gathered her things.

"Thank you so much for driving me back here."

I got out and hurried around to open her door. "It was my pleasure."

"It's been a really lovely couple of days. Please make sure to add the tolls and your gas to our final bill."

"I'll do no such thing. You've been my personal guest so there will be no final bill."

"That's unnecessary but thank you. You've been such a generous host. I hope I can return the favor someday."

I took her bag from the trunk and started to carry it to the front door but she took it from me.

"You don't have to do that. I can manage. Do you want to come in for a coffee or something to drink?"

"No thanks, I should get going to Emily's."

We stood on the driveway a bit awkwardly.

Maddie extended her hand. "I guess this is goodbye."

Then, with a shrug, she opened her arms and leaned in to hug me. I leaned in and gave her a hug and kissed her on the cheek.

Maddie smiled. "We'll do it as the Italians do." She kissed me on both cheeks. "If you're ever in Toronto, I hope I can return your hospitality."

"I would like that."

Maddie carried her bag up the walk. I stood by the car while she let herself in Anne's front door. Once she was inside, I got into the car and waved goodbye. I looked back as I drove away, and I could see her standing in the doorway still waving. The car felt empty. Too quiet.

I realized I'd not put Emily's address in the GPS, so I stopped at the end of the street to put it in. I thought how nice it had been to have someone else in the car. Despite having Wanda for directions, I missed having Maddie as my navigator.

Emily greeted me with an enthusiastic hug. With her mother in London and her in-laws still working full time, a little help and adult company was welcomed. Even without significant baby experience, there were lots of things I could do to help. That afternoon I did four loads of laundry, made dinner for Emily and Bob with whatever I found in her fridge and freezer. I even read Jake a story, although, I doubt he had any idea that I was reading, let alone what a book was.

Emily flopped onto the sofa beside me after putting Jake down. "Grandpa Nate, you're a godsend."

"I'm afraid I don't have much experience. When you were a baby, you lived in London, so we didn't see you very often."

"You're a natural. I can tell he already adores you. I'm so glad you came to visit. Do you have to leave tomorrow?"

"I have guests coming this weekend."

"Could you at least stay tomorrow? You drove all this way – it would be a shame to stay just one night."

"I have guests arriving Saturday…"

"You can stay one more day then…"

"You are your mother's daughter."

"Then it's settled. Tomorrow we'll have all day to give you some of that baby experience you missed out on."

"If it isn't an imposition…"

"It would be great to have you here. I want Jake to know you more than I did growing up."

Her words tugged at my heart. I hadn't made enough time to be with Ann and Emily.

"I'm sorry I wasn't around more. You lived so far away… and you grew up so fast."

She leaned over and put her head on my shoulder. "Well you're here now."

Bob came in and joined us in the family room. "Can I offer you a nightcap, Nate?"

"Bob's hoping you'll say yes so he has an excuse to break out the scotch on a weeknight."

"Maybe a wee one, for medicinal purposes, if it's OK with Emily." I gestured with two fingers how much Bob should pour.

Emily rolled her eyes but didn't protest. Bob went to the bar, poured us each a scotch, set the bottle on the end table, and settled into his recliner.

"So, Nate, are things busy at Hope Point these days?"

"I've got bookings for every weekend from now until Labor Day. Not full-up, but steady."

"Em and I were thinking it would be nice to come up with Jake this summer for a few days – guess we better book soon."

"I'll always have room for my family – you can always take my room. I'd love to have you. Any time."

"We could help out while we're there," offered Emily.

"You think I'm getting too old to be doing it on my own?"

"I didn't mean that! Only it's a lot to run a place by yourself. For someone of ANY age."

"I have help when I need it." I wanted to get off the subject of me, so I redirected. "How's work going for you, Bob."

"Busy but it's going to get even busier when Em goes back to work."

"Bob's going to be the one to pick up Jake every day because his office is closer to the daycare."

"Just call me Mr. Mom."

Emily shook her head and sighed. "Two hours a day hardly qualifies as Mr.

Mom, Honey."

"Well it's a lot more than I ever did, I'm sad to admit. Your Grandma Betsy did all that sort of thing."

"She didn't have a full-time job. Did she?"

"Heavens no! It was different back then. I earned a good living and Grandma Betsy took care of things at home."

"My career is important to me, but I'm not looking forward to leaving Jake."

"When do you go back to work?"

"Next week."

"So soon?"

"Yup. That's why it's great you're here this week. Next week you'd get – well I'm not sure what you'd get – I think I'm going to be a bit of a mess having to be away from Jake all day."

"I'm sure everything will be fine."

"I'm going to keep breastfeeding. So, I need to pump several times a day so I can give that milk to the daycare for the next day."

"Complicated."

"I've been practicing, and Bob's been giving Jake a bottle of breastmilk every day for the past week. He seems to be doing well."

"Bob or Jake?"

Emily giggled and gave me a playful shot with her elbow. "Jake, of course."

"We skipped the bottle stage with your mother."

"Why didn't you and Grandma Betsy have any other children?"

"Your grandma really wanted to have a baby, but she couldn't. She was pregnant three times and each time she miscarried."

"How terrible for you both."

"More for her. She gave up trying because the fear of losing another was just too horrible for her to bear."

"But then you adopted Mom. Why not adopt a baby brother or sister for her too?"

"Your mother was a big surprise. We had given up on the idea of having children, at least I thought we had, and then your mother came along."

"We've been talking about me doing one of those DNA tests, the ones that tell you your origins – because we don't know. Do we?"

"It never mattered to us. Ann was ours. End of story."

"Tell Bob the story of how you found out about Mom."

"You might need a little more scotch." Bob sprang up and poured us each another shot.

"Haven't you told him the story before?"

"Not the way you tell it. Please."

"Ok. Well, it all started back when I went to Japan for work…"

"What sort of work did you do?" asked Bob.

"Bob! Don't interrupt," scolded Emily.

"It's ok, I don't mind. At the time I was researching patents. We'd developed a coating that we hoped would be a big seller in Japan. It was a way to earthquake-proof glass panels. There'd been a big earthquake a couple of years before and quite a few American companies were making money helping to 'rebuild' Japan. It was quite common, starting after the war and then again after the earthquake, that American technology companies were invited to partner with Japanese companies. Bond, my company, was one of those."

"In those days, we had to go through actual books and microfilm to research patents. Of course, I needed an interpreter to do it in Japan, so it was very slow work. I was there for several months."

"Pretty unusual to be traveling overseas back then."

"And it was very different, especially communication. We wrote letters and on rare occasions a brief phone call if there was something really urgent."

"Snail mail!" said Bob.

"Your Grandma would write me once a week to keep me informed, even though the news was always out of date because it usually took a couple of weeks to get a letter from home. In the spring of 1966, I spent about 3 months in Japan. During that time, she had written several letters telling me about the work she was doing teaching art at St. Mary's Orphanage and School. I remember thinking how nice that she has something to get her out of the house and that she had reignited her love of art."

"In her letters, she always referred to "the girls" in general but the last letter I received before returning home from that trip was different. It was all about one particular girl named Ann. Ann this and Ann that. I'd been feeling a bit guilty about leaving her alone for so long. So, I wrote back, I'm really glad you're so excited about your work. Ann sounds like a nice girl. So unfortunate that she's at St. Mary's with no one to take her in."

"How did Em's mom end up in the orphanage?"

"We were told that she'd been with an aunt since she was a baby. Her parents had died but we were never told the circumstances. The aunt, who had been a spinster when she took Ann in, had married a widower with several children of his own, and he had insisted that she be given to the orphanage because she was not his responsibility."

"How barbaric of him."

"Ann was moved to St. Mary's Orphanage when she turned nine because she was too old for the one she had been living at previously. That's when your Grandma met her."

"So you came home from Japan…" prompted Emily.

"I got home a couple weeks after I'd received the letter. When I walked in, I noticed that your Grandma's sewing machine was set up in the family room. I thought it strange but figured she had moved it to work on something big because her sewing room was quite small. I was dead tired, so I didn't ask about it. I unpacked and went straight to bed."

"How long a trip was it then? From Japan to Boston," asked Bob.

"Three days, with one overnight stop in Hawaii."

"And you woke up the next morning…" Emily was getting impatient with me answering Bob's questions, but I didn't mind. It was bringing back a lot of memories.

"The next morning when I came down for breakfast, your Grandma was waiting for me, already dressed in a very smart suit with her purse and gloves, sitting at the kitchen table. I poured myself a cup of coffee and, because it was late morning, I asked her if she had a lunch date. She said no, but we had an appointment, and I should hurry up with my breakfast and get showered and dressed."

"I was surprised and somewhat annoyed by her springing something on me when I had just gotten home. There were things that needed doing around the house. I thought I'd cut the grass and then watch some golf on TV and relax. I was even more surprised and confused when she said we were going to St. Mary's to meet with Sister Theresa about adopting your mother."

Bob's eyes were wide and incredulous. "You mean you had no idea until that day?"

"Not a clue. Not in my wildest dreams would I have thought Ann would be coming home with us that day."

"Tell Bob the part about meeting Sister Theresa," prompted Emily. "That's the best part."

"We arrived at St. Mary's and rang the bell outside the big wrought iron gates. A young nun came and let us in. She knew Grandma and greeted us with a big smile. I remember thinking she seemed excessively happy to meet me when Betsy introduced me. Her name was Sister Helen. I remember how quickly she walked as she escorted us to an office, her robes flowing behind her, and she was giddy with excitement when she told us Sister Theresa would be with us shortly.

The office reminded me of my high school principal's office. Just being in the stark office with its uncomfortable chairs, wooden kneeler in front of a large crucifix and small stained-glass window made me feel like I was about to be punished or at least interrogated. I felt the same sort of dread I'd felt waiting for the nun who was our principal, coincidentally, also named Sister Theresa. She'd been a fierce disciplinarian who had once left large welts on my palms for laughing in choir practice. Even as an adult I shuddered at the thought of her."

"You mean like Sister Mary Stigmata in the *Blues Brothers* movie?"

I nodded. "She made The Penguin seem like a softie. The few minutes we waited made me antsy and I started to pace the room like a caged lion while your Grandma sat calm as can be, her gloves and purse in her lap, her legs crossed at the ankles.

She looked at me disapprovingly. 'Come and sit down. Sister Theresa will be here soon.' Which I did just as Sister Theresa entered the room."

"Was she really scary?"

"She came in with a swish of robes, arms open and a bright smile. Totally not what I was expecting. She hugged Betsy and then hugged me warmly.

She said, 'I'm just so happy to finally meet you. When Betsy told me you wanted Ann to have a real home and family, I was just delighted.'

I tried to disguise my surprise because up until then I thought we were there to discuss the possibility of adopting. It became clear we were much further along in the process when Sister Theresa sat down at her desk and opened the file in front of her saying, 'I have all the documents and forms Betsy had prepared while you were away, we just need your signatures on a few of them.'

She turned the forms to face me and handed me a pen. The lawyer in me took over and I start to say I couldn't sign the documents, but Betsy interrupted me. 'He just got back from his trip to Japan, so he hasn't had a chance to check to see if I got everything right.' Your Grandma was brilliant at social diversion. She didn't want Sister Theresa to know that I was completely blindsided.

'I completely understand, shall I give you a little time to review them? I'll go find Ann in the meantime.'

'That would be perfect,' said Betsy.

As soon as Sister Theresa left the room, she turned to me and said, 'Just sign them.'

I started frantically reading. 'These are guardianship with intent to adopt papers. This is serious business.'

'Your letter said Ann should have a family, and I agree. Sister Theresa agrees. She belongs with us. Just sign them.'

'You did all this without talking to me about it first.'

'You were away.'

'I was on a business trip. You could have waited until I got home so we could discuss it.'

'Then it would have been a long, drawn-out discussion. You would have taken forever weighing the pros and cons – this way you must decide right now.'

'But I don't know this girl.'

'But I do. And you will in a few minutes. Sign the papers.'

'Why don't I meet her first and then sign.'

'Don't you trust me.'

'This is a big, life-altering decision.'

Just then the door opened and in walked your mother with Sister Theresa who said 'Ann, I'd like you to meet Mr. Jacobs.'

She shyly extended her little hand. 'Pleased to meet you, Sir.'

'Very nice to meet you too, Ann. My wife tells me you're quite the artist.'

'I didn't know much about art until Mrs. Jacobs started teaching here. Now I like it.'

'We've been very lucky to have Mrs. Jacobs volunteering so much time to share her knowledge of art with the girls here at St. Mary's.' Sister Theresa was clearly a fan of your grandma.

Betsy beamed at Sister Theresa. 'Would it be OK if we asked Ann what she thinks about the arrangement we discussed?'

'I think that would be the next logical step.'

'Ann, Mr. Jacobs and I would like to adopt you. We understand this is a very big change for you but...'

'Yes. I'd like that,' interrupted Ann.

I asked her, 'How can you be sure?' I didn't believe that a nine-year-old girl could make a rational decision on the spot. I ignored the glare from Betsy and the disapproving look from Sister Theresa.

'Because Mrs. Jacobs has told me all about you and I can tell you're nice.'

I picked up the forms from the desk. 'Do you understand that once these papers are filed with the diocese and the courts, you will be our daughter and it's permanent?'

'How long will that take?' asked Ann.

'About six months,' answered Sr Theresa. Which I appreciated because I had no idea.

'So after six months you can't change your mind either?' asked Ann.

'We've already made up our minds, we won't be changing them,' said Betsy. 'We have a room all ready for you, so if you agree, you can come home with us today.'

I almost blurted out 'We have a room ready?' but then I remembered the sewing machine in the family room. Obviously, Betsy had converted her sewing room into a bedroom while I'd been away.

Sister Theresa tapped the forms on her desk. 'Everything is in order as soon as Mr. and Mrs. Jacobs sign these papers.'

Betsy picked up the pen and signed beside her name and then handed the pen to me while pointing to the line for me to sign. I looked over at Ann and the happy expectant look on her face melted my resolve to slow down and think through the process. I signed."

Bob let out a deep breath. "But you barely knew her? Weren't you afraid it wouldn't work out?"

"Terrified. But it would have been un-manly to admit it, and Grandma Betsy knew me well enough to know I'd never let anyone see how alarmed I was.

Betsy went with her to her dorm room to help her pack her things into a couple of cardboard boxes. Your mother didn't bring most of her clothes because they were the uniforms that all the girls in the orphanage wore and Betsy assured her that they could go shopping for some new clothes. She had a doll, all the art supplies Betsy had given her, a nearly bald stuffed unicorn named Fluffy and one nice dress for church on Sunday that she was wearing that day."

I didn't want to imply to Emily that I had any misgivings, so I didn't tell her and Bob about the conversation I had with Sister Theresa while Betsy was off doing the packing with Ann.

"Thank you Mr. Jacobs," said Sister Theresa. "I want you to know how happy we all are that you're adopting Ann. Girls her age are often overlooked."

"My wife is the one you should thank."

"I hope that doesn't mean you're not sure about this. It would be emotionally devastating if Ann felt rejected again."

My stomach turned over and my palms instinctively itched and hurt like they knew if I said the wrong thing there would be ruler marks embedded in them. "I promise you Sister Theresa; I won't let you down."

"So, you brought Em's mom home with you that same day?"

"Hard to believe but Ann said goodbye to the nuns and her friends and came home with us. We reassured her that if she wanted to keep going to the parish school she could, and I think that it helped knowing she would see all her friends on Monday at school."

"Whoa! Instant family. Straight to 'tween'. Yikes."

"I admit, it was a major adjustment."

"I thought Grandma Betsy deferred to you as the head of the household until you told me this story," admitted Emily.

"Grandma Betsy was very careful to keep up the appearance of family harmony in public. Back in the day, there was a lot of pressure to be the perfect wife and mother. But when she made up her mind about something, like adopting your mother, she wouldn't stop until she got her way."

"Lucky for me. Because I got you for a grandpa." Emily climbed out of the sofa and stretched. "I'm beat. We have all day tomorrow to be together so I'm going to hit the hay."

"Me too. The drive has me a bit tuckered myself and... I've finished my Scotch."

Bob picked up the scotch bottle and tempted me with it. "I could pour us some more?"

"No thanks. That's enough for me."

"I may not be the perfect housewife by Grandma Betsy's standards," said Emily, "but I've put fresh towels on your bed. Do you need anything else?"

"No, Sweetie. Goodnight."

"Goodnight, Great Grandpa."

CHAPTER 15

I always have mixed feelings when I get home from a trip. There's the relief of getting to the end of that day's journey and the comfort of being back in one's own home. But in equal measure, it's disappointing because an adventure has come to an end. Luckily today was a perfect June day and the city was alive with the sights and sounds of summer.

Standing on the sidewalk of the home I've lived in for decades, waiting for the cabbie to open the trunk, I surveyed my small front yard which, to my surprise, looked freshly mowed. I'd had my doubts about the dedication of my neighbour's son to his grass-cutting business. But so far, so good.

"Butter. Bacon. I'm home," I called out as I opened the front door. Bacon my brown and cream-coloured tabby came trotting down the hall and immediately started slithering between my legs and rubbing himself against me. Butter, my round fluffy yellow cat rolled over slightly so he could see me without leaving the comfort of the chair by the front window. I reached down and petted Bacon.

"Nice to see you too, Furballs."

Leaving my bags inside the door and kicking off my shoes, I headed straight ahead down the hallway to the kitchen at the back of the house. Bacon followed me meowing. He always complains when I get home from a trip. I imagine he's either yelling at me for leaving him alone with Butter or telling me what he's been doing since I left.

"I've only been gone a week, Buddy. I'm sure Julie was here to visit and keep your kibble topped up so what are you complaining about?"

Living alone for so many years, I've not had to worry about anyone judging me for talking to my cats like they actually understand me. I dropped a few treats on the floor for Bacon, who stopped complaining long enough to vacuum them up. I grabbed a bottle of water from the fridge, unlocked the door from the kitchen to the sunroom, slipped on the Crocs that were just outside the door and went out to the backyard through the sunroom.

My small turn of the century Tudor house had a good-sized backyard considering the proximity to downtown. Many of the houses in my High Park neighbourhood had only a sliver of green in the back, but I had quite a bit of room, even after adding the sunroom back in the eighties. I did a quick walk around the yard to check on things. Even after just a week away, my tomato plants had shot up. I threaded the new growth of the vines over the support cages and then checked on my zucchini plants. Lucky for me there were three small ones. Since my fridge was pretty bare, these made it possible to make dinner for myself without having to run out shopping or order in. Satisfied there was nothing that urgently needed doing in the garden, I grabbed a handful of basil and went back into the house.

The light on my kitchen phone was blinking letting me know I had voicemail. My first thought was maybe Nate had called to say he'd found the gift. I listened to the messages. Two appointment reminders and a robocall for window cleaning services. Nothing from Nate. I fought back a pang of disappointment rationalizing he would only have been back at the inn, best case, for a couple of hours and he may not have gone into my room yet. He had said he had guests this weekend, so presumably, he would find the package when he set up for them. I was anxious for him to find it. I like giving gifts almost more than receiving them. Almost.

"Should we take our stuff upstairs?" I asked Bacon, who ignored me and continued grooming his face. The thing I like best about cats is their independence, but it's also the trait that makes me wonder which of us is the pet and which is the master.

Will never liked cats. He tolerated my cat, Phoenix, who had been one of the friendliest cats I'd ever had. He was not pretty; gray with white patches, part of one ear missing and a short nose that looked like it had been pushed in. He'd had a difficult life before he showed up on the doorstep of my apartment in Kingston where I lived during university. He was bleeding, limping and very skinny. I took him to a vet friend, who I knew from the curling club, who told me it was likely he'd been hit by a car. Being a friend, and knowing I was a graduate student with a limited income, he offered to put him down free of charge because it was unlikely he'd recover from his injuries. We decided to wait and see if he got better. My landlady, Mrs. Bell, agreed to let me keep him if he was confined to my three-room apartment that was in a drafty addition at the back of her house. Like his namesake, Phoenix was reincarnated, as a fat, happy, lazy gray blob that lived another 10 years.

Will met Phoenix for the first time the night of our first date. He reached down to pet him, and Phoenix hissed and ran away. I suppose the cat knew something I didn't because I didn't run away, at least not soon enough.

I'd apologized to Will. "I'm sorry my cat was rude to you. It's not like him to hiss at people."

"I suppose he sees me as the competition."

"He does have me all to himself and I feed him, put a roof over his head and let him sleep in my bed…"

"I hope he appreciates how lucky he is." Will was charming and suggestive in a way I found attractive.

"He's a cat. He's aloof and ungrateful most of the time. But he's a good listener and keeps all my secrets."

"Do you have a lot of secrets?"

"Not many. I like having him around and he doesn't complain when I work late in the lab or library."

"I hope he won't be angry if I keep you out late."

"He sleeps a lot, I don't think he'll notice."

It was surprising that Phoenix didn't like Will because everyone liked Will. We'd met at a bonspiel, playing for opposing rinks vying for first place in the final round. He was tall, blonde, broad-shouldered with a large but athletic build, like a sturdy farm boy, which, as I later learned, he was.

He'd grown up in Verona, a small community north of Kingston. His father was a farmer who grew corn and vegetables in the summer and cut wood and drove a snowplow in the winter. His mother had been a homemaker but also ran their family farm stand. He smiled easily, had a quirky sense of humour and was the life of the party without being loud or overbearing. He was sweet and a little awkward when he first approached me after the prizes had been awarded and I was getting my things together to leave.

"Are you leaving already?"

"Yes, I'm heading out. It was nice meeting you, Will."

"Sure you can't stay for another drink?" His lovely blue eyes looked at me hopefully.

"I suppose I could… but just one more. I have an early start tomorrow."

"That's swell. What can I get you?"

"Rye and ginger, please."

We sat along the glass watching the ice-keeper tend the sheets.

"Did you get what you wanted from the prize table?" I asked.

"I did. I grabbed the Canadian Tire pocketknife. I can use a spare because I'm always losing them on job sites."

"What kind of work do you do?"

"I'm an electrician."

"Shocking!" I giggled.

"Hopefully never. But good one. What has you starting early tomorrow?"

"I'm proctoring an exam. I'm a graduate student at the university."

"So you're smart AND pretty."

I couldn't help but blush at his remark. He was charming and I was enjoying being paid compliments by a good-looking guy. It was a significant contrast to my daily experience at the university. There weren't many women in the Faculty of Engineering and Applied Science at Queen's University. Even fewer were graduate students. Being able to get my work done, without being impeded, is what I considered a good day. Bad days were the ones where I was fighting to be heard and taken seriously.

I was naïve when I enrolled, believing I could easily follow in my father and grandfather's footsteps. Both had graduated from Queen's, both mining engineers. Unlike many of their colleagues, they never discouraged me from following in their footsteps. I remember my grandfather handing me the keys to his almost new Glass Top Vickie when we returned from a family vacation in Florida the summer before I started university.

"An engineering student shouldn't have to take the bus to come home to visit her Pop," he'd said.

I drove that 1955 Fairlane Crown Victoria Skyliner for over 10 years. It was more than just a car to me. It was my independence and I felt empowered behind the wheel. It didn't hurt that it was also a great-looking car. Only a few of my classmates had cars and none of them were women. The cars they did have were unreliable. My Vickie needed the occasional boost, but I'd learned to do it myself because it had broken down on me the day I went to see Elvis Presley.

I'll never forget that day. Pops had given me two tickets and the use of his car to drive to the show. I invited the one girl I'd made friends with while staying with my grandparents in Florida to go with me. When we came out of the drugstore, where we'd stopped for a coke on our way to the concert, I couldn't get the car started. If it hadn't been for a good Samaritan who stopped to help us, we would've missed the show.

After that experience, I'd asked Pops to teach me how to jump-start it. He was so proud of me as he watched me hook up the jumper cables just like he'd shown me.

"You're too smart to do other people's typing. Don't be anyone's secretary. You're going to be an engineer."

Most of the male students and faculty at Queen's were less enlightened than my Pop. Being treated like I didn't belong was my daily experience. Will flirting with me in a way that wasn't degrading was a nice change. He wasn't at all turned off when he found out I was a graduate student, he asked me for my phone number and said he'd like to see me again.

He only waited a couple of days before calling me.

"Would you like to go see a movie Saturday?"

I tried to play it cool. "Yes. That would be nice."

"Groovy. I'll pick you up at 7. Guess you better tell me where you live."

I gave him the address and, despite Phoenix's rejection of him, we went to see a movie at the Capitol Theatre. Since it was on Princess Street and only a few blocks from my place, I suggested we walk to the theatre. I think he was a little offended. He thought I was avoiding getting into a car with him, that I didn't trust him. But I wasn't afraid, I just wanted to be able to bolt from our date if things weren't going well. It was a lot easier to slip away if I was walking distance from home.

As it turned out, I didn't want to get away. Will walked me home and, breaking all first date rules, kissed me goodnight. Our first date turned into a second and then a third and then a whole summer of spending most of my free time together.

One of the things I liked most about Will was that he always wanted to do something fun. For our dates, he arranged for me to see lots of Kingston tourist attractions I'd never taken the time to see even though I'd been living in the city for several years. One sunny Saturday in June he'd booked tickets on the Miss Kingston, and we spent the day cruising the St. Lawrence River and the 1000 Islands. I remember using a whole roll of film because I'd never seen so many fancy cottages. Ones with Victorian gables and towers, ones with boathouses like floating garages and modern A-frames with big triangular windows facing the river.

By the end of the summer, we were spending every weekend together and I'd even been invited to Sunday dinner at the farm with his parents.

It came as a total surprise when Will told me he'd accepted a job in Toronto and would be moving away in a couple of weeks. I was upset. I'd gotten used to having a steady boyfriend and was angry he'd made the decision without even mentioning the possibility to me. I questioned myself too. I felt stupid to have thought there was a future for us. Although we talked about keeping in touch, we didn't.

About a year later, I graduated with my master's degree; Dean's list, class of 1962. I was offered the position of staff engineer at DB Engineering, so Phoenix and I moved back to Toronto. Living with my parents, after being on my own, was very strange. Despite living in Kingston at school for most of the prior six years, my bedroom at my parents' house was exactly as I'd left it.

The conflicting values of my professional and personal lives made me feel like I was two different people. One was the independent woman carving out my place in a male-dominated workplace. I knew I needed to be twice as good to be treated as equal. So, I worked long hours, took on the hardest assignments and double-checked all my work. Any mistakes would give the boys ammunition to marginalize me and I was determined to not let that happen.

My alter ego, the now grown little girl who attended church with her parents, was doing her best to fit in socially. Unlike other young women my age, I wasn't married, raising small children, and looking after my home and husband. I was the subject of gossip. But I did my best to ignore the whispered 'Poor Maddie,' and 'Do you think she'll ever find a husband?' comments.

I reentered the social scene awkwardly that first summer in Toronto. As the third wheel, I tagged along with married friends to parties and events. I was set up on blind dates and given lots of unwanted advice like find a nice guy at work and then you can marry him and stay home.

When fall came, I was reinstated as a member of the High Park Curling and Lawn Bowling Club and curled in The Business Girls group on Wednesday nights. Most of the women who curled in those days were wives and mothers and they curled during the day. They took advantage of the club's nursery to watch their children for the couple of hours it took to play their games. The Business Girls group was made up of other women who had daytime jobs and careers. It was there I met Helen when I was assigned to her rink.

Helen had recently graduated from the University of Toronto and was hip to what was cool in the city. We would go out together on weekends to Yorkville, which, at the time, was the hub of the hippie counterculture in the city. I wasn't particularly rebellious, but the live music and the spectacle of students, artists, hippies, and bikers all congregating together, created an alternative scene to my otherwise conservative world that was interesting and exciting. The free-spirited celebration of individuality and acceptance was a relief from my structured and regulated work life.

Everyone on our rink, including Helen, was very competitive and we loved entering bonspiels. Helen and I often paired up with her brother and father to make up a mixed rink. Helen was a better skip than either her father or brother, so they were content to be lead and third. We played a very different game than rinks led by men, which sometimes confounded the opposing skip. We beat them with strategy rather than strength and it felt good.

We were active members of the club, and we supported many charity events. As I arrived for one such event, the St. Joseph's Hospital Charity Bonspiel, I heard someone call my name as I walked across the wide veranda that overlooked the club's bowling lawn.

"Maddie, Maddie. Is that you?"

"Will?"

Will hurried over and walked beside me. "What are you doing here?"

"My rink is playing in the bonspiel today."

"I mean what are you doing in Toronto?"

"I live here."

"When did you move back?"

"Last year."

I kept walking towards the door. I didn't want him to think I was happy to see him. I wasn't sure I was happy to see him.

Will opened the door for me and followed me into the club. "I had no idea..."

"You never called me, so how could you."

"I wanted to. I should have. I'm sorry I didn't."

I walked faster and headed towards the stairs that led up to the women's lounge and locker area. Will followed me across the room.

I called back to him as I climbed the stairs. "Sorry. Can't talk now. I need to go change."

I opened my locker and took out my curling shoes and sat on the bench staring into the open locker.

"Earth to Maddie."

"Hi Helen."

"Something interesting in your locker? You look like you just saw a ghost."

"Ghost no. Ex-boyfriend, yes."

"Here?" Helen looked into my locker, giggling. "I don't see any ex-boyfriends unless you dated your broom."

"I never expected to see him again."

"So he's kinda like a ghost?"

"He vanished like one."

Helen opened her locker. "You gotta tell me all about it later."

I focused on lacing my shoes and changing into my curling sweater, but I could feel my conflicting feelings welling up; hurt, angry, happy, excited. I started walking towards the stairs.

"You won't be much good without these." Helen held out my gloves and broom. "Cheer up, we've got some winning to do."

We met our opponents for the first game. We shook hands and introduced ourselves as is customary. I glanced over at the other sheets and there was Will, smiling at me. He gave a little wave.

Helen whispered to me as she slid by to take her place at the far end of the sheet. "Someone has an admirer."

"My ex!" I hissed back.

I was a jumble of emotions, but I did my best to focus on our game and avoided looking towards the other sheets. Helen didn't help matters. Each time we passed on the ice she whispered things like; "He's watching you," or "At least he's kinda cute."

When the match ended, in keeping with the curling tradition that each member of the winning team offers their opposing player a refreshment from the bar, Helen and I headed to the bar to purchase drinks.

"Who is this ex that can't keep his eyes off you?"

"His name is Will. We dated for several months a couple years ago."

"Did it end badly?"

"It just ended. He took a job. Moved away. Never heard from him again. I don't think we ever broke up officially."

"That's a bummer. Where did you find this guy?"

"We met at a bonspiel."

"Well, he's been looking at you like he's on the make. Maybe this is your chance for a 'do over'?"

"Why would I want a 'do over'?"

"Because you're not seeing anyone, and he's a hunk. You don't have to marry him….and …. he's walking this way…."

The bartender set our drink orders on the bar. Helen handed me money and grabbed hers and headed back to our teams' table. I told the bartender to put the drinks on my account so I could get away quickly, but I couldn't before Will made his way to the bar.

"Quite a coincidence, us meeting at a Bonspiel, again," he said with a nervous chuckle.

"It is."

"Do you think you could stay afterwards and have a drink with me?"

I lied. "I have plans."

"Maybe I could call you sometime? So, we could catch up?"

"I suppose that would be ok."

"Let me get a pen to get your number."

"Maybe later. My team is waiting." I escaped with my drinks and rejoined my team at our table.

Just before the last draw was about to begin, Will approached with a paper and pencil.

"Your number, please," he said with the sweetest pleading smile. I thought to myself – why not? As Helen said, it's not like I have to marry him, and we'd had fun together before…

Will called the next day. My mother answered and informed me there was a gentleman caller. I took the phone from her and stretched the cord as far as it would go down the hall away from the kitchen.

"It's been quite a while since we talked," he said.

"It was yesterday," I answered coolly.

"I mean really talked. It's great you've moved home."

"It's been an adjustment moving back into my childhood room after being on my own."

"Do you have a curfew?" he teased. "Or can you stay out past the gas lamps coming on?"

"I can stay out late. I get the odd disapproving glare, but that comes with the territory."

126

"Would you like to stay out late with me sometime?"

I was warming up to him, but I was trying my hardest to stay cool. "Maybe."

"Just maybe?"

"Are you asking?"

"Yes. I'm asking."

"Where would we go?"

"Anywhere you'd like."

"How about a movie?"

"I was just thinking; I should ask her to the movies on Saturday." I could tell Will was smiling by the tone of his voice. I imagined that boyish twinkle in his blue eyes.

"Well then, I accept."

"Great. I'll pick you up at 6:30."

"See you Saturday."

"Wait… I need your address."

I hung up after giving him my address and I sat on the floor in the hallway with the phone in my lap. I had mixed feelings. I was happy to be going out with him, but it had really hurt when he just vanished. I had been blindsided and I'd vowed I'd never let it happen again. I couldn't shake the feeling I was setting myself up for the same disappointment all over again.

Will slipped easily back into my life. Almost all our friends were already paired off, married, and having children. Everyone was pleased I was dating a decent, fun, good-looking guy and it made it less awkward that I wasn't the odd single girl.

Over the next couple years, we dated while we focused on our careers. I was gaining experience and building my reputation as DBs top engineer. Will started his own company that specialized in working with developers who were building fields of nearly identical homes in the newly sprouting suburbs outside the city. Will liked the simplicity and repetition of one or two electrical layouts that repeated over several streets of the new subdivisions. He could supervise several three-man crews who could do a whole street of houses in a week like an assembly line.

The money was good, and Will bought a house on Indian Road that was walking distance from my parent's house. He sought my advice as he furnished and decorated it. One evening we were lying naked on his living room floor, after making love on the new rug I'd picked out for him. Will rolled onto his side and faced me.

"Don't you think it's about time you stopped leaving every night?"

"You know I can't. Mother already worries about the neighbours seeing you walk me home when it's practically morning."

"Then why don't we just get married?"

I thought he was kidding, fishing for me to stay a little longer. "Are you asking me?"

"Maybe I am." He suddenly sounded serious and rolled up onto one knee beside me.

I giggled. Yes, his naked body was lovely, but he looked ridiculous with such a serious expression while his penis dangled inches from my face.

"How can I say yes to you? We can never tell anyone how you proposed to me."

"Does that mean you'd say yes if it was a better story?"

"I would think so."

"You'd say yes?" Will didn't believe me.

"Are you taking it back?"

"No, No!! Not at all. This is swell."

"Swell?"

"Great, wonderful. I didn't think you wanted to get married, ever."

"What made you think that?"

"Because you've never suggested it."

"Why would I suggest it? Aren't you supposed to do the asking?"

"This coming from the woman who defies all convention and bemoans inequality at work?"

"That's different." Although I had to admit, he had a point. I admired his observations and reasoning which wasn't usually his strong suit. I think being impressed by him added to the wonder of the moment, maybe more so than the fact that he'd just proposed to me.

"So, when should we do the deed?"

"Let's not make plans until I get back from Japan," I suggested.

"Should we tell your parents?"

"Shouldn't we wait until I've got, umm, a ring?"

"Oh, yeah, a ring. I wasn't planning on this tonight."

"Me neither. I would have worn something prettier." I slipped into the jeans and sweater I'd worn to go rug shopping.

Will pouted. "You're getting dressed?"

"It's getting late, I have an early meeting tomorrow."

Will tugged at my jeans playfully. "So, I guess you're not sleeping over at your fiancé's house tonight?"

"I'm still not convinced you're serious – do you really want to get hitched?"

"It's about time we did. Isn't' it?"

At the time, I couldn't think of a good reason not to marry Will. He was a good man, fun to be with, an honourable nice guy and we had great sex. What more could I want? Add to that I was approaching 30 and already considered a bit of an old maid. Marrying Will seemed like the logical thing to do. Remembering my naiveté that it could be as simple as finding someone who checked all the boxes, and everything would be ok, made me feel a little wistful. I could have spared myself a lot of heartache if I'd just gone it alone but then I might never have had Anne, the one good thing that came out of Will and my union.

Bacon jumped on the bed and climbed into my now empty suitcase.

"Sorry, buddy." I lifted him out, dropped him to the floor, and closed the suitcase. "You're not baggage. Unlike those thoughts you interrupted. Just for that, I'm going to get you some more treats."

CHAPTER 16

Visiting Emily was even nicer than I'd anticipated. She was so grateful to have me there, I was glad I'd decided to stay. She'd made us a pot of tea when she put Jake down for a nap.

I sat with her at the kitchen table. "Drinking tea always reminds me of visiting you in Oxford."

"We do love our tea."

"Do you miss living in England?"

"Tons. I loved being able to hop on a train and be in London in an hour."

"Remember when we took the train to London and went to the theatre?"

"Grandma Betsy wasn't feeling up to it. So just you and I went. I showed you the way."

"I let you think you were showing me. I was prepared if you got us on the wrong track."

"But I didn't."

"Your mother said you knew your way, but I couldn't believe my little Emily was so independent."

"I really miss Mom, especially now that I have Jake. She wanted to stay longer after the Baptism but having to care for Grandfather ... she just couldn't."

"I remember when I first met him and Mrs. Wardon at the engagement party they threw for your parents."

"What did you think when you met 'The Professor'?"

"They were very polite. At the party, they welcomed us to the family with a formal introduction and toast."

"I bet they served sherry and had uniformed servers with white gloves and aprons passing canapés?"

"Precisely!"

"It's hard to imagine Grandfather without Grandmother, she was the quintessential professor's wife: taking care of everything practical so he could be eccentric and brilliant. Mom said he couldn't boil an egg or decide what socks to wear without her."

"Hard to teach an old dog new tricks. Your mother hasn't told me much. But I get the impression it's stressful for her."

"She used to tell Grandma Betsy everything."

"They both liked to tell each other everything. I almost never knew the whole story... I suppose I preferred it that way."

"I can remember being mortified when she told her I'd had my first period and spilled all the gory details to her."

"Do you tell your mother everything too?"

"Not like she did. I think I'm a bit more like Father, some things are best unsaid."

Driving back to Bar Harbor after such a nice visit with Emily, I couldn't help feeling regret for how much of her and Ann's lives I'd missed living so far away. Betsy had been distraught when Ann applied to study abroad for a term. When Ann was accepted to the program at Oxford, Betsy hated the idea of her leaving, but she knew the opportunity to study art in a place with such a rich history was a chance of a lifetime. It was something Betsy would have loved to do as a young art major. She couldn't bring herself to discourage Ann, but she didn't push for her to accept either. Had she known that Ann would fall in love with England, and later with Lane, and would never move back home, she might not have been so supportive.

When we went to England to meet Ann's fiancé, in addition to the engagement party in Oxford, we also spent time in London. Ann was our tour guide. She wanted to show us everything that she loved about London. She took us to her favorite places. We went to the theatre and visited museums. While I enjoyed the Natural History Museum the most, Betsy was delighted by the Tate Gallery.

I remember feeling such pride as Ann confidently steered us through the vast collection pointing out important works and her favorites. When we got to the modern section, Ann had a special surprise for her mother.

She pointed to the wall at the far end of the room we'd just entered. "I thought you might take over the tour for these few paintings."

Betsy moved closer so she could read the plaque beside the painting. "They look like... they are Wilfredo Lam!"

"I thought these might bring back some memories of working in your uncle's gallery. You told me it specialized in Cuban art."

"I can't believe you remembered that. These are excellent examples. Lam's work often featured hybrid figures. He was significantly influenced by Picasso, who he met while living in Paris."

Watching Betsy's animated face as she told Ann about the artist and his work, I saw the young woman who'd shown me around the small gallery in downtown St. Petersburg.

"You talk about him as if you knew him," observed Ann.

"I did meet him once. He brought several of his paintings from New York to our gallery to show a collector who was a good friend of your grandfather."

"I had no idea!"

"Your mother swam in very elite circles before I took her north."

Ann looked awestruck. "But you never mentioned names."

"It was a long time ago, 1955 or 56. I quit working in the gallery before we got married"

Ann and Betsy had bonded over art when they first met, but that day in the gallery it was obvious that they both had a passion for it.

Because of the peculiarities of immigration rules, Ann and Lane decided it was simpler if they got married in England. When I was making our travel plans to attend the wedding, I suggested to Betsy that we take some time away from the festivities so she could spend more time touring the art museums. That only added to Betsy's anger that the wedding was not taking place under her control in Boston.

"If you were a good lawyer, you'd have things sorted so we wouldn't be the ones traveling," she'd said.

Although we visited Ann every couple of years, looking back, it wasn't enough. I used visiting Ann as a bribe to get Betsy to agree to accompany me on my business trips. Only twice did we take an actual vacation to visit her for more than a few days.

I was so focused on my career I convinced myself that working hard and being successful so that I could be a good provider, was the most important thing I could do for my family. What I now realize is the greatest contribution I could have made was my time and presence in their lives.

The trip to the Olympics with Ann, Lane and Emily was the only trip we'd taken as a family after Betsy died. I remember walking with Emily from the hockey venue to Café Al Bicerin dal 1763 for their famous 'bicerin" hot chocolate, coffee, and cream concoction. She had initially been suspicious of the fancy glass and dark-colored liquid under thick white foam, but she was completely hooked as soon as she took her first sip.

"It's like drinking a chocolate bar," she'd said.

"You like it?"

"What's not to like?"

"Perfect thing to warm us up. I was cold in the arena."

"You're just cold because your ladies lost to Sweden."

"It was still a good game. But I'm disappointed we won't play Canada in the final."

"Think of it this way; we couldn't get tickets for the gold medal game, so it's good they're not playing."

"What are your plans for this evening?"

"I'm meeting a bunch of people from London I met at the downhill event yesterday. We're going for dinner."

"Since when does your mother let you go out all alone with friends in a strange city."

"Since a while. I'll be leaving for university soon – and she knows she can't go with me everywhere anymore."

"It seems like yesterday that you were hunting for interesting rocks with me on the beach at Dover."

"I was 8. I stopped picking up rocks a while ago."

"You know you'll always be my little granddaughter; my favorite granddaughter in fact."

"I'm the only one."

"I'm really glad you'll be studying at Boston University."

"Mom isn't so keen."

"But it's her alma matter."

"She's doubly disappointed. I'm leaving and I'm not going to be an art major."

"I hope it means I'll see you more often."

"I'm sure."

"Any holidays you don't go home, I hope you'll spend with me."

"I'm happy to, but I don't want to get in the way of any lady friends…"

"I think I'm too old for lady friends."

"No you're not. You're pretty good-looking, for an old guy."

"You're pretty cheeky, for a young girl."

"Maybe someday the right lady will come along."

"I'm pretty set in my ways. I'm not sure anyone would have me."

Emily had been teasing, but I remember thinking I was happier than I'd been in a very long while. The first months after Betsy's death had been difficult. I'd been so busy looking after her that, without the daily routine of her care, I felt a little lost.

But, at the same time, our occupancy rate for the B&B was steadily increasing, and I was engrossed in developing a process to keep everything running smoothly. Activity is a good cure for most things and the steady flow of guests kept me from feeling alone.

It took several trips to carry everything inside from the Jeep through the back entrance. Emily had asked me to go with her to Costco while she had me there to help with Jake. She wanted to stock up before she went back to work. She pushed Jake and I pushed the big cart. Since we were there, I figured I'd pick up supplies for the Inn that we'll need for the busy summer season. Things like toilet paper, paper towels and cleaning supplies and a bunch of non-perishable things like flour, sugar, coffee, bottled water, and pop that could sit in the car overnight until I got home.

Despite being a bit tired from the drive, I had to get everything put away in the storeroom. I left out one pack of toilet paper so I could go replenish the rooms that Anne and Maddie had used. The gals were coming to clean all the rooms tomorrow morning, so I grabbed the keys and the toilet paper and headed up to make sure all the guest rooms were unlocked and restocked.

I unlocked Tokyo first. I was surprised to find that Anne had stripped the bed and had folded the dirty sheets neatly at the foot of the bed. I added two rolls of toilet paper to the bathroom and then opened the windows a crack to let the room breathe.

Dover was unlocked and the key was on the desk just as Maddie had said it would be but there was also a gift bag. She wasn't the first guest to leave something behind. She must have forgotten it when she was packing up. I repeated my post guest replenishment and window opening ritual and then picked up the gift bag and took it back to my office.

I checked the reservation book for Maddie's phone number but quickly realized that I had no contact information for her because Anne had been the one to make the reservations for both of them. I had Anne's phone number, so I called to explain that Maddie had forgotten something in the room and I wanted to get in touch with her to return it.

"I'll give you her address and my FedEx account number so you can use that to ship it to her," offered Anne.

"That's very kind of you."

"Least I can do for taking such good care of her. I'll email you the info."

"It was my pleasure."

I turned on my computer and, as I waited for it to start up, I went down to the storage room to get a small box of suitable size to pack up Maddie's forgotten item. As I put the package in the box, I saw there was a card that had slipped out of the bag. I didn't want to snoop so I pushed it back in and tucked everything into the box and taped it shut. A few minutes later, I had an email from her with Maddie's address and phone number.

It occurred to me when I was writing up the shipping label that I didn't know if the contents were fragile and could be damaged if the package was shaken or dropped in transit. Maddie hadn't packed it for shipping, but to carry with her. Since I now had her number, I could call and find out if I needed to put more packing material inside to protect the item. Fortunately, she answered when I called.

"Hello, Maddie. This is Nate Jacobs."

"Hello, Nate. Nice to hear from you."

"I'm calling to tell you I found the package you left in your room."

"It was just something small."

"Yes, it's quite small. I was wondering if it was fragile?"

"Fragile?"

"Yes, so I know how to package it to send it to you."

"Why would you send it to me?"

"I thought you'd want it."

"It's for you."

"For me?"

"Yes, I left a note. It's a little thank you gift."

"Thank you gift?"

"Yes, for you."

"I thought you forgot it."

"No. I left it quite deliberately; in a place I thought you'd find it."

"Well that part worked. I found it."

"Did you open it?"

"I didn't want to be nosey."

"Oh… Well… You can open it now that you know it's for you."

"I'll need to get scissors."

"Scissors?"

"To cut the tape."

"Tape?"

"On the box. I packed it up to send to you."

"It's a good thing you called before you put your present in the mail back to me. I'd take offence to that."

"I wouldn't want that."

I opened the box and untied the ribbon securing the gift bag. "Well look at that! The card says, To Nate". I pulled out the card and skimmed the thank you note that said she'd like to keep in touch and included her contact information.

"I should've put the card on the outside, to avoid confusion."

"I'm glad you want to keep in touch. I could have saved Anne the trouble of sending me your address and phone number if I'd opened this earlier."

I unwrapped the package that was inside the bag. On the box was a picture of a sailboat.

I read aloud. "Sea Cards. Over 450 nautical flashcards for mastering sailing and boating knowledge including nautical terms, sailing commands, gear and equipment, navigation rules and lights, safety procedures, buoyage, knots and more."

"I saw them at the Naturalist's Notebook. I thought they looked interesting."

"Will there be a test?"

Maddie chuckled. "No, no test."

"I look forward to going through them – I'll be a smart old salt next time you see me."

"Maybe when Jake gets a little older you can quiz each other."

"Thank you for the gift. It was completely unnecessary."

"Just a small token of appreciation for hosting me so graciously."

Since my computer was on and my email program open, I wrote a quick email to Maddie right after hanging up from our call.

> *Dear Maddie,*
>
> *Thank you again for the gift. It was a pleasure meeting you and spending time with you. I hope we can stay in touch. You'll find my particulars below. Do you Skype? Ann and Emily insist on seeing me when we talk so they set it up on my computer. It would be lovely to see you again.*
>
> *Sincerely,*
>
> *Nate*

Last year Emily had helped me set up an automatic signature at the bottom of my email with the contact information for the inn, so I didn't have to type it in every time. I reread my note and hit send.

Looking at the clock I realized it was already 6 pm. No wonder my stomach felt sour, I hadn't eaten since breakfast with Emily. I headed down to the kitchen to forage for something to eat.

The first thing I saw in the fridge were the cheeses I'd served Maddie. Taking them out, I thought of how zealously Maddie had eaten them. There wasn't much left of the Cyclone, she'd obviously liked it. I'll have to buy a nice blue cheese the next time she's here, I thought to myself. Then it occurred to me that maybe there would never be a next time. I hated the thought of not seeing her again.

It was a bit of a fluke we'd met at all. All the little choices we make, each day, can affect who we meet and when we meet them. Perhaps we were supposed to meet but we just kept missing each other until now. If Emily hadn't asked her daughter to be Jake's godmother, and if she hadn't been visiting Anne the same exact date as the Baptism, we might never have met. Discovering that we were in London at the same time when her photo had inspired my purchase of the inn, and then again both at the Torino Olympics made me wonder if we'd been just missing meeting each other for a long time.

"You're getting soft in the head old man," I said out loud to myself as I poured a glass of wine and turned on the kitchen TV. Even with the distraction of the evening news, I couldn't help but imagine Maddie sitting on the stool across from me. I bet we'd be bantering, or I'd be listening with awe at how she could talk about everything, anything or nothing at all and I would be happy just being there with her. I realized that I felt more alone now than I had after Betsy died. I felt guilty and ashamed to think it. Maddie had only been around for a couple of days, whereas Betsy and I had spent a lifetime together.

I'd "married up" socially. Not that I'd had that as a goal, but it was a fact that Betsy was from a wealthy well-connected family and had social connections I would never have had without her. I was the son of a bus driver. My dad was hardworking, an honest man, and I was proud of him. He knew every street in Baltimore, but he couldn't help me navigate the social networks that I needed to figure out to be successful in business.

From the first day I'd met her, she'd impressed me with who she knew and who she could introduce me to. My first job in the legal profession was a part-time clerk position she orchestrated through her network of contacts. At our country club, she went out of her way to meet every new member's wife or daughter and welcomed them by inviting them to have lunch or play a game of tennis. She had little interest in my business, but she was well informed about everyone else's. She wielded her social power with the skill of a swordsman, cutting through barriers dressed in a pillbox hat, matching purse, and white gloves.

I tried hard to live up to her expectations, but she often made it clear that I fell short. Like the night I took her to dinner at the Tiffany Room at the Belleview-Biltmore hotel. I'd planned everything in advance in excruciating detail as I was going to ask her to marry me. I wanted everything to be just perfect. Betsy dressed in an emerald-green evening gown, and I wore my one dark suit because it was the most formal thing I owned.

Several times when I was just about to initiate my proposal, some friend or friend of the family would stop at our table to say hello or ask her to give their regards to her father or her uncle whose gallery she worked at.

"There's something I want to ask you," I'd finally gotten to say.

"What's that?"

I reached into my pocket as I stood up from my chair. Holding the ring box out, I got down on one knee.

"Betsy Williams, would you do me the honor of being my wife? Will you marry me?"

Betsy looked around the room to see who was watching. "Aren't you going to show me the ring?"

I opened the box and showed her the solitaire ring in a white gold band. I'd researched what was in fashion and purchased the ring at one of the best jewelers in town. I'd spent more than I could comfortably afford but I knew she deserved something nice. She looked at the ring and smiled.

"Yes, Nate. I will marry you." She extended her hand, and I slipped the ring on her finger.

"That's wonderful." I leaned in to kiss her.

She kissed me politely and whispered in my ear. "I know you'll get me a better ring once you've finished law school and you have a real job."

I quickly learned that when it came to gifts for Betsy, status mattered more than sentiment. When traveling for business Ann was delighted by receiving postcards, strange, tacky souvenirs, and local candy. But for Betsy, it was Mikimoto pearls from Japan or a Cartier watch from Paris or don't bother.

I'd given Ann all Betsy's jewelry after she passed including, her Italian gold earrings, emerald, ruby and sapphire cocktail rings, and the diamond tennis bracelet I'd bought her for our 25th wedding anniversary. But nothing had meant more to Ann than the double string of pearls Betsy had worn so often they'd been restrung multiple times. She'd asked to borrow them to wear on her wedding day and of course, Betsy was thrilled to supply the 'something borrowed'. In the end, Ann didn't wear them because seeing her mother without them just didn't seem right. She'd taken them off and put them around Betsy's neck and asked to borrow her diamond bracelet instead.

I thought of the gift Maddie had bought me. It was playful and thoughtful, much like she was. I wondered what kind of presents she liked. She didn't seem the type to be impressed by the value of the gift in monetary terms. I'd have to work a little harder to pick out presents for her, but I looked forward to having the opportunity.

CHAPTER 17

I examined my face in the mirror, contemplating putting on makeup. Claire would be picking me up any minute for our monthly book club meeting. Claire always looked beautiful. That, coupled with her delightful French-Canadian accent, made her seem exotic and at least 20 years younger than her 80 years. She had worked for a famous plastic surgeon as his nurse. She regularly, gently, suggests changes I should make to my skincare regime to improve my complexion and makeup tips to accent my features. But I gave up looking glamourous years ago. I settled on a couple of swipes of mascara and some lipstick.

Perhaps, if Nate and I start Skyping regularly, I'll pay more attention to her advice so I can look good on screen. He'd emailed me his address right after we'd talked earlier this evening, but I'd not responded yet. I wasn't sure what to write back. I'd read his email on my phone so I decided to wait to respond when I could do so from my computer. I still prefer typing on a keyboard for important correspondence.

The doorbell rang and I hurried downstairs to let Claire in.

"You look lovely tonight, Maddie."

"Thank you. You look fabulous yourself, as always."

"I parked on the street. I'll wait in the car if you're not quite ready."

"I'm ready, just my purse and shoes… and the book." I gathered everything as I walked out with her, locking the door behind us.

"Did you have time to finish it?"

"I finished it this afternoon. I didn't have a lot of reading time in Bar Harbor."

"Did you and Anne have a nice trip?"

"Unfortunately Anne had to cut her trip short and get back to the office."

"I'd have thought that would have given you a lot more reading time."

"I stayed on in Bar Harbor without her."

"By yourself?"

"I wasn't completely alone. Nate, the owner of the B&B we stayed at, took me sightseeing and he drove me back to Boston on Wednesday."

"I hope he doesn't have a jealous wife."

"He's a widower."

"So that's why you're glowing. You have a new boyfriend."

I scoffed at Claire's suggestion. "Hardly. I've only known him for a couple of days and I'm far too old for a boyfriend."

"You're never too old to fall in love."

"I don't have a good track record with love."

"Maybe because it was never the right person?"

"You'd think after 78 years on the planet, I'd have found him by now."

"Maybe you did, but you just missed each other."

"Funny you should say that. We discovered we were in the same place a couple of times: in London in 1996 and at the Torino Olympics in 2006."

"Ahhhh... See! I told you. You just missed meeting him."

"It was just a coincidence."

"There's no such thing as just a coincidence. The choices you made led you to those co-incidences."

We'd arrived at the place for our meeting. Claire pulled in and parked in the driveway. "I want to hear more about your new boyfriend, Nate, after book club."

The book for this month wasn't exceedingly long, but the discussion about *Go Set a Watchman* by Harper Lee was spirited. Although desegregation and the injustices that fueled the civil rights movement in the American south were a prominent theme of the book, our discussion mostly centred around another aspect, the father-daughter relationship. Several women in our group shared personal stories about their relationship with their fathers. I was surprised how many had strained relationships or had pivotal moments of disappointment. The moment when their awe for their father who, in their eyes was omnipotent, was shattered as they discovered he had shortcomings and was human after all. I knew my father wasn't perfect, but he'd never let me down in any of the ways these other women had been disappointed.

"You were pretty quiet tonight," said Claire as we got back in the car.

"I didn't have any father-daughter trauma growing up – at least none that I remember."

"I thought maybe you were daydreaming about being back in Bar Harbor?"

"Didn't even cross my mind."

"Shall we stop at Tim Horton's for a coffee? You can tell me all about HIM."

We got our coffees and a donut to share and sat at one of the tables. Claire grilled me about what we'd done and what he looked like and if he'd kissed me yet.

"Of course there was no kissing!" I'd said indignantly.

"Hugging? Hand-holding?"

"We did hold hands running from the car in the rain – but that was just to make sure I didn't fall."

Claire's mouth curled into a sly smile. "Sure it was..."

"It really was. Completely innocent."

"But you liked it."

"Nate is easy to be with. We got along well. At least I enjoyed his company. It's possible he was just being nice to me for his granddaughter's sake."

"Oh, pisshaw. He wouldn't have done all that if he hadn't enjoyed your company."

"I suppose."

"So when are you going to see him again."

"Probably never. We don't exactly swim in the same waters."

"You obviously do since you've almost met twice – that you know of."

"It's getting late. I know you don't like driving late at night."

"It's only a few blocks. I'm not going anywhere until you tell me what your next move is going to be."

"I'm too old to be having moves."

"You're not dead."

"He emailed me tonight just a little while before you arrived."

"See. He's made a move."

"He thanked me for the gift, and he gave me his contact information."

"Did you write back?"

"Not yet."

"But you're going to.

"Aren't you supposed to wait three days or something so you don't seem desperate?"

"At our age we really shouldn't waste any days playing games. If you like him, answer him."

That was where we'd left it, or so I'd thought.

Claire rolled down the window and called out as she pulled away. "Don't forget to write him back."

I shook my head, smiled, and waved goodbye to her from inside my screen door. "Incorrigible," I muttered to myself.

Saturday morning, I woke up to rain. It was still pouring when I made myself coffee. I'd hoped to go to the garden center to get flowers for the front garden, but it clearly wasn't the day for it. I decided instead to download the pictures I'd taken while visiting Anne. I took my coffee to my desk, pulled the memory card from my camera, and copied the pictures to my computer.

Looking through them, I had several nice ones from the walking tour of Boston's historic sites that I'd done the day before we'd gone to Bar Harbor, while Anne was at work. Next came the pictures I'd taken outside the church, of Anne holding Jake, and the pictures I'd taken around Hope Point Inn. I laughed out loud when I got to the selfie with Nate where we were collapsing with Inny our stone man.

I decided that sending a few pictures to Nate was a good reason to email him. In addition to the selfies we'd taken, there were several views of and from his place that I thought were quite good and a cute picture of Jake in his baptismal outfit. I saved out smaller jpg files of a dozen pictures to make them more convenient for emailing. I opened Nate's email to reply. After several rewrites, edits, and deletions, I was finally satisfied with my reply.

Hello Nate,

I hope you and your guests are having better weather than we are! It's pouring rain here and they are predicting it will continue all weekend. The rain did give me a reason to do indoor activities, so I downloaded the pictures I took last weekend. I thought you might enjoy seeing a few of them so I've picked out some and attached them. If there are any you'd like to have in print form, I'd be happy to send them to you, either the prints or the high resolution files so you can print them however you'd like. If you have a photo gallery on your website, please feel free to use any you like. I've put that in writing because I'm guessing, as a lawyer, you'd be particular about having permission to use them. :)

Again, thank you for being such a wonderful host. I had a great time and I hope we keep in touch.

Cheers

Maddie

I attached the photos and hit send. It was still pouring outside so I continued to sort and touch up the photos that I'd taken. I was just about to get up and leave the computer when I noticed I had a new email. It was from Nate. I felt a thrill ripple through me as I opened it.

Dear Maddie,

Thank you for the pictures. They are excellent. I certainly would have asked permission before using them – but you beat me to it. I will ask Emily to add the ones of the inn to the website. She helps me with it when she comes to visit. They'll be coming in a couple of weeks and I'm looking forward to seeing them.

My guests for the weekend will be arriving soon. The weather is very nice here today and I hope the good forecast turns out to be correct. I've noticed that the better the weather is, the happier my guests are and the easier they are to please. This group will be leaving on Monday, so if you'd like to set up a time to talk, I'll be free that evening. I enjoyed our conversations this past week and I hope we can stay in touch.

Warm regards

Nate

I read it three times, and then I read it again. He'd answered so quickly. He wanted to keep in touch. I realized I was grinning and my heart skipping. I immediately hit reply.

Dear Nate,

I'm glad you liked the pictures. I too would like to stay in touch but Monday night I'll be away. I'm going to Montreal with a friend for a few days. Perhaps we could talk after I return? I get back on Thursday afternoon. You can reach me on my cell phone if you ever need to reach me. I also get my email on my phone while travelling. Anne likes to keep in touch by text and she worries if I don't answer her right away, so I've almost always got it with me. Remember when we had to write letters to keep in touch? It took ages to go back and forth, especially internationally. I guess that's why they call mail "snail mail" now. Hope to hear from you soon.

Maddie

Since I was still sitting at my computer, I decided I should book my train ticket for Monday. Looking at the schedule I wasn't sure which train to book, so I called Claire.

"Hallo"

"Hello. It's Maddie."

"How are you?"

"Great. I was just going to book my ticket for Monday – have you booked yours yet?"

"No. Not yet. I was going to call today."

"I just started to make my reservation online, but I wasn't sure which train."

"I told Cécile we'd be there in time for dinner…"

"We have two choices, the 8:35 arriving at 1:55 or the 11:30 arriving at 4:58."

"Which do you prefer?"

"The 11:30."

"Then that's what we'll do."

"I can book both our tickets if you'd like."

"That would be merveilleux. Let me get my credit card."

"Don't worry. I know you're good for it…"

"I am but thank you."

"Ok. We're booked. I'll print the reservations and bring them on Monday. Do you want me to email them to you too?"

"Don't bother. I won't be leaving without you. I can wait. Speaking of email, have you emailed your boyfriend yet?"

"He's not my boyfriend. But this morning I sent a few pictures I took while staying with him."

"That's an excellent excuse to email him. Clever lady."

"It wasn't an excuse. It was a reason."

"Potato, potaaato."

"He emailed me back already."

"I wouldn't be surprised if he was quite smitten with you. You're quite a catch."

"And you're hopelessly optimistic when it comes to love and romance."

"I can't help it. I'm French." She said it matter-of-factly as if this completely explained everything.

I redirected our conversation back to our trip planning, hoping to deflect Claire's curiosity. "I'm planning on taking a taxi to Union Station on Monday, would you like to go together?"

"Good idea. I'll leave my car at your house if that's ok?"

"Of course. See you Monday – say – 10 here?" I was momentarily relieved that she was off the subject of Nate. But of course, she didn't let it go.

"So, will you be answering his email?"

"I've already answered."

"Have you made plans to see each other again?"

"No, but he suggested we set a time to talk next week."

"When?"

"I don't know. He suggested Monday so I suggested after I get back on Thursday."

"Ahh. Making him wait. Playing hard to get."

I let out a big sigh. "It's going to be a long train ride."

"I'm just happy you've finally met a man."

"I've met plenty of men."

"Met THE man, I should have said."

"Men come and then they go."

"You've kissed your share of frogs, that's true. But perhaps Nate's your prince?"

Even now, at 80, Claire was still one of the most open-minded of all my friends. She'd been one of the few women who hadn't shied away from me socially after Will and I divorced. Despite being happily married to Theo, she'd been the one to help me move on by encouraging me to "keep living" when it would have been easier to just hunker down at home with Anne and give up on men altogether.

"I don't believe sex before marriage is wrong," she'd told me. "And it certainly is necessary afterwards. We are designed to be passionate, and it would be wrong to ignore such a vital part of what we are."

She was the only person I'd confided in when I'd stepped out with a college friend. Forty years ago, it was a scandalous thing to admit to someone.

Robbie and I had been in the same engineering class at Queens. He'd gone on to complete a Ph.D. and then had gone to work in Ottawa for the Ministry of Energy Mines and Resources. We'd kept in touch professionally since his research had been applicable to several of my more complex projects. We'd even collaborated on a few papers.

We didn't see each other that often. Once or twice a year at conferences like the PDAC or GAC. We'd meet for drinks or dinner, often with other friends and colleagues but sometimes just the two of us. We never had any difficulty picking up where we left off and finding things to talk about, often closing the bar because we'd been so deep in conversation, we hadn't realized how much time had passed.

So, it wasn't unusual for him to let me know when he would be in town. One time, when he was staying in town at the Royal York, we decided to meet in the hotel lobby bar. It was a hot, humid August evening. When I arrived, he was sitting at a table under one of the large ceiling fans, sharply dressed in light blue slacks; his sport coat draped over another chair and his shirt sleeves rolled up. He got up to greet me.

"Great to see you, Maddie. Hot day, eh? Can I get you a drink?"

"Yes on both counts."

The waiter appeared. I ordered a gin and tonic as I sat down at the table.

Robbie settled back into his chair. "Make it two."

"Have you been waiting long?"

"Just one drink ahead of you."

"I came straight from work. I should have stopped to freshen up in the ladies' room." I looked around to see where the washrooms were.

"Relax, you look fabulous. How is it you never change?"

"Older but not wiser. So, what brings you to town this time?"

"I'm spending a few days at U of T working with several guys in the geology department. We've got a joint research grant to develop a new airborne remote sensing technology for the Skyvan. We've just got the first samples in from this year's fieldwork."

"What's a Skyvan?"

"It's the ugliest plane ever. Looks like a van with wings."

"Interesting. It would speed up mapping if you didn't actually have to walk every mile."

"And saves on cutting thousands of miles of line through the forest. If we can zero in on the most likely targets from the air, we can focus our efforts on the ground."

"So you've been in the field then?"

"Not me personally. We flew several test flights over known hot spots, then we created anomaly maps based on the data. My field team has been out collecting samples to correlate the anomaly readings with actual specimens."

"How do you know they collected the specimens from exactly the right locations?"

"The site is a well-characterized uranium deposit in Alberta. We selected sample locations where we had high readings that coincided with defined geologic units based on existing mapping and air-photo interpretation."

"Sounds like you'll be working with some 'hot' samples."

He nodded. "I might glow in the dark by the end of this project."

"Guess you really shouldn't take your work home then."

He chuckled. "Funny girl. But true. And your work?"

"I'm spending more time supervising work than actually doing work. I miss getting my hands dirty so I try to get out to do site visits whenever I can. I'm the anomaly in my field – not your kind of anomaly."

"My anomalies are radioactive. You're just intoxicating."

I smiled and lifted my glass. "That's not me. It's the gin."

"So, any more international postings on the horizon?"

"Not for me. I can't leave Anne for a couple of months at a time."

"What about Will?"

"What about him?"

"Doesn't he take care of her when you travel?"

"His way of taking care of her is to drop her off at my parents."

"How is Anne?"

"She's at summer overnight camp this week and next. Since I've not had a phone call yet, I assume she's happy."

"So you don't have to rush home after drinks?"

"Nope. I'm free all evening. I'd just be home alone. Will's gone to Kingston for a baseball tournament."

"I was thinking of going to see that new Monty Python movie, The Holy Grail. But since you're free, do you want to do something else?"

"I'd love to see it. Will wouldn't go with me. He says he doesn't get what's so funny about that show."

"Wow. You really are amazing. I don't know any other woman who can talk about geology and Monty Python in the same conversation and who is beautiful on top of it all."

"Beautiful? Right. Are you sure you've only had one more drink than I have? Beer goggles perhaps?" I teased him but secretly, I was warmed by the compliment.

I'd never thought of Robbie as a romantic partner. We were just friendly colleagues. But in that moment, I felt a flicker of attraction for him, and I wondered if his smarts extended to the bedroom.

"You've always been a babe," said Robbie sincerely. "I hope Will appreciates what a catch he's got."

I didn't want to talk about Will. "What time is the movie?"

I didn't tell Robbie much more about my relationship with Will, but I think he knew me well enough that what I didn't say told him that I wasn't all that happy. Will and I had developed separate lives except for Anne. I worked long hours and he played sports and went out with the boys. Things had been rocky between us for a while; actually, for years. I found I was happiest when he was out or away. I turned into someone I didn't like when he was around. To keep the peace, for Anne's sake, I had to swallow my desires and needs and put up with Will's self-centeredness and preconceived notions of how things should be. I could never just be me with Will.

Talking and joking with Robbie was so easy. I felt no need to try to impress him. I knew he liked me just as I am and that he respected me. I knew he had no expectations. It was in stark contrast to my relationship with Will. Being around Will was like walking on eggshells, my nerves were stretched to their limits and my emotions barely under control.

We left the hotel and took a cab to the movie theatre, bought our tickets and popcorn, and took our seats. Robbie and I both started giggling from the very first scene. The movie had just reached the scene where they encounter the *Knights Who Say Ni* when the screen went dark. At first, we thought it was part of the movie but, a few seconds later, the emergency lights over the doors turned on and an usher came out and made an announcement.

"There's been a power failure. Please exit the theatre carefully. You may bring your tickets to a future show and they will be honoured."

Outside it was still quite light, even though it was after 9 o'clock. Almost everything had come to a standstill and the city was eerily quiet. On the road, in front of the theatre, I could see that the streetcars had stopped, and traffic was jammed up behind them.

"Guess I won't be taking the streetcar home."

Robbie suggested we walk back to the hotel and wait for the power to come back on.

The hotel bar was full of people. Seems no one wanted to be alone in their rooms. The atmosphere was reminiscent of a bygone era when there were no TVs or phones in hotel rooms and guests congregated in the hotel lounges and lobby. Strangers struck up conversations to pass the time. The staff kept serving drinks and, since the power stayed out late into the evening, the kitchen staff brought out and served everyone free ice cream that had started to melt when the freezers lost power.

Around midnight the hotel manager made an announcement. "Power is out across the city. It's unlikely we'll get it back tonight. Anyone who needs assistance finding their room, there are hotel staff in the lobby with flashlights who will escort you to your rooms whenever you'd like."

We headed to the lobby, and I checked with the Bell Captain about a cab. Without the streetcars and subway running, it would take a while so I suggested Robbie go to bed and I'd wait in the lobby until I could get a cab.

Robbie leaned in quietly so no one around us would hear. "I don't mean to imply anything improper. You're welcome to crash with me."

I accepted given my other options were a long wait or a very long walk at night.

"I'll head out first thing in the morning, or whenever the power comes back on."

One of the housekeepers helped us find our way through the pitch-dark corridors to Robbie's room. The only light was a single emergency bulb at the end of the hallway by the stairwell. We opened the curtains to let in what little light there was outside from the night sky. The city below was eerily dark. Union Station was just a big dark lump, devoid of any lights in its large windows or illuminating its columns. Thankfully, there was a bit of moonlight so we could navigate the room without bumping into the furniture.

"Here's a clean t-shirt if you'd like to not look like you slept in your clothes in the morning."

"Thanks."

"You can have the bed. I'll take the floor."

"I can't take your bed. I'll take the floor. It'll be just like camping. Give me a pillow and a blanket and it will be like a sleeping bag under the stars."

"I insist. What kind of a gentleman would I be if I let you sleep on the floor."

"Then we'll share. I'm going to change in the bathroom."

When I came out Robbie was in his undershirt and boxers on top of the sheet.

He pulled back the sheet on my side of the bed. "I'll take over and you can take under."

I giggled. "That sounds a bit naughty."

He pointed to his shirt and to me in his t-shirt. "Hey. What do ya know, we have matching pajamas!"

It might have been that we were both a bit tipsy from all the free drinks the hotel had provided, but we both found that hilarious and we giggled and laughed side by side in the bed.

I rolled on to my stomach and on to my elbows like a sphinx to look at him. "We're never going to get any sleep if you keep fooling around."

"You look pretty wide awake."

"I am. It's not my average Thursday night."

"Lie down. I'll rub your shoulders. Help you relax."

Robbie sat up beside me and gently but firmly started to knead my shoulders and back. He was a surprisingly capable masseur and it felt good. I could feel my body relaxing. I closed my eyes and enjoyed the feeling of his hands pulling the tension from my muscles. He was slowly working his way down my back. When he got to my bottom, he skipped over it and started working down my legs. As he massaged my thigh I relaxed even more, and my legs spilled a little further apart. I felt him pause and then his hands started a slow slide up my inner thigh. I didn't pull away because it felt nice. I remember thinking to myself, it would be nice to feel his hands a little higher. Just the thought made me feel a warm gush of wetness between my legs. Then I felt his hand slip briefly and brush my panties. My reaction was involuntary. I let out a little gasp and pressed myself into his hand.

Robbie whispered in my ear. "I can keep going?"

I mumbled an affirmative "Mmm hmmm."

His fingers slipped under the elastic edge of my panties and I felt his fingertips on my skin.

He tugged gently on the waistband of my undies. "Can I get these out of the way?"

"Uh huh." I lifted my hips up slightly so he could slide them off me.

For what seemed like a blissful eternity his fingers, tongue and lips continued to explore me until I had to beg him to stop. We didn't get much sleep that night. Once he had satisfied me, I returned the favour. After a short nap, I'd awoken to his hand stroking my bottom and we'd started all over again. First thing in the morning, I'd slipped out of bed, dressed, and left before Robbie woke up.

I'd confessed all this to Claire the next weekend when she'd come over for coffee, thinking she'd scold me. Rather, she'd encouraged me.

"If it's right for you, don't let anyone tell you it's wrong. Just be careful and discreet."

When I asked her if she'd ever strayed herself, she said that ever since she'd set eyes on Theo at the Café St Michel, she knew he was the only man for her. I asked her how she knew.

She smiled and said, "You'd never believe me if I told you."

"Try me."

"I saw Theo and I had this powerful déjà vu moment. Do you know it? When you feel like you've lived that exact moment before?"

"I know the feeling."

"Well, it was like that, only I not only felt like I'd been there before, but I knew I had to talk to him because I felt he was someone I already knew."

"You had met him before?"

She paused. "Not in this lifetime. I just knew that we were supposed to find each other."

"You believe in past lives?" I'd asked with considerable disbelief.

"I don't know for sure, but I knew, deep down in my soul, that I had to meet him. I walked right up to him and said, 'Hello my name is Claire' and he said, 'Hello Claire, my name is Theo. Would you like to dance?'. So, I said to Theo, 'Now that we're on a first-name basis, I'd love to.'"

"How bold. Weren't you afraid of what he'd think?"

"I just knew in my core that I should do it. And I was right."

When Theo died last year, just a few months after their 60th wedding anniversary I thought Claire would have been lost without him. What had amazed and inspired me was how she was so optimistic. Not that she wasn't sad he was gone. She was very sad. But she said she had lived almost her whole life with her soulmate, and she was grateful, and that she could not have asked for a more perfect life.

Claire told me "I'm happy to keep living because it gives me time to learn even more about life. I'll be even better prepared for the next time Theo and I meet."

CHAPTER 18

"Goodnight, Maddie. Sweet dreams."

"Goodnight, Nate. Sweet dreams."

Looking at my watch I was shocked that it was already almost midnight. I got up stiffly from my recliner to put the handset in the charging stand. We'd talked for almost two hours. It seems the more we talked, the more things we had to talk about. It's so easy to talk to her, or maybe, it's more accurate to say it's so easy to get Maddie talking. We have yet to find a subject that she has nothing to say about. I don't mean that in a derogatory way, I mean it in an awestruck way. There's so much interesting stuff in that pretty head of hers.

I replayed bits of tonight's conversation in my mind as I got ready for bed. I'd told her about Emily, Bob, and Jake's visit last week.

"Emily added some of the pictures you sent to my website."

"How sweet of her."

"She said yours are the best pictures yet, so I hope you don't mind we're using one for the front page."

"I'm flattered."

"Emily took all the pictures on a little stick. She said she'd work on replacing some other pictures with yours when she had some free time. I hope you don't mind that I gave them to her."

"Not at all. If I'd realized you wanted pictures for your website, I would have taken more pictures to increase the chance of getting something good."

I didn't tell Maddie about the little package I'd received in the mail today. The bright orange thick cardboard envelope with "Do not bend" on it had a printed card inside that said,

Grandpa,

I thought you might like to have these printed. You two look good together.

Thank you for taking such good care of us this weekend.

Love Emily

Emily had arranged to have prints made of the selfie pictures Maddie had sent. I had them propped up against the lamp on the end table beside my recliner and I'd been looking at them while talking to Maddie on the phone.

We'd talked about Toronto.

She said, "I've lived here so long it's like we're childhood friends who grew up together. Except one of us became world-famous and huge and I still live in the same neighborhood."

I told her that I hadn't been there in years, but that I'd spent a fair bit of time there in the late seventies. For several months I'd traveled back and forth between Boston and Toronto for business. Bond was investing in a major expansion into Canada, and I was in Toronto negotiating on behalf of the company. There were real estate deals, regulatory approvals for the new facilities and a host of other details that I was responsible for. It was interesting to think that Maddie had been living there when I'd spent so much time there.

There had been talk about me heading up the new Canadian division as president. I'd already been promoted to General Council when my mentor, Norm, had retired. He'd held the position for over 20 years, and he'd groomed me as his successor. One of his strengths was his fearlessness to take on things he'd never attempted. Taking the lead on the expansion north was exactly the type of challenge he'd inspired me to embrace. I threw myself into all aspects of the venture, hoping my hard work would pay off with another promotion.

I invited Betsy to come with me on one of my trips in July when I knew I'd have some time to take a few days vacation. I'd been commuting back and forth for several months and always stayed at the same hotel. I'd become acquainted with several of the staff including the concierge, Annette. She was super-efficient and seemed to know everything about, and everyone in, Toronto. She'd helped me make dinner reservations for business meetings and arranged everything including transportation. It was her that I approached to help me plan a special week of activities for Betsy and me.

I remember how impressed Betsy was when we stepped from the car and through the gilded doors of the Royal York held open by the Bell Captain, Sam, who said, "Welcome back Mr. Jacobs."

I thanked him by name and escorted her into the lobby. She barely moved her head, but her smile told me that she had noticed every detail and she approved. We walked up the marble stairs towards the reception desk. As we checked in, the clerk handed me an envelope, saying that the Concierge had left it for me.

When we got to our room Betsy asked what was in the envelope.

I didn't want to tell her too much, so I answered cryptically. "Tickets."

"Tickets for what?"

"Do you want to spoil the surprises?"

Betsy put her hands on her hips and ground her foot into the carpet. "I don't like surprises. I like to be prepared. You should know that by now."

"If you must know, I've arranged for us to see a couple of shows while we're here."

"That sounds lovely, luckily I packed evening attire."

"I knew you would. The first show is tonight. I thought we'd settle in, have a late lunch, and then get something light after the show. How does that sound?"

"I need to unpack... but, yes, that sounds alright."

"There are lots of things to do and see here in Toronto. I've made a list of a few you might like."

"Like what?"

"There is a brand-new tower, the tallest in the world, and you can go up it."

"You don't like heights."

"I'll go if you want to."

"Is there anything to do?"

"The view is supposed to be amazing and there's a restaurant that revolves. I could try to get us reservations?"

"That sounds nice."

"I'll call Annette, the concierge. She can work magic."

"So she's the one I should be thanking, not you."

Her words stung. I'd put a lot of thought into how to make this week special. I'd gone over all the shows that were in town. I'd picked the ballet, even though I detest it, because she enjoyed it, and *Romeo and Juliet* was one of her favorites. I'd also arranged for a Saturday day trip to the picturesque town of Stratford to see Oscar Wilde's *The Importance of Being Ernest* at the Avon Theatre. I thought she'd be delighted I'd arranged a private car to drive us there and back, a picnic by the river, and the best seats for the show.

Betsy stared out the car window as we pulled away from the theatre. We had about an hour's drive ahead of us so I thought we could talk about the show.

"Did you enjoy the play?"

Betsy turned in her seat and glared at me. "I know what you're trying to do."

"Trying to squeeze in a little vacation with my lovely wife while the company is paying for our hotel?"

"You're trying to make me like this place."

"I'm not. But do you?"

"I'm not moving to Toronto."

"It's a little soon to be making any decisions. I haven't been offered the position."

"I'm telling you now; I'm not moving."

"If we don't move, I can't accept the job."

Betsy was silent and looked straight ahead down the road. I could tell that as far as she was concerned, the subject was closed.

I tried to make her understand what it meant to us. "This is an important opportunity."

"For you."

"For us. I know it's a big change, But Ann starts university in the fall. The timing is perfect."

"Perfect? She leaves for school, and we abandon her and move to another country?"

"She can come home to us here. She'll love it. Remember yesterday, at the art gallery, you said she'd love the collection?"

"What about me?"

"What about you?"

"Precisely. You never think about me."

"That's not true. This whole trip is about you and me, together, getting to know Toronto."

"I don't know anyone here."

"We'll join a country club. You'll fit in perfectly. You'll make friends."

"I have friends. In Boston."

"We can invite them to visit us. Wouldn't that be fun?"

"Why should I give up everything for you to take this job?"

"Give up? It's a big promotion. If things go well, maybe they'll offer me the global presidency in Boston when Harold retires."

"If. If. If. What's the point of moving away just to go back?"

"Because what's good for my career is good for us."

"This is only good for you."

"You like nice things. You like shopping and expensive jewelry. Where do you think the money comes from?"

"Why can't you get promoted where you are?"

"If I don't take this job, I'll likely be passed over the next time around."

"You don't know that."

"This is my best chance. If I don't take it, someone else will, and I'll be off the fast track."

"If you take the job, you can move here alone."

"But you'd be the First Lady of Bond Canada?"

"That sounds like work."

"With the raise I'd get, I'll get you a full-time housekeeper."

"What I want is not to move. So, I won't need full-time anything."

"Maybe if we go see some of the neighborhoods, you'll change your mind. You might like what you see. I hear The Bridle Path is very nice."

"I'm not going to change my mind."

Despite my best efforts to convince Betsy of the merits of living in Toronto, and promising her many perks, she held firm. She refused to move.

My hard work did result in being offered the job as President of the new Bond Canada division. I asked Norm for advice. He said not accepting the position would be a career-limiting move, but he understood that there were legitimate personal reasons that must be taken into consideration. Declining the job felt like I was walking off the field mid-inning during the World Series. I was letting my team down, and I was giving up any hope of future advancement.

Fortunately, it wasn't a completely career-ending decision. I continued to hold the position of General Council up until my retirement. I oversaw the intellectual property, litigation and mergers and acquisitions departments. The expansion of the company globally and the massive changes in technology through the eighties resulted in many interesting and challenging projects. My legal team grew to more than 20 lawyers and their para-legal and administrative support staff.

But even with my successful career leading a large and diverse legal team, I always regretted never having the opportunity to take the top spot. I think I would have made a good leader, and I regretted not having the opportunity to be "the boss".

Betsy's outright refusal to even consider a move had made me feel like I'd no choice but to give in to her. I resented it. I wanted her approval even more than I wanted to make her happy. I wanted her support and when I didn't get it, I felt like I was failing, and that fueled my insecurities of being unworthy of someone of her social standing.

After our trip to Toronto together and in the weeks up until I was officially offered the job, a significant rift formed between us. Turning down the job was, in many ways, the breaking point for me. I was disappointed and Betsy didn't understand, or care, how much the opportunity meant to me. When Ann moved to university that fall, I dropped all pretense of sharing a bed with Betsy. I moved from the master bedroom to one of the other bedrooms. We'd not physically made love in years, but I'd kept up appearances for Ann's sake. Once she was out of the house, there seemed no reason to keep up the charade.

I'm not proud of having allowed myself to have relations with women other than Betsy. But she had no interest in a physical relationship, so it was hard for me to resist when the opportunity arose. I didn't seek out relationships, but I enjoyed the company of a woman and, occasionally, something that started innocently enough resulted in a more intimate connection.

When one of my business acquaintances, that I played golf with on weekends when I stayed in Toronto, gave me two tickets to the Toronto Argonauts game, I asked Annette the concierge if she'd like them. I wanted to thank her for all the help she'd given me setting up both personal and professional meetings and events. She accepted on the condition that I went with her.

From our interactions, I'd gleaned that she liked sports but what I didn't know was that she had three brothers who'd all played football, and the entire family were rabid Argos fans. On game day she wore a team jersey and tight bell-bottom jeans with her long hair loose. I remember because it was a stark contrast to her tailored work uniform, a severe dark suit with brass buttons on the jacket. She looked much younger, and prettier, as she jumped, cheered, and heckled beside me. It was hard to keep my eyes off her. I was surprised by how much fun this serious and efficient woman turned out to be.

After going to the game together, she smiled a little more broadly whenever we crossed paths at the hotel. I often stopped to chat with her when she wasn't with other guests and, a couple of times, she joined me for a cup of coffee at my invitation. It was nice to have someone to talk to outside of my daily work. We would talk about the weather or sports but, occasionally, being careful to maintain their anonymity, she would share guest stories about strange or funny requests she'd had to satisfy.

That's why I didn't think anything of it when she sat down beside me at the bar the night of a major blackout. It was late in the evening. She set her flashlight on the bar and asked the bartender for a coke.

She downed most of it one gulp. "What a night, eh?"

"Not your average Thursday?"

"No. I have escorted about 100 guests to their rooms. I'm beat. Sitting for a bit feels great."

"You're here really late."

"It's been an 'All hands on deck' sort of night, but I'm almost done."

"I'm going to finish up this drink and head to bed myself."

"I'll light the way for you."

"I'm sure I can find my way on my own."

"Doubtful. Besides, I don't want you tripping and falling on my watch."

"Then whenever you're ready; lead the way."

"Are you in a hurry?"

"No. I just thought you were very busy."

"My boss said I could leave, so you'll be my last trip up the stairs for tonight."

"If you're off the clock, someone else can see me to my room."

"Everyone's pretty busy. I'll take you now." She finished the last of her coke and turned on her flashlight.

Several flights of stairs later we arrived at my door. Annette stood very close to me, holding the light so I could insert the key into the lock. I paused and turned to her before going into my room.

"Would it be appropriate to tip you? I really appreciate you making that climb again."

"Here's a tip," she said, "invite me in."

I felt a tingle of excitement, although I dared not hope she was suggesting anything more than a rest before heading back down through the dark hotel.

I held the door and stepped aside to let her enter. "Of course. Please, come in."

She looked around the room with the flashlight and checked the bathroom. "Good, they did it."

"Did what?"

"When the power went out, housekeeping put a bucket of water in your bathroom and filled your pitcher and ice bucket. Without power, the hotel water system stops flowing as the pressure drops. They do it automatically for the suites, but I added you to our VIP list."

"That was thoughtful of you. Please, make yourself comfortable. Can I offer you a glass of ice water – since you've arranged for me to have it?"

Annette took off her uniform jacket, kicked off her shoes, and loosened her long hair that was tied in a tight bun.

She plopped into the armchair. "No water, but giving my feet a break, heaven."

I saw her rolling her ankles. So, I knelt on the floor in front of her and took one of her stockinged feet and started to massage it.

I felt her relax back into the chair. "Oh! That feels good."

I moved from kneeling to sitting on the floor and put both her feet in my lap so I could massage one then the other in turn. She didn't flinch when I moved from her feet to her ankles to her calves. I stopped when I reached her knees, not wanting to go too far and risk making her uncomfortable. I could feel her body relaxing under my touch. The way she yielded excited me. I'd become quite aroused by just innocently massaging her lower leg.

"You're not stopping are you," she said seductively.

"I don't want to… if you don't want me to."

She got up from the chair. "Let me make this easier for you."

Annette unbuttoned her blouse. I sat on the floor, in the dark, unable to move. I watched her silhouette as she removed her blouse and carefully laid it with her jacket. I felt myself getting harder and my pulse quicken when she turned around and bent over slightly as she stepped out of her skirt. I couldn't resist sliding my hand up the back of her leg and across her bottom that was now just a few inches from my face. She made an approving moaning sound as I did, and she turned around to face me again. I reached up to her waist and slipped my thumbs into the band of her stockings while my fingers massaged her lower back. I started to slide them down, carefully, so as to not ruin them. I'd made that mistake early on with Betsy, being overly zealous and ripping her stockings. Betsy had been angry, and I'd paid for it in frustration that night.

Still sitting on the floor, I slipped Annette's stockings off her feet. I ran my hands up the entire length of her leg and massaged her bottom. She leaned a bit forward as an invitation to continue, so I pulled her panties down and leaned in to kiss her upper thigh and nudge my nose between her legs. She lifted one leg and rested her thigh on my shoulder, opening herself to me. I wished I could see better, but I found my way in the dark. I explored her with serious disbelief that this was happening at all.

Annette was not shy about letting me know what she liked and wanted as she pressed herself forward onto my face, almost knocking me over. I slid a finger inside her, and she pulled back. I thought I had gone too far, so I backed away and started to get up. She reached for her jacket, and my mind raced to her leaving because I had offended her.

"I'm sorry. Are you going to go?"

"Why would I go now?"

"I just thought… you were taking your jacket…"

"I was just getting this. I thought we could use it." She handed me a foil pouch I immediately recognized as a condom. I practically leapt to my feet.

"Do you always keep these in your pocket?"

"A good concierge is prepared for anything."

Even in the dark, her eyes flashed with mischief and temptation. I started to undress and when I got to my briefs she reached over and tugged them down. I was hard and popped out of them enthusiastically. She took the condom from me and after running her hands deliciously along my shaft, she deftly rolled the condom over me.

"Is this how you treat all your guests?"

"You're the first to get this special treatment."

I wasn't sure I believed her but, at that point, I really didn't care. She was wet. I was hard. And she was crawling onto the bed just far enough to roll over and spread her legs. I stood at the end of the bed. She put her ankles on my shoulders and pulled me closer. I reached for her breasts and then her waist and pulled her hips towards me so I could slide into her. She moaned and swayed her hips. I knew I wouldn't last long. It had been so long. I came almost immediately, and it felt so good but also a little embarrassing.

"I'm sorry. It's just…," I stammered.

"I'll take that as a compliment." She rolled off the bed. "Come."

She led me to the bathroom, slid the condom off me. Taking a washcloth, she dipped it in the bucket of water and used it to wipe my still hard and very much at attention penis. The cool water sent a shiver through me.

She looked up at me from her perch on the edge of the bathtub. "I'm not done with you yet."

She leaned forward and began lightly licking the tip of my penis. She ran her tongue over the surface and then her lips along the shaft. I reached for her hair and stroked it. She opened her mouth, and I felt the warm wetness wash over my now cooled skin. I could feel myself hardening again. Sliding in and out of her mouth I couldn't resist grabbing her hair and tangling my fingers in it as I pressed forward slightly.

She pulled back from me. "See. I knew you had more in you."

She stood, led me back to the bed, and pushed me down onto my back. She pulled another condom from her jacket pocket and crawled onto the bed. She straddled my chest, facing backwards, and pressed her bottom towards my face. I grabbed her butt and ran my tongue up and down her folds as she leaned forward and gave my penis a suck. She sat up, slid the fresh condom onto me, and then swung herself around facing me and lowered herself onto me. I reached for her breasts and cupped them running my thumb over her nipples. She rode up and down, with one hand on my thigh to steady herself and the other rubbing herself. I pressed up into her and this time, held back until she was satisfied.

She leaned forward with a growl when she came and pulled me over onto her with one fluid motion. "Take me."

I was so excited by her words it took only a few strokes more for me to burst.

I rolled off her panting. "Wow. That was great!"

Annette rolled onto her side. "Don't expect this treatment all the time. This is a Blackout Special."

I stuck my lip out and pouted. "That's a shame."

"Well, maybe, if you're a very good guest, I can make an exception." She ran one fingernail across my chest making me shiver. "But now, I have to get home."

She got up, gathered up her clothes and went into the bathroom. When she dressed, she flipped on the flashlight and checked her appearance in the mirror, fixed her hair and straightened her skirt.

She opened the door just enough to slip into the hallway and said, "Good night Mr. Jacobs," in a very formal voice. And then she was gone.

The light of the moon that night left shadows just like tonight's moon. I wondered if Maddie had been in Toronto that night and if she remembered that blackout. I made a mental note to ask her sometime.

I shut out the lights in the sitting room and hallway. I paused in the dark to listen. In addition to the sound of the sea and wind, I heard a thumping noise coming from the patio outside the dining area. Most likely one of the guests had left an umbrella open and the wind was catching it. My management style had always been that I was willing to do any job that I asked others to do for me. Nonetheless, I grumbled to myself, "It would be nice to have someone else to go out in the dark and put the umbrellas away."

As I fastened the cords around the two unsecured umbrellas that were flapping against the window, I noticed what a lovely evening it was. I might have missed this starry sky if I hadn't come down to take care of the umbrellas. If Maddie were here, I'd suggest a nightcap on the patio under these stars. Maybe a limoncello, ice-cold, like they served it after our meals at the Scuola di Cucina in Torino. I should get a bottle and put it in the freezer for the next time she comes. If she comes again, I corrected myself.

"Maybe I'll just have to go to Toronto to visit Maddie," I thought to myself as I locked the back door and turned out the lights.

CHAPTER 19

I was changing into my curling shoes when Claire charged into the women's locker room. She simultaneously wriggled out of her coat and opened her locker.

"You'll never believe the day I've had."

"It's only 9 am."

"I know! I woke up at 5 to the sound of rushing water. The pipe for my garden hose burst and there was ice and water everywhere. The first really cold night we've had, and I already have an ice rink behind my house."

"What did you do?"

"I called a plumber."

"At 5 am?"

"I left a message."

"Did you shut the water off?"

"I have no idea how to do that."

"There's probably a main shut-off in your basement."

"Theo always took care of that sort of thing. If I had no water, how would I shower?"

"I hope the plumber came! The water's not still running is it?"

"He came at 7."

"So the water kept flowing for two more hours? Did you have a flood?"

"Only in the backyard. Luckily, the split was right where the pipe came out of the house. We could curl there today if there wasn't a hill."

Later that night I recounted the story to Nate including the colourful details about how Claire had flirted with the young plumber and offered to make him breakfast once he'd made the repairs.

"I hope I get to meet her someday," said Nate. "She sounds like quite the lady."

"Well if you come to Toronto, she won't let you leave without meeting her."

"It just so happens I'm coming in a couple weeks."

"Really? When? Why?"

"There's a toy show I've wanted to attend – it's the 17th to the 20th."

"I hope you'll let me host you. We did agree to that last spring."

"I was hoping you'd remember but I didn't want to assume. I would like very much to see you in person again."

His words made my heart leap. I felt exactly the same way. I was excited and I blurted out my thoughts as they came to me.

"It's not the nicest time of year to visit. We could get lucky. Some years we get a burst of nice weather in November but mostly it's just grey."

Nate chuckled. "Well I'm already grey, and the toy show is indoors so the weather won't matter."

"When are you arriving?"

"I don't want to inconvenience you if you already have plans."

"I don't think so. I'm looking at my calendar now. Nope. Nothing on it for that weekend. I curl in the morning Thursday, but after that, I'm open until Tuesday."

"I was hoping you'd be free. I was thinking of flying up on Thursday afternoon."

"So… What are your plans for the weekend?"

"I was thinking of going to the toy show on Friday. These shows can get very crowded on Saturdays and Sundays so I thought Friday would be less busy. Would you like to go with me?"

"I've never been to a toy show. Sounds fun."

"That's great."

"Is there anything else you'd like to do while you're here?"

"See you of course."

I could feel myself blushing. "Besides that."

"I haven't been to Toronto in many years. It would be nice to tootle around and see what's changed and what hasn't."

"When was the last time you were here?"

"It's been a while… before I retired. Late eighties I guess."

"30 plus years…"

"It sounds much longer when you put it like that."

"When you have your flight info, let me know so I can pick you up."

"I'm sure my hotel will have a shuttle, or I can take a taxi."

At the mention of him staying at a hotel I impulsively offered, "If you'd like to stay with me, you're welcome to."

"I don't want to impose."

"It's no problem. I have two extra bedrooms. But be forewarned, I'm not a professional host like you are."

"I gratefully accept."

"Email me your flight information. I'll just wait in the cell phone lot like I do when Anne comes home. She texts me when she's out, and I swoop in to get her."

"Texts?"

"Text message. With her phone."

"I'm not much of a text guy."

"You can call me. Just make sure you have my number in your phone."

"Will my cellphone work in Canada?"

"It should. You can check with your carrier."

"It's ATT."

"It'll work. You might need to notify them you'll be using it outside the US. Do you have my cell phone number?"

"On the card you gave me."

"Give me your cell number. In case I need to find you."

Nate gave me his number. "I'm looking forward to seeing you in a couple of weeks."

"So am I."

And I was, but shortly after I'd hung up, my mind started churning. I'd totally spaced and not asked him any questions to help me prepare. I resisted calling him right back – he'd probably gone to bed, and I'd be waking him up to answer random questions like does he like a foam or feather pillow.

I started making a To-Do list because it helped me tame the jumble of thoughts whizzing around in my head. First item, the guest room – it hadn't been used in a while so it could use help. Check the wine supply – and make sure I've got a few nice bottles in case we eat in. Groceries for breakfast, etc. Which caused me to start a second list of Things to Ask Nate because I realized that he'd served us breakfast, but I didn't know what he liked to eat. He liked coffee so I added 'coffee shop for beans' to the to-do list. I added 'pillow preference?', then scratched it off. I'll just get a couple of new ones so he can pick.

I also began to worry about entertaining him. I hadn't shown anyone around the city in a long time. He'd been so generous about showing me around Bar Harbor, I felt I should be prepared to be his guide in Toronto. I put 'prepare to be tour guide' on the to-do list.

I started to wander from room to room. Thinking about Nate being here and what I could do to make him feel at home. I was happy but also panicked. Simultaneously feeling excited, overwhelmed, and unprepared. Would it be awkward seeing him again? What if he's uncomfortable? What if the weather is terrible and we're stuck inside, and we run out of things to say?

Bacon had followed my wandering and was squinting at me with a puzzled look from the guest room bed.

"I guess I should ask Nate if he's allergic to furballs."

Bacon looked away, walked in a circle, and curled up on the guest bed. By the cat fur smudges on the bedspread, it was clear I'd been neglecting the guest room. I plucked Bacon from the bed and gave him a quick snuggle before ejecting him from the room.

"Sorry Pal, we're starting a cat-free zone until we know if Nate can be around you."

This had been Mother's room when she'd moved in with me after Father had died. The bedroom set was hers, and the black and white family photos, I'd hung on the walls when she moved in, were just as they had been. Although I'd packed up and donated all her clothing, there were many of her things still in the room. Her jewelry box was on top of the dresser. There were lace doilies under the jewelry box and lamps and over the arms of the rocking recliner we'd brought from her house. The secretary desk was a nice antique piece, in good shape outside but was stuffed with who knows what. There was an ancient TV on an even more ancient TV stand that was not antique, just old.

This room is a granny suite, not a guest room. I had only two weeks to make the room presentable for Nate. I didn't know where to start. My paralysis was broken by the phone ringing. It was Claire.

"Are you busy on Monday?" she asked.

"Nothing in particular, why? Do you need something?"

"I need a ride to my eye doctor appointment. I can't see after they check my eyes. I thought Andre could drive me, but he's got a meeting out of town and my daughter-in-law has the kids at home that day."

"No problem. I can take you but I'm going to ask a favour in return."

"What do you need?"

"To redecorate my guest room."

"What fun! When do you want to start."

"As soon as possible."

"Are you having guests?"

"Guest. Nate is coming to stay with me in a couple of weeks."

"We better start right away. Should I come by in the morning?"

"It's Friday. Don't you have a hair appointment?"

"Not until eleven. I'll come at nine. I want to know what you're thinking. I do good thinking under the dryer when I can't hear anything but the hot air whooshing."

"I'm thinking it needs to be less mother's room and more guest room. That's as far as I've gotten."

"We'll talk in the morning."

"You're a godsend."

"At nine."

"See you then."

The next morning Claire was at my door before nine. I opened the door, still unshowered, in yesterday's clothes I'd thrown on, with my coffee in hand.

"I'm so happy you asked me to help. I couldn't sleep last night thinking about it." She was carrying an armload of magazines. "So, I went through these to find examples for you to look at so we can decide on a style. Modern, traditional, transitional, French country, coastal…"

"I don't know…," was all I managed to say before Claire was halfway up the stairs.

"Show me the room."

"Do you want a coffee or something?"

"No thanks. I've had mine. I'm ready to go."

I followed Claire up the stairs and pointed to the door. I felt mild irritation at her energy level this early in the day, but I tried to disguise it because I was genuinely grateful for her help.

Claire dropped the stack of magazines onto the bed. "Tell me what you're thinking."

"Something less old-lady-like."

"What do you like or want to keep in the room?"

"The furniture, because I'm not going to buy new furniture. And… I like the family pictures…"

"What about the TV? Do you want a TV in the room?"

"I think it would be nice, but not that TV. It can go."

"The recliner?"

"It's sad. It can go."

"Have you thought about a colour?"

"For the walls?"

"We should paint."

"Do we have time?"

"I know a guy. I called him this morning. He's free Sunday to start getting the room ready and he can paint it on Monday. What colour?"

"White I suppose?"

"The curtain rods aren't bad, and you have a blind that is not offensive. We can probably work with them."

Claire was off and running and I was barely keeping up. She opened one of the magazines and turned to an earmarked page.

"What do you think of this. There are light walls and a basic traditional curtain. I know where we can get some ready-made ones. If we get them long, we don't have to worry about the length we can just let them puddle on the floor and we won't need to sew them. It'll be quick."

Claire continued to flip through the magazines asking me which I preferred and what colours I liked. After an hour of questions, she put on her coat and picked up her purse.

"I've got to run. I'll call the painter. He'll bring his boys to move everything.

You empty the closet and figure out where you want them to put everything while they paint. Tomorrow we'll get paint chips from Home Depot and pick a colour."

"Are you sure we have to paint the room?"

"Definitely. I must go. You look through these." She handed me the stack of décor magazines. "See if anything jumps out at you."

"Ok. Thanks for coming by."

"I'll call you later. I'll let you know if I think of anything else. I can see myself out – you get going on the closet."

It was like a small French-speaking tornado had just blown through the house. I felt a bit overwhelmed but not wanting to disappoint my generous and enthusiastic friend, I set down my coffee cup and started pulling apart the closet. I knew I needed to get rid of some things to make space for guests, but I don't like doing it. I keep things I think will be useful or have memories attached to them. Most things fit into one of those two categories, so things tend to accumulate.

This closet had accumulated a lot. There were several different sized suitcases. I wasn't planning on going anywhere for a while, so I put them in the hall to take to the basement. There were two heavy boxes under the suitcases. I opened them and both were filled with magazines. I was tempted to start looking at them. I didn't because I had to find something to purge. If I started looking through them, I'd be unable to part with them. I pushed them aside and made a note to get the boys to move them to the garage so I could recycle them.

This was the closet where I stored all my pictures, negatives, and slides. These were relatively well organized. I had a system of putting everything in shoeboxes and writing dates in marker on the sides. Fortunately, I'd slowed down adding to the shoebox pile a few years back because I'd switched to using a digital camera most of the time. I resisted the urge to look in any of the boxes because I knew I'd end up spending the whole day sifting through pictures and I'd never get the closet emptied. I moved all the photo shoeboxes from the closet and stacked them on the floor in my bedroom.

All the clothes in the closet were mine. My bedroom closet wasn't very big, and I'd overflowed to this one. I'd tried a system where you switched your clothes by season but I'd never really gotten into the habit so there was a mix of a little of everything from evening gowns to my big down coat. I moved the clothes to Anne's room putting as much as I could into the closet and piling what didn't fit on the bed.

I took down the last two dusty boxes from the top shelf of the closet. One was marked "office deco" and the other one "rocks". I knew exactly what they were even though I'd not touched them in ages. They were just as I'd packed them when I'd retired and cleaned out my office. These boxes I couldn't resist opening.

The "office deco" box had my collection of small items I'd gathered while travelling. There were a few from business trips, like the little temple Dave had given me in Japan, however, most I'd bought on trips I'd taken with Anne. Some were miniatures of famous landmarks like a tiny metal Eiffel tower, some were tacky like the little wigwam I'd bought at a craft fair in New Mexico. There was even a postage stamp-sized "Keep Calm" sign from London and one item I'd added to the box after I'd retired, a Torino 2006 mascot doll covered in pins which provided solid evidence it had been more than ten years since I'd opened this box.

The box marked "rocks" had my collection of special and interesting rocks I'd chosen to keep near me in my office. As I unwrapped each one, I remembered where and when I'd got it and why it mattered.

There was a piece of petrified wood I'd bought when I'd visited Arizona. It was shortly after Will and I split up. I'd planned to go to the conference for over a year. I'd envisioned that Will and I would rent a car and go sightseeing after it. Instead, I'd gone alone, and the little red and brown rock reminded me I'd ventured out on my own and it had turned out fine.

There was the tiny piece of black lava I'd picked up in Hawaii, ignoring all warnings of curses on anyone who removed lava from the island. I had marvelled at being able to hold a brand-new rock. I remembered how it made me smile when I read the sign describing the eruption, and I realized I was older than the nearby rocks.

There were several small but perfect examples of mineral crystals like pyrite, fluorite, and selenite. Among the small rocks, there was a larger chunk of drill core from one of my field projects. I'd kept it because it had a vug the size of a robin's egg filled with intact grey quartz crystals that had remarkably survived the trauma of being cut from the earth and dragged to the surface.

When I brought these boxes home from my office, I'd planned to do something with them but had just never gotten around to it. Altogether there were about two dozen rocks and travel trinkets. I loosely packed them all back into the two boxes and carried them downstairs to the dining room table. I decided to show them to Claire. Maybe she'd have an idea for a way to display them. I liked seeing them. More than just remembering, I got a feeling when I held each one. None of the items were valuable, but the way each one connected me to a moment in time was priceless to me. For someone less sentimental, these were two boxes of rocks and junk, but to me, they felt like pieces of my life, and I couldn't imagine getting rid of them. It's not just a collection of items, it's a physical record of places and events that were significant to me.

It was already one in the afternoon, and I was still unshowered and in yesterday's clothes. And I was hungry. I'd not eaten because I'd been focused on my closet task. I needed to eat something – now. Butter and Bacon, who'd ignored me most of the day, followed me into the kitchen. I tossed a frozen English muffin into the microwave to thaw and dug around in the fridge to find some cheese I could slice to put on it.

Butter and Bacon paced and meowed underfoot. When I moved the muffin to the toaster, I almost stepped on Butter who had thrown himself at my feet. While I waited for the muffin to toast, I gave them each a few treats, which they gobbled up ungratefully and then looked up at me for more.

"What? No treats? You two can't fool me. You ate them. No more." I turned my back on them and slapped a couple of pieces of cheese between the warm muffin halves. I ate my breakfast-lunch-snack standing at the kitchen door looking through the sunroom into the yard. It was time to dig up Romeo and Juliet my rosemary bushes and move them into their winter home in the sunroom. I picked up the to-do list I'd started last night and added 'call John' my garden/handyman and 'buy dirt' to the bottom.

Since I needed dirt, and Claire had suggested Home Depot for paint chips, I figured I could cross both off my list if I went this afternoon. There was a charity committee meeting tonight at the curling club, but I didn't have to be there until seven-thirty, so I still had some time.

Butter was grooming himself in a patch of sunlight on the kitchen floor.

"Do I need to shower?" I took his silence as a no. "You're right, I might get dirty handling the potting soil so I might as well go as I am."

Home Depot had about a million shades of white. I didn't know where to start. I played with the interactive decorating guide on a terminal in the paint department that let you pick a colour and see what colours were complimentary. I saw an example with a greyish-blue white I thought might look nice with Mother's mahogany bedroom set. I took the flyer with a bunch of different white options and picked up a bunch of strips with whites that ended in bluish grey so I could show them to Claire. I hoped I was on the right track.

I headed to the garden center where I was a lot more confident. I considered buying new pots for Romeo and Juliet but in the end, settled on two bags of potting soil. I would usually have bought one big bag, even though I'd struggle with it, to save a few bucks. But today the small bags were on sale, and I'd calculated they worked out to be the same price as a big bag.

I inherited the frugal gene from my mother. As a housewife, she'd always find a way to squeeze as much out of the allowance father gave her for the household expenses. She squeezed it so hard she actually had a nice little nest egg she used to treat herself to a new hat or dress without the bother of having to ask Father for money. He'd want her to have a good reason for the purchase and she'd learned that "because it's pretty" wasn't a convincing argument. Father didn't pay much attention to what Mother wore, so he rarely noticed when something new appeared, but if he did, she'd just brush it off and say he'd forgotten it and he never questioned it.

Within a week of asking for help, Claire had worked miracles with my guest room. She'd picked a grey for the walls and a bright white for the trim. The painters had emptied the room into my bedroom and Anne's and in two days they were done and moved the furniture back in. Claire suggested rearranging the room and I had to admit it was the right call once everything was in place. She even found a way to use my mother's doilies, making lace flowers that attached to the ties holding back the new dark blue drapes. The white, blue, and grey palette was fresh and modern and a huge improvement.

We'd taken three all-day shopping trips to find new drapery and bedding, a comfy chair, and a few accessories to, as she put it, "pull it all together". We hit all the usual home decorating stores, but we also went to flea markets, outlets, and antique stores that I never knew existed.

She'd even found a way to showcase most of my travel trinkets and rocks. She called it a memory box. We got a replica of a printer's drawer and hung it on the wall and then arranged all the pieces that would fit into the various slots. She said we had to leave at least one spot open, so I would always be open to making a new memory.

The room felt clean and bright. Everything that wasn't new had been deep cleaned, and Butter and Bacon had been banished so it was, so far, a cat-free zone. If Nate was allergic, at least I'd have one room in the house that would be a safe haven from cat fur and dander.

I was excited to show Nate to his room. I'd gotten used to calling it Nate's room because that's how Claire had referred to it. I'd initially tried to stop her from calling it that, but I gave in. She knew I was doing it for him. That's why she'd reluctantly agreed to the throw pillows with boats on them that we'd found in an outlet store. When she said they were wrong, I'd explained his collecting. She'd given in with the caveat "I suppose you can swap them out when you have other guests."

I took the new guest towels out of the dresser drawer and laid them out on the bed. Everything was as good as it was going to get. Butter and Bacon were meowing at the door.

"Back off boys, this is Nate's room." I opened the door a crack shooing them away so I could slip out before either of them could squeeze in.

CHAPTER 20

I recognized the CN Tower as the plane banked and turned to land at Pearson Airport. I'd flown from Boston to Toronto many times, but this time was different. Although I've traveled a lot in my lifetime, most was for business reasons. For many years, I was the person called on to hash out the final details and get agreement for important negotiations. I spent most flights preparing for battle, reviewing briefs or contracts, and making last-minute notes in preparation for my meetings. I'd be focused on my goals and how to come away with a win for our side.

Unlike my business travel, the goals for this trip were… fuzzy. I'd told Emily that the toy show just happened to be in Toronto, but she didn't buy it.

"You don't need to make excuses to go see your friend," she'd said.

It had been five months since I'd seen Maddie. It wasn't just because I'd been waiting for a plausible excuse to travel to Toronto to see her, the inn had been busy. It was the busiest season I'd ever had. Thankfully, I'd found a great helper in my neighbor's daughter Sarah, who was home from college for the summer and was looking for work. Both Ann and Emily were happy I wasn't doing it all alone, but they warned me not to drive the girl crazy with my schedules and routines.

At first, Sarah only came over on weekends we were fully booked to help me with breakfast service. She told me it didn't feel like work to spend her day with a view of the ocean, and she offered to help with anything I needed. She cleaned rooms, took out and put away lawn furniture and kayaks, and searched and printed out directions to local attractions and restaurants for the guests. By the time she left to go back to school in September, she'd become my full-time lieutenant innkeeper and knew everything from how to get the sticky lighthouse lock open, to my quirky replenishment routines.

Not only did she help with the day-to-day, but she also encouraged the guests to leave reviews on websites, something I didn't know much about. She showed me the comments and they were almost always glowing. She's a big part of the reason we have more advance bookings for next summer than we've ever had at this time of year. It had also been a financially successful season, so I'd offered her a full-time job next summer, with a pay raise. She promised she'd start as soon as she finished her exams.

The leaf-peeper bookings dry up as the leaves fall, so by the time November blows in I've got lots of free time. Without guests or Sarah around to talk to, I look forward to calling Maddie. She teased me about my regularity.

"If the phone rings at eight-thirty and it's Thursday, I know it's you."

I'm pretty sure she looked forward to our calls too. Whenever she had other plans for Thursday night, she always let me know so we could pick a different time to talk. Last Thursday I'd asked if I could take her to dinner tonight when I arrived.

She'd pretended to be offended. "You're afraid to eat my cooking?"

"Of course not. But you shouldn't slave over a hot stove for me."

"I let you cook for me. You gotta let me cook for you."

"Then I'm taking you to dinner one evening. I insist."

"We'll see," she'd said.

Part of my anxiety about this trip was about seeing Maddie for the first time in months. Even more anxiety came from the lack of a solid plan for the weekend. For both business and pleasure travel, I always had every detail mapped out long before we packed our bags. Where we'd stay, where we'd eat, what we were going to do, all planned out and organized. I'd have a file folder with reservations, confirmation numbers, addresses, directions, and any other details I might need. My file for this trip had my airline reservation, two passes for the toy show, the address of the International Center, and Maddie's address and phone numbers. It was unlike me to be so unscheduled. I felt unprepared and that made me feel anxious.

It didn't take long for the small regional jet to empty out. I thought I'd be able to just walk out and call Maddie. Instead, I had to wait, with about half of my fellow passengers, for my carry-on bag to be brought up by the ground crew. Then I had to wait in the customs line. When I finally arrived at the customs officer, she simply asked me the purpose of my trip. I told her I was coming to visit a friend and she said, "Welcome to Canada," and handed me my passport.

By the time I got through all of that, I had to go to the restroom. Fortunately, I found one in the baggage claim area. I was already feeling late and flustered by the time I walked out into the main arrivals concourse of the terminal.

The airport was much different than I remembered. I looked around, reading the signs, and trying to get oriented while I got out my cell phone. I had to wait for it to turn on and I chided myself for not thinking of turning it on sooner.

Maddie answered on the first ring. "I was worried you got lost."

"I'm just walking outside."

"Tell me what post you're at."

"Post? Oh, there's numbers…14."

"I'm on my way. Stay put."

I wished I'd asked Maddie what her car looked like. I peered into every car that approached. It seemed like ages, but, it was probably only a few minutes until she pulled up to the curb in front of me, hopped out of a red car, and opened the trunk. I should have guessed it would be red. It suited her.

There were cars all around us, pulling in and out. Maddie moved fast, grabbed my bag, and heaved it into the trunk before I could protest.

"Hop in," she ordered.

We got in and buckled up. She put the car in gear and pulled away. I was surprised and impressed that her car was a stick shift. She checked and double-checked over her shoulder as she pulled out and across multiple lanes of traffic.

"It's always a zoo here. How was your trip?"

"Quick. Emily dropped me at the airport. I drove down yesterday."

"Couldn't you fly out of a closer airport?"

"I could. But when I get back, I'm going to stay with them until after Thanksgiving."

"I bet she's happy to have you there for the holiday. Will you go for Christmas?"

"I'll have the whole family at the inn for Christmas. Ann and Lane are coming."

"How lovely."

I watched the road as Maddie pulled out onto the highway.

"This time of day it should only take about 30 minutes to get to my house. Are you hungry? Did you have lunch?"

"I was early for my flight, so I had something at the airport."

"I don't have anything planned for us this afternoon. Is there something you wanted to do? We're eating in tonight."

"I didn't make any plans, but I brought a book so, if you have things to do, I can amuse myself."

"I have a little prep work for dinner but otherwise, I'm all yours."

"I like the sound of that."

She glanced over at me, one eyebrow arched, and her lips flattened. "You might change your mind after three days with me."

"Not likely…but we'll find out."

Maddie had described the traffic as light, but the highway seemed very busy to me. I wasn't used to it. Other than driving down to see Emily, I didn't encounter much traffic in Bar Harbor except for pedestrians on cruise ship days. I squirmed uncomfortably while Maddie weaved her way through the multiple lanes of traffic. She seemed unfazed. I relaxed a bit when she pulled off the highway and into what seemed like a well-established and quiet part of the city.

"This is my neighborhood. It's called High Park, after the park in the middle of it."

'Have you lived here long?"

"My whole life, except for the years I was at university."

"A very long time then."

"When you say it like that, you make me feel old."

"That's not what I was implying!"

"Sure, sure. I invite you to stay and in no time, you're reminding me how old I am."

I was taken aback by her comment. I started to apologize when she burst out laughing.

She looked over at me with an evil grin. "I was just teasing."

This woman took me on an emotional roller-coaster like no one I'd ever known. I suspect that the more I'm near her, the more I'll get spun around. One second I'm feeling panic, like I've blown it, and the next my heart is soaring looking into her beautiful eyes. I am inexplicably drawn to her. It's like there's a gravitational force that pulls at me and holds me in orbit. Seeing her again, I already know I'm not going to want to leave her.

"I'm sorry. You're not upset, are you?" She looked over at me with concern.

"I'm thinking how good it is to see you in person and that I've missed you." It wasn't exactly what I was thinking, but it was true.

"I'm happy you're here too. And we're here."

She pulled the car into the driveway of a lovely home with a covered front porch and a detached garage that she opened remotely as we approached it.

"I hope you don't mind coming in through the back door. It's closer to the garage."

"Making me sneak in the back so the neighbors don't see you bringing a boy home?"

"I don't think the neighbors will think you're a boy."

"Ouch! Now who's being mean."

Maddie opened the trunk and we both reached for my bag, but I waved her off.

"I'll take it."

"I did say I'd carry your bag if you came to visit…"

"Well, I'm not going to let you."

"Are you here for an argument?" She giggled, presumably at the Monty Python reference.

"Not if there is an alternative," I answered with an exaggerated wink.

Maddie laughed. "You're a bad boy, Mr. Jacobs. This way."

She opened an unlocked door, and we entered a windowed sunroom. She then unlocked the house door.

"Don't you lock this door?"

"I hate standing in the rain or snow with my hands full trying to unlock it. I just lock the house. If someone is desperate enough to steal my patio furniture, they need it more than I do."

I thought of a bunch of terrible scenarios. Someone hiding in the sunroom, waiting to grab her when she came in. I locked the door behind us.

"What are you doing?"

"I just thought...I want you safe..."

She growled. "Don't! If you lock it, I'll end up locked out."

I unlocked the door and followed her into the house. We'd entered directly into the kitchen. Maddie slipped off her shoes inside the door and I followed suit. There were several pairs of shoes strewn on the mat by the door. I had to straighten a few to make a spot for mine. Maddie had already left the kitchen and was part way down the hall opening a closet. She hung up her coat and got a hanger for mine.

One side of the hall had stairs going up and the other side had two sets of French doors that opened into one large room that was both living room and dining room.

"Originally, this house had separate living and dining rooms, but we had them take out the wall between them when we bought this place."

"It's very nice. I love the wood floors."

"They're original to the house. So are these doors," she said pointing to the French doors. "But we had to replace the exterior windows because they leaked. The original windows had multiple panes like these doors. They were interesting but highly inefficient."

A large yellow cat looked up at us from the sofa, stretched and sat up watching me.

"You have a cat."

"Meet my furry children. That's Butter." She pointed to the yellow cat. "And that's Bacon." She pointed to a tabby that was crawling out from under the dining room table.

"Hello Butter. Hello Bacon."

"I hope you don't mind cats."

"I like cats." I reached down to pet Bacon as he walked around my legs. "Interesting names."

"Everything's better with Bacon... or Butter."

"Ohhhhh. I get it. Clever."

"They are friendly beasts. Especially if they think you'll give them treats."

"Of course I'll give you treats Mr. Bacon." Bacon showed his enthusiasm by flopping down and rolling over on my feet.

"Later. First, let's show you to your room."

Maddie again reached for my bag.

"Oh no you don't." I picked it up before she could and followed her up the stairs.

Maddie opened the door of the guest room. I immediately noticed the sailboat pillows on the bed.

"Did you add some boats for me?"

To my surprise, Maddie said, "As a matter of fact I did."

"I was kidding. Wow. Thanks."

"You can hang up or put away anything you'd like …" Maddie opened the closet and pointed to the dresser. "Your bathroom is the next door down the hall. Not en-suite, but at least you don't have to share. There's a shelf under the window you can use for your toiletries. I've left a set of towels on the bed."

"This is really nice. Thank you."

"If you need anything else, let me know. I'm not a pro, like you. You're my first guest in ages."

"I think you've thought of everything."

"I'll leave you to settle in. Do you want to have a rest?"

"I had a little snooze on the plane, so I'll just unpack."

"Just come find me when you're done. I'll be in the kitchen."

I didn't bring much with me, so it didn't take long to unpack. I hung up my dress shirts in the closet and put the rest of my clothes into a couple of the drawers. I took out my shaving kit and toothbrush and carried them down the hall to the bathroom. When I came back to the room, Bacon was settling into a ball on the towels Maddie had left.

"Those aren't for you." I carefully upended the cat and hung the towels over the back of the chair. I noticed Maddie had placed a bottle of water by the bed. It was sitting on a coaster with an anchor on it. I smiled because I got the feeling she'd selected that coaster specifically for me.

"I'm going downstairs now. Are you coming?" The cat just stared at me, so I left the door open and went downstairs.

Maddie had her back to me stirring a pot on the stove.

I wanted to let her know I was there, so I didn't startle her. "Something smells good."

She glanced over her shoulder. "Hopefully it tastes good."

"What are you making?"

"A mushroom sauce for polenta. I thought I'd dust off the recipe I learned in Torino because you said you'd enjoyed the food.

"I do. I'm sure it will be great."

"I've also got some gorgonzola and another cheese we can have with it if you prefer."

"Both sound good."

"I won't start the polenta until later. I can turn this off now. It's even better if it has a chance to sit and 'get married' as my cooking instructor would say."

"Funny. They told me the same thing. I thought it was just an excuse to take a break and have coffee … or wine…"

"Nothing gets done in Italy without first stopping for coffee," said Maddie laughing. "I suppose I should be offering you something. A coffee? Wine?"

"Nothing right now. I'd like to call Emily. She wanted me to let her know when I arrived."

"You can use the phone in the living room. It's free to call the US. It's on the desk."

I left Maddie and went to find the phone. The living room was relatively tidy, but the desk was a mess. I was afraid to dislodge the stacks of paper that covered it. Fortunately, the phone was at the edge and was a cordless type. I took it from its cradle and stood with my back to the desk to call Emily. I kept the call short so I wouldn't tie up Maddie's phone and returned to the kitchen.

"That was quick," said Maddie. "Did you reach her?"

"Yes. I just let her know I'd arrived safely and would call her if there were any changes to my return itinerary."

"It's nice out. I wondered if you wanted to go for a walk. It gets dark early, but we have a couple hours of daylight left."

"I could use a walk after a day of sitting."

Maddie wiped her hands on her jeans and put a lid on the pot. "I'll get our coats."

"The park I mentioned, High Park, is only a few minutes away," Maddie explained as she locked the house and opened the garage door. "We could walk in about 20 minutes, but I thought we'd drive just in case the weather turns on us." Maddie gestured for me to get into the car. Earlier at the airport, I'd only noticed it was a red sedan, but now that it was not in the frenzy of the airport, I noticed it was a BMW. An older model, but in good shape.

"Nice car, by the way," I said pulling on my seat belt.

"Thanks. We've been together for more than 10 years. I bought her when I was still working. At the time it represented that I'd arrived. Now, we're just hoping to age gracefully together."

"I'm surprised it's a stick."

"They don't make many like this anymore."

"I'd say that's true of her owner too."

Maddie smiled but continued talking. "I've always enjoyed driving. I feel more in control when I'm shifting the gears."

She backed down the driveway and onto the street. Within a few minutes, we pulled through the main gates of High Park. As we drove along the park road Maddie told me about it.

"There are several different things to do in the park, more in the summer than this time of year. But it's open all year round, every day."

"Do you come here often?"

"Not as much as I used to, but it's always been a great place to go wander with my camera."

"Is that a restaurant?"

"Yes, there's the café, zoo, special areas for children and dogs, a pool in the summer... something for everyone."

"How lucky to have this so close."

Maddie pulled into a parking spot across the road from the café. "I thought we'd walk here. It's called Hillside Gardens."

We wound our way through the garden area past small waterfalls and a bridge. The walkway headed generally uphill and after a while, we reached the top and could look out over the garden area.

"This is the best view of the maple leaf." Maddie pointed to the far side of the gardens below. "It's so big you can see it in satellite pictures."

"What's it made of?"

"Plants. It changes throughout the year. Flowers in spring and summer and evergreens and ivy the rest of the time."

I couldn't help but notice the perfectly mowed lawns and weedless flowerbeds. "It's very well kept."

We followed the paths down the hill and did a loop around the maple leaf. It was impressive to see how precisely the leaf had been constructed from living materials. We took one of the paths radiating away and linked up with a trail that followed the edge of a large pond.

"This is Grenadier Pond. When I was young, we would go skating on it every winter. Now they try to keep people off it. With climate change, it's iffy whether it freezes enough to be safe."

"Are there fish in the pond?"

"Yes. It's said that it got its name from a group of Grenadiers that were encamped nearby in the 1800s that used the pond for fishing. Over time it got contaminated and nasty but, back in the late eighties, the city rehabilitated it. There were lots of consultants hired to figure out how to clean up the pond and now it's got fish again."

"Was that the sort of work you did?"

"Similar, but not exactly. We did more structural and construction projects. More engineers than the bugs and bunny types."

"What are bugs and bunny types?"

"Biologists, entomologists, herpetologists, ornithologists…"

"I have trouble picturing you on a construction site."

"So did a lot of men." Maddie's voice was bitter. I'd unintentionally touched a nerve.

"I just meant you're so beautiful and always so well dressed, I can't imagine you in a hard hat and work boots."

Fortunately, Maddie laughed and took my arm. "You don't have to backpedal. I'll take it as a compliment you think I'm well dressed."

"Don't forget beautiful."

"Mr. Jacobs, you'll make me blush."

I couldn't think of anything to reply. Her touch had made all thoughts fly out of my head except for how good it felt. It was an innocent gesture, I told myself. She probably doesn't even realize that she's done it. It was so easy and natural the way she'd just wrapped both her hands around my arm and leaned in with her head almost on my shoulder.

She suddenly let go and leaned away. I shivered as if her touch was all that was keeping me warm.

"What's wrong?" I asked.

"Nothing. I just thought I was making you uncomfortable."

"No. I liked it. I was … just … surprised." I reached for her hand and she looked at me and smiled.

"Oh good. It feels warmer when I touch you."

"I was just thinking the same thing." I tugged lightly on her hand, so we walked a little closer together. We didn't say anything for a bit, but my thoughts were racing at light-speed through my brain. I felt a bit ridiculous that, at my age, I was acting like a smitten teenager. Just holding hands caused a tingling sensation, like my nerves were getting and sending too many signals at once. I realized I was excited by her touch and I had this strong urge to hold on forever and not let go.

"It's starting to get dark," said Maddie. "We should probably head back to the car."

"I honestly have no idea which way that would be. You have me lost in the woods already."

"We're hardly in the wilderness. Walk a few hundred meters in any direction and you'll end up on a city street."

"Or in the pond."

"There is a rather macabre legend about how the pond got its name. That it was named after several drowned Grenadiers who fell in while fighting in the war of 1812."

"Fighting your American enemies. Should I be worried you'll be seeking revenge?"

"I don't have any American enemies these days. None that I know of anyway."

A few minutes later we were back at the car, and after a few more minutes, we were warming up in Maddie's kitchen.

"Are you hungry?" she asked.

"Getting there. But not starving."

"Would you like a drink?"

"Yes please."

"Beer, wine, cocktail, water…?"

"You know, a beer would be great."

"Keith's ok?"

"I don't know it, but I'm sure it is."

"It's an IPA."

"Great."

Maddie opened the beer and got a frozen mug from the freezer and set both on the kitchen island in front of where I was standing.

"Thanks. Are you joining me?"

"I'm going to open some wine. A Barbera, like you served me. It will go nicely with the polenta later too."

"Sounds perfect. Can I open the wine for you?"

"Nope. You just sit there and relax. It's my turn to wait on you."

Maddie's kitchen was cozy but functional. On the left side as you entered from the hall was the business side with the fridge, stove, sink and a small island with two stools tucked under it. On the right was a rectangular table. It had a long high-backed bench against the wall and 6 chairs. It was narrow but long, and it looked like it could seat ten people.

"If you prefer you can sit at the table instead of here," said Maddie. "Wherever you're comfy."

I pulled the armed chair out from the end of the table and sat so I could look across at Maddie. I poured my beer. Maddie opened the wine and poured a glass. She then reached into the fridge and took out a platter that she uncovered and placed on the table near me describing it as 'Yorktown Antipasto'. It was an eclectic plate; Italian cold cuts, a couple of deviled eggs, tiny Asian style spoons with bite-sized appetizers like shrimp cocktail, hummus on a pita with feta cheese and a spicy Kimchee-like coleslaw.

"What makes this 'Yorktown'?

"It's an old name for Toronto. This plate has a bunch of different cultures on it. Even though they come from different places, somehow it all works together. Kinda like this city."

Maddie explained that the deviled eggs and shrimp cocktail would have been what her mother would have served. The rest, she'd learned to love through travel and experimentation.

I reached for a shrimp cocktail spoon. "It looks good."

Maddie helped herself to a deviled egg that she ate standing leaning against the kitchen island.

"Something to hold us over because the polenta will take a while to cook."

"Are you sure I can't help?"

"I'm sure." Maddie finished her egg and reached into a high cupboard over the fridge and brought out what looked like a copper cauldron.

"What's that?"

"It's called a 'Paiolo' or in the dialect of my cooking teacher a 'Cadernei'. It's the traditional Piemontese pot for making polenta. I figured I should pull out all the stops to impress you."

"You impressed me long before you pulled out the Caderknee."

"Wait until you see the stirrer that goes with it." Maddie rummaged through her utensil drawer and came out with what looked like a cross between a paint stirrer and a paddle. "If we're going to go authentic, we have to stir it with a 'Canè'."

"That Canay looks dangerous. I promise. I'll be good."

Maddie giggled and brandished the stick at me. "You better. Or else."

"No polenta for me?"

"No mushrooms or cheese might be a better punishment."

Maddie filled the pot with water and set it on the stove. She sat down with me at the table and helped herself to what was left of the antipasto I'd been nibbling on while she'd been talking about her polenta gear.

"So, tell me about the toy show tomorrow. What's the plan?"

"I thought we'd try to get ahead of the crowds, so I bought us each a 'Trading Pass' for tomorrow. It gets us in an hour before the show officially opens."

"What time is that?"

"It opens at noon, so the passes get us in at eleven."

"We should leave ourselves at least 30 minutes to get to the International Center and park."

"You know you don't have to go if you'd rather not."

"I've been looking forward to it."

The water had started to boil, and Maddie got up and whisked in a bag of polenta. I stood up and went over to watch her.

"Now I get my arm workout," she said as she whisked out all the lumps of cornmeal.

"You're pretty good at this, but do you want me to stir?"

"Not right now, it's easy now. I might ask you to take over when it's stiffer."

I thought to myself. 'This woman makes me stiffer' but I dared not say it. I was even shocked at myself at how being near her made me feel so… alive. She was stirring more than polenta. She was stirring up feelings in me that I hadn't felt in a long time. Standing close to her, it took a conscious effort not to reach out and touch her.

I tried to focus on the cooking, not the cook. "How long does it cook?"

"This type takes a good 45 minutes, maybe an hour. I got it at an Italian grocery store on College Street that imports it from Italy. They told me it's called 'Ottofili', organic, produced on small farms near Torino and it's the most authentic Piemontese polenta you can get on this side of the Atlantic."

"You spoil me."

"It's my pleasure. Literally. I've been looking forward to it too. Gives me a reason to make this polenta. It's too much effort just for one person."

"I didn't want you to go to this much trouble."

"I'm not. I meant I was glad to have a reason to make it. I enjoy cooking and having someone to cook for and it's the perfect time of year for polenta. It all came together perfectly."

"In that case, I'm glad I could be a good excuse."

"While the polenta cooks. Maybe you could answer a few questions?"

"I didn't expect the Spanish Inquisition."

"No one expects the Spanish Inquisition," answered Maddie without hesitation. I couldn't help but laugh and be in awe of this woman who responded so naturally and anticipated my odd sense of humor.

"Ok, so what questions?" I asked getting my giggles under control.

Maddie launched into a long explanation while she stirred the polenta. "You said you wanted to see what's changed since you were last here. I realized when I started to plan some sightseeing for you that I really knew nothing about where you'd been, so I've done a poor job planning your 'What's changed tour'".

"That isn't a question exactly, but you want to know where I'd like to go?"

"Yes."

"I used to stay at the Royal York Hotel."

"Nice. Probably hasn't changed much. What else?"

"I used to walk from the hotel to a private club where many of my associates were members."

"The Albany Club?"

"That's it."

"It's still there. If the weather cooperates, we could recreate that walk easily."

"I remember there was a sort of indoor farm market nearby."

"St. Lawrence Market. Still there."

"I always thought it would be a good place for a cook to shop."

"And for peameal on a bun if you're hungry."

"Peameal?"

"Bacon – the Canadian version."

"We have Canadian bacon…"

"It's not the same. That settles it. We're having breakfast at the St. Lawrence Market on Saturday."

"At least we have a plan."

Maddie scowled at me. "Are you suggesting that I haven't planned well enough?"

I shrugged – a bit worried that I'd say something that would sound ungrateful.

Maddie put her hands on her hips. "I'll have you know, I did a lot of planning, just not a lot of deciding until I could find out what you wanted to do."

"Which was very thoughtful of you." I hoped it sounded sincere and that my discomfort with the fluid program for the weekend wasn't showing.

"Would you feel better if we drew up a schedule?"

"Hmmm…well… yes."

Maddie sighed. "If that's what we need to do."

She stopped stirring and pulled a small notepad and pen from a drawer. She looked up at the kitchen clock. "Thursday. 7:45 pm. Dinner. Friday. 10:30 am. Leave for toy show… We haven't discussed the rest of Friday, but I made reservations at a sushi restaurant for 8 pm because they tend to fill up. Are you OK with sushi?"

I nodded and she continued. "Saturday. Breakfast at St. Lawrence Market, time TBD."

"We don't need to decide everything now," I said, but I was secretly pleased we were making a list and getting organized.

"Do you want me to map out a walking route for Saturday as well?"

I couldn't tell if Maddie was serious, annoyed, or teasing me.

"Let's just be spontaneous and see where we end up," I said because I thought that was what she'd prefer.

"Thank goodness." She turned back to stir the polenta. "I was starting to wonder if we were going to keep getting along or if we were going to have our first disagreement."

"I wouldn't dare disagree while you're holding that stick."

"This would probably leave a mark." Maddie held up the stick and dripped cornmeal on the stove. It didn't seem to bother her.

"Can I do anything to help?" I resisted the urge to grab a towel and clean up the polenta before it cooked onto the stovetop.

"If you'd like another beer, help yourself. Or, if you want to switch to wine…"

"I think I will. Can I top up yours?"

She set her glass next to the wine bottle. "While you do that, I'll set the table."

Plates, cutlery, water glasses, napkins, trivets, and cheese including a chunk of Parmigiano in a grater, gorgonzola, and some other cheese I didn't recognize all landed on the table in a flurry of activity.

"I suspected you had some cheese around here," I teased.

"A house without cheese isn't a home."

"I've never heard that expression."

"I made it up. But I believe it to be true."

"You make up a lot of your own rules?"

"Isn't that better than having to break other people's rules?"

Her response made my brain swim a little. "I never thought of it that way. I made a career of making sure my company played by the rules and I even enforced the rules."

"I made a career of ignoring a lot of rules. Like, little girls don't grow up to be engineers or run companies."

"But you did."

"And I ruffled more than a few feathers along the way."

I didn't know what to say but, thankfully, Maddie was focused on getting dinner on the table.

"The polenta is ready." Picking up the copper pot, she pointed with her elbow at a long shallow platter. "Can you hold that for me?" I held it as she poured the polenta onto it.

I put the platter on the table, and she transferred the pot of mushroom sauce from the stove to the table.

She put a large flat serving spoon into the polenta. "Get yourself some polenta then mushroom sauce, or cheese or both."

I took a small scoop of polenta and a spoonful of mushrooms.

She did the same. "I like to start with the mushrooms first to."

"I've been transported back to Piemonte."

Maddie smiled. "That's the best compliment I could ask for. You need to try it with the gorgonzola."

I did, and it was excellent.

We shared stories of our cooking schools and found we'd learned several of the same dishes and techniques. We'd both been introduced to the versatility of the anchovy with bagna cauda, vitello tonnato and lingua col bagnetto and the marinating and slow cooking techniques that turn less desirable cuts of meat into winter menu staples like brasato and trippa. Maddie of course remembered the cheese and chocolate tomini al verde and bunet while I reminded her of the warming properties of vinto brulé and bicerin.

"Imagine if we'd picked the same school," said Maddie. "We might have met ten years ago."

"We'd probably have shared a few bottles of Barbera together by now…" I lifted the bottle and topped up Maddie's wine and my own, finishing the bottle.

"A few more than a few I'd imagine. Shall I open another?"

"Not for me. This will be enough. Thank you."

Maddie began clearing the table. "I didn't make dessert, but I have some fruit."

"I'm full. But thank you."

Maddie picked up the notepad from the counter. "I don't have anything on our schedule for after dinner tonight."

"Then I suggest you pencil in 'Nate helps with dishes'."

"No. I'm just going to let the polenta pot soak and toss the rest in the dishwasher. It would take me longer to show you where everything goes."

"Then I'll excuse myself to the restroom. If I may?"

"You needn't ask permission. Make yourself at home."

By the time I returned downstairs, Maddie was walking towards me from the kitchen with our wine glasses.

"Would you like to watch a movie or some TV?"

"A movie?"

She set the glasses on the coffee table and opened a cabinet beside the TV. "Here's what I have in movies. Take your pick. I like them all."

The cabinet was jammed with DVDs and VCR tapes. Old movies, new movies, different genres from dramatic to romantic to comedic all stacked every which way. I pulled out a VCR tape of Monty Python and the Holy Grail and several DVDs tumbled out onto the floor.

"If you want to watch The Holy Grail, I have the DVD too."

Maddie scooped up the escaped DVDs and then reached into the cabinet and pulled it out. It seemed impossible that she could know exactly where it was given the lack of any apparent organization system.

She put the DVD in the player and grabbed three remote controls from the top of the cabinet.

She settled on the sofa with her legs curled under her. "The best view is from here. We can share." She patted the sofa beside her.

I watched in awe as she worked the remotes, pressing buttons on all three until the familiar opening credits started. She was smiling and giggling even before the silly subtitles appeared on screen. She noticed me looking at her and she blushed. "I'm sorry. I can't help it."

"Don't apologize. Betsy found it annoying that I laughed before the funny parts."

"Are there un-funny parts?"

We both giggled as we watched the movie. Maddie couldn't seem to resist blurting out the punch lines, she apologized several more times, but it didn't bother me. Her giggles made me laugh.

"Have you ever visited any of the locations where the movie was made?" she asked.

"No. Have you?"

"No. I would have if Anne had wanted to, but, she's not a fan. She thinks it's a silly movie."

"It is silly, but brilliant."

"Exactly."

"I'd go with you."

"Great. I'll add it to our to-do list."

"For this weekend?"

"No, Silly. We need more time than that."

"A quest. Lord be Praised."

Maddie giggled. "How many times have you seen this movie?"

"Probably 5 or 6 times. You?"

"In the last 40 years, probably 4 times as many as you."

"Has it been that long? I guess it has. You know, I first saw it in Toronto. I went alone one night when I had nothing else to do."

"The first time I tried to see it, there was a massive blackout partway through. At first, we thought it was a gag in the movie. As it turned out the whole city was dark."

"I was here during a big blackout around that time. Were blackouts common back then?"

"I don't remember any others. But I remember this one because it was unusual for such a big area to go out for so long. There was no power at our offices until mid-day the next day."

"It was on in the morning at my hotel. I was staying at the Royal York."

"That's quite a coincidence."

"Being in town for the same blackout?"

"Yes, but even more so that I was at the Royal York Hotel to meet a friend who was staying there, and we decided to go see the Holy Grail. But it didn't quite work out."

"Did she tell you about the free drinks and ice cream they served in the bar that night?"

"He didn't have to. I was there."

I don't know about Maddie, but my mind was flung back to that night. I pictured the candlelit bar and scoured my memory for the faces of the other patrons.

"I spent much of that night sitting at the bar chatting with other guests because there wasn't much sense sitting alone in a dark hotel room."

"As I recall, the bar was packed. Like a bygone era when hotel guests gathered in the common areas for entertainment. People who never would have spoken to each other were deep in conversation."

"I'm sure we'd have had a long conversation if I'd run into you."

"Because I talk a lot?"

"That, and because you almost got to see a movie I wanted to see. I'd have asked to accompany you the next time you attempted to see it."

"You? A married man. Asking to go to the movies with a married woman? How shocking!"

"You said you went with a friend. So not like a date."

"So you're saying a threesome?" she said with a sly giggle.

"Ms. Maddie you have a dirty mind."

"You suggested it."

"I did nothing of the sort. Evil Zoot! You will not corrupt this chaste knight."

Maddie laughed. "I think my evil temptress days are long behind me."

"So there were evil temptress days...I knew it!"

"I didn't say that."

"Yes you did."

"No I didn't."

"I've met my match. Run away. Run away."

We giggled, laughed, and bantered through the whole movie. When it was over Maddie asked if she could get me anything else.

"Nothing. Thanks. It's time for me to turn in."

"I'll be up for a little longer, so if you need anything. Just holler. If you're up before me, I'll leave the coffee pot set up. You just need to push the button. Please make yourself at home."

"Thank you. Goodnight."

"Sweet dreams."

"Sweet dreams."

I lay in bed thinking about the night of the blackout. I imagined myself looking around the dimly lit bar and seeing Maddie's face illuminated by candlelight. I imagined being bold enough to ask to sit at the table with her and her friend. I wondered if I'd met Maddie that night, would we have become friends? If I'd not given in to Betsy and taken the job in Toronto, would we have been friends all these years? Would our paths have crossed some other way? I fell asleep thinking of Maddie.

CHAPTER 21

My clock said 7:30 am. I rolled over and considered going back to sleep but then I smelled coffee. It took me a few confused seconds to remember I wasn't alone in the house.

"You're a terrible host," I muttered aloud as I groggily sat up and tried to shake off sleep and start to think. At least Nate knows his way around a coffee pot I consoled myself, feeling guilty that he was up, and I was not.

Bacon must have heard me moving because he started meowing and pawing at my door. He'd tried to bust in a couple times during the night, but I'd ignored him. He usually creeps into my room, after I'm asleep, to curl up at the foot of my bed. But last night I'd closed the door. I could tell by the look he gave me when I opened it he didn't approve of the new sleeping arrangements.

I started to head for the shower, then changed my mind, and threw on the flannel pajama bottoms and t-shirt that I kept beside the bed just in case I needed to dress quickly during the night. Only in the dead of winter was it cool enough for me to sleep comfortably wearing anything. I gathered my hair up in a clip to avoid brushing it and headed towards the coffee smell.

Nate was sitting at the kitchen table with a cup of coffee and his book. He was neatly dressed in khaki pants and a long-sleeved golf shirt. I could smell his aftershave. I hadn't heard him shower. Seeing him so put together, I regretted my choice to forego one.

Nate set his book down. "I hope I didn't wake you."

I yawned. "You didn't. I'm not really awake yet." I knew I sounded grumpy, but it was too early, and I needed coffee. I tried to sound cheery. "Have you been up long?"

"A while. I heard a noise at your front door about 4. So, I came to check that the doors were locked and that everything was alright."

"Probably the paper." I set down the coffee cup I was just about to fill and wandered to the front door to get the paper from the porch.

"The coffee is very good," said Nate, with a little too much enthusiasm for this early in the morning.

"Can I make you some breakfast?"

"I'm usually the one saying that." Nate had a goofy grin and wiggled happily in his seat.

"Do you want to make your own breakfast then?" I asked holding my coffee cup close to my face, hoping the rich earthy vapours would push the grogginess out of my head.

"I'd be happy to make us both breakfast." Nate got up from the table and stood at the counter. It was then that I noticed that the polenta pot I'd left soaking in the sink was cleaned and dried and sitting on the counter.

"Were you doing dishes this morning?"

"Well, it was still in the sink and needed to be done. So, I did it."

I suppose I did say make yourself at home, but it irked me that he'd just gone ahead and taken over. My better self whispered that I should be grateful. Despite my inner voice's caution, I scolded him.

"I was letting it soak overnight. You didn't have to do that."

Nate looked puzzled and deflated. "I guess all those years, getting up early on my own, working in the kitchen... I'm used to doing it."

"I'm sorry. Thank you," I said trying to be gracious.

"You don't need to worry about me. Pretend I'm not here and do whatever you'd normally do in the morning. I've got my book and, if I may, I'll read your paper."

"Help yourself." I topped up my coffee. "I think I'll go upstairs and shower."

I left Nate alone in the kitchen for an hour, even though showering and dressing only took me 20 minutes or less. I needed some time to wake up. I sat in the chair by my bedroom window and sipped my coffee while scrolling through the messages on my phone. Most of the messages were junk but there was an email with the bonspiel entry forms I needed to fill out and a text from Anne.

How's it going with Nate?

I had told her that he was coming to visit but by the time I did, Emily had beaten me to it. Anne had relayed that Emily was thrilled that her grandfather was getting away from the inn for a while. My daughter had teased me, suggesting she fly home for the same weekend so she could chaperone. Now she was being nosey and fishing for details. She would worry if I didn't answer so I texted a purposely vague response.

Nice evening. Toy show today.

Nate was washing a plate and cup when I returned to the kitchen. I think I scowled.

"I made myself breakfast," he said. "I helped myself. Like you said. I hope you don't mind."

"I'm glad you did, but you didn't have to do the dishes too."

He looked at me hopefully. "I could make you some breakfast too."

"No. I'm not hungry yet."

"You really should have breakfast."

"You sound like my mother."

"Is that a bad thing?"

"It's not a compliment."

Neither of us said anything for a few seconds so I asked, "Is there anything you need to do to get prepared to go to the Toy Show?"

"No. I'm all set."

"We have a little extra time then. Do you mind if we stop at the curling club on our way?"

"Never been to a curling club."

"I just need to print a couple forms and fill them out so I can drop them off."

Nate followed me to the living room. I sat down at my computer and turned it on to download the forms from my email.

"How do you work at that desk?" Nate's voice had a disapproving tone I found irritating.

"I work just fine. I have a stratigraphic filing system."

"I don't see anything in files."

"The older it is, the deeper it is."

I opened the forms on my computer, typed in the requested information and printed them out.

"Let me know when you're ready to go," said Nate.

"Just need to sign these." I grabbed a pen from under some mail and signed the form. "And I'm ready."

"That's it?"

"Yup."

"I'll go fetch my wallet and watch in my room."

"No rush. We have lots of time." I was worried he'd think we'd be late adding an unscheduled stop.

When we got to the curling club, I offered to give Nate a quick tour since he'd never been to a curling club.

"How long have you been a member here?" he asked.

"Forever. My parents were members before I was born."

As we passed the office, I went in to drop off the forms with the club secretary while Nate waited by the large glass windows overlooking the ice sheets. Our ice maker, Mac, was getting the sheets ready for the Friday morning senior men's league.

"Why is he doing that?" Nate asked when I joined him at the window.

"He's pebbling. The drops of water freeze and create the tiny bumps in the ice you need to curl."

"Why do you need bumps?"

"The combination of the concave bottom of the rock and the pebbles reduces the friction because the pebbles melt under the weight of the stone creating a micro layer of water that helps the stone glide and curl."

"It looks like a giant shuffleboard."

"The basic idea is the same, the team with their rock closest to the middle scores."

"Sounds simple enough."

"There's a little more to it because the rock doesn't travel in a straight line..."

Several members arriving for their league games said "Hi" to us as they headed through the clubhouse to the locker rooms.

"Seems you're pretty popular with the boys," said Nate.

I couldn't decide if his jealousy was flattering or annoying. I bristled at the idea that he thought I needed or wanted their attention.

"Curlers are generally a social lot."

"Betsy enjoyed the social events at our country club. Is a curling club like a country club?"

"A bit, with members and social events, but it's busiest the opposite time of year. We have tennis in the summer, and once upon a time they had lawn bowling."

"Our country club had tennis. Betsy never liked golf, but she played tennis."

The league teams were coming out onto the sheets.

"Do you want to watch a bit of the games?"

"If we have time."

I explained the game to Nate as we watched. By the end of the second end, I'd covered the basics of the game, and it was time for us to get going.

We hit the usual daytime traffic but arrived at the convention center ahead of schedule. There was already a line forming at the main entrance, but we found the much shorter Trader's line and we walked up just as they opened the doors. Nate handed our passes to the security guard.

"Enjoy the show," he said handing them back.

I didn't know what to expect at a toy show, other than there would be toys. The large convention room was filled with rows and rows of vendors. If a flea market and a trade show had a baby, it would look like a toy show. Some of the vendors had a single unadorned table with their wares while others had elaborate shelved displays with lights and professional-looking signs. Some of the vendors sat expectantly at their tables waiting for customers, while others were still frantically unpacking and setting up.

There was every imaginable type of toy. It was overwhelming.

"Where do we start?" I wondered aloud.

"I thought we would do a quick scout around and then circle back to any of the booths that look promising."

For the first few minutes, I just followed Nate as he moved quickly up and down the aisles of booths. At the pace he was moving, there was no way I could take it all in. Instead of trying, I watched Nate. He was a man on a mission. His head moved side to side as he went down the aisles. He reminded me of a bloodhound the way he seemed to be sniffing out what he was searching for. Suddenly, he stopped. He pointed to a boat that was still in the hands of the vendor who had just pulled it from a plastic bin.

I hung back and watched as Nate moved closer and the toy man held up the boat for Nate to see. It was a wooden runabout like the one in the movie *On Golden Pond*. It was about two feet long and looked quite heavy as the man braced his elbow on his hip as he turned it around so Nate could examine it from each side.

"How much?" asked Nate.

"Five hundred."

Nate wrinkled up his face and pressed his lips together. "I think that's a bit much."

"It's a good price for this piece. Accurate replica of a 1954 Chris Craft Runabout. Mahogany planking, chrome details, real leather seats; Even the flag is perfect. She's even got a name," he said turning the boat around again so Nate could take in all the details.

"How about $450?"

"I can't. The show hasn't even started officially and I'm sure to sell it."

"Ok. I'll take her."

The boat went back into its box and Nate paid the man with his credit card and he joined me in the aisle where I was waiting for him. His eyes were sparkling, and he was beaming.

"I'm sorry he wouldn't budge on the price."

"I'm not surprised. It was a fair price and even better because it's in Canadian." He leaned in as he said it like he was getting away with something and it was our little secret.

Nate tucked the boat under his arm and looked up and down the aisles as if trying to decide which way to go.

"Where to next?" I asked as Nate shifted the boat to his other side.

He looked uncomfortable. "Maybe I could put this in the car?"

"Tell you what, I'll take it to the car, and you can keep going."

Nate smiled, relieved, but immediately his face clouded. "How will you find me?"

"If I haven't found you in 30 minutes, department store rules."

"What's that?"

"When Anne was little we had a plan just in case she got lost in a big store.

If you don't see me, stop moving. Stand in the middle of the first main aisle you find and stay there until I find you."

"Yes Mom." Nate grinned as he handed me the boat. Now free of it, he scurried off down the aisle.

The box was much heavier than I thought. I juggled it and my purse as I stopped to ask the security guard about getting back into the show. He offered to have someone help me, but I declined. It made me even more defiant about not acting like an old lady when young people imply I can't do things on my own.

After locking the boat in the trunk of the car and returning to the convention center, I easily found Nate just a couple of aisles from where I'd left him. He was chatting with an older couple who had a booth that was filled with tiny toys. It made me think of Lilliput from *Gulliver's Travels*. Cars, houses, trees, people, animals...

Nate saw me and waved me over. "Maddie, I'd like you to meet Jane and Ray. Jane, Ray, Maddie."

"Nice to meet you." I extended my hand to each of them.

"Ray was just explaining that these are their own designs and are all handmade."

"Interesting." I stepped closer to the display cases so I could see the items inside.

"We do a lot of custom work for model railroad enthusiasts," explained Ray.

I moved past the wall of clear cases. "These are really neat. So detailed. Lots of hours of work I'd imagine?"

There were scenes depicting all aspects of life. There were blocks of buildings with sidewalks and streetlamps that lit, several different train stations and bridges, a football field complete with bleachers and tiny players, people of different ages, races and gender, standing, sitting, playing and working and finally a forest of trees and bushes.

"Jane does most of the painting and adds the details. I do the main structures. For example, this railway bridge, I built the structure, but Jane added the weathered texture to the wood and decorated the ends, so it has abutments that look like concrete and rocks."

I studied the end of the bridge. "It looks like those are actual rocks."

"They are real. We use real materials whenever possible to add to the authenticity of each piece."

"I like the kite flying boy." I pointed to a figure dressed in jeans and a sweater holding onto a string attached to a tiny gravity-defying kite.

"Jane is very proud of that one."

"It's incredible. It actually looks like the kite is flying." I could see Nate watching me reflected in the glass, so I turned back towards him.

"Are you ready to keep going?" he asked.

"Ready when you are." I could have kept looking, but I didn't want to hold him up.

"Thanks, Jane, Ray," said Nate shaking their hands. "Hope to see you guys at another show sometime. Let me know if you're ever in Bar Harbor."

"Will do," said Ray. "Bye now."

"Those were really incredible miniatures," I said to Nate as we walked away.

"I thought you'd like them."

"Definitely. Did I tell you that Anne and I always try to bring back something miniature from each of our trips?"

"Is that where the items in your guest room came from?"

"Most of them. Some I've picked up on solo trips, but most were with Anne." Nate looked at his watch. "The general admission hours have started."

I took that to mean we were not moving fast enough. "You lead, I'll follow."

Nate sprang back into search mode. We had breezed along three more aisles before he darted into a large booth that looked like a toy scrap yard with piles of similar-looking toys on each of their tables. Most were very old-looking, wooden trucks, cars, and dolls. The painted details were faded or missing, presumably from years of play. There were stacks of fragile-looking cartons that looked like the original packaging for the types of toys that were loose on the table. Nate had zeroed in on a table with several bins of small boats. He was going through each one, methodically."

"Are you looking for something in particular?" I asked.

"Ones I don't have," he answered, not looking up from his search.

Each of the bins had a variety of different boats, some had many of the same kind, but they varied in condition from very well worn to almost new looking.

"How old are these?" I asked.

"Tillicum toys were sold from the late twenties to the seventies. The all-wooden ones are pre-1960s," answered the booth man who was sitting in a chair watching us. "They were marketed as Tiny Boats for Little Folks." He stood and picked up one of the cartons to show me. "A complete set like this Convoy Set goes for $125 to $300 depending on the condition."

He handed me the box to look at. It said 'Table, Tub and Floor Play'. That explained the condition of the ones in the bins. It looked like they'd seen a lot of all three. I looked through the cartons. There was a Harbor Set, Ferry Terminal, Ocean Travel Set and it looked like there were multiple generations of them with slightly different packaging. Newer-looking boxes were glossier, and the boats had some plastic parts compared to the older boxes of blocky all wood boats with simple artwork.

"Ah ha!" Nate proudly held up a small lighthouse and two buoys.

"How cute," I said. "It's a bit like your lighthouse."

"How much?" said Nate to the man.

"Individual Tillicum are $10 each."

"How about $20 for all three?"

"I should charge more for the buoys – they are rare. The small ones were the most likely to get lost from the sets."

"$25," offered Nate.

"Ok, but only because I like you," said the man with a smile.

Nate paid the man and we left the booth.

The aisles were now jammed with people as the show had officially opened and the general admission crowds were streaming in. He cradled his acquisitions close to his body with both hands and was beaming like he'd just won a prize.

"Do you want to put those in my purse?" I offered.

"Yes please," he said placing them into the compartment I held open for him.

"That also leaves me a free hand to hold yours," he said with a wink.

"Just so we don't get separated in the crowd."

"Of course."

"So how many of these do you have?" I patted my purse to indicate the toys he'd just added to it.

"Almost all of them."

"That's not a number."

"About 40."

"That's quite a few."

"They're little. They don't take up much space."

"How do you know which ones you have and which ones you need?"

"These I keep in my office. I see them all the time. So, I just know."

Nate was full of energy as we wove our way through the crowd, darting into booths that looked promising, and then hurrying to the next when he didn't find anything that interested him. His face went from deep concentration to glee when something caught his eye. We saw several more vendors with the same little boats, but apparently, he had all of them already, so he didn't purchase any others. It was almost one o'clock when we reached the end of the last row of booths.

"How about we take a break from walking and grab a bite to eat?" suggested Nate.

"I'm not sure there's a lot of options here," I warned.

"How do you feel about hot dogs?"

"Who doesn't like hot dogs?"

"At the end of the hall, there's a guy with a hot dog cart. Can I treat you to lunch?"

"I should treat you since you bought the admission tickets."

"Least I can do. You've been so helpful, chauffeuring, carrying my purchases..."

There were a few tables near the hot dog cart. I took a seat while Nate ordered us each a hot dog and coke. "What do you want on yours?" he called over.

"Everything."

Nate delivered our meal to the table. His hot dog only had a strip of mustard but mine was piled with onions, relish, mustard, ketchup, and pickled hot peppers. We both sat facing the show and ate silently watching the steady flow of people streaming up and down the aisles. I'd not had a hot dog from a cart in a long time. It brought back memories of walking to the subway with Anne after taking her to the theatre and her pleading for one. The spontaneity and rebellion of giving in to temptation and the contrast of our evening attire and eating street food always gave me guilty pleasure. I relished the memory of the two of us eating a late-night snack that was bad for us, but we did it anyway.

"You like it?" asked Nate, just as I'd taken a large bite.

I answered with an affirmative mumble and a nod. It was surprisingly good. The wiener had a firm bite that burst with a snap and was meaty but juicy and the bun was soft and fresh but gave a firm foundation to carry the dog and condiments from plate to mouth. I couldn't resist a lick of the mustard and ketchup that was oozing toward the open end of the bun. I did my best to corral the condiments, but a few bits of onion escaped and landed on the napkin I'd placed on my lap.

He nodded at the stray onions. "I thought you only wore lobster for lunch?"

I know he was teasing, but I was embarrassed. I frowned and tried to eat what was left of my hot dog more daintily, but having to be careful took some of the pleasure from the moment.

Nate was still only halfway through his when I crumpled up my empty wrapper and paper plate.

"That was good. What's next?"

"Are you still hungry?"

"I meant, what do you want to do next?"

"Now we work our way back in the opposite direction."

"Why?"

"We might see something we missed and, there were a few booths that were not unpacked when we started, so I'd like to see those too."

As soon as Nate finished eating, we were off again. Despite the crowds, Nate plowed ahead. We spent the next hour or so looking at countless toy boats and talking to vendors about their collections. I learned a lot of new things about toys, like there are big premiums for old toys that are new in their original packaging, and toys that are no longer in their original packaging are considered 'loose toys' and can include new toys or ones that have been either well-loved or very abused by their young owners. I also started to suspect Nate had an enviable boat collection given the impressed looks on the vendors' faces when he talked with them about specific boats that he'd acquired or was looking to acquire.

I wasn't sure how to gauge whether the day was a success since Nate didn't make any other purchases. But, when we had been over every inch of the show twice, Nate led us towards the foyer.

"You've been a good luck charm. This has been the best show in years."

"So you're happy with what you found?"

"Absolutely. The shows have generally gone downhill. So many people buy and sell on the internet. We can go now unless there's something you'd like to look for."

"We can go." I started leading us back to the parking lot. "Do you buy on the internet too?"

"Rarely. I prefer to see things in person rather than pictures and descriptions."

"You go to a lot of toy shows?"

"Not anymore. But, once upon a time, I went to every show I could."

While rummaging in my purse for the car keys I pulled out the lighthouse and buoys Nate had bought and handed them to him.

"These will be easy to pack and take home. But the one in the trunk... Did you bring an extra bag?"

"If it's not too much trouble, could we take it to a pack and ship place?"

"There's a UPS store not far from my house. Would that work?"

"That would be great."

I dropped Nate and his toy boat in front of the UPS store on Bloor Street and then went to find a place to park. Nate was watching the clerk fill an enormous box with Styrofoam peanuts when I joined him in the store.

"You'll have a lifetime supply of packing material when that gets to your house."

Nate shook his head. "I'll unpack it in the garage and put them straight in the trash. I can't stand them. They get everywhere."

"I would save them. You never know when you need to pack something."

"If and when I need to, I'll go get it packed like I am now. No sense cluttering up the house with stuff I might never use."

"But you might use it. Waste not, want not."

"My mother believed that. She saved every empty jar, scrap of cloth, or piece of ribbon just in case she needed it someday."

"Thrifty."

"It took Betsy and me weeks to clean out her house after she died."

"I'm sure, like my parents, she lived through the rationing of two world wars and couldn't waste anything that could be useful."

"Betsy spent days sorting their house into piles of keep, donate and trash. I went on weekends to box up and move everything out of the house."

"My mother and I did that job together when she moved in with me. I still have all the 'keep' items stored in my basement."

Nate didn't say anything, but he shook his head and shivered like I'd said there was something frightening in my basement. The clerk finished packing up the boat. Nate handed him the paperwork he had filled out while we were talking and paid him for the shipping. Nate waved goodbye to his boat as we left the store.

"See you next week."

CHAPTER 22

Maddie suggested we 'Uber' to dinner. I'd heard of it, but I didn't know how it worked. She showed me how she used her cellphone to summon a car and how she could track it so we would know when it was arriving.

"You can't do it on your flip-phone. You need a smartphone."

"I doubt I'll be summoning Ubers in Bar Harbor."

"Uber's not the only reason to use a phone from this millennium."

I had to admit the Uber was convenient. We were dropped off right outside the restaurant. The place Maddie picked was very modern and bright and we had the option of sitting at the bar or at a table. I was surprised Maddie insisted we sit at the bar, but when she gleefully pointed out that our food options would float past us, I understood why.

"You picked a restaurant with boats?"

"I thought it would be fitting."

We ordered drinks. Sake for Maddie and a Sapporo for me.

Maddie looked 'upriver' at the boats approaching us. "I like pretty much everything here."

"How does this work?" I was uncomfortable not having a menu.

"We take whatever we want from the boats, and they tally the empty plates at the end."

"Simple enough."

Maddie was scrutinizing the contents of the boats going by us. "Do you like sashimi?"

"I prefer the kind with rice but pick whatever you like."

I didn't want to tell Maddie that I'd had my fill of eating sushi during my many trips to Japan. It's not that I don't like sushi but I associate it with forcing myself to eat all manner of strange, raw, fishy things so I wouldn't offend my Japanese hosts. I'd be happier with a bowl of noodles, or stir fry. But I didn't suggest it because Maddie was so enthusiastic about the sushi.

"I had my first sushi in Japan. I've craved it ever since. There were no sushi bars here back then. When the first one opened it was so expensive only movie stars and millionaires ate there."

"When I went to Japan the first time, I had no idea what to expect food-wise. It was quite the shock."

"I remember how surprised I was that raw fish could be so good."

"Or terrible, depending on the fish."

"I don't think there are any terrible fish on this menu."

"No cod sperm shots or raw octopus testes?"

"You ate those?"

"Unfortunately."

"Not your favourites then?"

"Not by a long shot."

"Good because you won't find anything that exotic here."

"I'm OK with unexotic, even cooked sushi."

"Did you know that the California Roll is a Canadian invention?"

"Why isn't it called a Canadian Roll then?"

"I suppose it's like French Fries, they aren't French."

"Should we grab a Canadian Roll when one comes by?"

Maddie laughed. "We're in luck. Here comes one now." She snatched it and several other items from the boats going by.

I helped myself to a piece of the California Roll. "So, you've been to Japan?"

"Once. Many years ago."

"Why?"

"For work. A soil investigation project. We were brought in by a Japanese company that was rebuilding an area destroyed by an earthquake. The earthquake liquefied the soils and the buildings collapsed. They wanted to avoid the same fate for the new construction."

"Sounds complicated."

"It was. Interesting, both professionally and personally. But I was totally naïve."

"I can't imagine that."

"I was used to being a woman in a man's world, but I had no idea how much worse it could be."

"So you didn't enjoy it?"

"Quite the opposite. I loved it."

"Really?"

"I had a chance to do and see things I never would have. But female engineers were unheard of in 1960s Japan. I had to be twice as good to be half as respected."

"That sounds terribly unfair."

"It's just the way it was. While the boys were off drinking with the Japanese guys, I was working in my hotel room."

"Must have been frustrating."

"It paid off in the end. I bought the company." Despite her words, she wasn't boastful. Her confidence was incredibly attractive.

We worked our way through the selections Maddie had picked for us; the California Roll, shrimp tempura, tuna and salmon nigiri, and some sashimi. I went for the roll and tempura and Maddie for the bare fish. It was good. The rice was mildly sour, sweet, and warm like fresh-baked bread, and sticky, so the roll held together even though my fingers were clumsy with the chopsticks. Maddie snapped up the pieces of fish, dipped them in soy sauce and popped them in her mouth without hesitation. I watched with more than a little awe at how quickly she made the fish disappear.

"You said you were in Japan a lot?" She set down her chopsticks, carefully arranging them so they didn't point at me and picked up her sake cup, cradling it as if she were warming her hands.

"Six or seven times. But only once for an extended period."

"Wow. Always work? Or on vacation too?"

"Always work. Betsy had no interest in going, but I did get to do some sightseeing while traveling on business."

"What kind of work were you doing?"

"The first few, and longest, trips were to research patents."

"When was that?"

"It was before we adopted Ann, so…1966."

"Whoa. I was in Tokyo the same year, in spring. Were you there for the cherry blossoms?"

"They made such a big deal of it. I remember I couldn't get any work done because everyone was off looking at trees."

"You sound like a grumpy workaholic American." Maddie picked up her chopsticks and dug back into the sushi.

"I was there to do a job."

"We were invited to join our client's family gathering in the park under the sakura trees. It was quite the experience."

"I saw the cherry trees. I just avoided festival days. Too crowded."

"I'm guessing you were in Tokyo too, based on the room name at the inn." Maddie stacked our empty plates and pulled a couple more from the boats.

"Yes. But I spent most of my time either in a library researching or in meetings."

Maddie shook her head. "All work and no play?"

"Not entirely. On my first trip, I saw the main sights of Tokyo, the oldest temple, the historic downtown and famous parks. I don't remember the names. My interpreter insisted on taking me sightseeing one weekend."

"I would have liked to go to Japan again. You're so fortunate to have been able to go multiple times."

"I suppose. Here's a bit of trivia for you. The boat that started my collection was a gift on my first trip to Japan."

"Exchanging business gifts is a very important ritual in Japan, eh?"

"It is. At the time, I didn't appreciate the significance of the ship they gave me. You may have seen it. It is in the Tokyo room Anne stayed in."

"I did. A lovely model. Very detailed."

"It's a replica of a Higaki Kaisen. They were the primary means of transportation in the Edo period that came to an end when Japan was forced to open up to the world. Historically this fundamental culture shift is blamed on Matthew Perry, of the US Navy, whose armada fired on Edo Bay."

"So they give the workaholic American a boat that represents the glory of the pre-American era … no, no symbolism there."

"I didn't appreciate the significance until many years later."

"So the message got through…just very late."

"I had it on a shelf in my office until I retired."

"And you blame your boat habit on that one boat?"

"After that, I started bringing home boats from business trips on a regular basis. At first, I kept them in my office at work, but it expanded to my home office. When I ran out of office space, Betsy made me store them in the attic."

"Does every boat have a story?"

"Maybe not a story, but there's always a reason I got it."

"Like completing a set? Like the little ones today?"

"Precisely. I had a set of boats when I was a boy just like the ones I bought today. I got them for Christmas. I remember playing with them on the stoop of our house."

"So the little boats remind you of those?"

"Actually, the ones I bought today will replace the ones I lost as a child."

"You have boats that were your childhood toys? I thought you didn't start collecting until your Japanese boat?"

"Betsy found a box of toys in the basement of my parents' house when we were cleaning it out. Inside were a few boats. I guess Mother kept them."

"So it's a good thing she liked to save things."

"She probably was saving them for her grandson, but she never got one. But she saved them anyway."

"Do you have any siblings?"

"Two older sisters. Both have passed."

"I'm sorry."

"Thanks."

"How much older were they?"

"My sister Jane was ten years older than me, and May was four years older than her."

"So you were a surprise."

"Yes. Apparently, my father was delighted to have a son to carry on the family name."

"Were you close to your sisters?"

"Yes and no. They were both married by the time I finished high school but they both lived their whole lives not far from my parents' house."

"Unlike you."

"We saw each other all the time until I moved to Florida. By the time I moved back north, they had big extended families of their own and I didn't make the trek to Baltimore to see them that often."

"I presume they had children."

"Yes. All girls. But by the time we adopted Ann, her cousins were getting married and having babies of their own."

"Do you keep in touch with your nieces?"

"I get Christmas cards with the updates but I haven't seen any of them in person since Jane's funeral."

"Weddings and funerals."

"At our age, mostly funerals."

"I feel guilty being happy to see people at a funeral. I'm sad for the loss but it's the only time I see some of my family."

"You shouldn't feel guilty about that."

"I always resolve to make more of an effort to keep in touch…"

"It's like New Year's resolutions. Easy to make but hard to keep."

"And time goes so fast."

Not only does time fly, I thought to myself, but around Maddie the sushi flies. All that remained were a couple of pieces and a large stack of empty plates. I put down my chopsticks and told her she could have the rest.

"Are you sure?" Her chopsticks were poised to snap up the last spicy scallop and piece of tuna roll.

"I'm done. Enjoy!"

As I watched her eat the remaining pieces, I sipped my beer and asked her about her career as an engineering consultant. I was struck by how unpretentious she was as she described how she had risen through the ranks to take over the firm. Despite her current humility, I imagined that she'd been rather terrifying to many of her male colleagues.

She told me a funny yet revealing story about an occasion in Japan. Apparently, they needed to visit a construction site as part of the project and the Japanese engineers assumed she'd stay in the office while the men visited the site. They'd informed her that her office attire was not appropriate for the field. She'd explained that even today, many Japanese companies' dress codes require women to wear skirts and high heels. She recounted how she'd ignored the glares as she removed her high heels, put on a pair of work boots, and got into the van with everyone else.

"I think they were just enough afraid of me that they didn't dare object. I could tell how upsetting it was to them. As much as I didn't want to annoy our client, I counted on them wanting to save face by not making a scene. I couldn't let them walk all over me. So, I pretended I didn't understand and did as I wanted."

"I can imagine their shocked expressions."

"It was more hostile than shocked."

"You are fearless."

"Not fearless. But I can be ferocious when I feel threatened. At the time, being left out was a real threat to my success. It wasn't fair. Nothing gets my hackles up like unfairness."

"They are pretty hackles…"

Maddie shrugged off the compliment. "Even after all these years, I still get irritated by inequality for women in the workplace. Things have changed, but not enough." She shot back the last of her sake. "Are we ready to go?"

"What about the bill?"

"Taken care of."

"I would have gladly picked up the check."

"Another time." She pulled out her cell phone. "If you're ready, I'll request an Uber."

"I'm ready."

Apparently, there was a car nearby. Maddie said we should go outside because the driver was only three minutes away. I took her coat and held it open for her to slip into it. Her back was to me and I could see her collar was askew. She didn't straighten it right away, so, I brushed her hair away and adjusted it as she buttoned her coat. As I stood there watching her back, I had to resist the urge to touch her hair again. It was fine and soft, and I wanted to feel it slip through my fingers. I imagined my fingers brushing against the skin of her neck as I combed through its length.

She looked over her shoulder and smiled at me. "Thanks."

I didn't say anything. I was caught in my reverie of running my fingers through her hair. Maddie started to walk away but noticed I hadn't moved. She looked back, nodded towards the door and then led the way out of the restaurant.

The Uber dropped us off at her house a short while later. Maddie excused herself to the bathroom. I also had to go but I didn't want her to think I was following her upstairs. I waited, uncomfortably, until I heard her door close to go up myself and use the other bathroom.

Maddie was in the living room when I came back downstairs.

"Thank you for coming to the toy show with me, for chauffeuring and dinner."

"My pleasure. I'm going to make some chamomile tea. Would you like some?" She put down the stack of CDs she was shuffling through.

"No thanks. I'm going to turn in."

"Had enough of me?"

"Oh no! I didn't mean that. I'm just wiped out all of a sudden."

"You were up a lot earlier than I was."

"I can't help it. Always been an early riser."

"Good night then. Sweet dreams."

"Good night. Sweet dreams and thank you again."

I went to bed, but I could hear Maddie downstairs. She'd put on some music and, even though she wasn't playing it very loud, I recognized the songs. Elvis had been one of Betsy's favorites. She would say she was too old for him, but she rarely missed watching re-runs of his movies, no matter how late they were on TV. I often heard his silky voice drifting out of our family room after I'd gone to bed without her.

I hoped Maddie hadn't been offended when I left her and went to bed. It's not that I didn't want to spend more time with her, but I could feel myself fading and Betsy had told me so many times that I was like an overtired toddler when I stayed up too late. Irrational, irritated and bad-tempered. Betsy would suggest I sleep in the guest room, so she wouldn't wake me when she came to bed, but I now realize it was more likely because she didn't want to put up with my angry outbursts.

I remember one time when Betsy was clearing up after a dinner party. She was holding three glasses in her hands and, as she set them on the counter, one caught the edge and tipped, breaking the glass, and spilling the contents on the counter and my pant leg.

"Watch what you're doing," I said. "You're like a bull in a china shop."

Tears welled in her eyes. "It was an accident."

"Don't start that." I hated it when she cried.

"Stop it! I'm not a child. Please, don't talk to me like that."

"Then I won't talk to you." The dishes I was carrying clattered as I set them on the counter.

"Please don't slam, you know it upsets me."

"You're the one breaking glasses. If you want slamming, I can do slamming."

"You don't need to be so mean."

"You just don't pay attention."

Betsy was silent and sobbing as she cleaned up the glass and spilled wine. I couldn't stand the sniffles and tears. I left the room. I was convinced I had done nothing wrong, and she was overreacting as usual. It was a familiar pattern. I would lose my temper; Betsy would react with tears and accusations that I was being critical or mean.

Exchanges like those gradually eroded our relationship. More than our differences, it was me that had driven a wedge between us. I'm a bit ashamed of my behavior towards Betsy. I would never have talked to an employee the way I talked to her. I wonder now if it was my insecurity, my feelings that she was above me, that made me grab on to any high ground I could claim. Putting her down and being critical was a way for me to feel superior.

Betsy learned to ignore my outbursts. She stopped reacting to them, but she also became more distant. We no longer touched. There was no intimacy, sex, or tenderness. The occasional night in the guestroom turned into the guest room being my room, except for the infrequent times when we had overnight guests. Once Ann had moved out, her room became the guest room. We were more like siblings forced to live together rather than husband and wife.

We started sharing a bedroom again when we moved to the inn. Betsy had insisted that the owner's suite have two bedrooms in case we needed an extra one, either for Ann or for me. She was already quite frail by then, weakened by the chemotherapy treatments and I think she felt comforted knowing I was nearby in the nighttime.

In the year that followed, she became more and more dependent on me. I'd vowed to be there in sickness and in health, so it was my duty and obligation to care for her, which I did until, near the end, she moved to a hospice that could administer medication to manage her pain.

Listening to Maddie listening to Elvis, I imagined meeting her as my younger self. I'm sure I would think she too was out of my league. I vowed if I had the chance at a life with her, I would try not to make the same mistakes.

CHAPTER 23

I felt a burst of relief as I drove away from the airport after dropping Nate off on Sunday. I'd worried about entertaining him for a whole weekend and if I could be as gracious a host as he'd been for me. But the weekend had gone well, and I'd enjoyed spending time with him.

"He left me a thank you gift he secretly purchased at the toy show. And now he's invited Anne and me to come to the inn for New Year's with his family," I reported to Claire who'd been pressing me for details over coffee at Chapter's bookstore, where we'd met to pick up copies of the latest book club book.

"Meeting the family is a big deal," said Claire. "This is getting serious."

"Serious? I don't know. Could be Emily invited Anne and my invite was an afterthought."

"Did you hear it from Anne first?"

"No. Nate asked me when he called me on his Thanksgiving Day from Emily's house."

"Sounds like Nate invited you and Anne is the add-on."

"He did sound pleased when I told him it was possible."

"Not too anxious or available. That's good. Play it cool."

"I'm not playing anything. I told him I needed to see about someone to look after Butter and Bacon and check on flight availability."

"But you didn't say no!"

"I didn't commit either."

"If you need to skip out on our Christmas plans to go be with Nate, Cécile and I will understand."

"That won't be necessary. Nate suggested I come the 29th or 30th and stay as long as I'd like, so I have flexibility to find the best priced flights."

"You don't have anywhere to be until February .... So you'll be gone for at least a month then?"

I shook my head and sighed at Claire's incorrigibility. "More like a long weekend, three or four days tops."

"I have a great idea!" Claire wiggled like an excited puppy.

"Dare I ask?"

"While you're there, if things are going well, you can invite him to come to Arizona. I have plenty of room for one more."

"Won't it cramp our style to have a man in the house?"

"We'll adjust. I'll get you a prettier housecoat."

"We'll see."

"First we need to figure out what you're going to get him for Christmas."

"Do you think I should?"

"What if he sends you something? You'll be scrambling."

"What if he doesn't?"

"Then you bring it as a hostess gift for New Year's."

"So it can't be something Christmas-y?"

"Something more personal. It doesn't have to be expensive, just meaningful."

Claire was not a hopeless romantic, she was a practical one. She wasn't fooled by my cool exterior and knew I cared what Nate thought about me. It took me a couple weeks but, following her suggestion, I'd put together a gift for Nate. I'd not wrapped it because I wasn't sure if it would be going in the mail or if I'd be hand carrying it to Bar Harbor.

I should have known her instincts about Nate would be spot on. A week before Christmas a package arrived and inside was a small, wrapped box and a card.

I didn't want him to think I'd sent a gift because he'd sent one, so I wrapped his gift and took it to the post office so it would be postmarked today. When I got back, I sat down and sent him an email.

Dear Nate,

The package you sent arrived today. It was a lovely surprise to get something from you. Thank you. I haven't unwrapped it. Unless you tell me otherwise, I'll open it Christmas morning. You should be getting something in the mail from me, but it may not arrive for a few more days.

Cheers

Maddie

Nate answered me almost immediately.

Dear Maddie

You can wait to open it until Christmas. Would it be possible for me to call you earlier this Thursday because Ann and Lane are arriving in the evening? Would it be OK if I called you around 3?

Cheers

Nate

On Christmas morning, Butter, Bacon, and I were sitting on the living room floor in front of the Christmas tree with our treats. Catnip toys for them, coffee and a generous slice of panettone for me. I was waiting to video chat with Anne so we could open our gifts to each other together. I decided to open Nate's present while I waited. I opened the card first. It was a 'for someone special at Christmas' type of card but Nate had written inside.

Merry Christmas Maddie. Looking forward to seeing you here for New Year's. Love Nate.

The words 'Love Nate' hit me like a flashing billboard, and I reread them several times. I told myself it was just a conventional way to sign a card, but I couldn't shake the feeling it was significant. He could have used 'cheers', our usual closing for emails. Would he be disappointed that I'd simply signed the card with the gift I'd sent him with a simple 'Maddie'?

I unwrapped and opened the box and found, nestled in a bed of foam and felt, two small tissue paper wrapped items. I opened the first one. It was a tiny house that reminded me of the inn. The second one confirmed my hunch as it was a replica of Nate's lighthouse. I checked the box to make sure I'd not missed anything. I found a small, folded card. On the front, it said, 'Custom Miniatures by Ray and Jane'. I recognized the names. They were the people we'd met at the toy show. Inside the little card, Nate had printed,

Since your picture inspired me to buy a lighthouse, I thought you should have one too.

The thank-you gift Nate had surreptitiously purchased in November at the toy show had also been one of Ray and Jane's figures. He'd given me a little girl with a kite similar to the kite flying boy I'd admired at the show.

I carefully studied the little models. They were utterly amazing. The house was light and made mostly of wood, but the lighthouse was heavier, mimicking the brick and steel of the original structure. I loved the tiny details like the curtains painted on the inside of the tiny glass windows and the rocks glued to the base of the lighthouse that looked like the outcrop it sat on. My study of them was interrupted by the electronic ring from my laptop.

"Merry Christmas Mom!!" Anne waved at me looking very festive with several bows perched on her head.

"Merry Christmas Honey. Great hairdo!"

"Linda put them on my head to keep her dog from eating them."

Linda came up behind Anne and looked over her shoulder.

"Merry Christmas!" The reindeer antlers she was wearing bobbed as she waved at me.

"Merry Christmas Linda."

"Can we open presents already," said Anne. "I've been waiting forever. I had to explain the eight AM rule to Linda."

"No present opening until I get up. And no waking me up until eight AM."

"She would only open her stocking until we called you," said Linda from the background.

Anne held up the present I'd sent. "I'm opening it now."

She unwrapped the box and opened it, only to find another present wrapped inside.

"You do this to me every year."

"Because you're a snoop."

"She's been poking at all her presents since they appeared under the tree," tattled Linda.

"Awesome. It's perfect." Anne held up the leather bag I'd bought her. It was a cross between a briefcase and a purse, big enough for her small laptop or a tablet, but streamlined and in a yellow-orange colour so it was more feminine than a typical briefcase.

"What a great bag," said Linda. "And it's the perfect colour for you."

"Thanks, Mom."

"You're welcome."

"Now open the one from me," said Anne.

"What about Linda? Does she get to open anything?"

"She already opened her presents. Show Mom what you got."

Linda held up her gifts from Anne.

"Now it's your turn, Ms. C," said Linda. She'd started calling me that from the first day I'd met her. I'd told her she could call me Maddie, but she never did.

I unwrapped the present Anne had sent. Inside there was a map of Arizona and an envelope. Inside the envelope was a printed page from a website with a helicopter on it.

"A helicopter ride?" I asked.

"Not just any helicopter ride," explained Anne. "A private flight over the Grand Canyon for you to take pictures. You have the whole thing to yourself, but you can bring up to 3 people with you. I called Claire to find out when you were going to Arizona. I have it tentatively booked for Feb 6th. But you can move it to any other day they have availability."

"Are you coming?"

"I was thinking you'd take Claire."

"But this is a first. We always do firsts together."

"Photography is your thing. I just get in the way."

"If you're not coming, you spent too much on a gift just for me."

"You're worth it."

"It looks amazing. Thank you."

I put the paper back in the envelope. "What are you doing the rest of the day?"

"We're headed to Linda's parents for dinner. You're going to Claire's?"

"She said to come any time after two."

"Are you bringing her a fruitcake?"

"Of course."

"Does anyone actually like fruitcake," asked Linda.

"Forgive her. She's never tried yours."

"If you want, I can bring you one at New Years?"

"You better," said Anne. Linda cringed.

"I only have a couple small ones left. The rest are spoken for."

"It will be enough to convert Linda, I'm sure. We better get going. Wish Claire a Merry Christmas for me."

"I will. I wish you were here."

"At least we'll see you for New Year's."

"Linda is coming too?"

"Yes, Emily invited her too."

"That's great. You won't have to make the long drive from Boston alone."

"It's not that far."

"But it's winter. And I worry."

Anne cut off my motherly fretting. "Merry Christmas Mom."

"Merry Christmas Anne. Love you."

After we'd hung up, I pulled out a notepad and started a to-do list for my New Year's trip, starting with 'pack Christmas cakes'. I'd already planned to bring a large one to share as it was our family tradition to eat Christmas cake all through the holidays. Anne liked eating it, but she didn't like making it. When she was a teenager, she would moan and make excuses why she was too busy to go to Ma's house to make it.

Every year in mid-November, Ma and I would make the fruitcakes for Christmas. We'd start in the morning weighing out the pounds of dried fruits, brightly coloured candied peel, flour, sugar, and spices. The quantity was so big Ma used an enormous pot to mix the cake ingredients. That pot was so big, that when Anne was little, she would hide in it and close the lid. She almost gave Ma a heart attack when she was 5 or 6, jumping out of the pot like a jack-in-the-box. I laughed out loud to myself at the memory of Ma cursing under her breath as the raisins she'd just measured went flying. Too big for the kitchen sink, Ma had to carry it up to the bathtub to clean it. Her punishment for Anne was she had to help wash and dry the giant pot.

Once the batter was poured into the paper-lined tins, the cakes would bake for several hours. The three of us would play cards while the cakes were in the oven. We'd play Rummy or Old Maid or if Pop was around, we'd play Euchre or Bridge.

Despite her aversion to cake making, Anne loved spending time at her Ma and Pop's house. It was a second home to her. After Will and I divorced, they helped me with Anne. She'd go to their house after school until I got home from work. There were many days I didn't get there until after she'd had dinner with them, but Anne didn't mind. Ma would set up TV tables in the living room and they would watch TV while they ate, something I never allowed her to do. Ma and Pop also liked to watch their soap operas and I blame them for Anne's continuing addiction to the Young and The Restless.

My iPad was ringing again. I thought it would be Anne calling back but to my surprise it was Nate. I hesitated to answer. I was still in my PJs. But I didn't want to miss his call, so I quickly ran my fingers through my hair to straighten it a bit and answered.

"Merry Christmas," I said, looking at the video of myself first to make sure I didn't look too scary.

"Merry Christmas Maddie. I hope it's not too early."

"No, not at all. I've been up for a while."

"I would have phoned, but Emily helped me set up Skype on the new iPad they gave me for Christmas and I wanted you to be the first person I called."

"I'm honoured."

"Have you opened gifts yet?"

"Yes. I just opened Anne's with her while we video chatted."

"Have you opened the one from me?"

"Yes, first thing this morning. Thank you for the lovely lighthouse. It looks just like yours."

"I sent them the pictures you took when you were here so they could get it as close as possible."

"You commissioned a custom lighthouse for me? Wow. That explains the resemblance!"

"I thought you might like it."

"I love it."

"I opened your gift last night. I shouldn't have been surprised we were thinking along the same lines."

"I didn't know what to get you."

"I recognized it right away. It's the picture that inspired me to buy the inn."

"I was hoping it was the one you saw. I had a moment of panic that there could have been another lighthouse picture in the exhibition."

"I love it. It's smaller than I remember."

"Yes, the one that was displayed was bigger – but I thought a smaller one would be easier for you to find a place for – even if it's in a closet."

"I would have happily found a place for it even if it was double the original size. Thank you. It's great."

Emily popped into the frame behind Nate. "Merry Christmas, Ms. Cole,"

"Merry Christmas! How wonderful your whole family is together for Jake's first Christmas."

"He won't remember it – but we're taking lots of pictures."

"That's great. Please wish Bob and your parents Merry Christmas from me."

"I will. I'll leave you to chat with Grandpa." She waved and disappeared from view, but I could hear her laughing and talking to others nearby."

"It sounds pretty busy there. I should let you get back to your family."

"We're all headed to church soon."

"To the church where Jake was baptized?"

"Yes."

"It's a lovely church and the pastor was so kind."

"They have a live nativity scene for the children so it will be a zoo. Literally. They have live sheep in the parking lot…"

"Oh my. That could be … messy."

"I'll tell you all about it when you're here."

"See you on the 29th."

"Thursday. Looking forward to it. I'll be there to collect you at the airport."

"Thanks for the call and the gift."

"Thank you. Merry Christmas, Maddie."

"Merry Christmas, Nate."

CHAPTER 24

I saw Maddie's plane approaching as I drove up the access road to the airport. I knew it was hers because there aren't many flights into our Bar Harbor airport. She couldn't fly direct from Toronto. Her itinerary through Boston with the layover was not much shorter than the drive from Boston to Bar Harbor. I know she'd considered driving up with Anne, but Anne had to leave on Monday to be back to work, so I'd convinced Maddie to fly so she could stay a few days longer. I was looking forward to having time alone with her after the others had gone.

She'd warned me she'd have a checked bag, so I made my way to the baggage claim area to meet her.

"Welcome back to Bar Harbor, Ms. Cole," I said as she approached me.

Maddie looked surprised. "I didn't expect you to come in to greet me!" She gave me an enthusiastic hug.

"Full-service airport transportation for our VIP guests. Your bag will be coming out over there. Can I take your hand luggage, Madam?"

"No need," she said striding alongside me towards the baggage carousel. "I guess this puts my swooping in to get you to shame."

"Not at all. It would make me dizzy circling this airport and the parking lot is right outside the door."

"Thank you. I appreciate the VIP treatment."

Her bag came a few minutes later and I waved off her protests and carried it to the Jeep while she pulled her rolling case.

I lifted her bag into the back. "This is pretty heavy for its size."

Maddie shrugged. "I pack tight."

"What's in here? Dark matter?"

"Close. Dark Christmas cakes. One for you, and one for my Anne."

"You didn't need to bring anything," I said, but I was thinking that she really shouldn't have.

"It's a family tradition," she explained, and, as if reading my thoughts, "If your family doesn't like it. I'm sure Anne will take it off your hands."

I didn't say anything as I was a bit surprised by the whole idea of Christmas cake. Wasn't it the cake everyone dreaded receiving? I'd never met anyone who admitted they liked the stuff. Maybe Lane would, it was a lot like Christmas pudding.

"I won't be offended if you don't like it. But I hope you'll at least give it a try." Maddie looked a little hurt and I was quite sure she would be offended if I didn't like it.

"Any other family traditions I should be aware of?"

"We eat grapes at midnight."

"Grapes? Why?"

"For good luck and prosperity in the new year."

"Any particular kind of grapes?"

"Doesn't matter. Just grapes."

"Does wine count?"

"It has to be the fruit, not the juice. But we can drink wine too."

"Remind me to put grapes on the grocery list."

As we drove, Maddie talked. I occasionally interjected but Maddie entertained me on the drive recounting what she'd been doing since we talked on Christmas day, including stories of escapades with her friend Claire who, I hadn't had a chance to meet when I visited Toronto.

"Claire's even invited you to come to Arizona in February. I told her it was a bit short notice to plan it, but she insisted I mention it," said Maddie.

We cut off the conversation there because we'd pulled into the driveway and saw Emily and Bob towing Jake in a sled across the front yard. When they saw us, they turned and pulled him towards us.

"You're here!" Emily gave Maddie a big hug as she stepped out of the car. Maddie smiled and hugged her and Bob and then bent down to coo at Jake.

"Oh my. You've grown since I saw you last! What rosy cheeks you have!" She grinned when Jake smiled at her. "He's just precious!"

"He's a whole big handful of precious!" said Emily. "It's been great having Mom to help this week."

"It will be a shock when we're back to reality next week." Bob took the larger of my bags out of the trunk while Nate grabbed the other.

Emily pulled Jake and his sled up to the front door and we all headed inside. Emily and Bob juggled Jake between them as they slipped off their boots and moved to the living room to unbundle Jake on the rug by the fireplace. Maddie waited until they'd cleared out to take off her boots and I helped her off with her coat.

"The place looks lovely all decorated for Christmas," she said.

"Ann and Emily deserve all the credit. They did the decorating."

"It looks great."

"I'll help you with your bags." I picked up both her bags and waved off her attempts to take one of them from me. "You're in the same room as last time if that's OK with you."

"Back to Dover. Perfect."

I let Maddie take the lead up the stairs. She paused outside the door.

"The name's gone."

"Yes. I need to order a new one. It's unlocked, you can go in."

Maddie opened the door and a huge smile came across her face. "What in the world have you done here?"

"It's a work in progress. Do you like it?"

Maddie walked towards the desk. "Is that the boat you bought in Toronto?"

"It is. Take a close look." I couldn't help but grin as I watched her examine the model. I'd taken extra care to clean it before she came. It gleamed with polished wood and brass and was a perfect replica of the sleek and elegant real thing.

"It looks great," she said.

"Look at it again." I nodded towards the stern as a hint.

"Madeline? The boat is named Madeline?"

"She is."

"Did you do that?"

"No. But, when I saw it was the Madeline from Toronto ON, it was a sign. I had to buy it."

"You didn't say anything! You're sneaky."

"I'd hoped I'd find a way to surprise you with it."

She turned and looked at the wall beside the window. "And that's the picture I sent you for Christmas."

"It is."

"So… a Canadian lighthouse and a Toronto boat. What will you call this room?"

"For now, Maddie's Room if that's OK with you."

She surprised me by giving me a big hug. "I'm honored. But you could call it Canada or Great White North?"

"For now it's your room. I'll let you unpack and settle in. Do you need anything?"

"Thank you, no. It won't take me long."

"No rush. If you want to rest or freshen up…"

"I'll just hang up a few things and I'll be down."

"I'm going to go light the fire. Make yourself at home."

"What about the room key?"

"I think it's safe to leave the room unlocked since it's only us here. But if you want a key, I can get you one."

"No need. I'm not worried."

I left Maddie and headed downstairs. I was a little annoyed that Ann and Lane hadn't come to the door to greet us. They knew I'd gone to the airport to pick

Maddie up and I'm sure they'd heard us arriving. Perhaps they'd decided to nap. Jake had been unusually fussy the night before. Having a baby in the next room waking up crying in the middle of the night was something they weren't used to. They had joked about it bringing back memories of their sleep deprivation when Emily was a baby.

There was no one in the living room when I got there. I had brought wood in from the shed earlier and had set the paper and kindling in place, so it only took me a few minutes to get the fire going. I moved the screen in front and then I started setting up a second low barrier of bricks and boards. Maddie came downstairs just as I was setting the last board in place.

"Is that the Jake fence?" she asked.

"Yes. He seems to be attracted to the fire and he's quick on all fours."

"Does it work?"

"So far so good. What have you there?"

She was carrying a large red and green cookie tin. "The Christmas cake I mentioned in the car. Where would you like me to put it?"

"Does it need to be refrigerated?"

"No, just someplace cool. It's quite well preserved at this point."

"Preserved?"

"Maybe 'pickled' is a better word. My mother's secret to a good Christmas cake is a solid month of regular soakings with Brandy before it's ready to eat."

"A month?"

"At least. I baked this batch on November 22nd, so they'd be ready to eat for Christmas. Personally, I think it just gets better with age."

"And presumably more alcoholic."

"My mother insisted that the alcohol evaporated and left behind only the flavor."

"So you're sticking with that story?"

"I am. Now, where do you want me to put this?"

"Would the storage pantry be suitable, or should I take it down to the cellar?"

"The pantry is fine."

"Here, let me take that." I took the tin from her. The weight of it surprised me. "No wonder your bag was so heavy."

Ann and Lane were both in the kitchen when we walked in.

"How lovely to see you again," said Maddie.

"Likewise, Ms. Cole," said Lane formally, extending his hand to her.

"Please, call me Maddie." She shook his hand and smiled.

"Did you have a good trip down from Canada," he asked.

"Uneventful. So that's good in my book."

I left the room to go put the cake in the storage pantry. I had to make some space for the cake tin on the shelf with the sugar, flour, and other baking supplies. I was only gone a couple of minutes but when I returned Maddie was alone in the kitchen.

"Where'd everyone go?"

"Ann said she heard Jake, so she and Lane went upstairs. She must have ears like a bat. I didn't hear anything at all."

"Can I get you anything? Some wine? Some cheese?"

"Nothing right now."

"Water? You should have water after flying."

"Water would be nice."

Before I could get Maddie a glass, the doorbell rang. "Do you mind helping yourself while I get that?"

"Go. I can fend for myself." Maddie waved me off and headed for the drink fridge in the dining area to help herself. She was sitting by the window at one of the breakfast tables looking out when I came back.

"Look what I found at the front door." I stepped aside so she could see who was behind me.

Maddie jumped up and hugged her daughter. "What are you doing here? You weren't supposed to be here until tomorrow!"

"We wanted to surprise you," said Anne.

"Surprise!" said Linda.

"And you didn't say a word." Maddie wagged her finger at me and gave me a scolding look.

"Don't blame him," said Anne. "I made him promise not to tell."

I escaped Maddie's glare by heading back to the foyer for the girls' bags. "Let's get you girls up to your room," I called back as I rolled their cases towards the base of the stairs.

"I'll get those," said Anne. "I'm the Sherpa on this trip. If it needs carrying, I carry it."

"I hope it's ok, but I've put you in the Maine Room instead of Tokyo this time."

"All your rooms are lovely. It'll be perfect," said Anne.

"It's a little larger, so I thought you might like the extra space."

Linda went straight to the window facing the lighthouse. "Wow. What a view."

Maddie had followed us upstairs. "Are you sure you want to share? If you want, you can bunk with me. You have to see what Nate's done in my room."

"I don't think so Mom. I've been bunking with Linda for a while. In fact, we'll be bunking together permanently come this spring."

Linda looked shocked and a bit worried. "You can't just spring that on her."

Maddie's forehead scrunched up and her lips were pressed together with concern. "Spring what?"

"It's good news. We're moving in together and… we're getting married!" Anne grabbed Linda's hand and showed Maddie the diamond ring on her left hand. She was beaming and Linda was grinning.

"Anne asked me at Thanksgiving, but we decided to wait to tell our parents until we could do it in person at Christmas," said Linda.

"Married?" said Maddie. "I … I didn't know you were …that serious."

I couldn't tell if she was upset or confused or just plain shocked. Anne had said they only needed one room, so I'd suspected that she and Linda were more than friends. It was apparent from Maddie's reaction that their early arrival wasn't the only surprise.

"When you find the person you're meant to be with, you gotta hold on to them." Anne squeezed Linda's hand.

Maddie's face cleared as Anne's revelation sank in. "That's wonderful!" She hugged both Anne and Linda.

"I know it's a little late to ask, and a little old fashioned, but we asked Linda's parents the same thing, do we have your blessing?" Anne looked into her mother's eyes. She and Linda were holding hands and I think we were all holding our breath waiting for her reaction.

"You don't need my blessing. Do you love her," she asked Anne.

"Like crazy," said Anne.

"Will you love her forever?" she asked Linda.

"Like crazy," said Linda.

"Then that's the only blessing you need!"

There was a lot of hugging and some tears, so I slipped away and went back downstairs. I went through the kitchen and straight down to the cellar to get a couple of the bottles of Prosecco I'd bought for New Year's Eve. An engagement warranted a toast.

CHAPTER 25

Anne's news had thrown me for a bit of a loop. I sat on the bed in my room for a few minutes to gather myself before going downstairs. It was wonderful to see Anne's excitement about her engagement but I couldn't help but feel like she was leaving me. It also didn't allay my maternal anxiety. Giving up her independence to make a relationship work would be a challenge for her, as it had been for me. On top of that, despite the changes in attitudes towards same-sex couples, not everyone will be accepting. I took a deep breath and silently promised I would do everything in my power to ensure my daughter's happiness.

There were eight champagne glasses and two bottles of Prosecco set up on the kitchen island when Anne, Linda and I came downstairs.

"I thought we should toast your announcement," said Nate to Anne and Linda. "I'll just run up and call the others to join us." Nate went upstairs and came back with Ann, Lane, Emily, and Bob in tow.

Emily launched into introductions. "Linda meet my parents, Ann and Lane, Mum, Papa, this is Anne's friend Linda."

"Actually…", said Anne, grinning as she grabbed and held out Linda's hand, "my fiancée Linda!"

"OMG that's awesome!" said Emily, grabbing Linda's hand and giving both her and Anne an enthusiastic bear hug. "When did this happen?"

"We've been keeping it a secret since Thanksgiving until we could tell our parents in person. We just told Mom now."

"So we should have a toast!" said Nate, opening the first bottle of Prosecco with a pop.

"This could get confusing," said Linda. "Anne and Linda. Ann and Lane."

"Maybe one of you is Anne-one and the other number two," giggled Emily. "But maybe not, because number two sounds bad."

"You're Anne with an E and Mum is just Ann. How do you feel about being Annie."

"I couldn't bear being called Annie," said Ann. "You can have it."

"How about you be Anne-T," said Linda to Anne. "Kinda sounds like Auntie."

"Only children don't get to be Aunts," said Ann.

"Maybe Jake will call me Auntie someday," said Anne with hopeful enthusiasm. My daughter seemed oblivious to Ann's snobbery that bordered on rudeness. I didn't think much of it at the time because Nate and Emily's warmth towards Anne more than compensated.

"Now that we have that figured out," said Nate, handing each of us a glass filled with the light gold wine, sparkling with bubbles. "I propose a toast." He lifted his glass. "To Anne and Linda. May the happiness you share with us today last a lifetime. Cheers!"

"To Anne-T and Linda," said Emily taking a big sip of the wine.

"Thank you, Nate," said Linda. "For the toast, and the lovely bubbly!"

"Would you like some more?" said Nate picking up the bottle.

No one protested as he made the rounds topping up everyone's glass. When he got to me, I said, "Thank you. It's sweet of you to do this for them."

"My pleasure," said Nate. "Life's moments should be celebrated. This is a big moment for your family. I'm honoured to be part of it."

"Have you set a date?" asked Emily.

"Not yet. We thought we'd figure out where first and then decide on a date."

"You could get married here!" said Emily.

"Nate doesn't do weddings anymore," I said, as a hint to my daughter that she shouldn't jump at Emily's suggestion.

"But I got married here," said Emily.

"That's different," interjected her mother. "You're family."

Emily wasn't letting it go. "Anne-T's family now. She's Jake's Godmother."

"I'm not sure Father would have approved if he'd known."

Emily looked horrified and embarrassed. "Mum! Please!"

There was a tense moment of silence. I wanted to defend my daughter, but I didn't know what to say. I was still processing the idea that she was marrying the girl I knew was her best friend, but she'd never portrayed as a romantic partner. It made so much sense. I should have clued in sooner.

"Is anyone hungry?" asked Nate.

"I'm not," said Ann, setting her empty glass on the counter and turning her back to us. "We should go call your brother before it gets too late there." She signalled for Lane to follow her upstairs.

Nate turned to me. "I have cheese. The ones you liked last time."

I couldn't tell if Nate was oblivious to his daughter's hostility towards Anne or if he was trying to diffuse the situation.

"As tempting as the cheese is, I think I'd like to take my camera and take a walk out back before it gets dark."

"You'll need snow boots," said Nate, looking concerned. "Bob shovelled our walk, but there will be snow on the path by the shore."

"I came prepared for outdoor winter activities," I reassured him.

"We have our snow boots in the car," said Anne. "We'll go too. Yes?"

Linda nodded and Anne left to go get their boots.

Emily, Bob, Linda, Nate, and I were left standing around the kitchen island. The sparkle of toasting my daughter's engagement had dissipated like the bubbles from the last sips of our Prosecco.

"Don't let Mum spoil this," said Emily. "Finding the person you want to spend forever with is definitely something to celebrate."

"Here, here," said Bob tipping up his glass and draining it. "Life is better shared." He put his arm around Emily and kissed her on the temple. "We think everyone should do it. Right, Ems?"

"Thanks, you guys," said Linda, although her eyes had lost some of their earlier enthusiasm.

"Thank you for the toast and the wine," I said to Nate, setting my empty glass on the counter. "Can I help clean up?"

"No. Get going. You'll run out of daylight. I was thinking dinner at seven?"

"We don't want to be a burden. We can go out somewhere in town and let you have dinner with your family."

"Of course you're welcome to go out, but I have everything ready for all eight of us tonight."

Emily put her hands on her hips. "No going out. You've got to be here for the big reveal tonight. Grandpa has been keeping his plans a secret until you got here."

"What's a secret?" asked Anne, back from the car with a big bag with their boots.

"Grandpa has something planned for us all tomorrow."

"Do we get a hint?" I asked.

"You probably want to wear those boots," said Nate.

"Finally, a clue!" said Emily. 'So, it's something outside."

"I'll tell you everything you need to know after dinner," said Nate mysteriously.

"You have to have dinner with us," said Emily. "We're having `Grandpa's lasagna. It's sooooo good!"

"As long as we're not imposing," said Anne. "We can go out to eat," she continued, echoing my earlier suggestion.

"If it makes you feel better, you can help with the dishes," said Emily.

"I'll do dishes for homemade lasagna any day," said Linda.

"Then it's settled," said Nate. "Now you girls run along for your walk before it gets dark."

It felt good to get outside. I'd spent my day in airplanes and airports and Anne and Linda had spent much of theirs in a car, so we all needed to move. I also wanted a little time alone with them. I felt guilty that I'd agreed to spend New Year's with Nate and his family when I could have, and maybe should have, spent it with just Anne and Linda. I didn't want anything to put a damper on their happiness. I was upset by Nate's daughter's comments, and I told them so.

"Nothing she says is going to shock us," said Anne.

"We've heard a lot worse," said Linda

"Besides, the only opinion that matters to us is yours," said Anne.

"Honey, I'm happy if you're happy. Now let's get some pictures of you two to commemorate this auspicious announcement!"

Despite the icy wind, the winter landscape made a lovely backdrop. The soft evening light reflecting off the snow was diffuse and flattering. The Atlantic was deep greenish gray, the rocks and ground snow-covered, and the evergreens along the shore dark and shadowed. Anne and Linda's puffy jackets were both blue, Anne's a conservative navy and Linda's a bright turquoise. Each had on a matching knit hat. The warmth of their faces as they looked at each other was a poetic contrast to the cold scenery. I snapped a few dozen pictures, moving them and myself around to try different poses, lighting and composition. I wanted to make sure I got a good one.

After I'd shot a series of pictures with them standing side by side holding hands, I told them, "Get closer." Linda put her arm around Anne and pulled her in. Being several inches shorter than Linda, Anne's head naturally rested on her shoulder when she leaned in. In my daughter's eyes, I saw a contentedness I hadn't seen before. I realized she'd found, in Linda, the kind of fulfilling partner that I'd never thought she'd find.

It soon got dark, so we headed inside. The three of us went to our rooms to freshen up and change before joining the others for dinner.

Nate's lasagna lived up to Emily's hype. It was excellent. What Emily hadn't mentioned was that Nate had prepared two kinds of lasagna for dinner. One meat, one seafood. Although he gave each of us the option of one or the other, we all ended up having some of both.

We pitched in clearing the table, loading the dishwasher, and washing dishes.

"This is the best seafood lasagna I've ever had," said Linda to Nate as she placed the one remaining piece into a container. "Will you share your recipe?"

"The secret's the sauce," said Nate.

"So… what's the secret?"

"Making the Bechamel with clam broth and cream instead of milk."

"Don't give away our family recipes to strangers," scolded Ann.

Linda either ignored or didn't notice Ann was being mean-spirited. "I promise I won't tell anyone. I just want to make it for my wife because she clearly liked it."

"Well, in that case, you should also know I use the same pan to sear the seafood as I do to make the sauce. While I cook the roux I scrape up all the good bits from the bottom."

"Scallops, shrimp, and lobster?"

"Yes. Sometimes I've made it with all lobster when it's plentiful and cheap."

"Any other hints?"

"Let's see… Under-cook the seafood, just sear it and let it finish cooking when it bakes."

"That makes sense," said Linda.

"Sounds like your fiancée is much more interested in the culinary arts than you are," I said to Anne.

"I'm into the culinary arts, just on the eating side, not the making side."

"Be warned Ms. C. I'll be hitting you up for recipes for all of Anne's favourites. She tells me you make the best pasta."

"No one compares to my father's pasta," interjected Ann. "He went to cooking school in Italy and came home a pasta master."

Nate looked slightly embarrassed. He reached over and put his arm around me. "Maddie went to cooking school near Torino at the same time I did."

Anne spoke up in my defence. "Mom's pasta was great before she went to cooking school."

"I'm sure you're both excellent pasta chefs," interrupted Emily. "But I want to know what Grandpa has planned for tomorrow."

"I never said I'd tell you what I'd planned. I said I'd tell you what you needed to know."

"What I need to know is… everything," said Emily. "How will I know what to pack for Jake?"

"Jake will need his snowsuit because it's an outside activity," said Nate.

"We know it's outside because you already said we'd need winter boots," said Anne.

"Hats, mittens, and warm layers and everyone ready to leave at 9:45 sharp," said Nate.

"You have to tell us more than that! Do we need to pack lunches?"

"Only for Jake. For everyone else, lunch will be provided."

"What time do you think we'll get back?"

"I expect we'll be back about two."

"Anything else we need to bring?" I asked.

"You'll want to bring your camera," answered Nate.

Emily looked at Bob. "We should have breakfast about eight, so we have enough time to get ready."

"What do you want for breakfast?" Nate asked Emily.

"I love your pancakes and sausage. If it's not too much trouble. And coffee, of course."

"No problem. I'll have the coffee ready by seven and pancakes by eight. And the machine hot to make Maddie's cappuccino."

"I'll be down for breakfast at 8 too," said Anne to Nate. "But I'm pretty sure she won't be down until at least 8:30."

The kitchen was cleaned up and Jake was getting fussy. Emily told us it was time for his bedtime snack before putting him down for the night. Emily picked up Jake and made the rounds for goodnight kisses, while Bob got his bottle ready, and then they, along with Ann and Lane, went upstairs.

"We should let you go be with your family. Would it be OK if we put on the TV in the living room for a bit?" I asked Nate.

"I'll come through with you," said Nate. "Can I top up anyone's wine?"

We took our glasses and Nate put on the TV in the living room and offered to light the fire.

"It's cozy in here already," said Anne. "We'll probably want one tomorrow after doing …. whatever we're doing outside."

"If you're fishing for more details, I'm not telling." Nate settled onto the sofa beside me across from Anne and Linda who'd claimed the loveseat. They leaned to one side to face the TV that was on above the fireplace. We decided to watch *It's a Wonderful Life* even though we'd missed the beginning.

When it was over, we thanked Nate for the lovely evening and walked our glasses back to the kitchen. Instead of going up to the owner's suite, Nate followed us back to the living room and turned out the kitchen lights behind him.

"Aren't you going up?" I asked, surprised that he wasn't going to bed.

"I hope you don't mind, but I'm staying in one of the guest rooms because I gave my family the whole upstairs."

"Do you snore?" asked Anne cheekily.

I scolded her. "Anne Tobias you behave yourself."

"Not that I've noticed," said Nate with a wink. "And hopefully you won't either."

We said our goodnights in the hallway and went into our respective rooms. Alone in my room, it really started to sink in that my daughter, at 46 years old, was getting married. I was still a jumble of emotions. I was happy for her and Linda. They were obviously excited and crazy about each other in a way I'd never seen Anne with anyone else. But I was used to Anne and I both being single. We'd been two unattached gals since she was a teen, and it was strange to imagine her having a family with someone else other than me. I couldn't quite put my finger on the emotion, not exactly jealousy, but a sadness that I was losing some of her. I felt ashamed that I could be so selfish. I worried that, by taking this step, she was making public what she'd kept private. She'd have to deal with the prejudices and negativity of others she'd avoided by keeping her relationships a secret. On the other hand, I was relieved and proud that she could be her authentic self. Yes, a jumble of emotions.

Anne knocked on my door at 8:10 and I heard her open it a crack. "Mom? Are you up?"

"I'm awake. Come in." I wasn't completely awake. My eyes were still closed but my ears were open.

"I'll just set this here." She put something on the desk. "Nate sent it up. He said to tell you that if you'd like anything else, he's happy to make it for you, but he'll be clearing up the kitchen at nine."

I squinted up at her and mumbled something resembling a thank you.

"Nate's making pancakes and according to Emily they're not to be missed, so, we're going to breakfast right now," she said in an overly perky voice as she left the room. I heard her and Linda talking in the hallway and their footsteps retreat as they headed downstairs.

I didn't immediately get out of bed. I stretched several different directions before crawling out of my warm nest. Once I'd gone to the washroom, I checked out the tray Anne had brought in. On it was an insulated thermos, a coffee cup, a ceramic cloche that was very warm, and a note.

Good Morning Maddie.

I thought you might not want to come down to breakfast so I took a guess at what you'd like. Please let me know if you'd like anything else.

Nate

I poured some of the coffee from the thermos into the cup and took a sip of a perfect cappuccino. Frothy but dark and slightly bittersweet. Peeking under the cloche I found open-face cheese and jam on toast. I marveled that he must have pre-warmed the cloche before putting in my breakfast. He'd thought of everything for this breakfast in bedroom surprise. Even though I wasn't hungry yet, I was touched by his gesture and that he'd remembered my preferred breakfast food from my last visit months ago.

Sipping my cappuccino, I puttered around in my room, making the bed, laying out the clothes I was going to wear and letting my mind and body slowly wake up as the day got brighter outside. After I'd showered, I again investigated the contents of the cloche. There were two thin slices of wheat toast neatly cut into triangles. I picked up one of the toast points and took a bite. It was still delightfully warm and crispy, and it was no ordinary cheese and jam. The jam was a black fig that was sweet yet had a savoury note, rosemary perhaps, and the cheese was salty and creamy and pleasantly funky that made me suspect it was made with sheep or goat milk.

I headed downstairs well before the designated 9:45 departure time so I could take my breakfast tray to the kitchen and wash up my dishes. Nate's daughter was there when I came in.

"Good morning, Ann," I said setting down the tray by the sink and turning on the water to rinse the cup and plate. Ann returned my greeting but looked displeased when I opened the dishwasher to add my breakfast dishes. Thinking that perhaps the dishes inside were clean I asked, "Should I not put these in?"

"You can but Dad is very particular about how his dishwasher gets loaded."

"That doesn't surprise me," I replied as pleasantly as I could.

Ann left the kitchen without offering help or suggestions. I was careful to conform to the placement of my plate and cup with the other dishes already inside the dishwasher. I certainly didn't want to leave a mess for Nate so I tidied up my breakfast dishes and tray as best I could, wiping down the tray and cloche and leaving them on the counter, and hand-washing the coffee thermos and placing it on a paper towel by the sink to dry.

I'd just finished when I heard a commotion on the stairs leading to Nate's rooms. Emily and Bob emerged loaded down with Jake, two big diaper bags and a pile of coats.

"Can I help?" I asked reaching to relieve Emily of some of her load.

She handed me the diaper bag from her shoulder while she juggled Jake from one hip to the other. "Thanks. We pack three times the stuff for him as we do for both of us combined."

"I remember those days. When Anne was a baby, we filled the station wagon with stuff just to go to the cottage for the weekend."

"I'm so preoccupied making sure I pack everything Jake might need, I sometimes forget my own stuff, like underwear."

"We've started a new family holiday tradition. Emergency clothes shopping for my Ems," said Bob.

We carried everything to the front hall where Anne and Linda were already waiting and starting to bundle up in their heavy coats and boots. Nate opened the front door and popped his head inside.

"Are we ready to go?" he asked, stomping the snow from his boots on the porch. I could see over his shoulder that he already had cleared the snow from the cars and the walkway.

"Just about," replied Emily. "Mum and Papa said they'd be down in a couple of minutes."

"Maddie, Anne and Linda, you can come with me," said Nate. "And Bob... if you could take Ann and Lane?"

"Sure thing," said Bob amiably. "I'll take this stuff to the car and warm it up."

Bob picked up the diaper bags and headed out. Emily followed him with Jake and started getting him strapped into his car seat while they waited for Ann and Lane. Anne and Linda jumped into the back of Nate's Jeep that was already running and warm. Nate held the door for me to get into the front passenger seat and then went back to make sure everyone else was settled into Bob's car.

It had taken almost as long to get everyone into the cars as it did to get to our destination. Within minutes of leaving Nate's place, we turned into a farm lane lined with high white wood fences that suggested it was an equestrian facility. We pulled into a large, cleared area beside a big grey wooden barn. A burly gentleman greeted us. He was wearing tall heavy rubber boots, dark green coveralls under a well-worn leather and sheepskin coat and a plaid hunting cap with flaps that came down over his ears. His cap and large mittens reminded me of the ones worn by Elmer Fudd the hunter in *Bugs Bunny* cartoons.

He waved. "Welcome! Great to see you Nate, and to meet the family." He extended his hand to Nate.

"This is Dave," said Nate. "Dave, this is my daughter Ann, her husband Lane, my granddaughter Emily, her husband Bob and my great-grandson Jake."

"Four generations of Jacobs – how fun," said Dave.

"And this is my friend Maddie, her daughter Anne and her fiancée Linda," continued Nate.

"Two Anns! That will cut down on the names to remember," said Dave. "Follow me, everyone."

Dave led us around the barn and standing, tied to a post, was a team of horses hitched to a big green and red wagon. The two horses were huge black beauties with white streaks down their face and white ruffles of long hair around their ankles. They had red leather harnesses with large brass bells that jingled when they shook their heads and snorted as we approached.

"We get to go on a sleigh ride?" asked Emily excitedly.

"Are you sure this is a good idea with Jake?" said Ann.

"We're going to take it easy today," reassured Dave. "Nothing to worry about, Mam."

"What a great idea," I said to Nate. "And the weather is perfect."

I was glad Nate had suggested I pack my better camera. Had he not, I might have opted for the point-and-shoot I'd used on my last trip. The sky was deep blue, and the sun was shining. The contrast of the white snow on the ground and the dark green of the pine forest would be a challenge for getting the exposure right. I snapped several pictures of the fields and forest anyway, but I focused more on taking pictures of us in the wagon, wrapped in the big blankets that Dave had provided, that smelled of hay and horses but were heavy and warm under and over us.

Dave sat above us on a bench seat at the front of the wagon. He steered the team down the farm lane towards the tree line and then along the edge of the field until we came to a lane that led into the forest. The wagon's large knobby tires made crunching noises as they rolled over the road's snow-covered gravel.

The woods were quiet, and it felt like we were transported back in time. Until Lane's cell phone rang.

He winced suggesting he felt bad about it. "It's Georgie. I need to answer it."

"His brother," explained Emily. "Uncle Georgie is looking after Grandfather while Mum and Papa are here."

"But he's alright?" Lane sounded concerned but calm. "Call me if anything changes. Alright. Goodbye."

Lane apologized for the disruption. "Father is giving Georgie a hard time. He's having a bad day. Nothing to worry about."

"No need to apologize," I reassured Lane. "It's a difficult transition when a child needs to take care of their parent. Difficult for both really."

"Uncle Georgie and your grandfather have never seen eye to eye, so he can be very difficult for Uncle Georgie when your Papa's not there to moderate," said Ann to Emily in a half-whisper as if none of us were there.

Dave unknowingly broke the tension calling over his shoulder, "If you keep your eyes peeled, we may see some deer along this stretch."

We all craned our necks away from looking at each other to peering into the trees as Dave turned the wagon down another even smaller lane. The trees changed from mostly pine to tall bare deciduous trees with much more open space around them.

"Jake seems to be enjoying this," said Linda. "It's like his little head is on a swivel."

"I think he's trying to figure out how to get at those bells," said Bob.

"Do you want to climb up there and ride the horseys my little cutie pie," said Anne in a sweet sing-song voice to Jake.

Ann rolled her eyes. "He's too young to ride horses."

"Of course you're too little. But you can still want to. Can't you?" Anne's funny faces and chatter made Jake giggle.

"Like a real-live carousel horse," said Linda.

"I wouldn't be surprised if he did," said Emily. "He loves his rocking horse from his Godmother." Emily smiled at Anne who looked a little too triumphant.

"He's still too little to ride it alone, but he loves to climb it," said Bob.

"So he's thinking, 'Man they have big rocking horses up here. I gotta get me one of those'," said Anne in a squeaky baby voice.

Emily laughed but her mother scowled and physically turned away and looked off into the trees. She and Lane were quiet while Emily, Bob, Linda and Anne bantered on about what was going through Jake's head. I presumed it was because they were preoccupied with concern for Lane's father, so I didn't try to engage them in conversation. I instead turned to Nate who was sitting beside me at the very back of the wagon.

"This is really super," I said. "Thank you."

"It's not over yet," he said with a gleam in his eye.

"You have something up your sleeve?"

"Just my arm," he said, laughing at his own joke and patting me on the knee.

Dave steered the wagon to the right again. It felt like we were making a big loop, but it was hard to tell since the road through the woods snaked back and forth.

"Whoa," said Dave quietly, and the horses slowed gently to a stop. He tied the reigns to the arm of his driver's bench, hopped down, came around the back of the wagon, and opened the back.

"Everyone out," said Nate getting out first and reaching back for my hand to help me down.

Nate and Dave helped everyone down from the wagon.

"Just head up the road a bit," said Dave.

"Do you have your camera, Maddie?" asked Nate. I nodded and held it up.

The road curved sharply ahead of the wagon and so we couldn't see very far down the trail. Anne, Linda, and I started off before the others as they took a few minutes to get Jake strapped into the front-facing baby-carrying apparatus that Bob put on while Emily secured Jake's mittens and hat. We rounded the bend in the road and, ahead of us, was a wooden covered bridge that spanned a small frozen creek. The dark grey trees, white snow, and red bridge in the sunshine was a scene right out of a storybook. As we stood there taking pictures, the others caught up with us.

"How cool is this?" said Emily taking out her phone and snapping pictures of the bridge and then a selfie of her, Bob and Jake.

"Do you want me to take a picture of you all together with the bridge in the background?" I asked.

Emily handed me her phone. "Oh yes! Please. Come on Mum, Papa, Grandpa."

Four generations together with the bridge and winter landscape behind them was a great shot.

"Stay there," I said taking several shots with my camera as well.

Emily took some of me and Anne and Linda and then we all walked over the bridge to the other side. As we did, I paused to take a picture of Anne and Linda walking hand in hand in front of me as they exited the darkness of the covered bridge. Their figures were silhouetted and framed by the bridge. I hoped I'd got the exposure right because they'd moved off to the side and out of view before I could take another shot. When I came out the other side, I joined them looking down into the shallow ravine at the abstract sculptures of ice and snow that had formed around the rocks in the creek below. We walked slowly beyond the bridge, turning back at regular intervals to photograph the scene as we moved away.

Nate came and stood beside me as I took a few more of the bridge. "Did you get some nice pictures?"

"I hope so. It's a lovely spot."

"Just wait here a minute," he said.

I heard the faint jingle of the sleigh bells. I held up my camera just in time to get a perfect shot of the horses and wagon exiting the bridge. The horses' breath, like steam from their nostrils, and the snow kicked up by their hooves, frozen in the air by the fast shutter speed I'd chosen because of the bright sun overhead.

Dave brought the wagon to a stop beside our little group. "Anyone looking for a ride, hop in."

Nate opened the back of the wagon and we climbed in and settled back into our same seats. Nate latched the door and called up to Dave that we were all secure. Dave snapped the reigns, and the team sprang into action jerking the wagon forward and starting us rolling down the lane.

It felt much warmer now. Maybe because we'd been walking or maybe because the sun had climbed higher overhead. As we went along, Dave told us there were lots of carriage roads and several interesting stone bridges in the National Park. For today, we were sticking to the farm roads that were mostly used in the spring to access the maple trees the locals tapped for syrup making. We passed a couple of old shacks Dave said once housed the sugaring pans. He explained that nowadays most people used tanks on wheels to collect the sap. Then, once they're full, they bring them to a central location with gas-fired boilers to reduce the sap to syrup rather than burning fires in the woods like the old days.

Dave also explained the history of the covered bridge. Although it looked antique, it was actually only about 10 years old. It had been constructed as part of a movie set and was now a popular destination for photo clubs and wedding photographers because it was easy to get to and, by design, there were ideal locations to set up a camera. As he finished explaining we emerged from the trees, and I recognized the big field we'd crossed when we'd first set out.

Dave brought the wagon to a stop in the barnyard and tied the horses to the post.

A tall sturdy woman wearing a bright red hat and coat had come out of the barn as we drove up.

She opened the back of the wagon to let us out. "Did you enjoy your ride?"

"It was great," I said.

"This is my wife, May," said Dave. "She's going to take over from here."

"Follow me," said May. "Dave's going to water and feed the horses, and I'm going to look after you."

She opened the door to the barn and ushered us into what may have once been a blacksmith's workshop. It was warm inside despite the concrete floor and stone and timber walls. There was a large black potbelly stove in the middle of the room with two simmering pots on top of it. Built into the stone of the long wall to our left was an oven with a wood fire burning inside.

"If you need the facilities, there's a restroom through that door," said May pointing to a wooden stable door that had "WC" in metal letters nailed to it.

It was warm enough that we took off our coats and, following May's lead, hung them on pegs by the door. There was a long table with benches on both sides to the right of the potbelly stove. At the end of the table was a tray of metal mugs, a stack of plates and a bucket with cutlery wrapped in cloth napkins.

May went to the wood oven and using a long paddle she had leaning against the wall pulled out a big flat bread from the oven. She slid it onto a wooden tray and put it on the table. Just the smell of the warm bread was enough to make my tummy rumble.

"Grab a bowl and mug and meet me at the stove," May instructed as she uncovered the two large pots.

May used two large ladles to fill our mugs with hot apple cider and our bowls with chili. The room felt even warmer once we had the steaming vessels in our hands. We collected utensils and settled on the benches on either side of the thick wooden table. May opened the door of what looked like an antique icebox and started pulling out items from the refrigerator hidden inside it.

She placed everything in the center of the table. "Sour cream, cheese, hot peppers for you to add to your chili as you wish. And butter for the rolls. Don't be shy. There's more of everything."

Bob reached for the hot peppers. "This chili is great."

"I might need a little of that sour cream," said Ann. "It's spicy."

I went for the cheese and watched it melt into strings around the bits of spiced meat and beans as I stirred. The big flat bread that May had pulled from the oven was, in fact, a sheet of rolls that were fused together into a large lumpy mass. I helped myself to a roll. It was soft in the center and slightly buttery, so it didn't need the extra butter I'd just added. But it was delicious with the salty creamy butter melting into the hot bread. I couldn't resist dipping it into the spicy red sauce that ringed the pile of chili in my bowl. The sweet cinnamon-laced cider was the perfect counter to the spicy chili. The two together had me so warm I removed another layer of clothing, tying my fleece sweater sleeves around my waist.

May offered second helpings as soon as anyone emptied their bowl. Most of us took her up on it. Bob and Lane appeared to be in competition to see who would eat the most hot peppers. It appeared to me that Lane wasn't enjoying the heat, but he matched Bob pepper for pepper on his second helping.

Confirming my suspicion Emily said, "Papa, you're going to hurt yourself trying to keep up with Bob. He loves spicy food, and it never seems to come back to bite him."

"Bites her in the butt," said Bob with a snicker. "Ems gets the ring of fire if she has too many."

"At least I don't emit clouds of toxic fumes after eating anything with beans in it."

Anne put her hands on her ears and shook her head. "TMI!"

"Change the subject," said Linda, "Before someone says something really embarrassing."

I didn't say anything, but I was glad I wasn't sharing a room with anyone tonight. We'd all had a lot of beans.

Dave came in and thankfully distracted us off the subject. "Everyone get enough to eat?"

Nate patted his belly. "More than enough."

"If you're done, anyone who'd like to take a walk through the barn and stables can come with me."

"Is it OK to bring Jake?" asked Ann. "I could stay here with him."

"Shor-enough is. Kids mostly get a kick outta the animals," said Dave.

We put on our coats and followed Dave out the door and across the farmyard to a larger barn. Dave slid open one of the big doors that hung from a metal track at the top and ushered us inside. It took a few seconds for our eyes to adjust to the dark interior after the bright sun on the snow outside. We'd entered a big room piled high with bales of hay.

"This is the hayloft. Of course, there's the hay and straw, but over here, in these bins, we keep the grain," explained Dave pointing to the various locations as he did.

"Do you grow your own hay?" asked Bob, hesitantly continuing, "Do you grow hay or harvest hay?

"We cut hay from at least one of our larger fields every year but it's not enough, so we buy some as well."

Dave led us to a narrow wooden staircase that led down. He suggested we turn around and go down backwards as it was very steep and more of a ladder than stairs. Bob went first with Jake, then Emily and her parents, then Anne and Linda and finally I started down. Nate was right above me and just as I stepped off the last rung, his foot slipped off the rung he was on, and he teetered backwards. I instinctively reached up to steady him and my hand landed squarely on his bottom.

"Yeow!" said Nate.

"Are you OK?" I asked thinking he'd hurt himself.

"Just fine. But you got a handful, didn't you?"

"Sorry."

"I didn't mind a bit," he said looking into my eyes directly as he'd reached the bottom of the stairs and had turned to face me.

He grinned and winked at me. "I know you wanted to – I just gave you an excuse."

His playful answer made my embarrassment vanish.

"Down here are all the animal pens," said Dave, "and if you come this way, we can go see the stables."

He led us along a walkway that had waist-high dividers separating it from the pens on either side. The barn was a maze of narrow walkways, pens, and gates.

The stable area had a much higher ceiling than the area with the pens and was much brighter. Each horse had its own tall stall with a half-height gate. There were six horses and all but two turned around and faced out looking at us as we walked the length of the stables. They appeared to be all the same breed of horse that we'd had pulling our wagon earlier. They were all tall and black with white blazes down their noses.

"Meet Fred and Aster, Ginger and Roger, and you met Gene and Kelly earlier," said Dave introducing us to the horses. "Gene and Kelly are being anti-social because I've just given them their lunch."

"Someone a fan of old musicals?" asked Linda.

"Do Gene and Kelly always work together?" asked Bob.

"Yes and yes," replied Dave. "Each pair works as a team, but we also use 4 or all 6 together when we pull different things. It takes all six to pull the fire wagon."

"You have a fire wagon? Cool," said Bob.

"We can go see it but first let's go through here."

At the end of the row of stalls, there was a wide sliding door like the one we'd entered upstairs. We didn't exit through it, but through a smaller door to the right of them leading back into the area with all the pens.

We walked by a pen with three goats.

"This is Rachel, Monica and Phoebe," said Dave. "Yes, they are friendly." He emphasized friend.

All three came towards us and put their heads over the short wall that divided the pen from the walkway.

"Is there a Ross, Joey or Chandler boy goat?" asked Linda.

"No. A neighbour lends us his billy goat when we need a boyfriend. Over here is my son's pig. He raised her from a piglet and hopes to win with her at the state fair this summer."

"What's her name," asked Ann.

"I'm embarrassed to say," said Dave.

"It's ok, we don't offend easily," said Anne.

"Bacon," said Dave.

"Ha!" said Anne. "Like your cat!"

"Bacon makes more sense for a pig," said Ann.

Emily frowned. "How could your son ever see his pet pig as bacon."

"I think he's thinking of all the piglets she'll have being bacon," said Dave. "He really likes bacon. I mean the breakfast food. But he also really likes his pig."

"Is it true that pigs are smart?" asked Bob.

"As farm animals go, yes."

"Then wouldn't she be offended to be objectified as simply a bacon producing machine?" said Linda.

"I've never given that much thought, Mam," said Dave. "Frankly, the only thing she takes offence to is not being fed on time. We took down the clock from over there because if DJ didn't feed her right after school, she'd bust down the door and come to the house looking for him. It's like she could tell he should be here by 4:30. Now that there's no clock she doesn't get ornery until it's dark. Could be a coincidence or she might just be able to tell time."

"That's Some Pig," said Linda laughing and looking for a response, "You know, Charlotte's Web, the spider writes 'Some Pig' to save Wilbur?" There was a collective groan and Dave took that as his cue to move on.

He led us out a door and back outside. From this side of the building, we could see that the barn sat on a hill with the lower level also being at ground level at the back of the barn. We could see the sliding door to the stable behind us on the left as Dave led us across another small patch of snow into a third building. I'd not noticed it before because it was behind and below the barn with respect to the upper level we'd entered at the beginning of our tour.

Before we'd even entered, I knew what was ahead. I could hear feathers rustling and clucking and expected to see chickens. What I hadn't anticipated was the spectacle of multi-coloured, ruffled, fluffy and strange-looking chickens squawking and jumping away from our intrusion.

"What kind of chickens are these?" asked Anne. "They're awesome."

"Several different kinds of Polish, silver and golden, Houdans, Sultan, Silkie Bantams and some I can't remember. They're May's girls."

Jake started to cry, and the chicken coop erupted in flapping and clucking.

"We better get outta here or there'll be no eggs tomorrow," said Dave. "Come through here." He pointed to a door leading out of the chicken coop into another part of the building.

"Look, Jake. A tractor," said Bob shaking Jake's little hands and using them to point at the big green John Deere that was backed into the big garage-like area we'd just entered. There were big doors that rattled with the wind and there were streaks of snow on the dirt floor that had blown through the cracks under and between the big door panels that were at least 15 feet tall. Jake stopped crying and stared wide-eyed at the big green machine.

"Kids always love tractors," said Dave.

We followed Dave around the tractor. Parked beside it were several pieces of modern farm equipment that Bob and Jake both seemed to be enjoying exploring as they detoured from our straight line to wander around each piece. We walked past a big red machine Dave said was a 'combine' and behind it, along with the wagon we'd rode in there were two other horse-drawn vehicles. There was a red fire truck complete with a big water tank, neatly coiled hoses, and two long ladders that ran down either side. The other was an actual sleigh – like one you'd imagine belonged to Santa Claus except instead of being red it was a gleaming black, gold and white.

"I bet that looks impressive hitched to your beautiful black horses," said Ann running her hand over the curved side of the seating cabin.

"It's like a carriage for a winter princess," said Anne.

"Or winter brides," said Linda nudging Anne as if to suggest it as an option for them.

"It's been booked for quite a few weddings. We have wheels to turn it into a carriage so we can use it all year round," explained Dave.

"It could be very romantic," said Anne slipping her arm through Linda's.

"Or it could be exceptionally cold and miserable," said Ann to Lane.

"I see a plan coming together," said Emily rubbing her hands together and obviously not sharing her mother's negative attitude, and continuing to push her vision for Anne and Linda's wedding. "Winter wedding at the inn, Dave bringing the brides in a horse-drawn sleigh to awaiting guests."

"I think you're further along planning than we are," said Anne, throwing her arm across Emily's shoulder and giving her an amiable sidelong hug. "We totally appreciate your enthusiasm."

"I just love love," said Emily. "And you guys are obviously in it."

"When you find the person you belong with, you shouldn't let her go," said Nate. He looked at me and smiled. I felt he was directing the comment to me, but I wasn't sure. He could have been referring to Anne and Linda or maybe he was speaking for himself. Thinking about it later that night when I was alone in my room, I was less sure it was about them and more sure he was implying he didn't want to let me go. I fell asleep with a warm heart thinking that Nate was as glad to be spending time with me as I was at having the chance to be here with him.

CHAPTER 26

I had a long shopping list for New Year's Eve supplies. I knew the shops would be busy, so I slipped out of the house at 8 am before anyone else had come down for breakfast. I wrote a detailed note saying I'd gone out and listed possible breakfast options. I left the note beside a large thermos of coffee and I hoped that, by now, Maddie, Anne and Linda would feel enough at home to help themselves.

I'd not shared all my plans for New Year's Eve with Maddie. I'd told her my fondest memories of New Year's Eve were from my childhood and teens when it was a neighborhood event. The families that occupied our block of rowhouses in central Baltimore would congregate in one house. There would be drinks and snacks all evening long as everyone brought something to share. The adults would play cards. The older kids would watch the little ones until they fell asleep, and then would try to sneak drinks and cigarettes when their elders weren't paying attention.

As midnight approached, we'd gather around the radio to listen to the count down. We'd shout Happy New Year and sing Auld Lang Syne; the couples would kiss, and we kids would point and giggle. Then, when the song was done, our host would start making breakfast.

"Breakfast after midnight? That's brilliant!" Maddie had said. "It makes perfect sense. I don't know why it never occurred to me to do it!"

When I'd run my plans by Ann and Emily, they thought it would be a fun change but they both insisted we not have a big dinner, so we'd have room for my pancakes after midnight. Emily, in particular, was excited to have a new family tradition based on my childhood memories. Ann didn't protest, but I could tell she was just going along with it because Emily had been so enthusiastic. Ann let it be known that she preferred to get dressed up and go to a party or a club but since that wasn't an option this year, whatever made Emily happy was OK with her. Just one of the many ways she was just like her mother.

Betsy always preferred to go out for New Year's Eve and as soon as Ann was old enough to join us, the two of them went all out to dress up in something new and glamorous. I always thought Ann was prettier without the makeup she and Betsy insisted they could not be seen without. Despite Betsy's explanation that going without makeup would be like being only half-dressed and her fear of what others would say if she showed up without it, I never understood it. But, it wasn't an argument worth having so I would work or watch TV while the two of them spent hours getting dolled up to go out.

The year Ann turned 21, Betsy insisted we buy her a fur coat for New Year's Eve. I couldn't understand why it was necessary because it was a few steps from the house to the cab and then another few to the country club entrance where we'd check our coats. Betsy had a rich chestnut brown full-length mink, and she selected an identical one for Ann. I protested, not because of the money, but because I thought Ann should decide what sort of coat she wanted or choose between a coat and some other substantial gift like jewelry. I was overruled.

Ann had been thrilled to have a matching coat. They'd even gone out and bought matching boots and gloves that also had to be changed to evening gloves and high heels that matched their dresses after making an entrance in their coats.

For my wife and daughter, New Year's Eve was about evening gowns and hairstyles and afterwards discussing who wore what. I was glad I could simply wear my same black tux and black bow tie and not get involved in all the garment drama.

So, it was no surprise when Ann insisted it wasn't a proper New Year's Eve celebration if we didn't get dressed up. I told her I'd envisioned a cozy casual affair and she was appalled. She'd conceded formal was too much but had taken a hard stance that it had to be at least cocktail attire including a jacket for the gentlemen. I knew I'd have the excuse of cooking to remove my jacket, so I agreed and vowed to myself to find an excuse for Bob and Lane to get out of theirs too. The week before she came, Maddie had asked about attire for the evening. I'd passed my daughter's requested dress code on to Maddie, Anne, and Linda, with my apologies. I hoped they hadn't gone to too much trouble or expense as a result.

My rounds to the butcher, bakery, cheese shop and grocery store didn't take me as long as I'd thought. Except for the grapes Maddie had requested, I'd pre-ordered everything. At each stop, my order was packed and ready to go so I was in and out in record time. By 10:30 I was back. I parked the Jeep by the side door where it would be easier to unload everything into the kitchen and storage area. Bob must have heard me because he was there, at the door, when I got out of the car.

"Looks like we aren't going to go hungry," he said with a happy chuckle as he helped me carry in the boxes and bags of food.

I checked the time on the kitchen clock once I'd finished putting away my acquisitions; it was 10:45. I was ahead of schedule and that gave me a little burst of pride in my efficiency and organization. I'd been thinking about and planning this evening for weeks. I'd worked out a timetable for today so I could be sure to get everything done.

I'd also prepared a schedule and a special New Year's Eve menu. I'd printed both out on heavy cream-colored stationery. The girls had wanted to know what we were eating. Apparently, it was important so they could pace themselves accordingly. Although the design was rudimentary, I was pleased with the way it had turned out. I'd even inserted a Happy New Year graphic at the top which had tested the limits of my computer skills. I could have asked Ann or Emily to help but I'd wanted it to be a surprise for them as well. I took out the schedule from the drawer with the breakfast menus and pinned it to the bulletin board in the kitchen.

"Good morning, Nate," said Maddie as she came into the kitchen carrying her coffee cup. "Thanks for the coffee." She rinsed her cup and started to put it in the dishwasher. I liked that she felt at home here and she knew her way around, but I still jumped in and took the cup because I liked to wait on her.

"Afraid I'll put it in wrong?" she asked.

I wasn't sure, but I think she was teasing. "No. But you're my guest." I turned the cup in the dishwasher, so the handle lined up in the same direction as all the other cups and rearranged several that were already in the dishwasher, so they were sorted by type. The big wide yellow cups at the front and the taller blue ones at the back.

I looked up and saw Maddie watching me with her eyebrows raised curiously. "I got it now. Yellow in front, blue in the back." She tapped her finger to her temple suggesting she'd made a mental note of it.

"I'm sorry I wasn't here to make you breakfast. I wanted to get my errands done before the stores got busy."

"I was going to offer to pick up anything you needed because Anne and Linda were thinking of going into town to look around."

"I don't need anything. And I got the grapes you wanted."

"You're too efficient. I guess you have the whole day planned out?"

"Of course. And it's all written out for you over there." I pointed to the bulletin board.

New Year's Eve Agenda

Day at Leisure
4:30   Afternoon Tea – Living Room
8:00   Cocktails
8:30   Grazing dinner
Midnight   Toast to the New Year
00:30   Breakfast Before Bed

Maddie went over and read it out loud. "At leisure until 4:30 afternoon tea, then cocktails and grazing from 8 until midnight, followed by breakfast before bed. Sounds lovely! How can I help?"

"I have everything under control."

"But I enjoy helping. Anne and Linda can go exploring and I can stay and help."

"You should go enjoy yourself."

"So…I'd be in the way?"

"I didn't say that. I just want you to do whatever makes you happy."

"I'm happy to help you."

"Ann's taking care of everything for tea, so I'm going to do prep for dinner now, so I'm out of her way later."

"Just put me to work," said Maddie. "I'm all yours."

I pulled my to-do list from the drawer. "Let's see." I looked over my list trying to decide what item I could easily assign Maddie. "How about cleaning mushrooms?"

"Sure." Maddie headed to the sink and started washing her hands.

I got out two white aprons and handed one to Maddie.

She tied it on. "Good idea. I usually don't think to put one on until I've got something all over me."

I picked up the large paper bag from the counter by the fridge and handed it to her. "Here are the mushrooms."

"Wash or brush?"

"I would rinse, wipe dry, then cut out the stem and a bit of the center to make room for stuffing."

"Got it. What are we stuffing them with?"

"Crab."

"Mmm. Sounds yummy. Do you want me to save any of the stems for something else?" She dumped the mushrooms into the colander I'd handed her.

"No need." I returned to the fridge to gather what I needed for the stuffing.

Anne and Linda waltzed into the kitchen. "Can we help?"

"I thought you girls were going to town?" said Maddie.

"We were. But it looks like Nate's put you to work."

"Her choice! I didn't make her. Go have fun. Just be home in time for tea." I pointed to the schedule on the bulletin board.

"We have something for you, Nate. Would this be a bad time to give it to you? You look busy," said Linda holding up a large silver gift bag with Happy New Year in big letters on the side.

"Now is fine, but you shouldn't have."

"It's nothing big." Linda passed me the bag.

"It might need an explanation," said Anne.

I opened the bag and, wrapped in silver tissue paper, was a puzzle. "1000 pieces and it looks challenging," I studied the picture of rows of vintage candy bar wrappers filling the whole picture.

"It's kind of a family tradition," explained Anne. "Every New Year's Eve Mom would get us a puzzle to do while we waited for midnight."

"This is great. I was going to set up a couple of tables so we could play cards. We can make one a puzzle table."

Anne and Linda followed me into the dining area. We shifted the long table closer to the buffet. Then they helped me move the smaller tables to make a couple of game playing areas. On the first table, I put out my card-playing tablecloth, the one with hearts, diamonds, spades, and clubs embroidered around the bottom. I set out two brand new decks of cards and card-themed coasters. I covered the slightly larger table against the far wall with a plain white tablecloth. I opened the puzzle and dumped out the pieces. Anne and Linda teased me, but helped, as I made sure all the pieces were face up. Then I propped the box against the wall, so it was all set and begging for someone to sit down and start assembling it.

"Can we do anything else?" asked Anne.

"You girls go have fun. Just don't be late for tea at 4:30. You may want to leave time to change."

I felt compelled to remind them of the time because my daughter had been emphatic that tea would be served at 4:30 sharp. Evidently, this was an important New Year's Eve tradition for Lane's family she wanted to share with Emily and me.

By the time I got back to the kitchen, Maddie had finished her mushroom task and was ready for another. We worked side by side checking items off my list. Mushrooms stuffed, skewers marinating after being soaked and threaded with strips of chicken, shrimp cooked, peeled, and arranged on a platter, lemons cut into slices and wedges, sauces made, cheeses grated, and Maddie's grapes washed. After we'd wrapped up and put everything in the fridge for later, Maddie helped me set up the bar and buffet areas in the dining room.

I looked over my list. "I think that's all for now."

Maddie looked disappointed rather than elated we'd finished. "Are you sure there's nothing else? Maybe Ann would like help preparing things for tea?"

"I have Emily to help me. I just need you both out of the way," said Ann coming into the kitchen from the back stairs.

"That's my cue. Will you be OK on your own for a spell?" I asked Maddie.

"Of course. I have my book, or maybe I'll get a head-start on that puzzle," she said with a wink.

240

"Oh, Dad! You remembered the puzzles," said Ann.

"I can't take credit. It was Anne and Linda who brought it."

"Really? How could they know?"

I had no idea what she was talking about.

"Don't you remember? Mom always left a new puzzle for me when I had to stay home with the babysitter on New Year's Eve."

"What a happy coincidence. A family tradition we share," said Maddie.

My daughter didn't look happy at the coincidence.

"Sorry Pumpkin," I said. "I remember your mother would always make sure you had something fun to do whenever we went out to a party. I just didn't put New Year's and puzzles together."

Maddie tried to help smooth things over. "But Nate told us about your tradition of dressing up."

"He remembers that because he was always pacing around, cross about being late, while we got ready. He never understood being fashionably late and making an entrance."

"I'm afraid I'm not fashionable and rarely make an entrance," Maddie said with a self-deprecating laugh.

"But you've not been late," I said to her.

"At least not yet," she replied with a grin.

"Watch out if you are." Ann switched to a deep voice mimicking me "If you're not early you're late."

"I don't sound like that."

"Fair warning. He can be a real pill when kept waiting," said Ann to Maddie.

"Unless I can do anything to help, I should get out of your way," said Maddie.

"Go. Besides, Dad needs his nap. Right, Dad?"

"Just going to recharge the batteries. A half-hour and I'll be good to go."

"Be down in time to get the fire going by four o'clock. Unless you want me to get Lane or Bob to do it?"

"I'm happy to set the fire," said Maddie. "Unless there's some trick to your fireplace I need to learn."

I sipped my arm through Maddie's and started leading her out of the kitchen. "We're leaving. I'll be down in plenty of time."

Maddie accompanied me through the living room and upstairs. She went into her room. I went into mine to lie down for a bit. I'd set my alarm, just in case, but I was up exactly 30 minutes later. I heard Anne and Linda giggling and whispering as they came upstairs and went into their room. It made me smile, hearing them, thinking about how happy they were together and how wonderful it was they'd found each other.

I was surprised that Maddie hadn't known that they were more than friends.

She seemed genuinely happy for them and very accepting. Many folks of my generation still find same-sex couples hard to comprehend. I remember the first gay couple that booked at the inn shortly after we'd opened. A man named Dan had called to book a room for the weekend for him and his partner John. Betsy had answered the phone and when he said partner, she assumed he was a business partner.

"Will your wives be joining you?" she'd asked.

Dan was not surprised by Betsy's assumption or question because it was not that unusual for him. He very politely said no and that he and John would only require one room. When Betsy hung up the phone she came out to the shed where I was trying to get the lawnmower running. I remember the moment well because she was terribly upset.

"I think we might have some problem guests next weekend," she'd said.

She'd been so agitated, I was relieved the phone call hadn't been bad news. "Why do you say that?"

"I think they might be gay."

"I don't see why that's a problem," I'd said. "This lawnmower… it's a problem."

"What will the other guests think when they see two men sharing a room? It could ruin our reputation."

"I doubt that."

"What about AIDS and all – won't the other guests be worried?"

I remember her going on about all the things the other guests might think while I continued to work on the lawnmower. As it turned out, Dan, an artist, and John, an architect, were delightful. They lived in Manhattan and were thrilled at the open space, hiking and beauty of both Bar Harbor and Acadia National Park. Contrary to Betsy's fears, they got along so well with the other two couples who were staying here that weekend the six of them returned to the inn together a couple of years later.

By then, Betsy had passed. After learning the news, Dan sent me a kind note expressing their condolences along with a painting he'd done of boats heading off into the sun. In the painting, he had christened one of the boats Betsy. I was surprised and touched by the gift because he'd done it despite the fact that Dan and John had barely seen Betsy. She'd confined herself to our quarters most of the time they were at the inn. She'd greeted all the other guests that weekend as they'd arrived but had not come to greet Dan and John saying she wasn't feeling well. I suspected she wasn't being entirely honest, but I couldn't be sure because she'd been having more frequent bad spells due to her treatments.

Betsy had always avoided situations that were new or uncomfortable. She would withdraw rather than risk not knowing exactly the right thing to say or do. It probably contributed to her avoiding travelling with me internationally.

Betsy was proud of not changing as the world around her evolved. Although she was reserved in public, I was appalled by the elitist, closed-minded attitudes she would spout when we were alone behind closed doors.

I was glad my granddaughter showed no signs of her grandmother's attitudes, but Ann was another story. She'd adopted many of her mother's rigid and narrow-minded opinions. Her insistence on dressing up for New Year's Eve was one of the more benign, but I feared her coolness towards Anne and Linda was also evidence of her mother's influence.

I grumbled to myself as I got my dress pants and shirt for later this evening from the closet to make sure they weren't wrinkled. I knew Ann would be disappointed if I wore the same thing for tea and for tonight. I changed from my jeans and polo to a pair of navy blue cotton pants and a blue plaid flannel shirt I'd recently bought. The clerk in the men's shop in town had said it looked 'dashing' with my gray hair. I wasn't convinced I was dashing. The deep blue did look good, and the plaid was understated so it wouldn't look ridiculous on an old guy like me.

It was nearly four. I'd assured Ann I'd have the fire going in the hearth on time, so I headed to the living room to light it.

"Oh good! You changed." Ann barely looked up from setting up what she had decided would be the 'tea cart', the narrow table that usually stood behind the sofa in my private sitting room. I'd removed the lamps and boats that usually occupied it, and put them in my office. I presumed she'd had Lane or Bob carry it down to the living room.

Earlier in the week she and Emily had gone through her mother's china and silver to select pieces for today. The centerpiece was the silver tea service Ann and Betsy had found in an antique shop in Oxford when we'd visited her there as a student. We'd shipped it home along with the boats I'd bought in the Portobello Market area in Notting Hill. Betsy had only used it twice that I can remember but it had sat proudly on our dining room buffet, polished regularly by our cleaning lady, until we'd packed it up to move to the inn. Fortunately, Betsy had insisted on wrapping each piece tightly in cellophane before wrapping it in the packing paper, so it hadn't taken Ann and Emily long to polish it back to its gleaming glory for today's tea.

"That fire feels great, Grandpa," said Emily coming from the kitchen carrying two of Betsy's tiered china serving towers. One laden with pretty sandwiches and the other with the tiny pastries I'd picked up at the bakery this morning.

"Thank you, my dear. I do as I'm told."

"We all do," said Bob who was wearing an apron smeared with what looked like jam and carrying a tray with glass bowls and a plate of mini scones.

"Put those here and go get the cups," ordered Ann.

"Yes Mum," said Bob, looking at me as he turned to go, raising his eyebrows as if to say, "help me". I shrugged in silent solidarity.

"And take off that dirty apron before you get back," Ann called after him.

While Ann finished orchestrating the tea set up, I took the wood carrier out to the shed to fill it up, so I'd have it handy for later should we need more. Coming back through the kitchen, I found Ann waiting by the stove with the kettle. The silver teapot and the box of tea she'd brought with her from England were on the counter beside the stove.

"Anything else I can do?" I asked.

"Just let everyone know tea will be served as planned."

Back in the living room, I was shocked at the transformation it had undergone in the few minutes I'd been gone. The furniture was shifted, and my boats had vanished from the coffee table and side tables; replaced with lace doilies and folded linen cocktail napkins. Eight multicolored and ornate bone china teacups and saucers sat in two neat rows beside the large silver tray. On the tray, were the silver sugar bowl and milk pitcher, a glass bowl of lemon wedges, a stack of silver teaspoons, and an open space for the teapot. At the far end of the table, there was the plate of scones with the glass bowls of clotted cream and strawberry jam and the three-tiered serving plates. Beside the food was a stack of eight luncheon plates from Betsy's finest china set. I hadn't seen those dishes in at least a decade. Ann must have found them when she unpacked the teacups and silver from the boxes stored in the basement.

Maddie came in just as Ann returned from the kitchen carrying the large silver teapot.

"It's as if we've been transported to an English manor," said Maddie.

"It's 4:30," said Ann. "Where is everyone?"

"We're here," said Linda.

Anne headed straight for Jake in his playpen. "Look at my handsome Godson all dressed up for tea!"

Jake was handsomely dressed in a pair of pale blue pants and a white shirt with a tiny pale blue bow tie at his chin. He was hopping up and down clinging to the sides of his playpen that they'd set up a safe distance from the fire and loaded up with several of his favorite toys. Emily and Bob took the seats on either side of the playpen. Lane was standing by the fire. He'd worn a tweed jacket and stood with his hands clasped at his back, seemingly waiting to be served. He looked comfortable, and it made me think this scene was very familiar to him.

Meanwhile, Maddie had gone over to the tea cart and was admiring and complimenting Ann and Emily on the décor and food.

"Since you've both already done so much," she said, "shall I be mother?"

Ann responded harshly, "You'll not be mother in this house."

Maddie stepped back from the table. "I'm sorry, I only meant to help."

I felt bad for Maddie. Although she pretended nothing had happened, I could see her expression was not the natural smile it had been before Ann's rebuke. Maddie took a seat at the furthest end of the sofa with her daughter and Linda between her and the remaining seats Ann and Lane would likely occupy.

Everyone except Ann and Lane looked uncomfortable. Ann poured the tea and formally invited each person to make their selections from the food. Despite the hot tea and warm fire, the room was chilly and the conversation measured.

"What does one usually talk about over tea?" asked Linda, obviously trying to break the tension.

"Traditionally, it's time to recap the events of the day or discuss details for the evening ahead," explained Lane.

"If it's only the ladies," interrupted Ann, "the topics include children and gossip."

"It was also the time for parents to see their children before bed, if the nanny brought them down for tea," added Lane.

"So strange. The nanny spent more time raising the children than their parents," said Linda.

"Not really different now," said Emily with a sigh. "I drop Jake at daycare and we don't see him again until dinner time."

"A nanny at least kept the children at home rather than shuffled around," said Lane.

"A nanny would be great," said Emily. "Especially if she did laundry."

"Did you have a nanny, Lane?" asked Bob.

"Nanny Meg. She looked after Georgie and me until we went off to boarding school."

"Glad you didn't send me off to boarding school," said Emily.

"Your Mum would have nothing of it. She insisted on staying home with you."

"As it should be," said Ann.

"Not necessarily," said Anne. "I think it was better to have a career woman as my role model."

"I was lucky your grandparents lived nearby and they wanted to take care of you while I was at work," said Maddie. "Not everyone has that luxury."

"I feel guilty enough leaving Jake at daycare," said Emily. "I admire women like you, Maddie, who showed us it's possible to be a good mother and have a career."

"I had career aspirations too," said Ann, "but my mother was always there for me, and I wanted that for you too."

I could see the conversation veering toward conflict. I quickly interjected to change the subject. "So... This evening we'll start with cocktails at eight."

My daughter glared at me.

"You said you wanted me to set up the bar," said Bob sitting up and leaning forward as if he were ready to sprint from the room.

"We have plenty of time for that," I said.

"Would anyone like more tea?" said Lane.

Like magic, the distraction of more tea seemed to break the tension and the conversation veered to the subject of food, how good the tea, pastries and sandwiches were and then to the menu for the evening.

"I'll have you all know I've typed up the menu. It'll be on display later for cocktails," I announced proudly.

"Impressive," said Emily.

"Do you have a cocktail menu too? I'm your man behind the bar, or in front of it in this case. So, I need to know," said Bob.

Ann and Emily accepted no help cleaning up the tea. So, Maddie, Anne and Linda decided to go for a short walk before dressing for dinner. Bob and Lane helped me set up the bar. I felt anxiously excited for the evening, and I checked my lists several times to make sure I'd not forgotten anything. I went over my plans in my head repeatedly, even while I was up in my room getting changed. It was my first New Year's Eve with my whole family together in a very long time and I wanted it to be perfect. I realized that even though Maddie and her daughter weren't actually family, I felt like they belonged here, and I hoped tonight would bring everyone closer together.

CHAPTER 27

"Air Canada Flight 1837, to Phoenix now boarding Group 4," announced the gate agent signalling it was my turn to make my way onto the plane. Once settled in my seat I sent a text to Nate letting him know I was on time. The flight was full, as I expected it would be, with Canadians escaping winter in Toronto for sunshine and golf in Arizona. I was grateful for my window seat, as I watched the snow-covered city fade away as we climbed into the clouds.

I took out my book to read to pass the time. I bunched up my scarf into a makeshift pillow and leaned away giving the person in the middle seat as much room as possible. But I couldn't concentrate on my book. When Claire had suggested I invite Nate to join us in Arizona I thought she was nuts. Even more of a surprise was Nate's enthusiasm when I'd extended her invitation to him. I'd only mentioned it in passing, but he'd obviously been thinking about it because he brought it up on New Year's Eve.

I ran into Nate in the hall outside my room after changing for dinner.

"You look stunning," he'd said.

"Thanks. Claire helped me shop. I thought the sequins were too much, but she insisted."

"They sparkle, just like you."

"That's what she said."

"Great minds. I can't wait to meet her. Perhaps in Arizona?"

I didn't think he was serious, and he didn't mention it again that evening. I smiled to myself remembering that night. Nate had escorted me downstairs, and he was grinning with pride at my surprise at the transformation of the inn's dining area.

I'd seen the tables he'd set up earlier for cards and the puzzle but, in the time we'd gone up to dress for dinner, four tall cocktail-height tables with black table cloths and barstools had materialized. Each had a tall silver pillar candle in the center with black cocktail napkins with Happy New Year in silver lettering fanned out around them. Large candelabras also stood on the bar and buffet area, each with five silver tapers. Small tea lights twinkled in glass holders around the serving area. The usually bright overhead lights were dimmed, and the room shimmered with candlelight.

"You'll find the menu for the evening on the buffet table," he said formally.

"And remember Bob has volunteered to tend bar this evening so please keep him busy." Nate gestured with his hand that I should move to the bar while he excused himself to the kitchen. Bob poured me a glass of wine, and I checked out the menu Nate had typed up.

New Year's Eve Menu
Cocktail Snacks
Assorted Olives and Pickles
Chips and Nuts
Hors d'oeuvres
Shrimp Cocktail
Smoked Salmon Canape
Chicken Satay with Peanut Sauce
Crab Mushroom Caps
Main Course
Cheese Fondue
Shabu Shubu Beef and Vegetables
Dessert / Late Night Snack
Maddie's Christmas Cake
Emily's Peanut Butter Balls
Cheese and Fruit
Breakfast Before Bed
Eggs Benedict
(choice of ham, crab or Florentine)
Buttermilk Pancakes
Sausage and Bacon
Toast or English Muffins
Assorted Jams

Even though I'd helped in the kitchen that morning, I had no idea that Nate had planned all this. I worried he wouldn't enjoy the evening with such an elaborate menu to manage.

Anne and Linda came in a few minutes later, dressed in coordinating black and silver cocktail dresses. They were as blown away as I was.

"Wow. This is amazing," said Linda.

"I'm glad you approve," said Nate returning from the kitchen followed by a young woman I didn't know.

"This is Sarah. She's been indispensable this past season and she's going to help me this evening."

We introduced ourselves. Sarah excused herself to go to the kitchen while Nate made sure Bob was on top of our beverage needs. Anne opted for Bob's 'New Year's Mule' he swore was sure to kick out the old year.

Linda was wary. "I'll stick with wine."

A few minutes later, Emily brought Jake down. She looked festive in a bright red dress, and he had on a black and white onesie that looked like a tiny tuxedo. Her parents came in last, just as Sarah began passing the cold hors d'oeuvres on large silver trays that she placed on the buffet table after offering us all our first ones.

Seeing Ann and Lane's attire, I was glad Claire had nudged me towards a dressier outfit. Ann wore a raw silk dress in deep emerald green. Her hair and makeup looked as if she'd brought in a stylist. She had on a diamond and emerald pendant and matching earrings that I couldn't help but admire.

"An extravagant wedding gift from Lane's parents," she'd said.

I got the distinct impression she was making sure I knew that the gems were real. Lane wore a black suit with a dark tie with flecks of emerald that matched Ann's dress. I was certain that wasn't a coincidence.

Nate rarely sat down the whole evening. He was in and out of the kitchen with Sarah as they set up each course on the buffet. Once we'd finished with the Main Course, Sarah left to spend the rest of the evening with her parents and boyfriend. Despite our repeated offers to help, Nate continued to wait on us. He cleared and replaced plates and refilled glasses when Bob wasn't quick enough at the bar.

Anne and Ann spent much of the evening working on the puzzle while Lane, Linda, Emily, Bob, and I played Hearts at the card table.

"Isn't it nice when the kids play so well together?" said Nate to me nodding towards our daughters as he refilled my wine glass. I agreed although I was a bit surprised our girls were laughing and chatting as the puzzle gradually took shape. I was also happy, for Nate's sake, that everyone seemed to really enjoy the party he'd obviously worked hard to arrange.

As midnight approached, Nate turned on the TV so we could watch the countdown and ball-drop in Times Square. Bob passed out glasses of champagne and Nate brought out a big bowl of grapes, the stems all neatly trimmed so the grapes were in little bunches of three or four grapes each.

The couples paired off as the countdown started. Nate stood next to me and put his arm around my waist. At the stroke of midnight, we all called out, "Happy New Year" and toasted and Nate took me in his arms and kissed me. Really kissed me.

I pulled back a little and quickly scanned the room. Ann and Lane, Anne and Linda, Emily and Bob were all kissing and not looking at us. Nate let go of me and I realized he thought I was pulling away from him. I smiled and reached my hands up around his neck and pulled him back in for another quick kiss.

He grinned. "I didn't need any of your grapes to be lucky this New Years' Eve."

"Everyone still needs to have grapes." I pulled away from him and picked up the bowl to pass them around.

"Why grapes?" asked Emily.

"For health, wealth and happiness all year," explained Anne.

Bob helped himself to another bunch. "I'll have extra then."

Ann wagged her champagne glass. "Does fermented grapes with bubbles count?"

"I can't imagine being any happier than I am right now," said Nate to me. "But I'll have a few, just in case."

It wasn't until everyone else had left, and it was just Nate and me at the inn, that the subject of this trip to Arizona came up again. We'd called Claire together to confirm dates and he'd stunned me by accepting her invitation to come for the full three weeks I was going to stay with her. We sat down together at Nate's computer and booked him an airline ticket departing and returning on the same days as I'd booked.

It's now been almost a month since we were together at New Years. We'd talked more frequently than our usual Thursday night calls and exchanged a lot of emails. Nate had been obsessed with making sure we discussed the details for the trip in advance. We'd talked about things we'd like to do, and he'd researched dates and times for various events we might want to attend. But now the moment was approaching, and I was feeling nervous about the whole thing. Three weeks is a long time to spend with someone you don't really know.

Nate's flight was scheduled to land about an hour after mine. We'd decided I would get my bags, pick up the rental car and then swing back to the terminal to pick him up. He'd called me just as I was getting settled in the white Nissan Versa they'd assigned me, and within minutes, we were in the car together.

"Wow! Look at that cactus!" Nate pointed to a huge prickly pear that loomed beside us as we drove out of the airport onto the interstate.

The sun baked down on us as we drove the long, straight, stretch of I-10 that ran through a very empty desert landscape. Other than a giant tumbleweed we watched explode, as it rolled into the path of the car in front of us, there wasn't anything exciting to see. It wasn't until we neared Tucson that the scenery shifted to include jagged mountains in the distance.

We chatted about our flights, the weather we'd left behind, and the time passed quickly. Closer to our destination, Nate read the directions to Claire's house from the map I'd printed out.

We pulled into the driveway of a boxy, sand-coloured brick house. It had a flat roof, bars on the front windows and a shoulder-height brick wall with a metal gate separating the house from the street. I worried I'd got the address wrong because it didn't seem like the sort of place Claire would like. We got out walked through the gate into the courtyard and up to a large wooden door with a heavy iron knocker.

Claire answered immediately, burst out the door with open arms, hugged me enthusiastically and kissed me on both cheeks.

"You made it! You must be Nate!"

Nate extended his hand. "Delighted to finally meet you, Claire."

"Welcome!" Claire ignored his hand and gave him a hug and kisses as well. "Where are your bags?"

"In the car. I wasn't sure we had the right house." I grinned at Nate who was looking stunned by Claire's effusive greeting.

"You, of all people, I can count on to find your way." She followed me back to the car.

I popped the trunk with the car's remote and Nate opened it while I got my purse and our heavy coats from the backseat.

"I'll take those." Claire grabbed the coats. "You won't be needing those for a while."

Nate groaned as he lifted my suitcase out of the trunk.

"I can take that. It's heavy," I said.

He snorted, handed me my carry-on bag, and waved me away. I didn't insist. I took my purse and carry-on and closed the trunk. Nate picked up both our suitcases and Claire led the way into the house carrying our coats.

Based on the outside, I hadn't expected to be impressed by the inside. The entrance area opened into a large living room that had floor-to-ceiling windows running almost the entire length of the room. To the right of the entrance was a hallway that Claire scooted down, disappearing into a room and emerging without our coats.

"I've hung your coats in the laundry room. Come this way." She headed through the living room and to the left. "Your room is this way."

At the end of a short hallway, she pointed to the furthest door. "That is your room. Both rooms have ensuite baths, but I thought you two would be more comfortable in this room." Then she pointed across the hall. "My room is this one."

Claire was oblivious to my rising panic as I realized she intended for Nate and me to share a room. I looked at Nate. He swallowed a couple of times and then smiled at Claire and carried our bags into our room without saying anything.

When he was out of earshot, I dragged Claire into her room. "You could have mentioned that your house only had two bedrooms."

"I didn't think of it," she said shrugging. "Is it really a problem?"

"A problem? Kinda. What's he going to think?"

"That he's a very lucky man." She patted me on the shoulder. "Now go to your room and unpack and change out of those winter clothes while I get ready for cocktail hour. The others will be here soon."

"What others?"

"My Green Valley friends. Everyone is looking forward to meeting you."

Claire left me standing in her room. I took a deep breath and closed my eyes for a few seconds to quell my racing mind before facing Nate.

Both our suitcases were on the one large king bed. Nate had opened his and had started unpacking it, making a stack of clothing beside it on the bed.

"I wasn't sure what drawers to use," he said as if the whole situation were perfectly normal. "There's quite a lot of space in the walk-in closet. There are empty drawers in there and in the dresser here." He pointed to the tall dresser in the corner of the room.

"Are you OK with this? I had no idea…"

"I am if you are. Just say so, and I'll get a hotel." He picked up a few items and placed them back into his suitcase.

"No. We can make it work…"

"So…do you want the dresser drawers or the closet drawers?"

We danced around each other unpacking. Thankfully, it was a large room with a large walk-in closet and a spacious ensuite bathroom that had double sinks, a shower, a separate soaking tub and most importantly, the toilet was in a closet-like space with a door. I decided to take over most of the walk-in closet because I figured I could use it as a dressing room. I tried not to think about our sleeping arrangements while I hung up my clothes and changed into a light sleeveless top and a pair of denim capri pants. Nate emerged from the bathroom as I exited the closet. He'd also changed from his travel clothing into a golf shirt and cotton pants

"You look lovely," he said. "Shall we go find our hostess?"

We heard the thumping of the door knocker and saw Claire rushing through the living room to the front hall as we emerged from our room. There was a burst of laughter and voices as a small group of people flowed into the room, each guest was carrying drinks or plates of food. Nate and I stood off to the side, near the large beehive fireplace. Claire greeted everyone and gave directions as to where they should put everything. Once the chaos of the mass arrival was over, Claire introduced us. There were two couples Mary and Marty and Fran and Bill from Wisconsin and Carl from Edmonton.

"They've not even had a chance to see the whole house yet," she explained.

"Then you do that while I open the wine," said Carl heading off towards what I guessed was the kitchen.

The other four went ahead of us outside to the back patio and began setting up the food they'd brought. Claire gave us a quick tour. From the living room, we walked past the wall of glass to the kitchen and then through the kitchen to another hall that had the door to the garage and in the opposite direction, led to the front door. She showed us the powder room by the front entrance, next to the laundry room where she'd hung our coats.

"Now the best part," she said. "Outside."

What I'd thought were large windows were, in fact, big sliding doors that opened up most of the back of the house. The large, covered patio extended the entire length of the house. There were three areas: a grouping of comfortable-looking wicker sofas and chairs that ringed a large low coffee table with a gas fire pit in the center, a large dining table big enough for at least eight people, and an outdoor kitchen complete with a bar area with barstools. Carl was behind the bar setting up glasses and filling them with wine.

In contrast to the gravel and cactus landscape at the front of the house, the view from the back included a swath of green beyond an open area of desert.

"That's the Green Valley Country Club golf course," said Claire. "Fortunately, we're far enough that we don't get many stray balls."

"Unlike our place. Did we tell you our bedroom window was broken this week?" said Mary.

"No!" said Fran.

"I thought I was going to have a heart attack," said Marty. "I was just closing my eyes for a little snooze… and wham. It only broke the outer pane of glass, but it still made a big mess."

Carl walked over to us and handed Fran and Mary glasses of white wine and turned to me. "What's your pleasure, Maddie? We have a Chardonnay and a Shiraz open and there's pop and beer if you prefer those."

"A Shiraz, please."

"I'll take a beer," said Marty.

"I'm busy taking care of the ladies. You know where they are," said Carl heading back to the bar to pour glasses of red wine for Claire and me.

"You're always taking care of the ladies," said Bill sardonically. "I'll get the beers. Nate, you want one?"

"Please." Nate moved closer to me as Carl delivered my glass of wine.

Claire explained that they got together a couple times a week for happy hour. They rotated hosting and it was always potluck, with the non-hosts bringing the food and drink. Today Mary had brought a layered bean dip that she served with tortilla chips and Fran had brought pinwheels made with spicy sausage in puff pastry. Claire set out napkins and cocktail plates and we settled around the large table to eat, drink and talk.

Much of the conversation revolved around advice about everything we should do while we were in Arizona. There were many more things than we could conceivably do in the time we were there but that didn't stop the group from coming up with ideas for local events, attractions and even excursions that stretched across state lines. Everyone agreed with my plan to spend a couple of days at the Tucson Gem and Mineral show.

"I have a couple of badges you could borrow to access the wholesale areas," offered Carl. "Claire and I used them last week and we don't plan to go again."

"I've got us covered," said Nate.

"You do?" I asked surprised.

"I do. I've registered us at the major wholesale venues. As long as you're OK being an associate of the Hope Point Inn, LLC."

"I guess you don't need me then do you," said Carl pretending to pout.

By 6 pm the sun had set, the snacks were eaten, and Mary, Marty, Fran, and Bill left to go home to the rental house they shared. As the temperature outside was quickly dropping, Claire suggested we move to the sofas so we could sit near the fire pit. Carl turned on the gas fire pit, refilled my wine glass and then he and Claire picked up the dishes and empty glasses and left Nate and me alone.

"Are you warm enough?" asked Nate.

"So far. The fire pit is nice."

"It's amazing how fast the temperature dropped when the sun set." He scooted over so that we were touching, shoulder to shoulder.

"Good excuse to sit close?" I teased.

"Do I need an excuse?" He put his arm around my shoulders.

Carl sat down across from us. "Aren't you two looking cozy. Claire and I were wondering if you wanted to go out for dinner? If you can pry yourselves apart for a bit…"

"We were just staying warm," I said, feeling like I needed to explain, perhaps more for Nate's benefit than Carl's.

"We hadn't discussed dinner plans. What do you think?" Nate turned slightly to look at me but kept his arm around me. "Do you think we can be pried apart?" He winked at me, and my embarrassment evaporated.

"I think so. But I'll need a sweater."

Claire decided that we should get into the spirit of Arizona by going to a Mexican restaurant. We had to leave right away. As Carl explained it, they roll up the streets early in Green Valley with most places closing by eight o'clock.

Carl drove us to Manuel's and we had what he asserted were authentic carne asada and enchiladas. The margaritas Carl insisted I try, went down all too easily with the salty chips and homemade salsa. By the time we left, I was a little woozy. The margaritas, the long travel day, and the time change, all caught up with me and I almost nodded off on the short drive home. As soon as we got in the door, I told Nate and Claire that I was ready to turn in.

"I'll just get you both a bottle of water to put by your bed," said Claire.

"You go ahead and get ready for bed," said Nate. "I'll bring the water in a bit."

I was grateful for a little privacy to use the bathroom and do my nightly routine. I turned on the lamps on both sides of the bed and turned out the overhead light but left the ceiling fan going on low. I wondered which side of the bed I should take. I decided on the one furthest from the door. Partly because it was closest to the bathroom but also there was an easily accessible plug for me to charge my cell phone. I'd just crawled under the sheet and was sitting up in bed when Nate knocked on the door and opened it a crack.

"Ok for me to come in?"

I checked to make sure I was decent. "Yes."

Nate came around to my side of the bed and placed a bottle of water on the nightstand.

"Ok if I use the bathroom now?"

I made an affirmative noise and nodded. Nate went to the dresser and took out his pyjamas and carried them into the bathroom. I shut out my light and settled in on my side with my back to Nate's side of the bed. I closed my eyes and, within seconds, I was asleep.

CHAPTER 28

Movement in my bedroom woke me with a start. It was dark, but there was just enough moonlight coming through the bedroom window for me to figure out where I was. As I took a few deep breaths to slow my heart rate, I realized it had been Maddie getting up to use the bathroom that had startled me. She hadn't turned on the light, but I could hear her moving around and the water running before she quietly slipped back into bed. I didn't want her to think she'd woken me, but now that I was awake, I too needed to go. I sat up slowly and looked around. I was a bit nervous walking in the dark and really wanted to turn on a light but didn't so I wouldn't disturb Maddie. Unfortunately, I forgot there was a bench at the foot of the bed, and I walked into it, with a big thump, almost falling onto it. Maddie sat up abruptly and turned on the bedside lamp.

"Are you ok?" she asked squinting and blinking from the sudden light.

"I'm fine. I'm sorry. Go back to sleep."

"Ok. Um. You can put on your light if you need it." She lay back down and pulled the covers over her head.

I put on the bedside light on my side, then shut off hers before going into the bathroom. My cell phone was plugged into the outlet by the sink, and I checked the time. It was only 4:30 but I felt wide awake, and my big toe was throbbing. I decided to shower and dress in the clothes I'd worn the evening before that I'd hung on a hook on the back of the bathroom door. That way I didn't have to leave the bathroom until I was ready to slip out, leaving Maddie to sleep in peace.

Thankfully, there were small nightlights in the hallway, so I made my way to the kitchen without tripping over anything else. The night before Claire had shown me where the coffee supplies were so I made a pot of coffee and looked around for something to do while it brewed. In the living room bookshelf, I found a couple of Arizona guidebooks, but without my reading glasses, that I'd forgotten in the bedroom, I gave up trying to read them.

I poked my head outside the patio door. It was surprisingly cold outside. The coffee pot gurgled and sputtered and gasped a burst of steam which I took as a sign the coffee was done. I went to the laundry room, got my heavy coat, poured myself a cup of coffee and headed outside. I sat on the sofa with my coat draped over my shoulders and my hands wrapped around the warm coffee mug.

The pre-dawn sky was a deep blue that brightened to a pale pink near the horizon. I could hear the high-pitched howl of coyotes that sounded a bit like babies crying and the coos of a family of quails that waddled along the back wall of the yard. There were quite a few rustling sounds in the bushes beyond the wall that I wasn't keen on investigating. The only human sound was the whirr of a golf cart passing on the course behind the house which I guessed was the groundskeeper making his rounds before the first golfers teed off.

The air smelled so different. I'd grown accustomed to the briny, fishy scent of the Atlantic as the scent of outdoors. The sweet, bright floral smell that wafted past me on the patio reminded me of the orange groves of Florida. Betsy and I had driven through them in full bloom on our wedding day as we headed off for our honeymoon trip.

We were married at Sacred Heart church at 11 am followed by a lunch reception at her parent's country club. After speeches and cake cutting, she'd changed from her wedding dress into her going away outfit; a crisply tailored white suit with a pencil-thin skirt and a jacket that cut in sharply at the waist and then flared out over her hips accentuating her perfect figure. Her ensemble was completed with a matching white hat with a spray of fishnet across her eyes, white gloves, and a small white clutch. Her outfit was glamorous and perfect, but I was more interested in seeing her out of it and what was under it.

Betsy waved like Princess Grace from her carriage as we drove off in her father's ragtop Cadillac. But, just a few miles down the road, she asked me to stop and put the top up because the wind was tugging at her hat. She glared at me crossly when I suggested she take off her hat. I pulled over immediately.

We had a four-hour drive ahead of us, across the state to Palm Beach. Because I still had a few weeks of school to complete, our honeymoon would only be three nights, which was a blessing as the hotel Betsy had wanted to stay at, The Breakers, was not the kind of place I could afford on my cook and bartender paycheck. Luckily, my father had given me a little money for the honeymoon, and I'd been able to negotiate a good price for the Sunday and Monday nights of our stay.

When the doorman extended his hand to her, Betsy stepped from the car looking like a movie star and I remember being awed by how graceful she was and how she floated into the lobby as if she owned the place. We showed our marriage license to the clerk at the reception desk for our identification and, noting the date, he congratulated the new Mr. and Mrs. Jacobs. He assured us that he could give us a very romantic room and that there would be a bottle of champagne delivered, compliments of the hotel. He then inquired if we would like him to make dinner reservations as it was nearly 7 pm. He told us the restaurant would be quite busy as it was Saturday night but we also had the option of room service up until 10 pm.

"What would you like, darling?" I asked Betsy.

"I'm not hungry just yet. I think we'll manage with room service."

I was relieved at her answer. I knew Betsy would want to be dressed up for dinner in the restaurant. I was looking forward to getting out of my suit and, getting Betsy out of hers.

The desk clerk handed a Bellman our key. The Bellman picked up our suitcases and we followed him to our room. After unlocking the door and holding it open for us, he carried in our cases and placed them on stands at the foot of the bed. He then demonstrated the light switches, how to open the blinds and the sliding door to the small balcony before handing me the room key.

"Is there anything else Mr. Jacobs?" he asked.

Betsy waved for him to leave. "That will be all." She nodded to me to give him a tip, which I was prepared to do. I was irritated she thought I needed to be reminded.

As soon as the door closed, Betsy began removing her gloves and hat. She placed them on the dresser and moved to stand in front of the glass door looking out at the Atlantic. Her silhouette was a perfect hourglass. I was just about to reach out and place my hands around her waist when there was a knock at the door.

"Room service," called a voice from the corridor.

I opened the door and stepped aside so the dark-suited waiter could wheel in a small cart with a bottle of champagne in an ice bucket, glasses, and a single red rose in a vase.

"Shall I open the wine for you?" he asked.

"No thanks," I said still holding the door open and fishing in my pocket for another bill to tip him. I wanted him to leave so we could be alone.

"Would you like some champagne?" I asked.

"I'd like to unpack first." Betsy turned from the window and opened her case. She looked very stiff and formal in her suit, so I suggested we change into something more comfortable.

"I'm comfortable. But you can change if you like." She started unpacking, hanging several dresses in the small closet.

I wasn't sure if she meant it. I stood there watching her unpack; unsure of what I should do. At the bottom of her suitcase was a neatly folded pile of white lacy material that started to unravel as she lifted it out.

I realized it was her nightclothes. "You should wear that."

"This is for bed." She refolded it and placed it in one of the dresser drawers.

Then Betsy opened my suitcase and began to unpack it as well.

"You needn't..."

"What sort of wife would I be if I didn't."

Betsy carefully removed my clothing from my suitcase. She shook out my dress shirts, smoothed them and hung them neatly in the closet and refolded my other clothes and placed them in the drawers.

With nothing left to unpack, there was an awkward silence as we stood looking at one another.

"Let's have a drink," I suggested.

"That would be nice," she said quietly, watching me as I opened the champagne and poured us each a glass.

"To you Mrs. Jacobs." I touched the rim of my glass to hers.

"Cheers," she replied and took a sip.

I opened the balcony door and we stepped outside with our glasses. Our room was several floors up and faced out to sea, giving us a bird's eye view of at least a mile of the coast. I suspected the desk clerk had given us a better room than the one I'd booked, which was described as having a partial view.

"We're so lucky to have this view," I said.

"What would be the point of staying at a beach hotel if you can't see the beach?"

"Are you hungry?" I asked, changing the subject, not wanting Betsy to know I hadn't booked this nice of a room, but made a mental note of her preference for future reference.

"I suppose we should eat something," she replied vaguely.

"I could order us some club sandwiches?"

She nodded.

I left her on the balcony to call room service. When I looked back, she was leaning on the rail, her back to me, slightly arched. Seeing her in that position stirred me. As soon as I hung up from ordering, I went to her and stood close behind her. She stood up. I reached my arms around her and held her as she continued to sip her champagne. I moved one hand up and brushed the hair from her neck and bent to kiss it. She giggled and pulled away.

She turned to face me. "That tickles."

"Maybe we should try it this way." I leaned in and kissed her.

She looked around. "Not here. Someone might see."

"We're newlyweds. I think it's OK if we're necking."

Betsy looked unconvinced. She moved past me back into the room and I followed. She pulled the curtains shut behind me. Then she put her arms around my neck and looked into my eyes.

"You can kiss me now."

I pulled her close and pressed my lips to hers. She puckered but kept her lips tightly together, so my kiss was brief. I slid my hands up her back and holding her head gently, kissed her cheeks and eyelids and nose.

"You're so beautiful. I want to kiss you all over," I whispered into her ear, moving to kiss under her ear and down her neck.

"Stop!"

I let go of her and stepped back. "How about a little more champagne?"

"Are you trying to get me drunk?"

I reassured her. "Certainly not. I know you like it. And we shouldn't let it go to waste." Although, I was hoping it would help her relax and enjoy finally being alone together.

I refilled her glass and she sat down in one of the armchairs.

"Perhaps you'd be more comfortable if you took off your shoes?" I suggested.

"I don't want to ruin my stockings."

"They have slippers for you."

I took the slippers from the bottom of the closet and got down on my knees at her feet. I carefully undid the strap of her right shoe and slipped it off. I gently rubbed her foot, massaging it before slipping on the pale pink hotel slipper. I did the same with the left, but I let my hands wander up her leg a little past the ankle feeling the softness of her silk stocking under my fingers. She didn't pull away, so I continued to massage her ankle and calf, moving to the other leg after a minute or so. She was just starting to relax when the room service waiter knocked again. She pulled her legs back and crossed her ankles. I got up to let him in.

While eating our club sandwiches I asked Betsy what she'd like to do while we were there.

"I'd like to visit the art museum. My uncle says the Norton's have put together a very good collection."

"I doubt it's open tomorrow, but we could go on Monday."

"What did you have in mind?"

"I thought we'd enjoy all the hotel amenities, the pool, the beach…our room with a view."

"You're just anxious to get me into bed."

"We've waited for this for a long time…"

I reached over and stroked her hand with my fingertips.

Betsy pulled hers away. "Could you at least wait until we're done our dinner?"

When Betsy said she was tired, I started to tingle with excitement. As anxious as I was, I didn't want to seem pushy or to rush her. I had read that a new bride might prefer to get ready for her wedding night with some privacy, so I suggested that I let her get ready for bed, and I'd take a walk down to check with the concierge about the museum times and maybe pick up some information on things to do tomorrow.

I left the room, went down to the grand lobby with its high arched ceilings decorated with paintings. I found the concierge who was happy to provide a folder of information about local attractions as well as a list of the hotel services that were available poolside and on the beach. I didn't know how long Betsy needed, but after about 20 minutes I went back to the room. I knocked as I unlocked the door and opened it just a crack so I could ask if I could come in.

"Yes. I'm ready," said Betsy.

She was sitting stiffly on the bed wearing a long white lace nightgown with a matching jacket that was belted shut with a wide white satin tie.

"That's so nice," I said. "Very pretty. You're pretty." I started to unbutton my shirt while I walked closer to her.

Betsy pointed to the bathroom. "You can change in there. I put your pajamas on the counter."

I changed as quickly as I could, putting on only my pajama bottoms and leaving my chest bare. I did a quick gargle with the hotel mouthwash and returned to the bedroom. Betsy was still sitting in the same spot. I sat down on the bed beside her and leaned in to kiss her while tugging at end of her sash to open the front of her jacket.

"I suppose we need to get this over with," she said standing up, facing me, and taking off the outer jacket revealing the lace nightie. It was sheer, but not see-through, and draped from two thin straps leaving her shoulders bare. I leaned towards her and put my hands on her waist running them upward towards her breasts. Betsy tensed up so I avoided touching them, instead, running my hands up her sides and reaching to caress the bare skin of her arms.

"Are you nervous?" I asked.

"Isn't that to be expected?"

Despite my reassurances that we'd take things slowly and there was nothing to fear, Betsy was tense. I led her to the bed and we lay down facing each other. I kissed her, stroked her face and hair, and told her how beautiful she looked and how much I loved her and was so happy she was my wife.

She gradually relaxed and didn't seem to mind when I slipped one strap of her nightgown off her shoulder. She'd allowed me to touch her breasts before, but I'd never seen them. She'd let me slip my hand up her blouse while making out, but I'd always had to work around her brassiere.

"Hello there you beautiful breast," I said looking at the one that was just peeking out and then grinning at Betsy. "I've waited so long to see you and you're even lovelier than I imagined."

My silliness seemed to relax her a little more and she smiled and wiggled so I could slide the whole top of her nightgown down to her waist. I kissed her deeply and then kissed her neck and while caressing her breasts, kissed across her collarbone and then nibbled my way down between her breasts.

Cupping one of her breasts in each hand, I brushed my lips over her nipples.

Betsy stayed very still but didn't pull away, so I sat up and rolled her onto her back and began caressing her legs starting at the ankle and slowly massaging and slipping her nightgown up as I went. When it was up to her thigh I slowed and ran my fingers up and down her outer thigh, gradually getting closer to her panties. I slipped one finger on either side into the leg opening of her panties and then up past her hip to the top so I could hook them and slowly slip them off her.

I continued to caress her legs, moving to touch her inner thighs but not going all the way up between them. I ran my hands up the front of her legs and slowly raised her nightie so I could run my hands over her belly. I stood up and took off my pajama bottoms and Betsy averted her eyes from my very erect penis that popped out of them.

"It's ok. You can look," I said.

She held up her hand and I hoped she would touch me, but I realized she was using it to hide my penis from her view.

I crept onto the bed from the end so I could kneel between her legs and then crawl forward until I was over her, supporting my weight on my hands and knees.

"Ok?" I asked and she nodded.

I touched the tip of my penis to her and using my hand slid the tip of it up and down between the lips of her vagina. I could feel her wetness and warmth and it took all my attention to not hurry and plunge into her.

"Ok?" I asked again, not wanting her to feel I was going ahead without her consent.

She nodded again so I slowly pressed into her. Betsy closed her eyes and lay completely still. I moved slowly, being as gentle as I could, working myself deeper, watching her face for any sign of pain or pleasure. I saw neither.

I didn't last long; the pent-up desire got the better of me and it was all over very quickly. I collapsed onto her and whispered I love you into her ear and buried my face in her hair while I caught my breath.

As I rolled beside her, Betsy gathered up her nightgown around her, took her robe and went into the bathroom. I drifted off to sleep waiting for her to return.

She woke me as she climbed into bed. "You're not going to sleep like that are you?"

"Like what?"

"Without your nightclothes."

"I can put them on if you'd like."

"Yes. Please."

I picked up my pajama bottoms from the floor and put them on and started to climb back into bed.

"What about your top?"

"How about we both go to bed topless?" I reached for the edge of her robe.

She pulled her robe tighter around her. "I think not. Your top is in the bathroom."

At the time I was so happy we'd just made love for the first time, I didn't hesitate to do her bidding. I didn't want to do anything to make her uncomfortable or feel pressured. I was determined to be a good husband and do whatever it took for her to open up and really enjoy sex.

I was anxious to get Betsy over her apprehension and fear. So, I tried asking her what felt good or what she wanted to try. But she couldn't or wouldn't tell me. Talking about it was distasteful to her.

We made love each night of our honeymoon at The Breakers. Betsy didn't resist my advances, but she never initiated physical contact nor was she enthusiastic about making love. I hoped that once she got past her initial fears that she would start to enjoy sex, not just tolerate it.

It was only two months into our marriage when Betsy got pregnant for the first time. She was so happy when she was 'late'. We had only just confirmed it a few days prior with her doctor when she started bleeding. It was devastatingly sad for both of us when she miscarried a few weeks into the pregnancy.

Her doctor had reassured us. "A miscarriage, although temporarily distressing, is a blessing in disguise. It's nature's reaction, preventing the birth of a child with birth defects. It's highly likely that another pregnancy and a healthier baby will soon follow."

When we were alone in the car after the appointment, I tried to console her. "We can try again."

Betsy huffed. "You just want a reason to start having sex again."

Betsy was always more open to me after we'd been out at major social events like weddings. At the time I presumed she was in a better mood after those types of events but, looking back, I realize I got lucky whenever she'd been around other young wives who were pregnant or had babies. Betsy really wanted a baby. If it weren't for that motivation, I doubt we'd have had sex as often as we did in the early years of our marriage.

We'd been married almost five years when Betsy had her third miscarriage. I sat on a stool beside her in the doctor's office as she struggled to hold herself together. He told us that the tests he had performed did not reveal any reason, but, after three miscarriages, it was unlikely she would carry a pregnancy to term. Betsy told him that she didn't want to go through it again. He offered to explain options for contraception, so we could continue marital relations without worrying about getting pregnant, but she declined saying it wasn't necessary.

Much to my dismay, it really wasn't necessary as our marital relations were infrequent from that time forward. Betsy liked being admired and complimented and she always took great care in keeping up her appearance, but she resisted my physical displays of affection. I could look but not touch, which was difficult for me to comply with. Perhaps on my birthday or after I'd given her a particularly expensive gift, Betsy would reward me by allowing me to make love to her.

The patio door opened bringing me back from my memories.

"There you are," said Claire. "I suspected it was you who had the coffee waiting for me."

"Good morning. I hope I didn't wake you."

"You didn't. Come inside, you look cold. I'm just going to pop out front and get the paper."

I hung my coat back in the laundry room and sat down across from Claire at the kitchen table.

"The paper only comes twice a week, and it's not great." She pulled out one section and passed the rest to me.

"I left my reading glasses in the bedroom. Don't want to wake Maddie."

"No problem. I have plenty. See if these work." She handed me the pink rhinestone-studded glasses she'd just put on and got herself another pair from a kitchen drawer.

We sat drinking our coffee and reading. As I finished a section, I folded it neatly and passed it to her and Claire would trade with a section that she'd finished. We had just traded the last sections when Claire looked up and said, "Good morning sleepyhead."

I turned to see Maddie strolling from the living room and into the kitchen. She was wearing red plaid pajama bottoms and a white t-shirt. Her hair was tied up with a clip and she was blinking as if the kitchen light was too bright.

"Mmmmm. Morning. You been up long?" she mumbled.

"Long enough to need to make more coffee." Claire got up from the table and pointed to a chair for Maddie to occupy.

Maddie smirked at me. "Nice glasses."

"Mine are in the bedroom. I didn't want to disturb you." I took off Claire's and went to get mine.

I returned to find Claire and Maddie huddled in the kitchen whispering. They stopped abruptly when I entered.

"So, what are your plans for today?" Claire asked me, obviously redirecting the conversation, trying to cover whatever they'd been discussing.

"Maddie's got a day of gem show exploring planned. Right?"

"Yes. I thought we'd check out the mineral exhibition and then visit some of the vendor locations."

"Are you shopping for something in particular? Maybe some jewelry?" asked Claire giving me a look that suggested it was more of a suggestion than a question.

Maddie frowned at Claire. "Nothing in particular, but I'd like to find an engagement slash housewarming gift for Anne and Linda. They're moving in together."

"You should at least visit the gem mall," said Claire to me. "Even if you're just window shopping. I saw the most spectacular sapphires when Carl and I went last week."

"Would you like to join us today?" I asked, although I was hoping she wouldn't take me up on it.

"I've got plans with Carl. We're going to the recreation center for our book club and then to the pool. You two are on your own today."

"I'm going to go shower and dress," said Maddie draining her coffee and refilling it. "Mind if I use our room for a bit?"

"I've showered already. All yours."

"Do either of you want breakfast?" asked Claire.

Maddie held up her coffee cup as she left the room. "Got mine."

"How about you?" she asked me.

"I do, but I'm happy to fix my own. I don't want to be a bother."

"Make yourself at home. Help yourself to eggs, bacon, toast… Whatever you find. I'm going to shower too."

Claire left me alone in the kitchen. I was just cleaning up the dishes after eating the fried egg sandwich I'd made for myself when Maddie came back. She was smartly but casually dressed in a pair of black capris pants and a bright blue top with pineapples on it and carrying a pair of sandals.

"I'm ready when you are," she announced.

I felt a little rush of excitement to be off on an adventure with her.

CHAPTER 29

I could tell Nate was uncomfortable in the passenger seat beside me as we made the half-hour drive to Tucson from Green Valley. I'd assumed he'd be OK with me doing all the driving. He'd been my passenger when he visited me in Toronto without incident and we'd agreed it made sense for me to rent the car for our trip. It was easier for me to rent since I was under eighty. He would be spared the hassle of getting a note from his doctor and copies of the driving and insurance records the car rental companies wanted for him to rent one.

So, I was surprised, and a little annoyed, that he continually gripped his armrest and pressed his feet into the floor like he was trying to brake for me. At first, I ignored it and tried to distract him with conversation, but that only made it worse.

"Are you sure this is the right way?" he'd asked as we left the highway and headed along the service road.

I pointed to the printed directions I'd folded and stuffed in the console between us. "You can read me the directions."

I didn't actually need help. The directions were simple, and I'd memorized the map. But it gave him something to do besides squirm in the passenger seat and question that I knew where I was going.

The convention center parking lot was jammed. We had to circle around a couple times before finding an open space.

"And now for something completely different, my first mineral exhibition," said Nate as we got out of the car and headed for the entrance.

I smiled at the Python reference. "Mine too."

Nate nodded and pressed his lips together with pretend seriousness. "Gem show virgins both of us."

I didn't know what to expect but I'd read this was a good place to start. It was described as part museum, part gallery, with mineral vendors and collectors from around the world all under one roof.

We started in the main exhibit hall and wound our way through the aisles of glass cases with displays of spectacular specimens. Most were lit with bright lights that showed off the colours and shapes of the minerals. We read the names and origins printed on labels adjacent to each piece. The theme for the show was 'Mineral Treasures of the American Midwest' so there were a lot of mineral names and locations I recognized. I wracked my brain to try to remember anything I could about the minerals we were looking at.

"So many minerals. Reminds me of how much I've forgotten and how much I never learned in mineralogy classes," I confessed to Nate.

"I would guess they've discovered a few new ones in the half-century since you were in school," he replied.

"Whoa Mister. You sure know how to imply the lady is old." I playfully swatted at his arm.

After we'd gone through the exhibits, we went into the adjacent hall where there were rows of tables with vendors selling mineral specimens.

"Who would want to buy these?" Nate pointed to the trays and trays of small black crystals. "They aren't pretty."

"We have many different kinds of buyers from amateur collectors to educational institutions and research organizations looking for reference specimens," answered the young lady behind the table who'd obviously overheard Nate's question.

"What are these?" I asked her.

"Pyroxene, augite specifically, and these here are olivine." She pointed to the tray beside the augite.

"Olivine? Green like olives?" asked Nate.

"Typically it's olive green but can range in colour from yellow-green to bright green; and even brownish green to brown for iron-rich specimens," the young lady explained.

"And there are a lot of green minerals that aren't olivine," I said as we moved to look at the next table in the row. "Like these tourmalines. I like tourmaline. It can be opaque black, or translucent and blue, green, yellow, pink, red, orange, purple, brown, or colourless."

Nate pointed to a tricolored crystal. "This is all tourmaline?"

"Watermelon tourmaline?" I asked the gentleman behind the table.

"Yes. We have quite a few nice ones left." He pointed to a tray with a row of boxes each with a single crystal.

"They are nice," I said looking over them, feeling quite pleased that I'd recognized it correctly, and feeling a little more confident as the cobwebs cleared from the geological information that had been un-accessed in my brain for a few decades. "I've always found it amazing that a single crystal can develop with multiple different colours. Watermelon tourmaline is an example from the natural world, that a change in the environment can shift the outcome dramatically. A little more of this element, or that, as the crystal grows, and you get a totally different colour. Life is like tourmaline. Just a slight change in circumstances can take life in a completely different and possibly more clear or colourful direction."

"Which of these do you think is the best?" asked Nate looking over the samples.

"Although this one is a little smaller, it has great colour and the clear nature of it makes it gem-like," answered the man.

"We'll take that one then," said Nate, "I like the idea that small changes in the past transformed this mineral from growing green to growing red."

"Or red to green," said the man.

"Either way. Still remarkable."

"What are you going to do with it?" I asked.

"Give it to you. To add to your guest room mineral collection as a memento of our first gem show together." Nate handed me the box and the man the fifteen dollars for the specimen.

"Thank you. But this is only our first stop. What if you find something you like better?"

"Then I'll get that too."

I popped the small box into my purse, and we looked over the remaining tables in the vendor area.

"Where to next?" asked Nate.

"The G&LW and JOGS sites are in the same part of town. Shall we head that way?"

Nate agreed and once back in the car I handed him a print-out of the directions. Within 15 minutes we were parked at the JOGS show. We picked it because it was the first one we came upon, and it was clearly marked with big signs along the road directing traffic into the parking area. Nate had printed registration confirmations, so it only took a few minutes for us to get the badges we needed for entry from the admissions desk.

Our plan had been to take a quick look around to get an idea of what was there, but it was impossible for me not to stop and look at the incredible displays. Near the entrance, there was an entire room of eastern European amber; everything from raw specimens to highly polished pieces set in gold and silver jewelry. In the main corridor, there was a long row of vendors with spectacular fossils: a huge polished agatized ammonite, trilobites the size of my fist and slabs of rock with fossil fish pressed into the silty stone. All these were distracting, but I really got stuck when we entered a large, warehouse-like area. At the entrance, on either side of the walkway, there were two pillars of rock. They were two halves of a huge cone, at least eight feet tall and with a hollow core filled with amethyst crystals.

"Wow!" I stopped in my tracks to peer at the large deep purple crystals inside.

"Wow is right," said Nate turning to look around the room.

The vast open area was divided up by the vendors. Some were demarcated by carpeted areas with fancy display signs and lighting, others with just bare tables or bins and still others with rows of what looked like wooden shipping crates. From the names on the signs, we could guess they'd come from all over the globe, many from China and Brazil but every continent was represented.

As we stood in the aisle, on the periphery of one of the more elegant booths, I pointed to a particularly interesting geode about the size of a basketball. It was sliced open to reveal the crystals inside and the cut surface of both halves had been polished smooth. The two parts were held open in a heavy metal stand so that the entire inside was clearly visible.

"How in the world did they get this open without damaging the crystals. Amazing," I wondered aloud to Nate.

"It's not as spectacular inside as the purple one over there." Nate pointed to a tall narrow rock covered in pale purple amethyst.

"The amethyst is pretty, but this one has a story to tell."

"How so?"

"Well, you can see there are larger, clear crystals underneath and on top of them there are tiny grey ones that make it look like it's sugar-coated."

Nate leaned in closer beside me to peer into the geode. "And that tells a story?"

"If I had to guess, it's evidence that there were multiple events that went into creating this. The larger crystals formed first and then sometime later, under different conditions, the grey ones were deposited."

"How do you know for sure?"

"I don't. But it makes me curious, and that's why it's interesting."

"So... like your tourmaline's story? Something changed and you got a different colour?"

"Different story, same idea."

We stuck to the perimeter of the booths, not wanting to suggest to the vendors that we were going to purchase any of the pieces. But I couldn't help but ogle.

Nate pointed to a spectacular coffee table made from a huge geode. "You wouldn't be moving that around to vacuum the carpet."

The geode was about a meter across and had been cut in half horizontally. It sat with the open end facing up, steadied by a metal ring with legs. The spectacular crystals inside were protected by a thick slab of glass that covered the opening and extended a few inches past the edge of the rock.

I leaned in to take a closer look inside. "I don't think I'd be moving it EVER."

"What are the yellow crystals inside?"

"I'd guess citrine. Yellow quartz."

"I thought quartz was white?"

"It has many forms. Amethyst is purple quartz; citrine is yellow quartz but there's grey smoky quartz and pink rose quartz and more colours I don't know the names for."

"I'm so glad you're here. They would all just be pretty rocks without you as my guide."

"They're pretty rocks to me too. It would be great to find something for Anne, but I think these are a little big for me to pack in my suitcase."

"I'm sure they ship," said Nate, with a shrug and a grin, tempting me to go for it.

"I don't need to find out. Let's keep looking."

"I'm just going to pop into the restroom," said Nate. "I'll catch up with you."

While Nate was in the washroom, I made a quick circuit around the rest of the booths. In the far corner was a young Brazilian woman with several tables filled with pieces of amethyst that had been fashioned into candle holders of various sizes and shapes. Some had small holes that would hold a taper but most had a tealight-sized hole. The amethyst ranged from a light, smoky, purple to very dark. I was pouring over them when Nate joined me.

I pointed to the tealight holders. "Anne would like these. She likes candles."

"Which one do you like?"

"I was thinking of getting two or three so she can use them as a centrepiece."

"But they're all different. They won't match."

"They're rocks. They're supposed to be different."

Nate looked unconvinced but I mixed and matched until I selected three that looked good as a grouping and individually. The young woman wrapped each one in bubble wrap and then brown paper and handed them to Nate and me. They were far too big and heavy for my purse, so Nate carried two and I had one. I now understood why there were so many people towing rolling suitcases around the show.

"I think we should drop these off in the car," said Nate.

The sun was directly overhead and scorching as we walked across the parking lot to the car. Something smelled delicious and my stomach grumbled in response. I noticed there was a ring of food trucks around the perimeter of the lot.

I pointed them out to Nate. "Those are making me hungry."

"Maybe a good time for lunch then." Nate tucked our purchases away in the back seat of our car and we headed over to investigate.

I decided on spicy fish tacos and a diet coke from a bright lime green truck and Nate got a hot dog and iced tea from one claiming to have the best dogs on four wheels. There wasn't anywhere to sit near the food trucks, so we carried our lunches back to the car.

Heat gushed out of the car when I opened the door, as if I'd just opened an oven. Rolling down the windows didn't help, so I started the car and cranked up the air-conditioning.

"Now I understand why all those cars we passed had big reflectors in their front windows," said Nate.

"Would be nice if they put one in the rental car."

"Like ice scrapers are standard issue in cars up north."

"Exactly," I said through a big mouthful of grilled fish and shredded cabbage.

We finished our lunch and decided to skip the G&GW show and head to the Granada Avenue area. Nate navigated, a little more at ease with our roles as driver and navigator. It got a little tense when we had to circle the block a couple of times, but we eventually found a place to park and Nate complimented me on my parallel parking ability.

This area had a different vibe than our previous stops. Walking towards Hotel Tucson, the epicentre of the Granada Ave show area, we came across several historic houses that had been converted to gallery spaces. They were very high-end with spectacular jewelry, artwork, and collectibles. We spent quite a while exploring one of the larger galleries. It was quiet and cool and museum-like inside which was a refreshing escape from the mid-day heat.

Several times we found we both admired the same pieces. It felt nice to be in sync with someone.

"I guess I shouldn't be surprised we have similar taste," said Nate echoing my thoughts.

"Seems we do."

"Betsy and I never agreed on art."

"That would make decorating difficult."

"Not really. She got to choose all the artwork for the whole house except for my office, which I decorated with my boats."

"From what I've seen, you have a lot of boats that are works of art."

"You get it. Betsy didn't see it that way."

When we got to the Hotel Tucson site it was much bigger than I'd expected. The ground floor hotel rooms, with doors that faced the courtyard, had been transformed into a sort of plaza where each room was a different shop. There were also large, tented areas that extended the shopping area well beyond the hotel grounds.

We'd only covered a few of the 'shops' when I needed to find a washroom. Inquiring, they told me I'd find them in the hallway just inside the hotel. Nate said he'd scout around the tents and if I couldn't find him, just to call his mobile, which he took from his pocket to make sure it was turned on.

I found Nate easily when I came back. But I was surprised to find him coming out of a tent selling gem show souvenirs carrying a small bag.

"What ya got there?"

He looked pleased with himself. "Postcards."

"You bought postcards?"

"I'm going to send them to Ann and Emily. It's something I started when Ann was little. Sending her a postcard wherever I travelled."

"I can't remember the last time I sent or received a postcard."

"I still do, on occasion."

"Did they have good ones?"

"I bought an extra one so if you want to send one to your daughter…"

It struck me that I'd never sent Anne postcards because she'd been with me for almost every touristy trip I'd taken. It was unfamiliar having someone new as my travel partner, but it wasn't bad. In fact, it was quite delightful.

CHAPTER 30

Claire was home when we got back, and Maddie launched into a recap of our day. After a full day at the gem show, all I wanted was to take a nap. I left them in the living room, went to our room and closed the door. I put the paper bag with the postcards on the dresser and took the small velvet bag out of my pocket that I'd kept hidden from Maddie and put it into the drawer with my undergarments. I slipped off my shoes and lay down on the bed. I closed my eyes and told myself to wake up in 20 minutes, which would be all I needed to recharge my batteries.

When I opened my eyes, I was startled by motion at the foot of the bed.

"Sorry. Did I wake you?" Maddie said in a whisper. "I'm going. I just wanted to grab my sweater."

"You didn't. I just closed my eyes."

"For the last hour or so."

"No… What time is it?"

"After six. The sun's going down. It's cooling off. We're out on the patio."

Maddie quietly closed the door behind her but creeping out wasn't necessary. I was feeling much better and ready to get up but puzzled why my internal alarm hadn't woken me. The heat must have tuckered me out. I got up, used the bathroom, ran a comb through my hair and then joined Maddie and Claire on the patio.

"Shhhh. No more talking about him," said Claire, winking at me.

"Sorry Ladies. I didn't mean to sleep so long. I just thought I'd rest my eyes for 20 minutes…"

"No worries," said Maddie. "We made good use of your nap time. We went to the store, prepped dinner, all while you were sleeping."

"What if I'd woken up and you were gone?"

"We left a note," said Maddie. "Help yourself at the bar."

Claire patted the arm of the chair beside her. "Then come join us."

I did as I was told.

"What did you think of our little gem show?" asked Claire.

"Impressive. Overwhelming. I'm glad I had a knowledgeable guide."

"Hardly. I've forgotten more than I ever knew," said Maddie.

"You impressed me." I looked directly into Maddie's eyes, hoping she saw I meant it. Then I turned to Claire. "I knew she was smart and beautiful and funny… but I got to meet Maddie the geologist and philosopher today. She's the most interesting woman in the world."

"I can't disagree with that." Claire raised her glass to toast, clinking mine then Maddie's glass.

Maddie grimaced. "Knock it off you two. I suspect you're buttering me up because you want something."

Claire laughed and I protested, "I meant it. No ulterior motives. I promise."

That evening Maddie and Claire cooked dinner for the three of us. We had chicken and potatoes baked in the oven with garlic and some rosemary plucked from the bushes growing along the edge of the patio and a simple tomato and onion salad. To make up for sleeping through dinner prep, I volunteered to do the dishes while Maddie and Claire finished their wine on the patio. A little later, I also offered to serve the dessert of lemon gelato they'd picked up from a gelateria Claire had wanted to try because it had recently opened to rave reviews.

The weeks flew by. Claire was plugged in to everything happening in Green Valley. She attributed it to knowing who to ask.

"Just ask Jane Hansen or Evie Olsen," she'd told us. "They know everyone and if they don't, they make it their business to find out."

"They don't know us," said Maddie.

"Don't be so sure. They've been gathering intelligence. Carl told me they cornered him at Starbucks to press him for information on who my houseguests were."

"I can't imagine we're big news. We're not celebrities or anything,"

"To them, everything is news. Lots of folks avoid them because they're busy-bodies. But I say, Nourrir les poulets pour qu'ils pondent quand vous avez besoin d'un œuf."

Maddie laughed but I had no idea what Claire was saying.

"Feed the chickens so they lay an egg when you need it," translated Maddie.

Claire was an excellent hostess. She kept Maddie and I busy every day, often giving us multiple options for what to do and who to do it with. Several afternoons we headed to the local pool. Maddie and Claire made fun of me because I readjusted our chairs into a straight line each time we got up to go swim.

"You're as bad as the Pool Boss," said Claire, referring to the elderly man who was the self-appointed enforcer of the pool rules.

We played golf at a couple of the Green Valley courses. We went to the Sonoran Desert Museum, which was part zoo, part museum, documenting the natural environment of the area. We even visited an observatory where we had a lecture on what was visible in the local night sky and had a chance to look through a big telescope and see far-off galaxies that looked like glowing cotton balls.

I started to become more of a night person because Maddie loved sitting on the patio or taking a walk on the golf course cart path at night so she could look up at the stars. I couldn't let her go off into the night alone and she wouldn't be stopped.

"You just don't ever see a night sky like this in the city," she said multiple times, her head tilted back, and her face pointed up at the heavens. She would point out the celestial objects we'd learned about at the observatory: Venus, Orion, the Pleiades, Polaris, and the Milky Way.

I've always been more of a morning person, but there I was, lying in the grass in the middle of the ninth fairway scouring the sky for meteorites because Maddie had spotted a falling star and wanted to see more. She'd suggested it would be more comfortable than standing with our necks bent over backwards.

The grass and ground were warm and dry, but the evening air was cool. Maddie inched closer to me so we were shoulder to shoulder.

Maddie pointed to a cluster of stars. "I bet somewhere out there, on a planet whizzing around one of those stars, there's a couple lying in the grass looking back at us."

"How do you know their planet has grass?"

"Good point. Maybe they have grass, but it's purple... Oh! There's one!" She pointed to the streak of light crossing the sky directly over us.

"There's another," I said pointing a little to the left of us.

"No wonder they worry about light pollution. I wouldn't want anyone to wreck this view."

I rolled over onto one elbow so I could see her better. "It is a lovely view." I reached out and ran my fingers along her jawline.

"You're not looking at the sky. You might miss the next falling star."

"There are no more beautiful stars than the sparkle in your eyes."

Maddie smiled. "Does that line work on all the girls?"

"First time I've used it. Guess I better find out."

I leaned in and gently touched my lips to hers and immediately pulled back.

"I think it might be working," said Maddie with an inviting, playful smirk.

I took that as permission to kiss her again. This time a little longer with a little more pressure and my free hand stroking her cheek as lightly as I could.

"Yes. It's definitely working," said Maddie when I leaned back.

I continued to trace her features with my fingertips as she looked up at me. I wanted to memorize every detail of her face. I traced along her temples, eyebrows, cheekbones and down her nose to her lips. As my fingertips passed over her lips, her tongue darted out and she playfully nibbled on my finger. That caused a tremor to run through my body and a definite stirring in my briefs. I

275

rolled over a little more towards her and we kissed like teenagers making out for the first time. A little awkwardly at first but gradually letting go with our hands finding a grip to pull each other closer.

Just then we heard the whine of tires and the electric hum of a golf cart and saw the flash of headlights as it turned a corner heading towards us.

Maddie hopped up quicker than I and extended her hand down to help me up. "We better scoot."

We were smoothing our clothing and starting to walk back to the path when a very bright flashlight temporarily blinded us.

"What are you two doing?" said a male voice.

I squinted and held my hand up to block the light so I could see who it was. "Just out for a walk."

"Are you alright Ma'am?" said the voice with the flashlight pointed at Maddie.

"Yes of course. I wanted to see the meteorite shower they told us about at the observatory."

"Well, the course is closed. You should head home," said the voice.

I took Maddie's arm. "We are on our way now, sir."

The golf cart made a U-turn and headed back the way it had come.

"We got in trouble," said Maddie in a low singsong voice.

"You are definitely trouble, Ms. Cole."

"You started it."

"No I didn't," I peppered back, setting us both off giggling.

We were still exchanging "yes you did" and "no I didn't" and laughing as we came into the house.

"What have you two been up to," said Claire.

"Nothing," said Maddie, sounding guilty.

I tried to explain. "We just got chased off the golf course."

"That's odd," said Claire. "They usually don't bother with people walking."

Maddie started to giggle. "We weren't walking at the time."

"Dare I ask what you were doing?"

"Just looking at the stars," I said as innocently as I could, but the effect was countered by Maddie giggling again.

"You two are acting like two teenagers caught making out," said Claire, which set us both off laughing so hard Maddie crossed her legs and then excused herself to run to the bathroom.

Claire looked at me sidelong. "You didn't?"

I didn't answer but shrugged and ran my finger across my lips to indicate I wasn't telling.

Claire wagged her finger at me playfully. "Quelle folie!" Then winked and gave me a thumbs up.

I looked at my watch. "It's getting late, so I'll say goodnight." I made a quick exit to avoid further conversation on the subject.

Maddie had left the bedroom door open, so I went in, and as I did, she came out of the bathroom.

"Claire scold you for being a bad boy?"

"I think she might approve. But it was in French, so I'm not a hundred percent certain."

"I guess I could go find out, let her know we didn't do anything naughty."

"I'd rather we picked up where we left off." I closed the bedroom door and reached for her hand.

Maddie took my hand and I gently tugged so she would come closer.

"Mr. Jacobs, whatever do you mean?" she said in an innocent but teasing voice.

"I mean to kiss you some more."

Maddie folded so naturally into my arms I knew she wanted to kiss me too. Her face turned up, smiling, her eyes looking squarely into mine, was irresistible. I pressed my lips onto hers and as I did, I slid my hand up her arm, just barely touching her skin. She shivered at the touch and pressed into me even closer, returning my kiss enthusiastically. Her lips were softly parted and the way we connected felt so perfectly natural. We just fit.

I pulled back from her lips to look into her eyes. Bringing my hand up from her shoulder to her face and brushing my fingertips across her cheek. I moved slowly so I could memorize the contours of her face and the softness of her skin. My fingertips traced her cheekbone and brow.

"You have the most amazing eyes."

She closed her eyes, and I brushed my fingertips over her eyelids and lashes. I could feel her breathing and thought I heard a tiny moan of pleasure as I continued to trace her face, my index finger running down her nose to trace her perfect lips.

Holding her close and touching her was having an effect on me, one I'd not felt in many years. I could feel myself expanding and my briefs get a little tighter. I moved away slightly, not wanting Maddie to notice my reaction. But she did.

She leaned her hip gently forward. "I get the feeling you're enjoying this as much as I am."

Her words excited me even more. I kissed her again, and, buoyed by her encouragement, ran my hand down her neck and across her collarbone to the top button of her blouse. My fingers were trembling as I fumbled to undo the top button. Maddie leaned away and I felt a flash of concern that I'd read her signals wrong. I hadn't. Maddie looked me squarely in the eyes and began to undo the top button I'd been struggling with.

"No. Let me," I pleaded.

Maddie dropped her hands to her sides and watched my face intently as I started to undo her blouse one button at a time. I was dizzy with excitement and my heart was pounding so hard I could hear my pulse thumping in my ears. As I slipped her blouse off her shoulders, I paused holding it awkwardly in my hands, not sure what to do with it and simultaneously struggling with where to look; my eyes roaming from her bare skin to her face and to the blouse in my hand.

"Here. Give me that." Maddie took the blouse and tossed it onto the chair by the dresser and then turned back to me putting her arms over my shoulders and leaning in close. "Now what?" she said seductively, sending my mind spinning. Was this really happening? What is she thinking? I opened my mouth, but no answer came. Maddie giggled. "You're speechless? I hope that's a good thing."

"You're amazing."

"Really? Amazing?"

"Yes. Really amazing. And exciting. And beautiful. And if it's OK with you… I'd like to explore a little more of you."

"It's OK with me." Maddie leaned in to kiss me, sending tingles through my whole body.

I felt like I was the luckiest man in the world. This woman standing here, kissing me was the whole package. Smart, beautiful, and to my delight, exciting in ways I thought I'd never feel again.

I hugged her close and whispered in her ear. "Turn around."

Maddie turned and I wrapped my arms around her at her waist and kissed her neck from her ear to her shoulder. She leaned back into me and her head tilted, leaving more of her neck for me to nuzzle and kiss. I slid my hands across her belly and up her body to the base of her bra. I paused, waiting to see if she would stop my hands. Her hands moved, not to block me, but to reach behind her and rest on the outside of my thighs. She pressed her shoulders back, as if to open herself to me. It had been decades since I had been with a woman this way, but my desire to touch her overcame my fear of not knowing what I should do.

I drew my hands up and around her, following the edge of her bra, but letting the back of my hands brush the outer curve of her breasts, until my hands met at the clasp at the back. I struggled a bit, tugging at it to free the hooks securing it. Once it opened, I moved my hands across her back and up to her shoulders. I kissed the cap of one shoulder as I slipped the strap off, letting it fall to her elbow, and then did the same to the other. Her brassiere fell forward, and she caught it before it hit the floor and tossed it to the chair with her blouse.

Still standing with her back to me, Maddie leaned back, her head tilted to one side and resting on my shoulder. I again reached my arms around her. I drew my hands slowly up her sides and then, as gently as I could, slid my hands under her breasts to cup them. My thumbs moved over her nipples, making her squirm a little.

"Is this OK?" I asked.

"Mmm ... yes," she said drawing in a deep breath and melting a little more into my arms.

We just stood there for several minutes. Me stroking her breasts and kissing and nibbling her neck and shoulders, and Maddie leaning into me with her eyes closed letting out the occasional sigh or soft moan letting me know she was enjoying my touch as much as I was enjoying touching her.

"Should we make ourselves more comfortable?" she asked not pulling away but opening her eyes and craning her neck so she could look up at me.

"OK."

Maddie took my hands and slid them off her.

"I'll be right back," she said with a little wink and went into the bathroom and closed the door. I wasn't exactly sure what 'more comfortable' meant, but I quickly decided that I was overdressed for it. I stripped down to my undershirt and briefs. I pulled back the comforter on the bed and slipped under the sheet.

Maddie was wrapped in a towel when she came out of the bathroom a few minutes later. She turned out all but the one bedside lamp and then quickly climbed into bed dropping the towel at the last second. I couldn't help but reach out to touch her naked body.

"Not fair." She tugged at my undershirt. "You need to lose these too."

I was more than happy to oblige and soon we were tangled together naked and kissing. I rolled Maddie onto her back and then gradually kissed my way down her body. I took my time. Drawing the covers slowly back to reveal a few more inches and then kissing and stroking her. I could feel her breathing deeper as I worked my way lower.

I paused when I reached her hips and looked up at her. "Is this OK?"

She opened her eyes and looked into mine with a sexy smile. "Oh yes, very. But it could be perilous..."

I couldn't help but break into a huge smile and reply with a reciprocal Holy Grail reference. "Oh, let me have just a little bit of peril."

I wanted so desperately to please her. I stroked her thighs, gradually working my way between her legs. Kissing and nibbling until she let out several whimpers, clamped her legs on my ears and stopped my movements. I felt a swell of pride that I'd been able to please her. It was exciting the way she'd opened up to me. So exciting in fact, that to my surprise, and delight, I had sprung completely to life. Crawling up over her, I slid into her. Her hips pressed up to meet me. It felt so good to be this close and moving together was so easy and natural I never wanted it to end. I could feel Maddie moving with me and her fingers pressing into my back. She looked up into my eyes and I thought I was going to explode. But my arms and knees reminded me I wasn't as young as I used to be, and I got a cramp in my calf. I winced.

Maddie looked concerned. "What is it?"

"I have a cramp. I … I have to stop. I'm sorry." I rolled off and lay beside her.

Maddie rolled onto her side and slipped out of bed to the bathroom. I sat up at the side of the bed and stretched out my leg trying to relieve the painful knot in the back of my calf.

"Try pulling your toes towards you," suggested Maddie returning from the bathroom and slipping under the sheet.

"I'm OK." I got up and gingerly walked to the bathroom. I felt disappointed in my performance as I cleaned myself up, but I hoped Maddie wasn't. I brushed my teeth and put on my pajamas that I'd left folded in the drawer of the bathroom vanity.

Even though I hadn't been gone long, Maddie was fast asleep when I came out. She'd pulled the sheet up to her underarms, but her bare shoulders revealed that she had not put on her nightclothes. The thought of lying all night beside her naked body sent a ripple of excitement through me. I removed my pajamas as quietly as I could and slipped into bed beside her.

As late as it was, and as tired as I was, I couldn't sleep. All I could think about was Maddie's body. The room was quite bright with moonlight streaming in. I rolled onto my side towards her, and I stared at her naked back and shoulder. I wanted to pull the sheet back and run my hands over her. I resisted. I didn't want to wake her, or, God forbid, have her think I was taking advantage of her. Suddenly she flipped over and faced me. I was startled at her movement, and I sat up.

Maddie groggily opened her eyes and squinted to see me. "Are you OK?"

"Yes. Are you?"

"Mmmm, yes. Why are you awake?"

"Because you're naked and I just want to touch you."

"Oh. Mmm. OK." She rolled over again and her breathing slowed and deepened letting me know she'd gone back to sleep.

My mind raced. She'd said OK. But was she awake enough to know what she was saying? Did she want me to touch her? I took a chance. I moved closer, lying behind her in the same position as she was. I reached out under the covers and placed my hand on her bare waist. Maddie squirmed, not away, but closer, backing into me until her whole body rested against mine. She was close enough for me to reach all the way around her. I slid my hand across her belly. I could feel it rise and fall with her breathing. I wanted to touch every inch of her. I slipped my hand up slightly so I could cup her breast. She didn't pull away. Her breathing slowed and her body melted into me a little more. Holding Maddie like this felt impossibly good. A wave of relaxation washed over me, and I fell asleep.

CHAPTER 31

Nate lifted my suitcase and handed it to the rental car shuttle bus driver who stacked our bags, one by one, into the rack. It was a relief to settle into the seats of the bus. We had plenty of time to spare to catch our flights. I'd been a bit concerned when we'd hit traffic around Phoenix on the drive from Sedona where we'd spent the last three nights.

Nate checked his watch before reaching for my hand. "We made good time."

I nudged him playfully. "Plenty of time for a long, very expensive lunch, eh?"

Nate had doubted my suggested departure time was early enough. I'd capitulated, leaving an hour earlier with the stipulation that if we were early, he was buying lunch.

Fortunately, we were both flying from the same terminal. We checked in at our respective airlines and met at security and then together chose a place to eat lunch. The hostess seated us at a booth and our waitress came immediately with tumblers of water and took our drink order. Nate excused himself to go to the washroom. I reached to pick up the menu and the bright spotlight over the table made the bracelet on my wrist sparkle.

I smiled remembering what Nate had said as he'd clasped it onto my wrist over dinner last night.

"This bracelet is to remind you of how I see you. Remember you explained quartz comes in many colours, each lovely in its own way? You are amazing in so many ways." Nate had pointed to each of the colours. "You're smart, beautiful, funny, exotic and strong."

It was similar to a tennis bracelet but with a repeating pattern of different quartz gemstones; citrine, amethyst, rose, smoky and clear quartz. The stones were set in silver and large enough that you could see they were clear and well-matched in colour. I turned it slowly on my wrist, watching how the spotlight over the table made each of the stones flash with colour.

Nate caught me studying it when he returned to the table. "I'm glad you like it."

"I do. Thank you, again." I stopped myself from playing with it and opened the menu.

"It's me that's thankful." Nate pushed aside the menu and reached across the table to take my hand. He looked into my eyes and continued in a soft but earnest

282

voice, "You've made me happier than I can ever remember being. I'm going to miss you. I've gotten used to having you near me all the time."

"You've even gotten used to being a passenger while I drive," I teased.

"OK, not used to everything, but most things."

I put on my best pout. "Most? Maybe I should reconsider our summer plans. Are you sure you want me around for even longer?"

"I wish you were coming home with me today and I didn't have to wait months to sleep with you in my arms."

"It'll go fast."

When it was time for me to head to my gate, Nate paid the bill and then accompanied me there. He stood very close with his arm around my waist until my group was called.

"That's me." I turned to him and gave him a quick kiss.

Nate pulled me back and kissed me again. "I miss you already."

I freed myself and stepped into line to board. "I'll text when I land."

Nate stood watching me. I looked back as the gate agent scanned my boarding pass and he waved. My hands were full, so I smiled and winked and then he was out of sight as I walked down the jet bridge to the plane.

A few hours later I was unlocking the front door of my house.

"You're here! Let me give you a hand with that," called Jane from the living room floor where she'd been sitting surrounded by books and papers with her computer in her lap, which she set aside and jumped up to help me move my large suitcase from the porch to the front hall.

"Thanks. Everything OK here?"

"Yes. Sorry I didn't realize it was this late. I meant to have this cleaned up." She nodded at the papers on the floor.

"Don't worry about it. Working on a paper?"

"Yes. This is heavy. What's in it, rocks?"

"A few, yes."

"Want me to carry it up to your room?"

"Please and thank you."

Jane was an undergraduate student at the University of Toronto. I knew her parents through the curling club. She'd jumped at the chance to house sit for me because it was just as close to campus as the house she shared with several other students and was, as she put it, 'way better digs'. Not only was her place in a sketchy neighbourhood and crowded with five housemates, it had temperamental heat and hot water, and was cold and drafty in the winter. Her mother had told me that she'd dropped in to bring her some home baking, to motivate her during exams before Christmas. She told me she'd found her in her room, studying, with her winter coat and mittens on, because the landlord hadn't been around to fix the boiler and it was below freezing outside. When I heard the story, I suggested that Jane could help me out by house sitting and her mother was thrilled to give me her number. Jane came by the house and we made a deal that she could keep my house as warm as she wanted and take as many hot showers as she wanted as long as she fed the cats, made sure the walk was shovelled if it snowed and didn't have any parties.

Jane put my suitcase just inside my bedroom door. Butter and Bacon had followed us up and were sniffing at the bag suspiciously.

"I'm all packed and can be outta here in a few," she said.

"There's no rush. If you want to stay tonight, you're welcome to."

"That would be awesome Ms. Cole."

"Go back to what you were working on. I'll just unpack a bit and then figure out some dinner. Have you eaten?"

"No. I'm afraid there's not much in the fridge."

"You let me worry about that. Worst case, we order pizza."

I unpacked only what was necessary from my carry-on bag and I was just about to open my large suitcase when I remembered that I'd told Nate I'd call when I got home. I dug my cell phone from my purse and called him.

"You're home safe and sound?" he asked as soon as he answered.

"Yes. Jane is still here. I'm going to make us some dinner now."

"Emily and Bob say hi. We're about to sit down to dinner."

"Call me before you go to bed?"

"Certainly. I miss you, Maddie."

"Talk to you later."

Jane had tidied up the living room floor and was sitting on the sofa working on her laptop when I came back downstairs. She put it aside and followed me into the kitchen.

"I should have asked you if you wanted me to go shopping for you," she said apologetically as she watched me do a quick inventory of the fridge, freezer, and cupboard.

"Do you like fish?" I asked.

"I like everything," said Jane.

"Girl after my own heart. Be a dear and go downstairs to the fruit cellar and get me a couple of onions. They're in a basket on the floor."

Jane went for the onions, and I put water on to boil to make rice. I took a couple of tilapia fillets from the freezer and ran them under cold water to thaw them.

"Anything else I can do?" asked Jane handing me the onions.

"Have a seat and fill me in on what I've missed."

"Not much. The boys behaved themselves. They didn't throw any wild catnip parties. They started sleeping with me after about a week of waiting on your bed for you. I noticed you had a couple of bulbs out in your front hall light, so I got Dad to come help me change them. Mom came too, and vacuumed because she was afraid you'd think I was messy."

"I told you not to bother with that. My cleaning lady will be here tomorrow."

"I told her that, but she insisted."

"I'll have to thank them." I got a chef's knife and started chopping the onions I'd peeled.

"How about you? Good trip?"

"Very nice."

"Do anything exciting?"

"We took a helicopter flight over the Grand Canyon."

"Did you go with a group?"

"It was a private flight. Just me and my friend Nate."

"That's amazing!"

"Funny thing happened… We were filling out the release forms before the flight and they said, if we were married, we only needed one form. Nate pointed out it was one more reason he should marry me. I told the pilot we needed a second form and started filling it out. Then Nate asked me what I would say if he asked me to marry him. I told him he wouldn't know until he asked me."

"So then did he ask you?"

"He did. I said I'd think about it."

"Oh my God! That's huge."

"I'm not sure if it was an actual proposal or a hypothetical. He could have just been kidding around."

"Then what happened?"

"We got in the helicopter."

"That sounds so cool."

"I thought it was fantastic, but I didn't realize his fear of heights included looking down while flying. It turns out he spent the whole flight watching me because he couldn't look down."

"That sucks."

"He almost fell asleep in the car as we drove back to where we were staying in Sedona because the stress of the flight completely wiped him out."

"So what about the proposal?"

"It never came up. We talked about our plans for this summer and I kinda forgot about the whole proposal thing until I was on the plane home."

"What plans did you make?"

I handed her napkins and silverware to set the table. "Actually, that brings up something I'd like to talk to you about. What are your plans for this summer?"

"I've been talking to one of my professors about working for her this summer."

"Would you be living in the city or moving home with your parents?"

"I would prefer to stay in the city, but the University job doesn't pay very well. I'll probably commute. I can take the GoTrain."

"Would you be interested in house sitting for a month or so?"

"Absolutely! Any time you need me. I think the boys are getting used to me too."

"Anyone who gives them treats will win their hearts."

"Boys will be boys," said Jane chuckling.

I made a plate of fish and rice for each of us and set them on the table. "I haven't decided if I'll take the boys with me."

"Whatever. They're good company, but they might prefer to be with their mom."

It was a relief to know Jane was available. I explained to her over dinner that Nate and I had decided that I would come down around the fourth of July and stay for a few weeks. I'd questioned the timing, given that it was his busiest time of the year.

I taunted him. "You're just trying to get some free help."

"I've got Sarah to help me with the inn," he'd replied. "But you definitely will help make every day better just because you're near."

Jane offered to help me clean up after dinner. I refused. She said she didn't want to eat and run, but she was really under pressure to get her paper done. I told her to run along. She let me know she'd be up and out early in the morning. She had a class at nine and wanted to stop at her place beforehand to drop off her things. She left me in the kitchen and took her laptop and papers up to the guestroom.

Leaving the dishes I'd washed by hand in the rack to dry, I decided the kitchen was tidy enough for tonight. I wandered through each room of the main floor, looking around to see if anything was amiss. It wasn't that I didn't trust Jane, I just needed to reconnect with my home space. I cleaned up a hairball from under the dining room table and straightened the sofa cushions in the living room before deciding that I should finish unpacking while I waited for Nate to call back.

Heaving my large suitcase onto the bed, I opened it and began unloading it. I pulled out my dirty laundry; starting a heap on the floor that I would deal with tomorrow. I'd used it to cushion the amethyst candle holders I'd bought for Anne and Linda from the drops and tumbles of the airport baggage handling systems. I unwrapped each of them and was relieved that they were still perfect.

Next, I took out the stack of maps and fliers I'd saved from the places we'd gone. I flipped through them thinking about the trip. The Mount Lemmon

Skycenter where we'd looked through the big telescope, the Sonoran Desert Museum where I'd learned Nate was terrified of snakes, our scorecard from golfing that reminded me of how Nate had insisted we call the front tees the "silver tees" after the marker colour and not refer to them as the "ladies tees" as he was playing from them as well, the map of galleries in Sedona that Nate had marked with stars on the ones we'd liked, and the map of the Grand Canyon with the flight route our helicopter pilot had sketched so I'd be able to map where I'd taken my photos.

It had been an interesting trip that's for sure. I put the stack on top of my dresser and went back to unpacking. Pulling out the little box with the tourmaline Nate had given me, I put it on top of the dresser too, making a mental note to put it on display in the guest room tomorrow after Jane had gone.

I heard my mobile ringing in the distance, and I realized I'd left it in the kitchen. By the time I got to it, it had gone to voice mail, but I saw that it was Nate's number. I didn't wait to listen to his message, that I was certain he was leaving. I called him back.

"I was worried when you didn't answer," he said as he came on the line.

"I was upstairs unpacking. My phone was in the kitchen. I didn't make it in time."

"You can ignore the half-message I left."

"I'm sure it was a half nice message."

"It would have been nicer, I was just getting to the good part and your call interrupted me."

"I can hang up and let you get it done if that's better?"

"Funny lady. No way. I'm not letting you get away that easy."

"So, what were you going to leave in this great message?"

"I would have said how much I miss you. That I'll miss waking up beside you and watching you sleep. I'll miss your kitten snores."

"I don't snore."

"OK, your nighttime breathing."

"You won't be bothered by it tonight."

"Bothered? I was wondering if I'd sleep at all because you're not in bed with me."

"I think you'll be just fine. You must be tired, it's pretty late for you …"

"You've turned me into a night owl."

"Or it might be the jetlag."

"No, I changed my watch."

"Exactly. I bet you're looking forward to being on your own, getting back to your routines."

"You have disrupted my routines, but I've rather liked it."

"I have good news then, Jane is interested in house sitting."

"That's great. But I don't want to wait until July to see you."

"You can see me any time. We can Skype tomorrow – it's Thursday after all."

"I was going to ask you to come sooner. A short visit? An extended long weekend?"

I was surprised and didn't answer right away.

"I'll pay for your airline ticket," said Nate.

"That's not necessary."

"So? Will you come sooner?"

"I suppose we could discuss it. When were you thinking?"

"Is tomorrow too soon?"

"Tomorrow is too soon."

"The day after tomorrow then?"

"You don't mean that. Seriously, when were you thinking?"

"I was thinking that we should have changed your ticket and you should have come home with me forever."

"You could have changed your ticket."

"I might have. If you'd asked me to."

"You wouldn't. You've got an inn to look after."

"I guess you'll never know."

"Why don't you come here then."

"Are you inviting me?"

"I suggested it didn't I?"

"That's not a very heartfelt invitation."

"Would you rather I rescinded it?"

"Absolutely not. I accept. When can I come?"

"Is tomorrow too soon?"

"It's not soon enough. But I wouldn't put you on the spot like that."

"Let's try this again. When would you like to come?"

"Practically, it would be best if I came before my busy season starts."

"When is that?"

"Mid-April."

"How about early April? Before Easter?"

"That would work. We're fully booked for Easter."

I had walked to my desk with the phone while we were talking and opened my desk calendar to April. There wasn't anything on it for the weekend of April 1st or 8th.

"I'm looking at my calendar now. The first Saturday is April 1st."

"Do you have any engagements around that time?" asked Nate.

"Other than curling on Wednesday nights, my schedule is open at this point."

"Then consider yourself engaged for a long weekend."

"If you want to come longer..."

"How about Thursday to Tuesday?"

"I'll pencil you in then. March 30th to April 4th."

"I think you can safely use ink," he said, which made me chuckle. He continued, "I'm going to hold you to it because I don't want to wait until July to see you again."

"You can see me any time you want. We can Skype," I repeated.

"What I meant is, I won't have to wait until July to hold you in my arms and to sleep with you again."

"Oh. I see. This is a booty call."

"A what?"

"A booty call. It's when you call someone because you want sex."

"I would never do such a thing," he said with exaggerated indignance.

"Too bad."

"Bad Maddie! I like bad Maddie."

"You started it."

"I did not. I just said sleep. You brought up sex."

"You started it.

"I think Claire started it. Putting us in the same room. That reminds me, I must thank her specifically for that."

"You can tell her in person when you come. She'll be back from Arizona by then."

"All kidding aside, I would like to do something to thank her. She was a very gracious hostess."

"She doesn't expect anything. She wouldn't let me contribute to the house rental fees because she said she was renting it whether or not I came to visit. So, I definitely want to do something."

"Perhaps we could do something from both of us? Did you have any ideas?"

"I was thinking I would invite her to high tea at either the Royal York or the King Eddie. But that's more of a girly thing."

"Does she like the theatre? Perhaps high tea and then a show. That wouldn't be too girly for me."

"She enjoys all the performing arts; music, dance, theatre. So that might work. I can see what's coming up in April."

"If you'd permit me to plan something, I'd be happy to."

"I'm happy to help. I want to pay my share so let me know what I owe you if you buy tickets or anything."

"I'll check on travel first and then I'll work on an agenda."

Nate told me he'd call me the next day when he was home in Bar Harbor.

We said our goodnights, but before hanging up, Nate added, "Thirty-five sleeps until we're together again. Not that I'm counting."

"Sounds like you just did."

"Did what?"

"Count."

"Can't slip anything past you, eh?"

"You're starting to speak Canadian now?"

"You're rubbing off on me."

"You should go. If you get to sleep, when you wake up it will be thirty-four sleeps."

"I'll be counting sleeps instead of sheep for the next six weeks."

Nate's enthusiasm to spend more time together was infectious. I thought about his last visit and how much had changed since he'd come to stay with me for the toy show. For starters, it's unlikely he'll be sleeping in the guest room this time.

It had been a very long time since I'd shared a bed with a man. In fact, it had been decades. Which made what happened between Nate and me even more surprising. Delightfully so. We got off to a bumpy start. Nate's cramp brought things to a halt prematurely on our first attempt. I wondered if we were too old for that sort of activity. But during the remainder of our trip, Nate proved me wrong on several more occasions.

"Just like riding a bike," Nate had said after our second attempt that left me delightfully spent and him panting beside me.

The biggest change, though, was not in the bedroom. It was that Nate, with my permission, began to make public displays of affection. He would reach out and place his hand on my thigh when we were sitting side by side, take my hand while we were walking and even kiss my cheek when something I'd said or done inspired him to do it. They were innocent enough gestures but what surprised me the most was that I tingled when he touched me. It woke up feelings I'd long ago given up on experiencing.

I have no doubt that Anne will approve of the evolution of Nate and my relationship. Years ago, when she moved to Boston, she told me she wished that I had someone because she'd feel less guilty leaving.

She'd once asked me, "Dad remarried. Why didn't you?"

"I'm not cut out for it," I'd answered. "I have everything I need."

When Anne was growing up, I'd been so busy with work and trying to be a good mother, I didn't have time to go looking for love. I carried a fair bit of guilt that I chose to keep pursuing my career instead of staying at home to raise my daughter. From the first day they put her in my arms, I worried that I was doing it wrong. From worrying I'd stab her with a diaper pin to watching her drive off in my car for the first time, I questioned if I was doing it right and if I was qualified for this motherhood job.

I didn't see that doubt in my mother. She blamed my father for putting ideas in my head that ruined me for motherhood and marriage. If she'd had her way, I would have studied something more appropriate like nursing or teaching and then abandoned it when Anne was born.

On top of the bad mother guilt, there was the nagging feeling of failure because Will and I had not stayed together. Although I don't regret the choices I made, my career contributed greatly to the unravelling of our marriage. My success gave me financial stability, independence and now in retirement, the freedom to do pretty much anything I wanted. But what I'd had to do to achieve that success had come between Will and me on many occasions. Through the years I'd formed a belief that I was just not cut out to be anyone's wife.

I'd not come to that conclusion entirely without suggestion. My mother's not-so-subtle comments to Anne with advice on how to keep your future husband happy so he doesn't go looking elsewhere angered and hurt me. I suspect my mother would have had a difficult time accepting Linda and Anne getting married but I'm fairly certain she would attribute it to me not being a proper role model for my daughter.

When Anne left for university, I tried dating. The men who were interested in dating a 50-year-old woman were either trying to replace someone, looking for a mother for their children or confirmed bachelors who would require a significant amount of house-training before they'd be suitable to live with.

I just couldn't see letting any of them live in my house let alone marrying them. I didn't mind the occasional sleep-over but as soon as they hinted at making it a more permanent arrangement, I broke it off. It felt like they were invading, taking over what was mine, and what I'd worked so hard to build on my own. After several attempts, I concluded that I was happier being single than struggling to fit into someone else's idea of the ideal wife.

I'm sure many of them thought it was me that was the problem. I struggled with my emotional baggage that manifested in contradictory behaviour. I would drop everything to help my daughter, which would suggest to my companions that I'd be a good mother for their children. But when they would try to bring me into their children's lives I would resist because I didn't feel I was qualified to take on that responsibility.

I'm not saying I lived like a nun. I've always enjoyed the company of men. During my career years, most of my closest friends and confidants were men. I felt more aligned with their daily life and work than I did with their wives who were, more often than not, stay at home moms or housewives. I did envy my male colleagues, often wishing I had a "wife" at home to take care of Anne and the house while I was at work. There were a couple of these confidants with whom I had both an intellectual and physical relationship. I wouldn't consider them lovers; they were what Anne would describe as 'friends with benefits'.

I wondered what Nate would think if he knew about my past love life. He hadn't asked me about past relationships. Other than the odd reference to Anne's father we hadn't discussed Will and me.

Would he have hinted at marrying me if he knew that I'd been with other men? Or were my experiences and open attitudes in the bedroom exciting to him? I yawned at my reflection in the bathroom mirror. For tonight, those questions would go unanswered. Butter and Bacon were already circling the bed waiting for me to get under the covers so they could settle into their favourite spots. I didn't keep them waiting any longer.

CHAPTER 32

Maddie pulled off the highway and onto the access road to the Toronto airport.

"Do you want me to park and come in with you?"

"You can just drop me at the curb."

"It seems wrong to drop my brand-new fiancé," she said with a giggle. "I don't want to break you."

I grinned hearing her refer to me as her fiancé. "You've already broken me. I can't live without you anymore."

Maddie pulled up to the curb. "I guess we'll find out if you can live with me in a few weeks."

"I wish it were sooner. But you're stubbornly refusing to come until July."

"Are you stalling because you want to miss your flight and stay longer?"

"I wish. I better go." I leaned towards her and we kissed briefly. "I'm going to miss you."

I got out of the car and Maddie did as well. She came around to the passenger side as I pulled my two small bags from the backseat.

She stepped between me and my bags and put her arms around my waist. "I might miss you too."

"Might? I'm crushed." I pulled her closer.

"OK. Probably miss you."

"Probably?"

"Likely?"

"You'll miss me. You just don't realize it yet."

"I guess you better kiss me goodbye like you're trying to make me miss you."

I didn't need any encouragement to kiss her.

"That'll have to hold you until July," said Maddie as I released her from a lingering kiss.

"It's going to be 12 long weeks. But who's counting." I gave her hand one last squeeze before picking up my bags.

"We can video chat every day."

"We have a lot of details to work out. How about twice a day?"

"You might be an innkeeper, but the lawyer in you just can't stop negotiating for a better deal."

"You've said yes." I nodded towards the ring on her hand. "I've already got what I came for."

"You may find out you got more than you bargained for," said Maddie in that teasing voice that was charming and sexy all at once. "You better run along. The traffic cop is coming to shoo me away."

Sure enough, the traffic control policeman was approaching us and pointing at Maddie's car and waving his fingers clearly indicating that she should move on.

"One more kiss from my fiancée and I'll go," I said with a final peck on her lips before turning to head for the entrance.

"Travel safe," Maddie said as she walked back to the driver's side of the car. She stood and watched me and waved to me when I turned back before going through the sliding door to the terminal.

With two flights and a layover in Boston, I had a lot of time on the trip home to replay the weekend in my mind. As Maddie and I had agreed, I planned our thank-you gift for Claire. I made reservations for the three of us to have tea at the King Edward Hotel and bought theatre tickets to *The Book of Mormon*. I was a little concerned about the choice of show, but Maddie had assured me that Claire would enjoy it.

There were moments when I cringed, having accompanied two ladies to a highly satirical show with mature themes. My discomfort was unwarranted as neither Maddie nor Claire was scandalized by the show, rather they recounted to each other their favorite 'naughty' humor over drinks after the show.

"Thank you, Nate," said Claire. "Maddie told me you planned everything, and it's been a lovely day."

"The least I could do to repay you for hosting a stranger in your home."

"I'd heard enough about you beforehand. I knew what I was getting into," said Claire.

"Strange perhaps, but not a stranger," said Maddie teasingly.

"Hey!" I pretended to be hurt.

"Ungrateful wench," said Claire.

"Keep it to yourself, you old bat," said Maddie sending them both into fits of laughter.

"You two are bad," I said getting up. "By the time I get back, you better settle down."

"You're leaving us?" asked Claire.

"Just for the men's room."

When I got back, I could tell they'd been talking about something they didn't want to share with me. They'd been leaning back in the booth with their faces close together. When they spotted me coming back to the table they separated and sat up straight.

"Am I interrupting something?" I asked.

"Nope," said Maddie

"Would you like another drink," said Claire a little too obviously trying to change the subject.

We decided against another round, and I got out my phone to request our ride. Maddie had been surprised when I'd declined her offer to get us an Uber earlier. I showed her that I had installed Uber and a couple other car service apps and I was all set to take care of our transportation. I didn't confess that Emily had helped me get the buttons on the screen and set up my accounts and payment information. Emily had been delighted that I had replaced my "antique" with a smarter phone that was good for more than just calls.

"You planned a super day for us," said Maddie as she crawled into bed beside me that evening.

"It was my pleasure." I took off my reading glasses and placed them and my book on the nightstand.

"I didn't mean to interrupt your reading."

"Now that you're in bed, I can't concentrate on anything else."

"It's pretty late. Past your bedtime," she teased.

"I'm a changed man with you. I'm doing things I never imagined."

She snuggled closer. "And liking it."

"Definitely liking being back in bed with you." I turned towards her and reached out and ran my fingers from her temple along her cheekbones to her lips. "I've missed this face."

"Just the face?" she said in a sultry voice.

"No. All of you." I leaned in and kissed her on the nose.

She smiled, bunched up her pillow and scooted further down under the covers, laying on her side facing me with her head on her pillow. I leaned away and turned off the bedside lamp and by the time I turned back she'd closed her eyes and fallen fast asleep. I watched her sleep by the light of the streetlight coming through the bedroom window. She was so lovely, and I felt so lucky to be there with her.

I was tired and relieved that today had gone well but I had a hard time falling asleep. I was both nervous and excited about the plans I'd made for Monday. I rehearsed every detail in my mind. Going over the details must have had the same effect as counting sheep because I drifted off to sleep.

I'd told Maddie very little about Monday except that she should be ready to head out at two. She asked what she should wear. I told her I'd be wearing dress pants, a dress shirt, no tie but a jacket.

"So, business attire but not formal business?" she asked.

"That sounds right. But wear comfortable shoes for walking and standing."

"Finally, a clue. Not a good clue, but a clue." She looked at me curiously but didn't fish for any more details. I got the impression she was enjoying that it was a surprise.

Maddie came down carrying her jacket, dressed in black suit pants and a red silky blouse that had a draped neckline that drew my eye to her chest, and I had to force my eyes away. I smiled seeing she had the bracelet I'd given her in Arizona on her wrist. She'd worn it every day we were together. I'd commented when she picked me up at the airport that I was glad she was wearing it.

"Is this alright?" she asked.

I realized that I'd been just standing there, staring at her. "You look lovely. Perfect."

Our first stop was the Art Gallery of Ontario. I'd arranged for a private guided tour of their photography collection. Our guide was excellent. She focused our attention on specific photographs explaining both their technical and cultural significance. I'd toured many art galleries with Betsy, but we rarely looked at the photography exhibits.

"That was really interesting," said Maddie as we left the gallery. "How did you find her?"

"I contacted the curator of the collection and asked her about it. She suggested this gal because she volunteered at the AGO and was a graduate student in Art History at the University of Toronto."

As we Ubered to our next stop, Maddie said several times how much she'd enjoyed it. I felt buoyed by my successful plans so far. As we entered the Lobby Bar at the Royal York, I was relieved that, despite the passing of the years, it still had the same quiet elegance that I remembered. Maddie excused herself to use the ladies' room after we'd placed our drink orders.

I'd planned to wait until dinner, but when I saw Maddie walking back towards me, smiling, I knew I couldn't wait any longer.

"From the first moment I met you, I knew I had to get to know you better."

She peered at me over the rim of her glass as she took a sip. "So how's that going?"

"I like what I've seen so far," I replied, taking a sip of mine.

Her lip curled into a mischievous grin. "You've seen pretty much everything."

"Correction. I love what I've seen so far, and I never want to stop seeing you."

"That may be a bit difficult since we live in different countries."

"That's exactly what I'd like to change." I slipped from my chair and down on one knee beside her.

"What are you doing?" She looked confused.

"I'm asking you to marry me." I took the small box from my pocket and opened it facing her. "Maddie Cole, will you do me the honor of being my wife?"

"Are you serious?" She looked at me wide-eyed and barely looked at the ring.

"Yes. But my knee is starting to hurt."

"Get up then."

"Not until you answer, or my knee gives out."

"I don't know what to say."

"How about yes."

"You're crazy."

"I'm crazy about you."

"OK. True. Yes."

"Yes, you'll marry me or yes crazy?"

"Yes, Nate Jacobs, I will marry you."

I had to lean on the table and the seat of her chair to push myself up from the floor, but I got up and immediately pulled her up from her seat and kissed her with delight. I took the ring from the box and slipped it on her left-hand ring finger.

"It fits!" she said with surprise. "How did you know my ring size?"

"I have my ways. Do you like it?"

"It's beautiful."

"I thought you should have a ring as unique and exotic as you are. But if you'd prefer something more traditional…"

"I couldn't imagine anything more perfect. What an amazing color."

"It matches your blouse. They told me that the color is called pigeon blood."

"It's a lovely stone," She tilted her hand back and forth letting the light pass through it from different angles.

"I knew the geologist in you would examine it closely."

"I'm not examining. I'm admiring."

"It is one of a kind, like you. I had it made for you. Remember the gallery in Tucson with the jewelry you liked?"

"You got this in Tucson?"

"No. It's by the same artist. I got her contact information from the gallery owner and worked with her to design something especially for you."

"Wow."

"It took me a while to decide on the right stone. I decided on a ruby because red is your favorite color and it's the color of love and passion which is why I want you to wear this ring, because I love you."

"Ruby for love and diamonds are forever?"

"And the two bands cross each other and then become one."

"Our lives intersecting and then we finally meet?"

"I knew you'd understand." I kissed her again, oblivious to the people around us.

Thinking back, I'm surprised I didn't stick to my plan of asking Maddie to marry me over dinner. Yet another example of how she inspires me to be spontaneous. I'd made reservations at a casual but highly rated Italian restaurant called Piano Piano. I'd told them I hoped we would be celebrating a special occasion but not specifically that it was an engagement. As she seated us, the hostess asked us what we were celebrating. Maddie announced that we had just gotten engaged. The young woman, at first, looked a little confused; perhaps because she expected it was a birthday or anniversary given our ages.

"That is definitely something to celebrate. Can I bring you each a glass of prosecco to toast your engagement?"

"Are we crazy?" asked Maddie as we sat sipping our wine, waiting for our antipasti.

"How so?"

"Getting engaged at our age."

"Not crazy. It just took us a long time to find each other."

It's not surprising that our dinner conversation, and most of our discussions over the next twenty-four hours, until I had to leave, revolved around the subject of us getting married. Not just the wedding itself. That was the simple part.

"I suppose you've got the wedding planned already," Maddie had teased me during dinner.

"Not entirely. But I have some ideas," I'd said attempting an air of mystery by raising my brows and looking at her intently.

"Do I get a say in this? Or will you spring a wedding on me like you have this engagement?"

"Would that be all bad?"

Maddie smiled and looked at me suspiciously. "I'd like to have a little notice. So I can be prepared."

"So, if we agree to where and when, you'll leave the rest up to me?"

"Within reason."

"Just give me a list of your requests, and I'll take care of the rest."

In my mind, it had been simple. She marries me, we move in together and live happily ever after. Maddie didn't see it that way. I could feel her stress and resistance when I casually mentioned her moving to Bar Harbor. As certain as I was that we should be together, I realized it was going to take some time for us to work out the details. The independence and confidence I loved about her had been forged by her hard work to build a life that was secure and happy for her and Anne all on her own.

"I can't just drop everything and everyone to be your wife," she'd said.

"Are you having second thoughts?"

"No. But you have to want to marry me as is."

"I love you as is."

"I'm not going to turn my whole life upside down to be with you."

"I would for you."

"Are you sure I'd like you as much if you did?"

We agreed to keep our engagement quiet for the time being. At first, I'd resisted. I wanted everyone to know. She pointed out that Anne, Ann, and Emily would have a million questions and that we should wait until we'd been able to work out some of the details. We decided it was safer to just look ahead to July and make plans for Maddie's stay. Take things one step at a time.

Since returning from Arizona, I'd called Maddie almost every day. I'd even started texting her. She'd been so delighted the first time she got a text, she replied with hearts and happy faces. Before Maddie, I saw no reason to have a phone that did anything but make calls. Now, I can't imagine not being able to send her messages throughout the day. Today, during my layover and when the flight crew announced that we could use our phones, I sent her several messages with ideas and questions.

I got into my car at the airport and texted Maddie again while I waited for the car to warm up. She doesn't always answer right away. Sometimes I get worried until she replies. This time she answered immediately.

Glad you're there. Drive safe. XO

Driving back to the inn I listened to the radio and was happy to hear that the weekend weather forecast was looking promising. The B&B rooms were fully booked so there was a lot to get done in the next couple of days. I'd been so focused on packing the ring I'd completely forgotten to put a notebook in my satchel. On the plane, I wished I'd brought it so I could jot down the lists that had been forming in my head all day. It had been some time since I'd reviewed the booking information and I wasn't sure if there were any special requests, so I'd need to check that as well. First item on the list, make a list.

I was happy to see Sarah's car parked by the back door as I pulled up to the house. I hoped she had managed to get all the rooms ready while I'd been away.

"Welcome home, Boss!" she called out to me from the dining room as I came in.

I put my bags at the foot of the stairs and went through the kitchen to the dining room. "Thank you. Everything under control?"

"I think so." She got up from the laptop she was working on and handed me a file folder. "Here's the scoop on the guests for this weekend. There's one couple who have noted they are vegan on their special requests section. The only other request was for non-feather pillows, so we can put that couple in either Tokyo or Lighthouse because I checked when I made up the rooms and all the pillows are hypoallergenic in both."

"Anything else?" I asked, relieved that she seemed to be on top of everything.

"I've gone through the inn email. I've responded to the ones with general questions, but there are quite a few new booking requests, so I want to go over them with you before replying."

"I haven't taken any new bookings, so the reservation book is up to date. I'll get it." I went to the living room to the small desk where we kept the room keys and the reservation book and brought it back to the dining room.

She took the book and opened it. "We could replace this with an online calendar." Sarah had suggested this several times before.

I shook my head and smiled at her. "Maybe someday, just not today."

The reservation book worked. The calendar pages were large enough that each day had space for me to write in the guest names for each of the four rooms. I could see which rooms were occupied and how many rooms were booked for each day.

"I'll reply to the emails today before I head out. And before you say it, I'll update the book in pencil with the date requests and put the confirmed ones in pen." She pulled the writing utensils from the sleeve at the front of the book and held them up for me to see.

I gave her a big thumbs up. "See. The system is perfect as it is."

With Sarah looking after the reservations, I could focus on the kitchen. Over the years I'd developed a system for the breakfast menus. I had a basic menu of things I would always have on hand. I also have menus and recipes for a variety of dietary requests. Every year there seems to be some new diet that people request, and I try to accommodate them if I can. I pulled out my recipe binder and flipped to the vegan section to select some options for this weekend's menu.

The next week was hectic with the inn full for Easter weekend. Saturday was cold and cloudy so most of our guests spent the day indoors. I kept a fire going in the living room all day and kept replenishing the coffee, tea, and beverages in the dining room. It was such a dreary day that Sarah offered to bake a batch of cookies for an impromptu afternoon tea to help brighten the day.

Fortunately, Sunday and Monday were warmer, so the guests were happier. But that also meant that they wanted to cram as much into the days as they could. There were a few hiccups, like the mouse nest we discovered in one of the kayaks and a mix-up with a fishing charter reservation that I was sure I'd made but the boat had no record of it. Sarah worked much longer than her usual 7 am to 3 pm every day, but she never complained, and we got through our first big weekend of the season without any major mishaps.

It wasn't until Tuesday night, when all the weekend guests had left, that Maddie and I had a longer video chat, and we could pick up discussing our plans.

"I've decided to drive down," announced Maddie.

"That's a long drive. I don't think it's a good idea."

"I won't do it in one stretch. I've talked to Claire and I'm going to take her to Montreal which is about halfway. I'll stay with her at her sister's and then the next day I'll drive from Montreal to Bar Harbor."

"But then you'll be alone for all that way."

"I don't mind driving alone."

"I could buy you an airline ticket."

"I don't need an airline ticket. This is better. I'll have my car."

"You don't need a car. I can pick you up."

"I don't want you to have to drive me around."

"It's no trouble. Or you can take my car."

"I don't want to have to use your car. And it will be easier for packing compared to flying."

Nothing I said was going to change her mind, so I changed the subject. "Is there something in particular that you'd like to do while you're here?"

"What do you mean?"

"I just wondered if you wanted to have Anne and Linda come for a while or if you had some things in mind you'd like to do or see?"

"I would like to see Anne. I was thinking I could drive down to Boston one weekend and go see her new house."

"I thought you were coming to see me?"

"We don't have to spend every minute together." She paused, squinted and leaned in towards the video screen. "What's the matter?"

"Nothing. Why?"

"Because you're scowling."

I was thinking that spending every day together was exactly what I was expecting we'd do.

"You're beautiful," I said intentionally attempting to change the subject but she didn't let it go.

"I just thought you'd be busy with guests, especially on the weekends, and I could get out of your hair. It would only be for a couple of days, the rest of the time I'd be with you."

"I won't be too busy to spend time with you if that's what you're worried about."

"You told me that your summer weekends are the busiest time."

"Have you already arranged something with Anne?"

"Not yet. It was just an idea. I need to check with her."

"Have they set a wedding date?"

"I was going to tell you. They told me on Easter. It's Jan 27th."

"That's an unconventional time of year for a wedding."

"That's what I thought."

"Where are they getting married? Someplace warm?"

"Nope. Boston. But they plan to honeymoon in Hawaii afterwards."

"So, will we be attending as husband and wife?"

"I'm sure you're invited either way."

"But will I be step-father to the bride?"

"I don't know. Will you?"

"With pleasure. I want to marry her mother as soon as possible."

"You're crazy."

"Crazy about you. Now that I've found you, I don't want to waste time being apart."

"Then we need to figure out if we can live together. And where."

"I want to but you're already planning on leaving as soon as you get here."

"Not as soon as I arrive. Just before you're tired of having me around."

I knew she was joking, but it underscored the challenges ahead of us; merging lives that were well established individually, figuring out the when, where, and how we would build a life together further complicated by the fact that we lived 700 miles apart.

CHAPTER 33

It was still pouring rain as I pulled into Nate's driveway. My neck and shoulders were tense from the stress of driving in a storm for the last three hours. As I approached the house, the door near the garage opened and Nate came out opening a large umbrella and pointing and waving to direct me to back the car in close to the door.

I put on my raincoat that I'd hung over the back of the passenger seat to dry after my last gas stop. I opened the car door and Nate rushed over to hold the umbrella over me as I got out. He pulled me into his arms and kissed me.

"I'm so glad you're here. I was worried about you driving in this weather."

"It was slow going." I stretched and reached back into the car to grab my purse from the front seat.

"Should we get the boys inside and settled first and then come back for the rest of your things?"

"I'm sure they're anxious to get out, but I need the washroom first."

"You go on in." Nate handed me the umbrella. "I'll get them."

"The carrier is buckled in," I said over my shoulder, but my full bladder wouldn't allow me to stick around to give instructions.

I got back to the door just as Nate, soaking wet, maneuvered the long double carrier into the entryway and set it down.

"Should we take them upstairs before letting them out?" he asked. "I've got their food and litter box setup in the laundry room."

As if to respond, there was a long low growl and a hiss from the carrier.

"Yes," I said. "They've had enough confinement."

I took one end of the carrier and helped Nate carry it up the stairs and into the small laundry room. We had to shift it around several times to get us and the carrier inside and the door shut. I unzipped the two openings but neither cat came out.

I picked up their new food bowl and gave it a shake to rattle the kibble and called to them.

"Butter, Bacon. Snacks." There was no movement. "We can just leave them to explore on their own."

Nate opened the door so we could slip out. "I think the rain has let up a bit. We should unpack your car now; in case it picks up again."

303

I made one final trip to the car for the last few items in the front seat after Nate had helped me unload everything from the trunk.

"I can't believe all this came out of your car." He looked dismayed by the pile of storage bins and suitcases that we'd hurriedly stacked up in the entryway.

"You'd think I was moving in or something."

"I'm not suggesting I don't want you moving in. I'm astonished by your packing skills. This pile looks much bigger than your trunk."

"I guess it's bigger on the inside."

Nate looked puzzled, so I explained the Dr. Who reference. "Dr. Who is a time and space travelling alien with a ship called a TARDIS that looks like a police phone box but inside it's much bigger. The catchphrase whenever someone new enters is they always say it's bigger on the inside."

"Sounds rather far-fetched," said Nate.

"It might grow on you. We can watch a few episodes sometime."

Nate picked up a suitcase and garment bag. "I'll start taking things upstairs."

"First you need to see what Claire sent you." I pointed to the insulated cooler bag and a large brown paper shopping bag that I'd set on the kitchen counter. I was excited for him to see what she'd sent.

Nate looked irritated but set the bags down and came to look.

"What's this?" Nate opened the paper bag. "Bagels?"

"Not just any bagels. Real Montreal bagels. Fresh baked this morning from St. Viateur bakery. Arguably the best bagels on the planet. At least according to Claire."

"There's a lot of them."

"Three dozen. Minus three. I got hungry. There are bags to freeze what we don't eat today."

"What's in here?" he asked tapping the cooler bag.

"Open it!"

Nate unpacked the contents onto the counter "Smoked salmon, cream cheese, pickles, mustard and ... corned beef?"

"Not corned beef. Montreal smoked meat from Schwartz's deli. It's famous."

"And more bread?"

"Claire said we had to have everything, to have the complete experience."

"She didn't have to go to all that trouble."

"I couldn't have stopped her. She left the house early this morning and was back by 9 am with all this."

Nate put the meat, cheese and salmon in the fridge but frowned at the other items.

"We can deal with those later." I grabbed one of the plastic bins and started carrying it upstairs. "I know you want this stuff out of the way."

"I suggest we put it all in the guest bedroom. Until you decide where you want things." Nate followed me up with another bin.

It took several trips for us to carry everything up to the guest room, a room I didn't know existed before today.

"I thought you could use this desk for your computer or writing," said Nate.

"Still not letting me in your office," I teased.

Nate looked confused. "What?"

"Other than your sitting room, I've not seen any of these rooms before."

"I guess we better remedy that." Nate lifted his bent arm and extended it to me. "Allow me to escort you on a tour of your home for the next few months."

I took his arm grinning at his overly formal gesture. "Lead on."

We both chuckled as we crunched together to fit through the door arm in arm.

"Although you've previously seen the sitting room, we'll begin our tour there as there have been a few adjustments since your last visit."

The old recliner that Nate had sat in the night we watched TV was gone as was the old loveseat. In their place was a new longer, comfortable-looking sofa with a large square ottoman in front of it. There were also two matching wide chairs. The upholstery was a solid neutral colour and the style was what I would describe as comfortable but still classy and it reminded me a bit of my own living room furniture.

"Do you like the new furniture?" asked Nate.

"Yes. When did you get it?"

"It arrived just last week. I thought you'd probably hate my recliner as much as my daughter and granddaughter do."

"Will you be comfortable watching TV without it?"

"The sofa is exceptionally comfortable. And it has room for two." He squeezed his arm to his side pulling me closer. "And being close to you is very comforting."

"You got a new TV?"

"Bob and Emily helped me set everything up. It's apparently a smart TV... But I haven't really worked out all the smart things it can do. I expect my tech-savvy fiancée will have it figured out in no time. Shall we move on to the next location on our tour?"

Nate led me out of the sitting room and back past the guest room door. "You've seen the guest room. Which you may choose to use as your office. This," he paused dramatically and then opened the door across the hall from the guest room, "is my office."

In the center of the room, there was a large wooden desk with a wood executive chair with wheels. The desk was almost completely clear. There was a computer monitor, keyboard and mouse, a couple of paperweights and a letter opener.

As clear as the desk was, the walls of the office were, by contrast, completely full. One wall was filled with glass-fronted display cases that went from the floor to nearly the ceiling. On the other three walls were a combination of bookcases and shelves that extended from wall to wall, right up to and even over the door. Every inch of every cabinet and shelf was filled with boats.

"Wow," was all I could say.

Nate released my arm. "Feel free to look around. I'm not hiding anything from you."

"Except maybe the boats you told me you stored in the attic."

"That's not on the tour today. But you're welcome to explore on your own to satisfy your curiosity."

I started at the nearest wall and started to make my way around the room. There was far too much to take in all at once. The boats seemed to be very well organized. There were groupings of like-sized and styled boats that I assumed were sets or series. The boats were also very efficiently arranged to make best use of the space. The smallest ones were lined up in tight rows inside the glass-fronted cabinets, while the larger ones were docked on the shelves and bookcases. One bookcase was entirely filled with ships in bottles.

"I went through a bottle collecting phase," explained Nate when I leaned in to examine them closer.

"I can see that. They're amazing. This one even has tiny sailors working on deck."

I'd worked my way around the whole room and back to Nate at the door.

He again extended his arm to me. "Shall we continue on?"

He led me back across the hall to the next door.

"This is the main bathroom." He stepped aside for me to enter ahead of him. "It has both a tub and shower, so if my lady would like to soak, she'll have to do it here."

I scrambled to say something nice about the room. "I don't take many baths. But it's a nice tub." I kept silent about the rose wallpaper and pink tile that was nothing short of hideous.

"I think it's time this room was re-done," said Nate.

"It is a bit... dated."

"I've already hired someone to redo it, but I was hoping you'd help me select the colours and fixtures and tile..."

"I don't know that I'm an expert. But I'm happy to help."

"Thank you. It hasn't bothered me because I never used it. But now that you're here, I expect it will get a lot more use. Now, if you'll step this way..."

Nate led me to the next door, across the hall from the laundry room where we'd confined Butter and Bacon.

"Our bedroom," he said ushering me into the room.

"I took the liberty of having it repainted, hopefully, you approve of the colour. I thought perhaps you and I could decorate it together and you could select or change anything you want so you feel at home."

The room was very sparsely decorated. The walls were a soft creamy white and the trim was painted bright white. The bedroom set of dark wood looked solid and classic and included a four-poster bed with nightstands and dressers with turned legs that matched the posts. There was a large window on the wall opposite the door. I noticed there were curtain rods with no curtains but there was a shade. The shade was pulled up halfway and I could see there was a great view of the ocean. In front of the window, facing out to sea, were two leather wing-backed armchairs with a long narrow rectangular table between them. The table was positioned longways, so it extended from behind the chairs to just slightly in front of them. On the end of the table closest to us, there was a large wooden boat I recognized.

"You moved the Madeline from the guestroom?"

"As soon as we were engaged." He looked at me with a very mischievous look. "I couldn't think of anywhere more appropriate than my bedroom to put my Madeline."

Nate showed me that one nightstand and the larger of the two dressers were completely empty and he'd cleared a section of the closet. He pointed out the set of new red hangers he'd bought for me to use. It was obvious he was trying to make me feel welcome. It was sweet but also a little overwhelming.

"Do you want to unpack?" he asked.

"I should check on the boys first," I said.

"Do you need anything?"

I shook my head no. "You've already gone to a lot of trouble."

Nate smiled. "Not at all. I'll start working on dinner and leave you to settle in."

Nate went downstairs and I slipped into the laundry room being careful lest a cat tried to escape. Neither did. Butter was perched on top of the stacked washer-dryer and Bacon scooted back into the carrier.

"I know. It's kinda freaky to be in a strange place," I cooed at them taking the bag of treats from the side pocket of the carrier and sitting down on the laundry room floor. I shook the bag to get their attention. Butter jumped down from the top of the dryer to the counter but didn't come any closer. Bacon's nose emerged from the carrier opening, sniffing suspiciously.

"Treats." I shook the bag again before opening it and put two pieces on the floor beside me. Their love of freeze-dried chicken overcame their distrust of the evil woman who'd confined them for the better part of two days.

"I'd love it if my fiancée would come and stay for the remainder of the inn's season," Nate had said on the phone just days after we'd gotten engaged. I'd dismissed the idea initially. How could I just drop everything and move to Bar Harbor for five months? I'd advocated for sticking to our original plan of a month or so. But he'd been persistent; determined to remove any roadblock I put up.

Suggesting I bring Butter and Bacon had helped convince me I could stay longer. Nate had asked me to tell him what he should have on hand to make them feel at home. I'd given him a detailed list with their brand and flavour of food, type of litter and litterbox and their favourite treats. I'd recommended we keep them in a limited space to start so they could gradually acclimatize to their new environment. I'd considered their need to adjust a lot more than I'd thought about my own. Sitting there on the laundry room floor, coaxing the cats with treats, it suddenly hit me that this wasn't a visit. This was a new life. I understood the cats' instinct to hide.

CHAPTER 34

I didn't have much to do while I waited for Maddie to come down. I'd had so much pent-up excited energy waiting for her to arrive I'd been going a million miles an hour all day. I'd started out the day by giving the entire upstairs an extra once-over, even though the cleaning girls had been there on Monday. I'd already done the prep work for dinner, set the table in the dining room, selected wines from the cellar and even run out to the florist to get flowers to welcome her.

I couldn't help humming along to the music I'd put on as I pulled together the crab cakes and pre-heated the oven. I thought it would be appropriate to serve the first thing I'd cooked for Maddie. I'd considered taking her out for dinner, but I really wanted it to be just us tonight.

"Are you done unpacking?" I asked, surprised to see her downstairs so soon.

"I only unpacked my overnight bag with the essentials and hung up the garment bag in the closet."

"If you need more time…"

"The rest can wait. Mmmm you're making your famous crab crumble cakes." Her voice was playful and teasing.

She suggested we have a taste of Montreal for an appetizer. She assembled a bagel with cream cheese and smoked salmon, and I opened the chardonnay I'd selected to have with the crab cakes. We toasted her arrival with the wine and bagel.

I touched my glass to hers. "Welcome home, future Mrs. Jacobs."

She suddenly looked quite serious. "Thank you. But you know I'm not going to change my name."

"Really?"

"It would just complicate things at this point in my life. It doesn't make me any less your wife… when the time comes."

"And have we given any more thought as to when that time might be?"

"Have you?"

"Every day."

I didn't want to press her on the subject so soon after her arrival. We'd had several discussions during our phone calls over the past few weeks. We'd gone around in circles and not gotten any closer to a decision about where and when we would get married. On top of that, we'd still not told our children of our engagement, because Maddie had insisted we keep it quiet.

"I'm very comfortable living in sin with you," said Maddie with a mischievous grin and a wink.

"That's good. If there's anything I can do to make you feel more at home…"

"I'd like to do some of the cooking."

"You mean for us? Or for the guests?"

"I meant for us. But if you want me to help with the guest meals, I'm happy to."

"Morning isn't your favorite time of the day."

"True. I could help with prep work the night before."

"I already know you're a great cook, so *mi kitchen, su kitchen*." I opened my arms and spun around making Maddie giggle.

"I was hoping you'd be OK with it because I had an idea for a project that necessitates using the kitchen."

"What sort of project?"

"I want to make a gift for Anne and Linda. A cookbook of family recipes."

"Linda was constantly asking how things were made. I bet she'll love it."

"My thought was, I'd make each dish. As I do I'll measure and write down everything I do and take pictures of the steps. Then I'll put it all together in a book."

"Sounds like a big project."

"I thought I could start on it while I'm here. As long as I won't be in your way."

"An opportunity to discover your family's secret recipes, I'll make room for that." I was already thinking about where and how I could rearrange things to make space for Maddie's supplies in our pantry.

We continued to chat about the cookbook project over dinner. I suggested we pick a section of the pantry, fridge and freezer for her ingredient storage. I think my enthusiasm for her project assured her that I genuinely wanted her to make herself comfortable here.

"So, your next guests arrive tomorrow… Need me to do anything tonight?" asked Maddie as she helped me clean up after dinner.

"Everything is taken care of," I assured her.

Maddie maneuvered herself between me and the kitchen sink where I was trying to do the dishes. "Then you're all mine tonight."

At first, I felt quite irritated that she was in the way but, seeing her impish grin, my annoyance melted.

"So, this is how it's going to be? You, distracting me from my chores, with your feminine wiles?"

"Life is more than a to-do list." She hooked her fingers through the belt loops of my pants and pulled our hips together. My brain wanted me to protest but my will was completely shattered by the playful twinkle in her eyes.

"What if I put you at the top of my to-do list?" I struggled, but failed, to reach around her for the dish towel to dry my hands.

"What do you want to do with me?"

"If I could just get these dishes done, we could go upstairs, and I'll show you."

"Why do we need to go upstairs?" she said in a sweet tempting voice.

My brain scrambled to process the situation. I felt a shiver of excitement at the unexpectedness and a wave of panic that she might be suggesting we have sex right then and there in the kitchen.

"You look terrified."

"You're terrifying, but in the best way."

"So terrifying is a compliment?"

"When it's the combination of excitement and fear…"

"So I'm 'fear-citing'?"

"You are uniquely fearciting. We need to invent new words to describe you."

"A little fearcitement sounds like a good thing."

I took a step back to lean against the kitchen island, tugging Maddie with me as she was still hanging on to my belt loops. I dried my still wet hands on my pants before reaching up and sliding them into her hair, drawing her face to mine. The intensity of emotion that welled up from deep inside me, made it impossible for me to think of anything but how much I wanted to kiss her.

After a deliciously long kiss, Maddie pulled back. "Don't you need to finish those dishes first?"

"What dishes?" I slid my hands over her shoulders so I could stroke the soft skin of her collar bone, inching towards the top button of her blouse. It was Maddie's turn to shiver as my fingers lightly skimmed along the edge of the fabric. She tugged again on my belt loops and pressed her hips seductively against mine and leaned in and nuzzled my neck.

"Shall we take this to our bedroom?" she said in a low voice into my ear.

I unhooked the fingers of one of her hands and led her upstairs.

After making love, Maddie curled up in my arms and fell asleep. I slipped out of bed, put on my pajamas, robe and slippers, and crept back downstairs to the kitchen. I worked as quietly as I could so I wouldn't wake Maddie. I imagined she would tease me that I couldn't leave the dishes until morning, but I knew I'd sleep much better knowing they were done.

I was back upstairs in 10 or 15 minutes. Passing the laundry room door, I heard a rustling noise. I felt bad that the cats were confined. I didn't want to give them free rein just yet, so I closed all the other doors leaving only our bedroom and bathroom doors open. I opened the laundry room door just a crack and both cats dove for cover in their carrier. I opened the door wide and slipped a doorstop under it to make sure they wouldn't get shut out if they ventured out.

"It's OK guys," I whispered. "You can come out when you're ready."

Maddie hadn't stirred. She was still curled in the same position I'd left her in. I stood just inside the door watching her sleep. Her face was towards me. Her expression, so peaceful. She looked like an angel. The way the bedsheet was draped revealed her shoulder and just a hint of the curve of her breast. It made me want to reach out and caress it. I resisted, not wanting to wake her. It was hard to believe that she was finally here. I smiled remembering the delight I felt when she called this our bedroom.

Waking up and finding her beside me felt like everything was finally as it should be. Then there was a soft thud and motion at the foot of the bed. I leapt out of bed with a start, my heart pounding, only to find Butter on the floor stretching, blinking, and looking at me as if to accuse me of disturbing him.

I was now wide awake. I shut off my alarm and decided not to lay back down. As I came around the bed to go to the bathroom, I found Bacon curled up in Maddie's jeans that we'd hastily cast aside as we'd undressed last night. I smiled and my heart swelled with a little pride remembering Maddie's contented sighs as we cuddled together. I dressed quietly in the bathroom and then headed downstairs to turn on the coffee machine so I would be ready to make Maddie's favorite cappuccino when she came down.

CHAPTER 35

Waking up in Nate's bed the first morning, I was a bit confused. It was not unlike the feeling of waking up in a hotel room and being startled by the unfamiliar shapes and shadows in the room. I was quickly oriented by a familiar meow.

Butter and Bacon were sitting on the bed looking at me.

"Did you two break out of jail or did you get an early release?" I asked them. In response, Bacon rolled upside down to have his belly rubbed and Butter turned away in disgust, leaving the bed for a sunny spot on the windowsill. I looked at my phone to check the time and realized I'd forgotten to plug it in, and the battery was almost dead. I hadn't been thinking about my phone at bedtime. I couldn't help but grin remembering how enthusiastically Nate had responded to my brazen advances after dinner.

I wasn't surprised Nate had woken up before me, but I was surprised I'd slept until almost nine. I opened the blind higher. It was a glorious sunny summer morning. I retrieved my jeans from the floor and pulled on a t-shirt and went to find Nate. Passing the laundry room door, I noticed it was propped open. I was relieved Nate had apparently let the boys out rather than they had escaped and intruded uninvited into our bedroom.

"Good morning, Beautiful," he'd said, making me smile, although it was hard to believe I was, given my dishevelled-ness.

"Morning. Sorry I slept so late."

"You had a long day of driving yesterday. I expected you'd need a good sleep. Cappuccino?"

"Please." I perched on a stool while he made it.

Over the past few months, Nate has gone out of his way to help me settle in and be comfortable in what he calls Our Maine Address. We've established a comfortable routine. Nate is up before me but, when I get up, I join him in the kitchen, where he's either cooking for guests or going over details and to-do lists with Sarah. He never leaves to run errands until he's at least made me my first coffee.

Learning to live together hadn't been all smooth sailing. The hardest incidents for me to accept were ones where he'd become irritable and mean over seemingly insignificant transgressions on my part. The first of these incidents was the Thursday after I'd arrived. I'd stood in the pantry doorway chatting to him thinking that I was keeping him company as he made his shopping list. He'd snapped.

"Do you have to always be talking?" he'd said in a dismissive and rude tone.

Shocked and hurt, I retreated upstairs to the spare room where I'd been unpacking what I'd brought to spend the next few months with Nate. I paced back and forth choking back anger and disappointment, and questioning my sanity being engaged to and now living with someone I really didn't know.

My stomach was in knots. I moved things from one pile to another debating if I should start packing to go home. When he came looking for me an hour or so later, he acted like nothing had happened.

"Are you ready to go to the store?" he'd said.

I was afraid I was either going to either scream at him or cry. I wasn't sure which, so I just said, "No."

"How long do you need? I need to get to the bank before four."

"Just go. I don't want my talking to disrupt you." I opened my laptop and flipped through the binder on the desk to release some of the nervous energy generated by the churning thoughts in my brain. I was angry at Nate for talking down to me. I was angry at myself for feeling hurt and vulnerable.

"Are you mad?" he'd asked.

Despite knowing he was genuinely confused, I exploded. Unloading with a barrage of words that I don't recall. Spewing my raw thoughts, from brain to mouth, without filter.

"There's no reason to raise your voice," he'd said.

His scolding tone just infuriated me more; the anger and disappointment caused tears to well up and I could feel my throat closing. I wouldn't have tolerated anyone speaking to me in the tone he used let alone someone I was considering marrying. I turned away and took several breaths trying to compose myself and decide what to do. Should I say more? Say nothing and start packing?

Nate came up behind me and put his arms around me and nuzzled my neck.

"Don't be upset," he'd said.

"Too late," I answered, not wanting to let him off the hook.

"I like that you have a lot to say," he said in a teasing voice that made me smile despite still being very annoyed with him.

"Then you shouldn't tell me to shut up."

"I never said that."

"Might as well have."

"I did not."

"Did to."

"Did not. And I'm not here for an argument," he said with a chuckle at his own Python reference.

I couldn't stay mad at him. He was genuinely contrite.

I eventually figured out that he can't focus on more than one thing at a time without getting frustrated. When he gets frustrated, he snaps. He's not snapping at me. He's angry at himself that he's been overwhelmed.

Today as I sipped my coffee, Nate gave me the run-down of what he planned to do.

"I'm going to go up and change and then I'm going into town to the bank. Then I have a meeting with our accountant."

"I didn't know we had an accountant."

"We do. She's very efficient so I expect I'll be done with her around lunchtime."

"Do you want me to make lunch for us?"

"No. I won't be back until later because this afternoon I've got a service appointment for the jeep and afterwards I'm going to get a haircut."

"And our guests?"

"They're heading out for the day so they shouldn't need anything."

"So the coast is clear for me to make a mess in the kitchen?"

"All yours. I won't need it again today. I suspected you might be working on the cookbook today so I got everything for tomorrow out of the way early."

Nate left a short time later with his briefcase and his to-do and shopping lists in hand. After I'd waved goodbye from the back door, I started pulling out everything I needed to get back to work on my project. I laid out the ingredients for the first recipe for today and set up my camera on the tripod at the far side of the counter to document each step as I went along.

"What are you making?" asked Shelly, one of the guests, who'd poked her head into the kitchen from the dining room.

"I'm working on a cookbook of family recipes for my daughter. Today 'appetizers'."

"I wondered why the camera. Pictures for the cookbook?"

"Yes. I'm taking pictures of the steps and the final result. Unfortunately, I don't have my mother's skill at presentation. She was meticulous about her cocktail parties; she rivaled Martha Stewart in her day."

"I love cocktail parties. Especially the food."

"We won't be able to eat everything, so if you'd like to have a taste before you head out to dinner, you're more than welcome."

"Taste what?" asked Dan, Shelly's husband who'd joined her in the kitchen doorway.

"Maddie's making appetizers. Says we could have some later."

"Then we'll bring the drinks and make it a party."

"You can't just impose like that," scolded Shelly.

"It's no problem," I said. "I'll try to get through at least a couple of recipes so there will be enough for everyone to have a taste."

"Then it's a plan. I'll tell the others," said Dan leaving.

"Did you need anything?" I asked Shelly who was lingering in the doorway. "Nate's out but..."

"No. We'll get out of your hair. See you tonight."

I'd developed a process for documenting each recipe. For each one, I typed up the ingredients and instructions either from memory, my mother's recipe cards or from my own cookbooks where I'd scribbled in the margins with notes for modifications. I'd printed each recipe on a separate sheet of paper. As I made each recipe, I wrote notes and made changes on the paper copy as I measured ingredients that I would normally 'eyeball' or add 'to taste'. I also took pictures of each step along the way. After I finished testing and documenting each recipe, I updated the file on my computer based on my notes. I'd figured out how to put pictures into the word documents and lay out each recipe, so it looked nice on the page.

I was proud of the way the book was coming along. Since starting the project in July, I'd finished the soups and salads recipes as well as most of the vegetable side dishes and fruit desserts. I'd made a schedule for myself in approximately the order that the different ingredients would come into season.

I'd planned to make only two recipes today because any more would be too much for Nate and me to consume. Now that our guests were expecting a cocktail party, I figured I'd try to do a couple more while I had a crowd to feed. I shuffled through my stack of appetizer recipes to see which ones I could make given the ingredients I had on hand. Then I pulled out one of Nate's notepads from the drawer and started to figure out how to get everything done in time. I smiled thinking, if Nate saw me making a checklist, he would tease me that his habits were rubbing off.

Nate had given me free rein to go through all the kitchenware, china and serving pieces of Betsy's he'd stored in cupboards and boxes in the basement. Based on her collection, I imagined that Betsy had been an excellent homemaker and hostess or at least had acquired all the right tools and accessories.

When I'd come across her collection of jelly moulds, I knew I had to make one of Anne's childhood favourites, my mother's shrimp spread. One of the other reasons for upping my list of offerings today was that I was a bit hesitant to serve it because although it was tasty, it looked a bit weird. I was glad I'd planned to start it first because it needed time to set.

I'd copied the recipe for the shrimp spread from a worn and stained recipe card but it probably originated on the side of a tomato soup can or in a magazine ad for cream cheese. It used those ingredients along with chopped celery, green onions, gelatin, mayonnaise and four cans of tiny shrimp, which were a lot more luxurious in the 1960s than they are today. When I'd purchased the cans of shrimp last week, Nate had asked me if they were for the cats. He'd been horrified when I told him it was an ingredient for the cookbook.

My mother had added some kick to the recipe over time adding horseradish and Worcestershire sauce and, when that wasn't enough for her anymore, several dashes of Tabasco. It was this 'refined' version of the recipe that Anne had loved. I measured what I thought was the right amount of each but tasting it, I had to add a little more horseradish before packing the pink mixture into Betsy's jelly mould with the starfish pattern on it.

With that out of the way, I put eggs on to boil for the deviled eggs. Then I cleaned the mushrooms, lining the caps in rows on a baking sheet and chopping the stems to sauté for the stuffing. Once the mushrooms were stuffed and ready to bake and the deviled eggs chilling, I started on the Swedish meatballs because they could be fully cooked and then reheated when I made the cream gravy later.

I had cleaned all the serving dishes for the appetizers already. Not because I'd expected to be serving them to the inn guests, but because I'd planned to photograph the finished recipes as they should be served. Betsy's deviled egg tray, with the dozen egg-shaped indents and small blue flowers around the rim, reminded me of my mother's china. I photographed the deviled eggs in the dish on the kitchen counter and put them back in the fridge for later. I moved my camera and tripod to the dining room so I could photograph the final presentation of the other dishes there.

Shelly had popped into the kitchen around four o'clock and asked what time they should come down and I'd told her that I needed about an hour more. A little before the hour was up, I set out the small, rimmed cake stand with the shrimp mould surrounded by crackers and two chafing dishes with the mushrooms and meatballs on the buffet in the dining area. Nate came back just as I was climbing up on a chair to get a better angle to photograph the meatballs.

"What's all this?"

"I'm taking pictures of the appetizers I made today."

Before Nate could respond, Dan and Shelly came in carrying several bags.

"Where shall I set up the bar?" asked Dan.

"Bar?" said Nate.

"For the cocktail party. Are we too early? Do you need more time?" asked Shelly.

"Just need a couple more pictures and I'm all set," I said, snapping several shots of the meatballs from my perch on the chair. "Sweetie, could you show Dan where to put things while I take these pictures."

Nate furrowed his eyebrows and scowled at me but directed Dan to the second buffet table and got out glasses, plates, and cocktail napkins from the cabinets. I disassembled my camera and tripod and carried it to the pantry.

"How did this happen?" whispered Nate as I zipped up my camera bag and tucked it behind the door.

"I told them they could help themselves to the dishes I was making, because I knew we couldn't eat it all, and they suggested they'd bring drinks."

"But I made dinner reservations for them."

"I assume they're still going. I didn't ask."

"They can't just have a few snacks. They'll need dinner," huffed Nate.

"They didn't seem worried about it."

"I suppose we could pull something together if they don't… There's only four of them."

I left Nate rummaging in the pantry fridge and I went back to the dining area.

"What can we get the chef to drink?" asked Dan amiably. "We've got wine and beer and some alcoholic apple juice that Shelly likes."

"It's cider, not apple juice. And it's good," said Shelly, obviously used to Dan's teasing because she just shook her head and laughed.

"Red wine. Please." I noticed that they'd not touched the food. "Why aren't you guys eating?"

"We thought we should wait to toast the chef," said Robin who was sitting with her friend Shelly at the long table the group had been using to eat breakfast together.

"To the chef!" said Steve, who delivered my wine while Dan topped up Robin's glass with white wine.

"Thank you. Now please, dig in."

They helped themselves and invited me to join them at the table.

"Shelly told us you're working on a cookbook. Can we get the recipes, or do we have to wait for it to be published?" asked Robin.

"I'm happy to give you the recipes. I'm not planning on publishing it. It's a gift for my daughter."

"So. Um. What's the pink stuff?" asked Dan looking suspiciously at the shrimp spread.

"It's a shrimp dip."

"Kinda like shrimp cocktail and chip dip had a baby," said Shelly. "Try it. It's good."

"I'm sorry. It's a bit strange. But it's my daughter's favourite," I explained.

"So you're giving her recipes for her favourites?" asked Robin.

"I'm trying to document family recipes for her and her fiancée."

"What a great idea. I wish my mother would do that. Nothing I make turns out quite like hers," said Shelly.

"I wish she would too," said Dan, eliciting a glare from Shelly.

Steve shook his head. "You're on thin ice, Buddy."

"Can I get you another cider, Dear?" asked Dan looking penitent.

"That's not going to get you out of the doghouse," said Robin with a giggle.

"Did you enjoy the fall colour wagon ride today?" I asked changing the subject.

"Yes. They apologized that it was a bit late in the season, but it was still great," said Steve.

"I got some good pictures of the horses," said Robin getting up to help herself to seconds.

"We could move the food to this table," I suggested. "I just set it up on the buffet to take pictures…"

"Awesome," said Dan, who picked up the chafing dish of meatballs he was just digging in to and moved it to the center of the table. Steve picked up the other chafing dish and moved it, and then they moved the cold dishes over as well.

"I don't need more of this…" said Shelly scooping shrimp dip onto her plate. "It's weird but addicting."

The five of us chatted, sipped our drinks and the appetizers slowly disappeared. They were nice young people who were enjoying their weekend getaway without their kids. Dan was very funny as he recounted the story of the drama of dropping their daughters at his parents for the weekend. Steve was the quiet one, but he was the perfect straight man to Dan's comedy. Robin and Shelly got me talking about Anne and her wedding and about my cookbook project.

"What can I get you, Nate," said Dan jumping up from the table when Nate finally joined us in the dining room.

"Nothing right now. Thanks," said Nate. "I was wondering about dinner?"

"Is it time for us to leave already?" asked Robin.

"No. You have plenty of time. But if you'd like to stay in for dinner…"

"We have lots of booze," said Dan heaping four more meatballs onto his plate.

Shelly elbowed Dan. "We couldn't possibly impose any more than we already have."

"We'll be making dinner for ourselves; we can just add another ladle of water to the soup as my mother would say," said Nate.

"What's for dinner?" I asked Nate, thinking that might help them decide.

"We have a few options. We've got plenty of pasta. Or there's breakfast for dinner, we're always stocked up for that."

"Pasta with pesto and then quiche and a salad?" I suggested.

"I don't think I need all that," said Robin. "I'm pretty full already."

"We love pesto," said Dan who got another elbow in the ribs from Shelly.

"We should cancel your dinner reservations if you're not going out," Nate suggested.

"Are you sure it's OK?" asked Shelly.

"As long as you're not expecting a gourmet meal," I cautioned.

"Oh, we are," said Steve with a chuckle. "You've proven you're both great cooks. We've loved Nate's breakfasts and your appetizers are da bomb!"

After dinner, they offered to help clean up, but we declined. They took their Spanish coffees and went to watch a movie in the living room.

Once we were alone behind the closed kitchen door, I could tell something was wrong. Nate was scowling and taking his frustrations out on the dishes, rattling them as he slammed them into the dishwasher.

"What's the matter?"

"It could have been a disaster," he said in a tone that made me bristle because it sounded like he was lecturing me.

"But it wasn't."

"That's not the point. We can't just throw something together when it's for guests."

"Why not? We had everything we needed."

Nate didn't look convinced.

"They're happy with their nightcaps. Let's break into that new bottle of limoncello, bundle up and sip it under the stars on the patio," I suggested, hoping to get him to stop worrying about it.

Somewhat begrudgingly, Nate got the limoncello from the freezer and we put on our jackets and grabbed one of the big wool blankets from the chest. Once we were snuggled under the blanket Nate started to relax. I thought about how, in the past, I would have not let go of trying to convince him I'd been right. I didn't feel the need to prove myself to Nate even though he'd hurt my feelings. I just wanted to make him happy. I avoided the subject as we sat close to keep warm, focusing instead on searching the clear night sky for falling stars.

The following week Sarah showed him the glowing review they'd left about their stay.

I overheard him telling her, "We should always look for opportunities to spontaneously respond to our guest's ideas whenever possible."

It made me smile and I felt both vindicated and a little delighted that Nate was also changing as a result of my influence.

CHAPTER 36

I'd called Ann early in the morning; before Maddie had gotten up. I wanted to ask her if she and Lane could come for Thanksgiving. We'd already mentioned it to Emily and Anne, and they had enthusiastically agreed to come. As I'd feared, Ann had been less keen.

"It'll be pretty crowded won't it?" she'd said.

"No more than last Christmas."

"But you didn't have your girlfriend living with you then."

I wanted to correct her, but Maddie and I had agreed to tell everyone of our engagement once we were all together in person.

"Won't you please come?" I'd asked again adding, "We'd really like to get the whole family together at Thanksgiving because Emily and Bob are going to his parents for Christmas. So, this is the only long weekend they can make it up to the inn."

She'd been noncommittal. "I'll talk to Lane and get back to you."

I knew it wasn't a matter of money, or time off, that was holding her back. Last summer, when I'd told her how busy the inn had been, she'd committed to coming to visit in the fall, when things were slower. She'd told me that they had set aside some vacation time and they were looking forward to hugging their grandson that they'd only seen on video chats since Christmas.

I filled Maddie in later that morning while she had her coffee at the kitchen counter, and I finished cleaning up after breakfast service.

"What if she doesn't come?" said Maddie, her brows scrunched together and frowning.

"I guess we just do it without her."

"Are you sure you're OK with that?"

"If she can't come, she can't come."

"Is it because she can't come or she doesn't want to come when I'm here?"

"She may as well get used to it. You're here to stay!"

"But she doesn't know that … yet."

"Are you suggesting we tell her?"

"No. I want to keep it a surprise. Should I call her?"

I appreciated that she offered, but I could tell she wasn't convinced that it was a good idea. We ultimately decided I would talk to Emily to ask her to encourage her parents to make the trip. As much as I wanted Ann to be here, I wasn't entirely sure she'd be happy about Maddie and I getting married. Our weekly phone calls had slipped to every other week since Maddie had come to stay at the inn. At first, I thought it was a coincidence that whenever I started to tell her about something Maddie had said or started to describe something we'd done together, Ann made an excuse to end our call. It didn't occur to me that she was doing it on purpose until one morning last week. Ann and I were just starting our call when Maddie walked past my office door, and I invited her to come say hello.

"I must ring off, Dad. My kettle is boiling. Love you. Bye." She'd abruptly hung up before Maddie could make it from the door to my desk.

"I get the feeling she didn't want to talk to me," said Maddie half-joking.

"Why would she not want to talk to you?"

"Maybe she thinks you're cheating on her mother."

"That makes no sense."

"Or she just doesn't like me."

I couldn't tell if it upset Maddie. She was careful not to say anything disparaging about Ann.

"We can't force her to like me, or like the idea that we're going to be together," she'd wisely pointed out, adding, "But I worry that she'll be even less happy with me when she finds out why we want everyone together at Thanksgiving."

Whether or not Ann was coming, I had a lot to get done in the next four weeks. Maddie and I had decided that, after Thanksgiving, I would go stay with her in Toronto. We'd arranged for Sarah to move in as caretaker. It was the perfect arrangement. She was excited to have her own place for a few months as she'd been living with her parents since graduation, and we wouldn't have to worry about leaving the place empty in winter. She was thrilled when I offered to pay her a small salary to manage the inn.

It would be my first full winter away from the inn in twenty years. I usually continue to take bookings through the winter, only shutting down completely for the weeks I'd go visit Ann and Emily. I've developed a system over the years to scale back on inventory of food and supplies as the season slows, in anticipation of shutting down.

Initially, I'd assumed that I would shut down as usual and Sarah would just be there to make sure the snow got shoveled and the pipes didn't freeze. But she wanted to contribute rather than simply rattle around the house with nothing to do. When I'd expressed my concern to Maddie, she'd asked me what I was afraid of? And, I really didn't have a good answer. We agreed we would continue to accept bookings at least through December and then decide if we should continue based on how things were going.

For my own peace of mind, I had to be sure that Sarah was ready to take it on by herself. I'd spent many hours this past month trying to imagine every possible scenario she might encounter. I started a notebook and wrote out what I thought she would need to know. When appropriate I made checklists or wrote out step-by-step instructions for her to follow.

Instead of running down the inventory, this year I was scaling it up so that Sarah had much of what she needed for the whole winter. And, as of this coming weekend, she would start planning and serving breakfast to our guests while I was still there to help.

I'd also had to make sure I could do all the accounting and banking for the inn from Maddie's house. I preferred to go into the bank and speak with the manager who I'd relied on since she started working there as a teller. When I explained the situation to her, she'd shown me how I could do everything remotely.

"It's very simple Mr. Jacobs," she'd said turning her monitor screen to show me the online banking website and walking through logging into my accounts.

"And I can do this from Canada?"

"From anywhere in the world. But I wouldn't use a public computer to log in. It might not be secure."

"Can I use my fiancé's computer?"

"Yes. That would be fine. You can also download the banking application to your phone or a tablet."

Maddie helped me practice logging into the bank site on her laptop after I'd gotten it set up at the bank. She said I could use her laptop whenever I needed it, but she also helped me set up the application on my phone and showed me how to use it. In doing that, we started to think about what I should do about my cell phone being in Canada for several months. She'd arranged for a special plan to cover her while traveling. I added a trip to the mobile phone store to my list of things to do.

I knew that getting everything set up this first time was going to make it easier in the future. We'd established that Maddie was not going to give up her home in Toronto and move here with me on a full-time basis. So, I was going to have to go to her. It had taken many long, and sometimes heated, discussions but we'd finally settled on spending five months at each of our houses with the remaining two months of the year as 'negotiable'. We agreed on summer in Bar Harbor and winter in Toronto. Once we'd come to a mutually acceptable arrangement, we started making plans to make it happen.

I hadn't started packing yet, but I'd been making lists of things that I wanted to bring with me. I had separate lists for personal items like clothing, toiletries, and prescriptions and then for business and recreation. We planned to drive to Toronto. It would be a bit cramped, with me and my things added to hers and the cats. I tried to convince her that we could store her car and take my Jeep because it had more space, but she was adamant that she was driving her car back. She suggested that it was best to leave the Jeep behind for Sarah so she could use it to get around when the snow got deep. In the end, I relented. I didn't want to drive separately and there was no way Maddie was going to leave her car in Bar Harbor.

On top of all the preparations to relocate for the winter, I had a lot to prepare for Thanksgiving weekend. I wanted everything to be perfect. After months of keeping it a secret, I was finally going to have a chance to tell everyone how proud and happy I was that Maddie had agreed to marry me. I also had some little surprises planned for Maddie because I wanted it to be a memorable and special occasion for her too.

CHAPTER 37

I didn't want to do anything to discourage Ann from coming so I hadn't considered inviting anyone but my daughter and her fiancé to the inn for Thanksgiving. But since Ann declined, I asked Nate if it would be OK to invite Claire. He thought it was an excellent idea.

I was thrilled that Claire was here. I'd missed spending time with my best friend these past months, and I'd missed our usual Thanksgiving rituals back in October when Canada had its Thanksgiving weekend.

"Oh Maddie! This place. The view. C'est magnifique!" gushed Claire heading straight to the window.

"This was the room I stayed in the first time I was here. And I had the exact same reaction."

"And so it is a very lucky room."

"It might be a little lonely tonight. Are you sure you don't want to stay in the guest room near me?"

"I wouldn't want to cramp the newlyweds."

"We're not newlyweds yet. And it might go from lonely to chaotic once the others arrive."

"I will enjoy the solitude tonight and revel in being part of your extended family tomorrow."

I set her suitcase on the stand next to the desk. "Do you want to unpack? Freshen up?"

"Yes. A little. I won't be long."

"Take your time. Join us in the living room when you're ready and I'll give you a tour of the rest of the place."

I could feel there was a blast of cold air coming from the front hall when I rounded the corner from the guest stairway into the main room. The front door was wide open, and Nate was directing two delivery men one carrying two tall pedestals and the other two enormous bouquets of red roses and white orchids.

"Could you place one on either side of the bay window, please," said Nate.

It now made sense that Nate had insisted I go alone to pick up Claire at the airport, and why he'd been evasive when I'd asked why he didn't want to come.

"You ordered flowers?"

"We can't have a wedding without flowers," he replied with a grin. "You like them?"

"They're beautiful. What a nice surprise."

"The first of many." He looked at me with a mischievous smile. He accompanied the delivery men to the door, thanked and tipped them, and closed the door behind them.

"I thought we were surprising the kids, not each other."

He walked towards me still grinning like a Cheshire cat. He took my hands and pulled me in close, so we were nose to nose. "But you love surprises. And I love you."

"Surprises are great. And so are you." I leaned in and kissed him.

Claire came in carrying a garment bag. "You two just can't keep your hands off each other can you."

"Can I take that for you?" asked Nate.

Claire held the bag close to her chest. "Not a chance. No peeking."

Nate's face contorted with a confused expression.

"Follow me," I said to Claire. I led her down the hall, through the dining room and kitchen and up to our bedroom.

Claire unzipped the garment bag and pulled out the dress. "I can't wait to see it on you. You should try it on right now. So, if I need to make any adjustments, I can work on it tonight."

I shut the bedroom door and changed into the dress.

"Come here, I'll zip you," ordered Claire and I obeyed. I was relieved the zipper closed easily confirming that my measurements hadn't changed in the months I'd been away. Claire had worked her magic yet again. The bodice was perfectly snug and the A-line skirt with the soft pleats draped perfectly from my hips. Claire ran her hands along the pleats of fabric that wrapped across my body and checked for gaps along the V-neck.

"Lift your arms," she instructed, studying the movement of the dress as I did. "Now turn." She got down on her knees to study the hem as I rotated. "Put on the shoes to make sure," she said nodding at the garment bag.

In the bottom of the bag, each wrapped in tissue paper, were my favourite scarlet suede pumps. They were a perfect match for the dress. I slipped out of my socks and into the shoes and did another turn as Claire studied the hem.

"It's good," she said using the arm of the chair to climb up from the floor.

"Are you sure it's not... too red? For a wedding?" I said catching my reflection in the dresser mirror.

"You look hot! It's perfect for you. And practical. You can wear it to Anne's wedding, and no one will know it's a wedding dress."

I ran my hands over the skirt as I walked to the mirror. "You're a miracle worker. When you said you found the perfect material... I had no idea it would be so rich feeling."

"We got lucky. My guy at King Fabrics just did a huge Chinese wedding and had brought in an extra shipment of red satin and peau de soie. This piece was the last of the best stuff he had. I got a fabulous price because it was technically a remnant."

"No wonder it feels a lot more expensive than what I paid you for the material."

"It helped I'd made you this dress before, so I knew exactly how much we needed."

"This one is much nicer than the black one."

"Practice makes perfect."

"How will I ever repay you for this?"

"Getting to see you get married in it is more than enough reward."

"Help me out before Nate comes up." I turned to have her unzip me. "He has no idea I got you to make me a new dress and I don't want him to see it before Thursday."

Claire carefully put the dress back in the garment bag while I got dressed. I took it to the guest room closet. Then I showed Claire around the rest of our rooms, ending with Nate's office.

"Oh my," said Claire making a slow circle around the room, much like I had the first time I'd seen it.

"I thought you were kidding when you told me there were about a thousand boats in his office."

"So, this is where you girls are hiding," said Nate coming into the office behind me and sneaking a stroke of my bottom which made me jump as I wasn't expecting it.

I stifled a giggle. "I was just finishing showing Claire around."

Nate stopped stroking me and clasped his hands behind his back with a not-so-innocent grin.

"Do I need to leave you two alone?" asked Claire, observant as usual.

"I just wanted to let you know that I have everything set for dinner and we can begin whenever you're ready."

"Superb," said Claire. "You can fill me in on all the plans for the weekend and give me my assignments."

"But there will be no working on an empty stomach at my inn," said Nate extending his arm to Claire. "Come along young lady I've prepared something special for you."

Claire looked at me curiously and I shrugged. "Don't look at me. This is all his doing."

I really didn't know. Nate had told me earlier in the day he'd take care of dinner for tonight. I'd been out much of the afternoon as I'd run a few pre-wedding errands and then made the drive out to the airport to get Claire.

Nate seated us at a table in the dining area that he'd set for three and poured us each a glass of wine.

"You sent me a taste of Montreal, so I thought it would be fitting if I welcomed you with a taste of Maine."

I picked up my glass. "But first, we should toast our guest. To Claire, the first to know our secret."

"You mean I was the first to know you were sleeping together?"

"To Claire, who is always the first to know," said Nate touching his glass to Claire's and taking a sip. "Now if you ladies will excuse me for a minute, I'll get your appetizers." Nate left for the kitchen.

"OK," said Claire after he'd left the room. "Tell me how this is going to go."

I explained that we planned to wait until Thanksgiving morning to tell everyone about the wedding. We had made up a story that we would be going out for Thanksgiving dinner. We told them the location was a surprise but that we would be dressing up so they should come prepared with a nice outfit.

"Won't they be suspicious tomorrow when they see the flowers?" asked Claire. "Is there someplace we could hide them?"

"We could move them to the garage. They'll keep better in the cool. We could bring them out Thursday when we rearrange the furniture for the ceremony."

"That's a good idea," said Nate returning from the kitchen with a platter. He set it down in the center of the table and turned to Claire. "Number one Maine dish, lobster rolls. These are miniature ones, but I guarantee the filling is one hundred percent authentic."

The lobster rolls were the cutest, tiniest ones I'd ever seen. The small brioche buns were hollowed out and generously stuffed with lobster. They were perfectly sized to be eaten in one bite, or several if you were trying to be ladylike.

"These are delicious," said Claire. "Did you make them?"

"The filling is my secret recipe," said Nate, "but I bought the rolls."

I helped myself to a second one being unable to resist a little more lobster. "Where did you get these buns? They're yummy."

"Maybe once you're my wife, I'll tell you all my secret sources," teased Nate getting up and heading back to the kitchen with the now empty platter.

Claire peppered me with questions. "Are you going to tell everyone together? What exactly are you going to say? What about Nate's daughter in England? Are you going to tell her before or after?"

I explained that we had decided that once everyone was up and had come down for breakfast, we would tell them together and then we would call Ann and tell her too.

Nate returned from the kitchen carrying a covered cast iron pot with big oven mitts. "We need to make sure everyone is ready by three o'clock because the wedding officiant needs to be home for her Thanksgiving dinner by five. Don't touch. It's hot." He set the pot in the center of the table and went back towards the kitchen.

"Sounds like one of my jobs is making sure you're ready by three o'clock," said Claire.

"This is one day I definitely need to be ready on time."

"Are you going to get your hair done?"

"I didn't want to impose on anyone on Thanksgiving Day. Besides, I'm not planning on doing anything fancy with it."

"I'm sure between the four of us ladies, we can make sure you look presentable."

"I'm counting on it."

Nate came back from the kitchen, this time carrying three dinner plates, each with a small bowl perched on it. Setting them down in front of us he opened the lid of the cast iron pot.

"The second Maine dish, baked beans." He served a scoop into the small bowls on each of our plates as he explained, "Traditionally they would be served with hot dogs or ham but today, for my sophisticated ladies, I've paired them with pork tenderloin. Bon appetit."

"Good thing I'm sleeping on the far side of the building given the effect beans notoriously have on the digestive system," said Claire which made me laugh because I had just thought that it would be unfortunate if one of us had to sleep in the guest room if either of us were afflicted.

"No matter how stinky Maddie is, I'll still marry her," said Nate.

"Gee thanks," I said. "I'll have to see how stinky you are. I could change my mind."

Nate feigned being stabbed in the heart. "I'm crushed." He got up and picked up our empty plates and left us giggling at the table.

"I suppose you haven't farted in bed yet?" said Claire chuckling. "My Theo would tease me terribly. He would make gagging noises and pretend to be dying. The first time he did it I hid in the bathroom and cried but after a while, I would let it go and then try to fan it in his face just to get him to put on his little show."

"That's too much information."

"Being able to survive each other's farts is the sign of a strong marriage," said Claire causing both of us to laugh.

"I hope you have better marital advice than that to share with me."

"Marital advice?" asked Nate coming back from the kitchen.

"You don't want to know," I said.

"Maine dessert for tonight," said Nate setting a tray down on the table. "Whoopie pie. Unlike the famous Maine blueberry pies, they are not a pie."

"Whoopie? Like Making love? Maybe you should serve Whoopie pie for your wedding!" said Claire causing us to burst out laughing again.

CHAPTER 38

"Good Morning, Granddad," chirped Emily coming into the kitchen carrying Jake on her hip and towing the highchair from the dining room behind her.

"Good morning to you! You're both up early!"

She yawned. "Your great-grandson takes after you, not me."

"Coffee?"

"Yes please." She sat Jake in the highchair, strapped him in and handed him a bright orange truck and then added a couple more toys to the tray of the highchair.

I handed her a cup of coffee with milk and sugar, the way she liked it. "What can I get the little man for breakfast?"

"Can I make him a hard-boiled egg? He's been into them lately."

"I'll make it for him. How about you?"

"Just the coffee for now. After Jake's had his egg maybe he'll have half a banana and I'll eat the other half."

"Surely that's not enough."

"If this weekend is anything like previous Thanksgivings, I'm surely going to eat too much. Starting off slow on purpose."

I couldn't help but grin because she had no idea I'd gone to great lengths to make this weekend unlike any other Thanksgiving. I didn't want her to suspect anything, so I turned to the stove to check the timer for Jake's egg while I composed myself.

I manned the stove, toaster and coffee machine filling orders as each family member wandered in. No one sat in the dining room, instead, they gathered with their coffees in hand around the kitchen island. By the time Maddie came down, the kitchen was buzzing with activity.

"What a happy sound to wake up to," said Maddie giving her daughter a big hug and leaning over to kiss Jake on the head. "How did everyone sleep?"

"Not as late as you," teased Anne.

"I need more beauty sleep than you." Maddie messed up Anne's hair playfully and looked at me with a grateful smile when I handed her a steaming cappuccino in her favorite mug.

"Shall we tell them now?" I asked her in a loud whisper, pretending to be sharing a secret but intending them to overhear.

"OK," Maddie loud whispered back. "Are you going to tell them or should I?"

"You guys are too cute," said Linda.

"Out with it," said Anne. "What are you two up to?"

"We need to confess." I made my voice sound as somber as I could.

"Oooo sounds serious," said Emily sarcastically.

"It is. We lied to you about today. We won't be getting dressed up to go out for dinner."

Bob scowled at Emily. "You made me pack a tie for nothing!"

"You'll still need the tie," said Maddie which made Emily shoot Bob an 'I told you so' look.

"We just won't be going out," I continued.

"We're having a party here?" asked Anne.

"Yes. Of a sort. You are the party. You're our wedding party," I announced opening my arms with a gesture to include all of them.

There was silence. They stood there looking confused or maybe stunned.

"We're getting married today. Surprise!" Maddie clapped her hands and grinned madly and then held out her left hand with her engagement ring.

"Whoa! That wasn't there last night!" said Anne.

Emily leaned in for a peek at the ring. "When did this happen?"

"April. But we waited until we'd worked out the details and we wanted to tell you all together."

"You!" Anne shook her finger at Claire accusingly. "You knew about this!"

"I was sworn to secrecy." Claire ran her finger across her lips as if to zip them shut.

"We wanted to have your parents here too," I said to Emily, "We'll call them today and let them know."

"We can FaceTime her right now." Emily pulled out her phone. When it started to ring, she turned her back to me and held the phone up so the camera had both her and I in view.

"Hello Mum," she said with a wave to Ann.

"Happy Thanksgiving, Honey. Happy Thanksgiving, Dad."

"We're all here," said Emily turning the phone and panning it around the kitchen.

"Hello Ann," chimed Anne and Linda.

"Nice to meet you," said Claire.

"Happy Thanksgiving, Mum," said Bob.

"Wish you were here," said Maddie.

"You're going to wish you were here too," said Emily.

"Maybe next year," said Ann.

"Next year won't be the same because, here, I'll let Grandpa tell you…"

Emily handed me the phone. "We just told everyone that Maddie and I are getting married."

Ann didn't say anything so I wasn't sure if she could hear me.

"Did you hear me?"

"Yes," she said.

"And the wedding is today!" said Emily "Isn't that super fun?"

"It's very sudden," said Ann.

"They've been secretly engaged for months," said Emily very dramatically.

"I asked Maddie last April. We wanted to wait to tell everyone in person," I explained.

"And you're getting married... today? Was that her idea?" said Ann.

"We thought it would be fun to surprise you all. And we thought it was the perfect day because we have one more thing to be thankful for this year."

"We considered eloping," added Maddie, "But family will make our day even more special."

Emily leaned in over my shoulder. "They haven't even told us any details yet. We called you right away."

"I see," said Ann.

"Now it makes sense that Grandpa was so adamant he wanted you guys to come."

"It does," said Ann.

"Don't worry. I'll fill you in on all the details," said Emily.

"How's Jake?" asked Ann.

"He's great." Emily took the phone from me and turned the camera to show him in his highchair. "Say hi to Grandma."

Jake waved excitedly and knocked bits of banana off his tray and onto the floor.

"I better let you go take care of that," said Ann.

"Ok. Talk later. Love you," said Emily and we all chimed in goodbyes to Ann.

"We need details," said Emily as she wiped up banana smudges from the floor below Jake.

I explained that the ceremony would be at three-thirty and afterwards, we'd have a little party here to celebrate.

"What do you need us to do?" asked Linda.

"Make yourselves scarce but be on time for the ceremony. I want everyone ready by three fifteen because we have to get Mrs. Hunter home in time for her thanksgiving dinner."

"Will there be other guests coming?" asked Emily.

"Just us," I answered.

The doorbell rang and I left the kitchen to answer the door. I could hear the ladies peppering Maddie with questions. By the time I got back, only Bob and Jake were left in the kitchen.

"Where'd they all go?"

"They started talking about hairstyles and clothes and … I don't know… they just all went upstairs."

"Just as well," I said as I continued through the kitchen to the back door. "I don't want Maddie to see these. I'm going to unpack them in the garage."

The rest of the day flew by. Sarah arrived shortly after breakfast. She helped Maddie and I rearrange the furniture in the living room. We opened up the space in front of the bay window and set up the flowers we'd hidden in the garage. We placed six chairs, three on each side, in a triangle pattern, with one in front and two behind.

Once we'd arranged everything for the ceremony, we moved on to the dining room. We shifted the tables together to make one long table in the center of the room. Maddie had washed and polished all the glassware and silver we'd not used since last New Year's Eve. We set the table starting with a long white linen tablecloth. Sarah laid out the place settings while Maddie arranged the centerpiece. She and Claire had come up with the design after looking through the decorations and tableware stored in the basement. They'd put a dozen white candles in short cut-glass glasses and nestled them in loops of red, white, and silver ribbons.

"Do you like it?" Maddie asked.

"Once those candles are lit, the only thing that will sparkle more is your eyes."

"And my ring… that I better give to you now before I go start getting ready." She took the ring from her finger and put it in my hand.

"You go on. Sarah and I will finish up."

Sarah pulled out the list I'd given her. "Should I set up the champagne glasses now?"

"Don't forget the sippy cup with water for Jake. We don't want to leave him out of the toast!"

"Got it," she said.

"What about Mary?"

"She texted. They're on their way. They'll be ready to serve the bubbly as soon as you say, 'I do'."

Sarah started getting the glasses out. I looked at my watch. It was already 2:30. I was a little worried that Carl and Bella had not arrived, so I left Sarah and went to the front door. I opened it just as they were walking onto the porch. Both were laden down; Carl with his guitar, music stand and towing a cart with his amp and a duffle bag on it and Bella with a camera bag slung over each shoulder and carrying a large flat case and a tripod in her hands.

"Happy Wedding Day!" said Bella.

I held the door open for them. "Thank you. Come on in!"

I showed Carl where to set up and handed them a schedule of the timing and sequence of events in case they didn't bring the one I'd given them previously.

"Just point me towards the bride," said Bella. "I'd like to get a few pictures now, if she's ready."

I led Bella to the back stairs and called up to Maddie to let her know Bella was on her way up then I went back to check on Sarah.

"Let's go over the list," I suggested.

"We're good to go. Except, you can't get married in that." Sarah pointed to my outfit of dungarees and a sweatshirt.

"Of course not. But… Everything good to go?"

"All set. Now go. I got this." She shooed me from the dining area.

I told Maddie that I'd get ready in one of the open guest rooms so she could get ready in our room. She was adorably mysterious about what she was going to wear but I knew she'd asked Claire to bring her a dress from home. Claire, Anne, and Linda had gone upstairs with her and had come down together giggling like little girls, so I took that as a sign that things were going well with my bride-to-be.

It didn't take me long to change into my suit and tie. When I came back down just before three, Sarah was just hanging up Lynn's coat.

She gave me a big hug. "You look dashing!" And then seeing Carl she said, "Hi! I didn't know you were doing this one too."

"Thank you both for doing this," I said. "Especially on Thanksgiving."

"Nothing better to be thankful for than true love. And I get to witness it," said Lynn. "Now show me where you'd like me."

I walked Lynn over to the center of the bay window. "I thought you could stand here facing into the room. Maddie and I will stand in front of you and our witnesses in these two front chairs."

"It's lovely. With the ocean view and the flowers, perfectly lovely."

Sarah had been standing by watching as I walked Lynn through the setup.

"Shall I go see if Maddie is ready?" she offered.

"Please get her bouquet from the garage and bring it to her," I reminded her.

"I'm on it," she said with a little salute.

Emily was the first to come down to the living room. She had on an elegant black cocktail dress.

She looked troubled. "I'm sorry I only brought a black dress. I didn't know we were going to a wedding."

"It matches my suit perfectly. Having my best person in a matching outfit is particularly important."

"You want me to be your best man?" she said with a big smile.

"Best person? Best woman? Best granddaughter? Will you?"

"I'd be honored."

"Good, then you should hold on to these." I gave her the red velvet box from my pocket that had Maddie's ruby ring and the simple white gold band for me we'd picked out together at the jeweler in town.

"Good thing this dress has a pocket!" She slipped the ring box into her pocket.

"Maddie said to tell you she's ready and she loved the bouquet," said Sarah coming back just as Claire, Anne, and Linda all came down together from their rooms.

"I'll go check on her," said Anne, continuing through the living room towards the kitchen. "I wouldn't want to fail in my Maid of Honor duties."

"Where do you want us?" asked Linda.

"There are two chairs for you ladies here." I pointed to the two chairs on the left. "And this one is for my Best Person and behind her, those are for Jake and Bob."

"The booster chair was a dead giveaway, Grandpa," said Emily taking Jake from Bob who'd just come in carrying him. Emily strapped Jake into the booster chair and gave him a storybook that he took and started turning the pages as if he was reading it.

I nodded to Carl who was set up near the fireplace and he started playing a lovely classical piece on his guitar. I went to stand in front of Lynn, just slightly ahead and to the left of Emily's chair. Anne came back grinning and took the single chair on the left, followed by Bella with her camera, who positioned herself near the pedestal of flowers with her back to the window.

I'd tried to anticipate every detail for today. I'd been going non-stop for the past few weeks with the singular goal of making today perfect. And finally, the moment had arrived.

"I think we're ready to begin," said Lynn.

Carl started playing a little louder and transitioned to *Pachelbel's Canon*. We'd decided that would be Maddie's cue to make her entrance. Seeing Maddie looking into my eyes as she walked toward me, I couldn't help but gulp for air. She looked gorgeous. I could feel my chest tighten and I felt a rush of pride that this beautiful woman was going to be my wife. I was shocked at the vibrant red of her dress. But it captured her fire and passion and was a perfect choice. Her hair was clipped back with sparkly clips but fell in loose curls to her shoulders and framed her face perfectly.

"Wow," was all I could muster to say as she came to stand beside me in front of Lynn and our family.

Maddie handed her bouquet to Anne and then took my hand as we listened to Lynn welcome everyone.

"Today we celebrate the separate journeys that have brought Maddie and Nate together, and we usher them toward the new journey they will embark upon as husband and wife. Will you, Nate and Maddie's family and friends, as witnesses to this day, stand by them, with support and encouragement for this union?"

"We do!" responded Anne, Linda, Claire, Emily, and Bob in unison.

"Goooooooopa," said Jake waving his book at me.

"Even the youngest of your family have spoken up on your behalf," continued Lynn with a big smile. "And so, I will now ask you to declare your intentions for a lasting partnership in love and marriage. Are you prepared to do this?"

"We are," we answered, and we turned to face each other. I took Maddie's other hand so I could hold both. I looked into her eyes and my mind went completely blank. There was a brief moment of panic that I couldn't remember the vows we had planned.

"As Maddie and Nate exchange their vows today, they do so from a place of deep love and commitment. Nate, please make your solemn vow to Maddie."

Maddie smiled at me and I took a deep breath. "I, Nate, take you, Maddie, to be my wife. You are the light in my life and the beat in my heart. In the good times and bad, there is no one I'd rather have by my side. I will love you as my best friend, lover, and partner. I promise to show you, day in and day out, that you are my everything. On this day, I give you my heart."

"And now Maddie, please make your solemn vow to Nate," prompted Lynn.

Maddie squeezed my hands and looking into my eyes said, "I, Maddie, take you, Nate, to be my husband. You are the light in my life and the beat in my heart. In the good times and bad, there is no one I'd rather have by my side. I will love you as my best friend, lover, and partner. I promise to show you, day in and day out, that you are my everything. On this day, I give you my heart."

"Please present one another your rings," said Lynn. "The shape, a circle, has a universal, centuries-old meaning, representing eternity, infinity, timelessness, and wholeness. These rings symbolize your never-ending commitment to this marriage and the love you share. May they be a constant reminder that you are loved."

Emily pulled the ring box from her pocket and handed it to me. I put Maddie's ruby ring back on her finger and it slipped easily into place as if that was where it belonged. Maddie had to wiggle my ring to get it over my slightly crooked knuckle. I felt a rush of excitement as I looked down at my hand with the bright metal band on my finger.

"By the power vested in me by the State of Maine, before your families and your friends, I now pronounce you husband and wife. Please seal your marriage with your first wedded kiss," said Lynn.

Still holding hands, I pulled her in closer and kissed her while our little gathering applauded.

"Woo hoo," said Bob.

"Maaaaa Goooo," said Jake, which made everyone laugh.

"Don't move," said Bella. "I want to get a picture with Lynn." Handing Sarah a large reflector and positioning it where she wanted it held, she stepped back and took several pictures of us. Carl continued to play while Bella worked through different combinations of our little group. Us with our witnesses, with Emily, Bob, and Jake, with Anne and Linda and finally ending with the whole group together.

"OK. Say Yippee," she instructed, and we all did.

Sarah waved towards the dining room and Mary and her daughter, who we'd hired to take care of the food and serving, came in with glasses of champagne. Bella moved back as Mary served each of us our champagne. Emily sat Jake back in his booster chair and gave him his sippy cup.

Carl ended the song he was playing with a strum that sounded like 'ta da'.

"I'd like to propose a toast," I said. "Thank you for being here to share our special moment. I'd like to propose a toast to the forming of this new blended family. I..."

Maddie interrupted me with an elbow nudge. "We..."

"We are grateful this Thanksgiving wedding day for the gift of all of you. To you. Cheers!"

There was the tinkling of glasses, and everyone said, "Cheers."

Emily cleared her throat to get our attention. "As the Best Person, I believe it's my privilege to propose the toast to the bride and groom. Since Grandpa gave me no notice, I've not had time to prepare a speech that wittily conveys all his most endearing flaws. So, I guess I'll just say that I'm so happy that you've found each other. I extend to you the toast Grandpa gave us on our wedding day. 'May you be friends to each other as only lovers can, and may you love each other as only best friends can.' Please raise a glass to the bride and groom."

Bella continued to circle our little gathering taking candid pictures as we'd discussed. I was just about to give Carl the 'signal' for the little surprise I'd planned for Maddie when Anne tapped her ring on her glass making it tinkle.

"My turn to make a toast," she said. "As the Maid of Honor and daughter of the bride, I would like to propose a toast to the groom. Thank you for hosting us all here and, based on what I've heard from Mom today, for all your work planning and arranging this surprise wedding. Thank you, Sarah, and ... I don't know your names," she gestured to Lynn, Bella, Carl, and Mary. "For keeping Nate from doing everything himself and especially for being here on Thanksgiving." Anne turned to face Nate. "Welcome to our little family, Nate, or should I say, Dad? To the groom!"

There was a cheer from everyone, and it made me smile. As I clinked glasses with Anne I said, "You can call me Dad or Pop or Nate just don't call me your old man."

She laughed and gave me a big hug saying, "You got it, old man, I mean Dad."

I could see Carl had taken the microphone from the stand in front of him and had it in his hand. He raised his eyebrows and waved the microphone and I nodded back to let him know it was time. I put down my glass and took a deep breath. Carl turned on the mike and in his best radio voice said "And now, Nate has a special request for his new bride Maddie. And he's going to start us off."

Carl handed me the microphone and started to play the song we'd practiced together in his basement in secret several times over the past month. I cleared my throat and took a deep breath and then started to sing to my lovely Maddie.

Maddie was wide-eyed and obviously surprised. Looking around at the others they too looked shocked. I wondered if this had been a bad idea. But Maddie was beaming, and I felt better continuing to sing *Can't Help Falling in Love.*

When I reached the end, Carl continued to play an instrumental bridge and I set the mike into the holder in front of him.

"I'd like to invite the bride and groom to share in their first dance," said Carl.

I took Maddie by the hand. "Would my wife do me the honor of a first dance?"

"With pleasure," she said folding into my arms as Carl began singing the song again from the top. "That was really good. I never knew you were an Elvis impersonator too."

"First time."

"How long have you been planning this?"

"Since I heard you playing Elvis records when I visited you last year."

I didn't notice at the time, but Bella snapped pictures of us while we were dancing. At that moment all I could see were Maddie's eyes. The way she looked at me made me feel like I was the luckiest, happiest man in the world. When the music stopped, everyone clapped, cheered and Bob made a loud whistle with his fingers.

"I guess you figured out that Mom loves Elvis," said Anne.

"It was pretty obvious given the number of times I've heard his voice over the past year," I said.

"Did she tell you the story of how she almost missed her one chance to see him?" asked Anne.

I didn't have a chance to answer her as Sarah approached Maddie and me and let us know they were ready for us to come to the dining room. Sarah also nodded towards the front door.

"Excuse me for a minute." I left them and went to the front door to help Lynn with her coat and thank her. Carl and Bella had started packing their gear and I thanked them as well. Meanwhile, Maddie ushered everyone to the dining room where Mary and her daughter were standing at the ready to pass out the hors d'oeuvres.

As we sat down to dinner Maddie picked up her wine glass and announced, "I think it's my turn to propose a toast." Everyone around the table picked up their glasses.

"To Anne and Emily for standing up for us at a moment's notice. To Claire for making sure I had something special to wear. To Linda and Bob for their loving support of our daughter and granddaughter and to Jake… who is asleep. But most of all to my husband who has made my heart throb from almost the moment I met him, who's now replaced my teenage heartthrob as my favorite singer of all time. To all of you who have made this one of the happiest days ever. Cheers!"

"To all of us," said Bob in a fake whisper, "Quietly toasting so we can eat dinner in peace." He looked over at Jake who was fast asleep in the portable bed they'd set up in the corner of the dining room.

"I hear there's a story about you almost missing seeing Elvis?" I said remembering what Anne had said earlier.

"It's true," said Maddie. "My girlfriend and I stopped at the drug store for a milkshake because it was a sweltering hot August afternoon. When we came out to drive to the show my grandfather's car wouldn't start. It was too far to walk there and make it in time for the 3:30 show, so I put the hood up and we both stood by the car. We hoped we could flag someone down."

"When was this?" I asked.

"It was late summer 1956. I was so distressed we might waste the tickets my Pops had given me."

"Was this in Toronto?" I asked.

"No. I was in Florida with my grandparents. St. Petersburg."

"So did you hitch a ride?" asked Bob.

"No. A nice young man stopped and gave us a boost. We just barely made it to the show. I tried to get tickets lots of times after that, but they were always sold out and I never saw him perform live again."

"Incredible," I said.

"I know eh?" said Anne. "Almost missed her one chance."

"No. I mean it really is incredible."

"Are you OK?" asked Maddie looking at me concerned.

"Ah huh," I said. "So did this young man drive a Studebaker?"

"I don't remember. Why?"

"Was your car light blue?"

"How did you know that?"

"Were you wearing a dark blue skirt and a blue and white striped top?"

"I could have been. I had an outfit like that. I don't remember."

"It was me," I said not believing it as I said it.

"What was you?" asked Maddie looking at me like I was talking crazy.

"It was me who stopped to give you a boost."

I went on to explain to them that I remember seeing two girls standing by a car with the hood up. They both looked into my side window as I drove past them. They looked distressed, so I pulled over to ask them what was wrong. They explained their car wouldn't start and they were in a terrible hurry because they were going to miss seeing Elvis. I said I would try to help but I wasn't great with cars.

I got into the driver's seat of their car, checked the fuel gauge to make sure it wasn't out of gas, and then turned the key. The engine barely cranked so I thought it might be the battery. I told them I'd try to jump-start it for them. I moved my car so it was nose-to-nose with theirs. I got out my jumper cables and connected them. Then I started my car and then told them to try theirs. Lucky for them, it started right away. I took the cables off, shut their hood, and gave them a signal that they were good to go. They yelled 'Thank you' and waved to me as they took off."

"Mind. Blown," said Emily.

Bob scrunched up his face like he was thinking very hard. "So, you've actually met, like… sixty years ago?"

Claire raised her glass. "There's no avoiding your soulmate. You just met for the first time at the wrong time. Here's to finally getting it right!"

Anne raised her glass to us. "Here here!" And we all drank to that.

I turned to face Maddie. "I waited a very long time to find you, again. I won't be letting you get away ever again." I leaned over and kissed her neck and she giggled.

Mary and her daughter started to serve the next course and the conversation gave way to eating. I didn't mention that I'd watched for that blue Crown Victoria for several weeks after I'd given it a boost, hoping to run into the pretty driver again. Nor did I tell them how I'd wished I'd asked her name so I could try to look her up. I knew it was inappropriate, given that I had a wife at home, but I still couldn't help slowing down to peer at the driver of every pale blue car in St. Petersburg.

CHAPTER 39

Nate was already in bed, so I slipped in beside him and snuggled up to his back.

"Husband," I said softly into his neck.

"Mmmm. Yes, Wife," he replied with a chuckle.

"Fantastic Thanksgiving-Wedding-day, eh?"

Nate rolled over, and we lay nose to nose on my pillow. "Yes. Thank you for finally marrying me." He reached over and brushed my hair away from my eyes.

"We've only been engaged a few months. That's not very long."

"I mean making me wait sixty years."

"I was too young for you sixty years ago."

"And I had just married Betsy."

"So it's your fault then. You didn't wait for me."

"I didn't know you were coming." Nate stopped playing with the ends of my hair and started to trace my eyebrows and cheekbones with his fingertips.

"Well, next time, you'll know better," I said with my eyes closed enjoying the sensation of his caresses.

"Next time?"

"Our next lifetime."

"I'm not finished living this one." He scooted closer and ran his fingers along my jawline and down my neck to my collarbone.

"Mr. Jacobs. What are you doing?"

"I'm just about to kiss my beautiful wife. If she'll permit it."

"Maybe I'll kiss you first." I leaned over and touched my lips to his.

Nate again wriggled closer, so our bodies were almost completely in contact from our lips to our toes.

"You were the most beautiful bride ever."

"That's very sweet of you to say."

"I calls 'em as I see 'em," he said starting to stroke my face again. "You caught my eye then and you're every bit as irresistible tonight as you were standing by your broken-down car."

He started to tug playfully on the buttons on the front of my pajama top. "Could we maybe...keep each other warm without these?" He unbuttoned my pajama top and started to slip it off my shoulder.

"As you wish." I rolled onto my back so I could slip out of my pjs and shove them out of bed and onto the floor. Nate did the same and then rolled back onto his side to face me.

"I love you, Maddie." He ran his hand down my side and then cupped my breast.

"I love you too, Husband. I'm glad you've made an honest woman out of me. Now we can sleep together guilt-free."

"I'm not thinking of sleep. I'd like to make love to my wife. If that's OK with her."

"Definitely OK."

I was surprised at the tenderness and closeness I felt as we joined together. Nate moved slowly, not because he lacked enthusiasm, but for maximum pleasure. Every movement was deliberate and sensual. I started to close my eyes as the sensations washed through me.

Nate said, "Look at me."

Looking into his eyes, I could feel my heart pulling in my chest like it was expanding with every breath. Emotional and physical sensations were jumbled together. I could feel the way he looked at me. I could feel his love for me making every inch of my body tingle.

Lying with our legs and arms entwined in a post-coital embrace I whispered to him, "That was the best... ever."

"You'll make my head swell with those compliments."

I snuggled closer and purred in his ear, "That sounds like a good thing."

I fell asleep on our wedding night in his arms with my head on his chest. Even in sleep, neither one of us wanted to let go. Nate's arms were still wrapped around me when I woke up the next morning.

"Good morning, Sexy," said Nate as I squirmed to roll over to face him.

"Good morning, Husband."

"I didn't want to wake you, but my arm is asleep and I had to move." He rolled onto his back and rubbed his arm and wiggled his fingers.

There was knocking on the door at the base of the stairs, and we heard it open.

Anne called up, "Are you decent?"

"Give us a minute," I answered getting out of bed a little too fast, wobbling, and knocking the water bottle on the nightstand to the floor with a crash.

"Are you OK?" called Anne. "Can I come up?"

"Yes. Fine. Just give us a minute."

Nate had sat up and was hastily putting on his pajamas as I was putting on mine. Seeing we were both decent I called down to Anne that she could come up. She came in carrying a tray with cups of coffee and two small cloches.

"Breakfast in the honeymoon suite for the newlyweds." She set the tray down on the table near the window.

Nate picked up one of the mugs and handed it to me. "What a nice surprise. Thank you."

"Sorry, we thought you'd be up by now." Anne gave me an odd look. "Didn't mean to rush you out of bed."

"You didn't. We were up," I said.

"Then why are your pajama bottoms inside out?" she said with an impish grin. "I'll just leave you lovebirds alone."

Anne closed our bedroom door behind her as she left the room.

Nate lifted one of the cloches. "This one's definitely for you."

"Our first breakfast as husband and wife with the first breakfast item you made me."

"Hopefully mine's not cheese and jam." Nate lifted the other cloche and uncovered a hard-boiled egg and a buttered, toasted English muffin.

"Someone down there knows your breakfast habits."

"Or it was a lucky guess. Either way. Bon Appetit."

We sat in the wing chairs with our coffees and breakfast. The sky outside the window was grey but we couldn't help but be cheery.

Nate chuckled. "Guess we got caught with our pants down."

"I should keep mine this way when we go down."

"They might think you're losing your marbles."

"Which is worse, them thinking we're crazy or horny?"

By the time we'd eaten, showered, and dressed, only Sarah was in the kitchen. She was loading the dishwasher.

"Everyone's been through for breakfast," she reported to Nate very business-like and not letting on if Anne had said anything to her.

"Thanks," said Nate. "I appreciate everything extra you've done to help out this week."

"It's been fun. Maybe you'll rethink the no weddings at the inn policy?" She raised her eyebrows raised with hopeful expectation.

"We'll see," said Nate in a tone that clearly said no-way. "You can head out. I'll finish up here."

"That would be great. Thanks. I'm driving over to Blue Hill to Mark's grandparents' place. They've invited me to spend the weekend at the farm with the whole family."

"That sounds fun," I said. "Is it still a working farm?"

"Yes. Blueberry farm. Mark's uncle runs it now."

"Is it a big family?" asked Nate.

"Pretty big, Mark's got two sisters and there are several cousins, and one of them has a couple of kids too."

"Wow."

"It'll be cozy, but there's room for everyone because Mark's uncle and aunt have their house right beside his grandparents'. I just hope everyone gets along as well as you all have."

I didn't say anything but couldn't help thinking if Ann and Lane had come, things might not have been as harmonious.

As if reading my thoughts, Nate said, "Well, my daughter didn't come ...she's not so thrilled about it."

Sarah got her coat from the hook by the back door. "I'm sure she'll come 'round once she sees how happy you are."

Nate draped his arm over my shoulder and pulled me in and kissed my temple. "That I am. Now get going. Drive safe. Have fun. See you Wednesday."

After she left, we cleaned up the last of the breakfast dishes including our tray. Nate started his Thursday replenishing routine. He was already muttering about being behind as it was Friday today. Knowing I'd be in his way or anger him with my disregard for the correct number of napkins in the dispenser, I went to find Claire and Anne.

I found them in the living room. Claire was in the wing chair reading and Anne and Linda were seated at the small desk.

"What are you two up to?" I asked.

"Addressing invitations," said Anne shuffling through the stack of envelopes in front of her and handing me one. "I hope you won't be offended. Quicker than mailing it and I'll save a stamp."

She watched me as I opened the outer envelope and broke the small heart-shaped wax seal that held two flaps of creamy paper together over the printed inner page. Their names, Anne and Linda were embossed at the top and then there was a quote followed by the invitation text.

"Until my last day, I'll be loving you."
Because you are special to us
We would be honored if you would join us
To celebrate our wedding day.
The ceremony will take place at
Saturday, January 27, 2018 at
Three o'clock in the afternoon at
The Charles River Museum
Celebration reception and dinner to follow.

There was an RSVP card and envelope and a separate details and directions page with addresses, maps, and accommodations suggestions.

"It's perfect," I said. "I love it."

"So I can mark you as a 'Yes', then?"

"Wild horses couldn't keep me away."

"And Nate of course."

"Yup. We're a package deal."

"I spoke with Dad last week. He'll be coming as well," said Anne a bit hesitantly.

"I assumed he would. Hoped so, for your sake."

"He was surprisingly on board. He also offered to help pay. But we declined."

I'd offered to contribute to the wedding, but Anne had refused. She said she and Linda had it covered.

"Who's next on the list," said Linda handing Anne the envelope she'd just finished addressing for her to stuff with the invitation pieces. Anne turned back to their task and, not wanting to distract them, I sat down in the matching wing chair beside Claire. She'd pulled the afghan from the back of the chair down around her shoulders.

"Are you cold?"

"I'm fine, Chérie. It's just cozier under a blanket on a grey day like today."

"I should start a fire. That will help. Be right back."

I headed out to the shed to get some wood and kindling.

"What are you doing?" asked Nate as I passed the pantry door where he was straightening cans, turning their labels facing out and making his restocking notes on his clipboard.

"I'm going to start a fire. Claire's sitting reading and Anne and Linda are addressing wedding invitations in the living room. I haven't seen Emily and Bob."

"I can carry the wood in," said Nate putting down his clipboard.

"No. You finish your inventory. I've got it," I said leaving before he could take it from me.

It wasn't in my best interest for me to interrupt his inventory. I'd learned, the hard way, that it was best to leave him alone whenever he's got that stupid clipboard in his hand.

CHAPTER 40

"Your daughter is quite the planner," I said, opening the large envelope the hotel receptionist had given us when we'd checked in. It was the same stationery as the wedding invitation and was addressed to us. Inside there was a handwritten note from Anne along with several pages of pre-printed information. The note read:

> *Dear Mom and Nate,*
> *We are so happy that you're here with us to celebrate our wedding day. We can't compete with the surprise factor of your wedding, but we hope that you'll be as delighted by ours as we were to be part of yours. Our goal for all our guests is Maximum fun, Minimum stress. We wish we could have hosted you in our home but given its size it was impossible. So, we've tried to anticipate what will make you feel at home in your hotel. If it hasn't been delivered already, a cooler and box of kitchen supplies will be delivered to your room today. If there's anything more you need, please let us know. We can't wait to get this party started!*
> *Love Anne and Linda*

There was a wedding day itinerary indicating that they'd arranged for transportation to and from the hotel and gave the pickup times. The earliest time was circled on our card with a note saying we should try to be on the first one. The printed pages also included suggested tourist attractions and nearby grocery and liquor stores. They'd even suggested restaurants for dining out and ones that delivered or did take out.

"I think Linda might have had a big part in that." Maddie continued to unpack and inspect the clothing she'd brought. "She's very dictatorial when recommending a restaurant or store."

"You know you aren't supposed to upstage the bride," I said, as Maddie carefully pulled the red dress she'd worn for our wedding out of the garment bag and hung it on the front of the wardrobe.

"I think it might need steaming."

"You'll look perfect."

"I can run the shower and steam it in the bathroom if it doesn't fall out on its own in time," she said still scrutinizing the dress and ignoring me.

We had plenty of time to get the dress sorted before the wedding on Saturday. Anne had reserved a room for us at the Crescent Suites Hotel. She'd suggested it to all the guests from out of town because it was walking distance to the museum where the wedding would take place. Our suite had a full kitchen and the cooler and box the girls had sent us was filled with kitchen essentials. We had everything we needed to fix ourselves breakfast or a snack without having to request supplies through the hotel grocery service. While Maddie fussed with her dress, I unpacked the cooler and put everything away in the fridge and cupboards.

The first official event for us was on Thursday; lunch at Anne and Linda's house so we could meet Linda's parents. Anne had strongly recommended that we not rent a car given the horrific Boston traffic that could be confounded with heavy snow in January. We had taken a taxi from the airport to our hotel. For the short drive to Anne's, I'd ordered us an Uber. Unfortunately, it took longer than I'd anticipated for the driver to show up.

"Sorry we're a bit late," I said to Anne as she helped Maddie off with her coat.

She took our coats and headed down the hall with them, calling over her shoulder, "No worries. You're not the last to arrive."

Maddie unzipped and slipped off her boots and I took off my galoshes.

"Hey Mads," said a deep voice. I looked up to see a tall broad-shouldered man pulling Maddie into in a big bear hug.

Maddie extricated herself from his arms and introduced me. "Will, this is my husband Nate. Nate, Will, Anne's father."

Will extended his large hand and grasped mine with what seemed an overly firm grip.

"Nice to meet you." He pumped my arm then said to Maddie, "So you finally broke down and did it again?"

Maddie careened her head to peer around Will. "Where's Rita?"

"She and I are taking a break. I'm flying solo this week. We could have hooked up for our daughter's wedding."

"Never going to happen," said Maddie sharply, shaking her head and rolling her eyes but with a smile and a familiarity that made me uncomfortable.

"Guess not. You up and married this guy out of the blue," said Will, leaning in towards Maddie and pointing at me with his thumb.

The way Will looked at Maddie was a little too chummy for my liking. Maddie turned away from Will to get her dressy shoes from her bag.

"By the way," continued Will following her every move with his eyes, "marriage agrees with you. You look great Mads."

Just then another couple came in the front door and we all had to shuffle forward into the hallway to make room for them to enter.

"It's wicked cold out there," said the woman shaking snow off her fur coat with a full-body wag. "I'm Barbara, but you can call me Barbie, and this is Jeff." She tugged off her gloves, kicked off her boots, slipped out of her coat, dropped it in Jeff's arms, and came towards us with open arms. "You must be Anne's parents! So happy to finally meet you!"

The three of us formed a line along the hallway. I positioned myself between Maddie and Will and placed my arm around her waist. Barbie hugged each of us in turn as we introduced ourselves. Jeff followed her with their coats, shaking hands awkwardly under the thick wet wool and mink. Jeff continued down the hall to dispense with the coats. Not waiting for our hostesses, Barbie ushered us into the living room. She seemed very much at home as she directed us to sit in the chairs and sofa around the coffee table. She presided over us, standing in front of the gas fireplace facing the grouping of seats.

"Do you live in the area?" I asked her, suspecting from the way she replaced the Rs in her name with Hs that she was a Boston, or at least Massachusetts, native.

"Born here, just like our Linda. We've lived in Brookline forever."

"Where's Brookline?" asked Maddie.

"Just west of downtown, about 30 mins from here. Not far from Boston College," explained Jeff who'd slipped in silently behind us.

Anne came into the living room carrying a tray of glasses followed by Linda with a bottle of champagne and a carafe of orange juice.

"We wanted to start off with a toast." She placed the tray of glasses on the coffee table. Picking up two glasses she turned to Barbie and asked, "Mimosa, champagne or fresh squeezed tangerine-orange juice?"

"I suppose it's not too early for a Mimosa," said Barbie.

"Mom for you?" asked Anne.

"Mimosa sounds lovely," said Maddie.

Anne held the glasses while Linda poured the beverage of choice for each of us. Champagne only for me and Will, juice for Jeff and mimosas for all the ladies.

Anne held up her glass. "To our parents!"

"Who made us. Perfect for each other," said Linda with a giggle.

Anne affectionately nudged Linda with her elbow. "We are thankful to have you all here with us and we are blessed to have your love and support as we connect our two families through our wedding."

"Here! Here!" Jeff stood so he could touch his glass to his daughter's and then turned to us as we stood to toast, making our glasses ring happily.

"Best thing we ever did was make you," said Will kissing Anne affectionately on the cheek before downing the champagne all in one gulp.

"Need a refill?" Linda asked Will lifting the bottle up to her eye level. "There's a little left in this one and we have more."

"Top up the ladies' glasses with that," said Will. "But I wouldn't be opposed to a beer if that's an option."

"Absolutely. Anne picked out a couple of beers she thought you'd like. Follow me."

Linda handed Anne the champagne bottle so she could dole out the remaining champagne.

"Bring the other bottle," Anne called after her as she drained it topping up Maddie and Barbie's glasses.

"I understand you lived in Boston for some time," said Jeff moving to position himself next to me.

"Yes," I answered, watching Will come back carrying a beer and the fresh champagne bottle.

"And now you're up in Bar Harbor?" asked Jeff.

"Yes. Moved there after I retired."

"What line of work?"

"I was General Counsel for Bond Technologies."

"Ahhh a lawyer. Guess I better take the lawyer jokes out of my Father of the Bride speech then."

"Only if they're not funny. I love a good lawyer joke."

"You know my Linda is a lawyer…"

"Then you better get her permission for the jokes, not mine."

"That's what the wife said. Lucky you're not on the hook for a speech."

I tried to focus on what Jeff was saying but I was distracted watching Will huddled with Anne and Maddie. They were laughing and toasting and seeing them made my stomach churn.

"Lunch is served," announced Linda from the doorway. "If you want to set your glasses on the dining room table… and come make yourselves a plate in the kitchen."

I moved in between Maddie and Will. "I'll set yours down for you." I took Maddie's glass and quickly headed to the dining room to place it next to mine on the far side of the large square dining table. The others followed. Will chose the end of the table where there was a single seat.

The girls had put out enough food to serve 20 people. Every flat surface in the kitchen was covered with platters, bowls, and chafing dishes.

"Start here," said Linda pointing to the end of the kitchen counter closest to the door.

After we'd all settled around the table with our plates, Linda said, "We have a little activity planned."

"This was all her doing," said Anne. "Just in case it goes very badly."

"It'll be fun," said Linda.

"That is our wedding theme," said Anne.

"Maximum fun, Minimum stress," they said in unison.

It was sweet to see these two grown and successful women giggling together. This was the first time I'd seen them in their own home with their guard completely down. It was clear they were madly in love. My heart was filled wth delight for Anne as if she were my own daughter.

"Here's the deal," said Linda bringing the table to order while pulling a bright yellow straw hat from under her chair. "In this hat, we have a bunch of cards with questions. We want each of you to pick a card, without peeking, and answer the question on it." She held the hat high above Barbie's plate. "Mom you go first."

Barbie reached up, swirled her hand in the hat, and pulled out a card.

"I see you printed these for old people." She turned the card to us so we could see the giant type on it. "It says, 'What song comes to mind when you think of your daughter? And why?'"

Barbie didn't hesitate for a second. "That's easy. The red shoes dance song. She had posters all over her room of what's his name..." Barbie nudged Jeff who shrugged helplessly.

"David Bowie," said Linda looking down and putting her head in her hand. "We can skip the why part and move on..."

"Oh no we can't," said Barbie. "She begged me for red pumps and a leather ragged edge dress like in the video and she would dance in her room to the song while staring at his pictures. Then she moved on to wanting to get her hair bleached and cut just like his. His hairstyle was rather feminine so I was OK with it, but I drew the line at the bleach."

"Why have I never seen pictures of this?" asked Anne.

"It was the eighties," said Linda. "Not my best decade." Linda handed the hat to Anne.

"Who's next," asked Anne. Linda nodded towards Maddie and Anne held the hat out so Maddie could pick a card.

"I hope it's not a musical question." Maddie shuffled through the cards and drew one. "Mine says, 'What's your favorite vacation memory with your daughter?' That's a tough one since we've had so many great trips together. I'd have to say our first London trip. It was your first international trip, and it was for your 16th birthday. "

"That was a great trip," said Anne. "We saw Cats and we stayed at a fancy hotel where they put little chocolates on my pillow every night."

"Where did you stay," I asked.

"The Savoy," said Maddie. "We also went to museums and shopping."

"And I started to drink tea," said Anne.

"What year was it?" I asked.

"I was 16, so 1986," said Anne.

I made a mental note to tell Maddie that I had also stayed at the Savoy in 1986. Betsy and I had made a stop in London to visit some galleries while we'd been there for our Ann's wedding. I'd bought several antique toy boats at a shop in Notting Hill. Seeing the very old toys in the antique markets of England had inspired my collecting bug.

"Dad, your turn," said Linda taking the hat back from Anne and holding it up for Jeff to select a card.

"Mine says 'What advice do you have for your daughter's fiancé?' This seems like dangerous territory, but I suppose I should remind Anne that there's a reason that she argues for a living, she loves a good argument."

"Hey," said Linda with an exaggerated pout. "I don't argue. I debate."

"Good thing we're on the same page about most things," said Anne placing her hand on Linda's and looking at her with a sweet but playfully patronizing smile.

"Don't you worry Jeff, my Annie's not one to back down from a good fight if needed," said Will.

"We've never had a major disagreement," said Anne.

"Let's hope you never do," said Jeff. "Happy wife, happy life, times two." He picked up his glass to toast the girls and we all joined in.

"I guess I'm next," said Will reaching for the hat.

"Pass the hat," said Linda giving it to her Dad to hold it for Will who pulled a card.

"I am the wrong person to answer this question," said Will shaking his head. "What advice for a long and happy marriage would you give your daughter?"

"I think you definitely should pick another question." Maddie's tone was teasing but had a bitter edge.

"No, no. I picked it I'll answer it." Will drummed his fingers on the table and looked at the ceiling searching for an answer. "I would have to say… don't give up too easily. I really should have kept asking Maddie to remarry me and not given up when she turned me down the first time. I didn't know how good I had it. So yeah, hold on and don't give up."

"Don't worry Pop, I'll not be letting this one go. Never ever." Anne put her arm around Linda and kissed her cheek.

"Shall we do another round?" said Linda taking the hat back. "We have plenty more questions in here," she added shaking it invitingly.

Despite the odd embarrassing story, Anne and Linda seemed to enjoy putting their parents on the spot with the questions. Their goal had been for us all to get to know each other better, and in that regard, the luncheon was a success. The food was very good, but the best part was watching how sweet Anne and Linda were together and their delight hosting their parents in their home.

CHAPTER 41

Nate was stiff and silent during the short ride back to our hotel from Anne and Linda's house.

I asked him, "Are you upset?"

"No," he'd answered but I could feel the tension. I sensed his mood like it was a force field, radiating out from him, making my nerve endings twitch under my skin.

"Did I do something?" I asked, wanting to put things right if I had.

"You've done nothing." There was an edge to his voice that surprised me in its harshness.

"But you seem upset." I reached for his hand across the back seat of the car.

"Will you just let it go," he hissed, glaring at me. He turned away and stared at the back of our driver's head.

I started to feel panic that it was something so serious he didn't want to discuss it in the presence of a stranger. For the rest of the ride, I turned my focus out the side window, running back over the past few hours in my head, trying to identify the source of Nate's annoyance.

Instead of hurrying to open my door, as he usually did, Nate stood by the car fiddling with his phone. I presumed he was having trouble with the app to pay our driver. I slid across the backseat and out his door.

"Do you need help with that?"

"Why would you think that? Because I'm an old man?"

"Not because you're old, you're just not the most... tech-savvy." I had no intention of being mean, just teasing him a little, trying to lighten the mood.

"I don't need help. But if you'd prefer someone else paid your car fare maybe you should have ridden back with Will." Nate opened the lobby door and went in ahead of me instead of holding it open for me.

"Why would I do that?" I was baffled as to why he was behaving rudely and speaking to me as if I'd done something wrong.

He walked ahead of me through the hotel and back to our room as if I wasn't even there. I could feel my irritation building at his behaviour while concern and confusion swirled in my head. As soon as our suite door closed behind me, I grabbed Nate's arm, so he had to stop and face me.

"What's going on?" I asked.

354

"You tell me," he said pulling away from me, taking off his galoshes and hanging his coat up.

"I have no idea what you're upset about. How could I possibly tell you?" My voice got louder with my frustration.

"Why do you always have to yell?"

"I'm not yelling. If you want yelling, I can do yelling," I seethed, breathing heavily through my nose to keep my composure, but feeling my temper starting to boil over.

"I don't want the whole hotel to know our business."

"What business? What is wrong with you?" I said stepping in front of him, so he had to look at me.

"Wrong with me? Yes. Of course. It's my fault."

Nate turned away and walked from the sitting area of the suite to the bedroom. I followed him.

"I never said it was your fault. I want to know what's wrong."

"Just let it go."

"I can't let it go. You're obviously upset and angry at me and I want to know why."

"I'm not angry with you." He sat down on the bed and started to take off his dress shoes.

"Then why the hell are you being mean and rude to me?" My voice cracked as my emotions got the better of me and tears started to well up.

Nate took a deep breath and let out a long sigh. "I'm sorry. It's just... seeing you and Will."

"Me and Will? There is no me and Will."

"Seeing you together. It makes me a little crazy."

"This is a little crazy? I'd hate to see a lot crazy." I knew I was lashing out, but I was swinging more towards anger from hurt.

"Until now, I could pretend he didn't matter."

"He doesn't matter to me other than he's Anne's father."

"But he did."

"That was a lifetime ago. You were married too. For even longer than I was. Why should you be angry with me?"

"I'm not angry with you. I'm angry at me. At life."

Nate looked up at me. My heart softened and my anger dissipated seeing his pained expression and imploring eyes. I sat down on the bed beside him and took the shoe he was holding from his hand and tossed it on the floor so I could take both his hands in mine.

I looked into his eyes. "Talk to me."

"It makes me crazy when I think about how much time we missed out on.

When Will started telling stories of you and Anne... all I could think is you should have been with me all those years."

"You should have found me sooner."

"Oh, right. It's always my fault?"

"Well, I kept showing up in all the same places as you and you didn't see me."

"I think you didn't see me. I'm the one that remembered what you were wearing the day your car broke down."

"Touché. But you were already married. You didn't wait to find me."

"I'll know better next time. I'll find you sooner."

"Next time?"

"In our next lifetime. I'll find you sooner, so we have more time."

"That sounds like a really good plan. But we need to make the best of the time we have. We can't waste it being angry about things that happened before we met."

"I don't like Will."

"You have to play nice for a couple of days. He's Anne's father and she wants him here and I want Anne to have whatever and whoever she wants at her wedding."

"But you don't have to be so chummy with him."

"You're not jealous, are you?" I was shocked by the absurdity of Nate being jealous of Will. We'd been divorced for decades, and Nate knew that.

"He still wants you."

I laughed. "That's ridiculous. And even if he did, I've found the love of my life and he's sitting here on the bed being ridiculously jealous and it makes me love him even more."

Nate put his arm around my shoulder and kissed my cheek. "I just can't lose you now that I've finally found you."

"I'm not going anywhere. You're stuck with me."

The obligations of being the bride's parents thrust Will and me together numerous times over the course of the weekend. Anne and Linda wanted their parents to participate in the wedding ceremony. As we walked through the details at the rehearsal, Will made numerous comments emphasizing how lovely it was to be there together for our daughter. Now that I was aware that Nate was jealous of Will, I was more sensitive to Will's comments and innuendos that I'd dismissed as simply Will being Will. I reassured Nate repeatedly that there was no reason for him to be jealous and he repeated it made him angry he had to share any of the precious time we had together with that 'clown'.

Sticking with tradition, both brides had decided to be escorted down the aisle by their fathers.

"You won't be upset if I ask Dad to walk me down the aisle, will you?" Anne had asked me a few weeks before the wedding. She explained that she'd tried to convince Linda that they should walk in together, but Linda had always dreamed of being walked down the aisle by her father. Anne was conflicted about how she should make her entrance.

"I'm fine with whatever you decide," I'd answered automatically but I did feel disgruntled. Will had left us both, then floated in and out of Anne's life when it suited him whereas I'd been the one to provide the stable home for her. He hadn't earned it.

"Are you sure?" said Anne, sensing my hesitation. "The other options are for you to walk me down the aisle, or for both of you on either side of me, or for me to walk in alone."

"I think it would be strange for Rita and Nate if your father and I both walked you down the aisle," I'd answered not knowing, at the time, that Will's marital status had changed.

"I feel guilty leaving you out."

I did my best to reassure her that it wasn't something I'd always hoped to do and if Will walking her down the aisle is what made her and Linda happy, that's all that mattered to me.

Because Will had come alone, and he didn't know many of Anne and Linda's guests, he spent much of the rehearsal party and the wedding reception hanging around Nate and me. I marvelled at how Nate concealed his dislike for Will, joking boyishly with him while they waited at the bar for their drinks. I frequently found myself in the awkward position of having both Will and Nate vying for my attention. Nate was demonstratively possessive of me whenever Will was around. Will treated me like I was a long-lost best friend with complete amnesia of the mess he'd made of my life. Being around the two of them made me feel both flattered and annoyed in equal measure.

Other than the 'Nate versus Will' drama, we had a fantastic time at Anne and Linda's wedding. It was a beautiful celebration of two people, in love; committing their lives to each other. My eyes welled up as they exchanged their vows. Nate was at the ready with his white handkerchief and squeezed my hand affectionately as he pressed it into my hand so I could dab my eyes.

In a break with tradition, Anne and Linda had a mix of bridesmaids and groomsmen as their attendants. Anne had her longtime friend as her Matron of Honour, but Linda had asked her brother to stand up for her, so she had a Best Man instead. They invited the wedding party, their partners, and their parents to join them on the dance floor for their first dance.

As Nate and I danced in a circle around the brides, he held me close and whispered in my ear, "Next time I hope we're younger than them when we have our first dance as husband and wife."

I looked into his eyes. "We'll dance at our wedding and our daughter's wedding, and they won't be months apart."

"Definitely not," he agreed and he spun me around on the dance floor with renewed enthusiasm.

We danced until my feet hurt. Even though Anne and Linda made a point of letting us know we could leave early as they planned to party into the night, I didn't want to leave until the very end. Nate and I settled into a couple of chairs facing the dance floor and we watched my daughter and her wife dance and laugh and sing with their friends.

Nate was holding my hand and playing with my engagement-wedding ring. The stones flashed with the strobe lights from the DJ stand.

"You can offer me the same ring next time."

"Do you really believe in multiple lifetimes?"

"I believe that every possible reality is happening simultaneously so every possible life we're living is always happening. We just happen to be observing this one."

"We need to observe one when I meet you sooner."

"It might not be that simple. We need to make the right combination of choices so our paths cross at the right time, under the right circumstances."

"But we've crossed paths many times. We were supposed to meet."

"It's possible we have met many times, in many different realities; we just didn't observe any of them."

"At least not yet…"

"Each of us made decisions that shaped who we are and led us to meet at this time in our lives. Maybe this is the perfect moment?"

"I don't think I'd have made the same choices if I'd known you sooner."

"Like what?"

Nate turned his chair slightly to face me and looked at me quite seriously. "From the moment you walked into my inn, I wanted to spend every minute getting to know you better."

"And I thought you were just being nice to the old lady who tagged along with Jake's Godmother."

"I fell for you before our first selfie falling with Inny."

"We'd only just met."

"Now we know that's not true. Think of all the near misses over the years. We took the long way around to finally being together."

As lovely as it was to imagine another lifetime, where Nate and I found each other sooner, I didn't want to miss out making as much as we could of our time together.

"We should make as many memories as possible this time, so you don't forget to find me next time," I said.

"What sort of memories should we make?"

"Is there something you've always wanted to do? Someplace you've always wanted to go?"

"Norway."

"Pining for the fiords?" I said in a poor squeaky imitation of John Cleese that made Nate giggle.

"I am. Are you?"

"Never been to Norway. Definitely pining."

CHAPTER 42

Lane packed our small suitcases into the 'boot' of his car. "Is that all the luggage?"

"We sent our heavy clothing ahead to Norway. We're traveling light, for now," I explained.

"Thanks for coming to pick us up," said Maddie.

"After your long flight, we thought it would be easier on you," said Lane opening both the front and back seat car doors.

"We were all set to take the train. I hope it's not too much trouble," said Maddie starting to get into the back seat to let me sit with Lane.

"You can take the front seat if you like." I held the door for her.

"I've been putting off a client dinner meeting in Canterbury because it would require an overnight stay. This gave me a good reason to schedule it. It's just a quick side trip to gather you here on my way home."

"Killing two birds with one stone," said Maddie.

"Precisely," said Lane. "Are you hungry or in need of a coffee?"

"Not for me. But if you do…," said Maddie.

"I stopped at a rest area on the motorway while I waited for your flight. If you change your mind, there are a couple of rest areas between here and Oxford. Just let me know."

It started to rain as we pulled away from the airport. I leaned my head back, closed my eyes, and listened to Maddie chat with Lane and the rhythmic thwap of the wiper blades. I must have fallen asleep as I woke up with a start when we drove onto a very bumpy cobble street.

"We're almost there," said Lane looking into the rearview mirror. "Sorry about the jolt awake. I barely notice the teeth-rattling roads until I've been driving the motorways for a while and I get spoiled by the smooth pavement," he said with a wry smile.

Ann and Lane's house wasn't visible until we pulled into the driveway past the thick high hedgerow that ringed their entire property.

"What a beautiful house. I love the stone," said Maddie leaning forward with her nose practically touching the windshield of the car so she could see it better.

"Thank you. It's small but it has its charms. And quirks."

"It looks like a postcard," she said admiringly, and I could tell she was plotting where she would set up to take pictures of it.

"Let's get you in and settled," said Lane, cracking his door and popping an umbrella open above the car. He came around the car and opened both our doors and then held the umbrella over us as we moved in a huddle under it to the front door and inside.

"You stay here," he instructed. "I'll fetch your bags."

Lane put the umbrella down and put on a large hooded yellow rain poncho that was hanging on a peg by the front door and headed back out into the rain. We slipped off our coats and hung them on the pegs. I stayed near the door to hold it open for Lane.

Maddie wandered into the kitchen from the hall, calling out to Ann to let her know we'd arrived. There was no reply except the squawk of a bird I couldn't see from the front entryway.

"Well, hello Polly," I heard Maddie say from the kitchen. "Where's your mommy?"

"I'll take these to your room," said Lane carrying the suitcases in. "I'm sure you'll want to freshen up."

"Where's Ann?" I asked surprised she wasn't there to greet us.

"I'm not sure. Her car is gone. She'll have left a note."

"There's a note here," said Maddie from the kitchen.

Maddie came back to the entryway and handed Lane a folded paper with his name on it. Lane opened it, read it, and then stuffed it into his jacket pocket.

"It seems she had to go to the gallery today. You'll be on your own here for a spell because I have a meeting at the college this afternoon." He picked up our suitcases and led us through the kitchen, along a short hallway, and through a glassed-in breezeway that connected two parts of the house.

Lane explained a little about the house as we went. "Nate, you might recall that this used to be the garage until we annexed it to add another bedroom and Ann's studio." He led us up an open wood staircase to the second-floor loft space that had a high-pitched open beamed ceiling and a stone wall at either end.

"The loo is here," he said opening the door adjacent to the stairs. "Only a shower," he said to Maddie. "If you prefer a bath, you can use the tub in our bathroom."

"Shower is perfect," said Maddie. "This is a lovely room."

"I'll leave you to settle in. I'll put the kettle on and plunder the icebox to see what I can rummage up for lunch."

As soon as Lane left, I started to unpack my suitcase that he'd placed on a long wooden bench under the window across from the stairs in the center of the long wall of the room.

"Can I use the loo first?" asked Maddie emphasizing the word 'loo' with a silly grin.

"Of course," I said carefully lifting my folded shirts from my bag and turning to put them on the bed but running into Maddie instead. "What are you doing?" I said, almost dropping my shirts.

"Oops," she said. "I just want my toiletries. I'll get out of your way."

The room had no closet but there was a large armoire and a matching dresser. I remembered how Betsy had divided the drawers, three large ones for her and 2 small ones for me, and that we'd had to put her hatbox on top of the armoire because she didn't want to stack it with our suitcases on the floor. Opening the armoire, I was surprised to find it quite full. I shifted the contents to one side one at a time and pulled out all the empty hangers I could find. Since there were only four, I hung my shirts on top of each other and my pants on another and saved the remaining two for Maddie. Of the five drawers in the dresser, there were only two empty ones. I took the smaller one which easily held the rest of my things.

I'd finished unpacking and was just tucking my empty suitcase under the bench when Maddie came out of the bathroom.

"I feel one thousand percent better with my teeth and hair brushed." She nodded at the bed where I was stashing the suitcase. "You're already unpacked?"

"Yes, Darling. There weren't many hangers. I only took two, so you'd have two."

"I can leave most things folded," said Maddie pulling out her clothes and stacking them on the bed.

"There's only one more empty drawer," I said pulling it open for her.

"I suppose I could leave some things in my suitcase," she said sorting the folded clothes into two piles on the bed.

"I'm surprised Ann didn't clear out some space. We told her ages ago we were planning to come."

"Perhaps she was hoping that we'd change our minds and go straight to Norway," said Maddie sighing.

"I'm sure that's not it," I reassured her, but I wasn't at all sure Ann was happy we'd come to visit.

Lane had put out a plate of sandwiches on the kitchen table and had made a pot of tea by the time we joined him in the kitchen.

"I'm sorry the pickings are slim," he apologized.

"This is perfect," said Maddie, ever the grateful guest. I knew she was bitter when it came to Ann, but she didn't let it show, at least not with Lane.

At first, Maddie had been understanding; Ann needed time to get used to the idea that her father had remarried. But as the months had gone by, and Ann still couldn't bring herself to be happy for us, Maddie had lost patience. That's why I'd been so surprised when she suggested we visit her as part of our trip. She'd explained that she wanted to try to get to know her and that she didn't want to be the reason that I didn't spend time with my daughter. I had argued against it. I didn't want anything to mar our first big adventure as husband and wife. I had my doubts that Ann would come around. The fact that she'd not been there to meet us, she'd left a note only for Lane and there were no welcoming touches in our room as there had been when Betsy and I had visited, were all clues that my fears were well-founded.

"Ann should be home by teatime," said Lane. "In the meantime, make yourselves at home. The telly is in the living room if you want to watch a program. And here's a key, just in case the rain lets up and you want to go for a walk. Anything else you need before I head out?"

"We're all set," I said.

"Thank you again for coming to pick us up," said Maddie pouring a cup of tea. "And for the lovely tea. It smells heavenly."

"Enjoy. Help yourselves to whatever you find. Ann and I thought we'd go to the pub tonight for supper, but we'll go a little early since you're probably a bit jet-lagged."

"We'll be fine. Don't worry about us," I assured him, not wanting to make him late for his meeting taking care of us.

"Just think," said Maddie once we were alone eating our sandwiches and sipping tea, "less than twelve hours ago we were in a taxi heading to the airport in Toronto and now we're in Oxfordshire sipping tea, soon to be headed to a pub for a pint."

"Flying buses planes these days," I said, feeling the effects of the lack of sleep and not sharing Maddie's sense of wonder.

"I think someone needs a nap," said Maddie with a teasing motherly tone.

"I just need twenty minutes to close my eyes."

"I can tidy up here once we're done."

"Are you going to come up?"

"I'll either wake up feeling worse or not wake up until tomorrow."

"What are you going to do?"

"I'll find something. Watch the telly maybe," she said imitating Lane's accent.

When I opened my eyes, it was already starting to get dark outside. I was surprised I'd slept so long and a little anxious that I'd left Maddie on her own for so long. I got up and found her sitting in a chair in the glass breezeway, wrapped in a blanket, reading.

"Well hello, sleepyhead," she said putting the book down.

"Why are you sitting here? It's cold."

"There's nice light and I like listening to the rain."

"Why didn't you wake me?"

"I came up after you'd been gone for about a half-hour. You were snoring and looked so comfy I didn't want to bother you. I just got my book and came back down."

"I was sure I'd only sleep thirty minutes."

"You always say that, but it's never true."

"It's not never true."

"Is too."

"Here for an argument?"

"No I'm not," she answered automatically, making me chuckle.

CHAPTER 43

"It was absolutely magical," was my response to Anne asking about our trip to Norway. We were lucky. We had clear skies on the nights we were above the Arctic circle and there was only a sliver of moon; perfect conditions for viewing the aurora borealis. As much as he enjoyed the experience of seeing the northern lights, I think Nate was even more delighted that everything he'd planned had worked out.

After our short and somewhat cool visit with Ann, we flew to Oslo and started our Norway adventure. When we'd first discussed taking a trip to Norway, I'd picked up a blank leather journaling book from the clearance bin at Chapters bookstore. Using a gold paint pen I'd written "Norway Adventure" on the cover and had given it to Nate as a gag gift for his birthday. I'd included a note saying that I looked forward to writing the story of our trip together. I think he took this as a challenge and he immediately began filling the book with notes and lists and ultimately with a detailed day-by-day itinerary.

Nate had worked hard to fit as much into our two weeks as he could. We toured Oslo, Bergen, Trondheim, visited the Lillehammer Olympic site, cruised the fjords, and then spent several days in nearly complete darkness visiting Tromso and the Lofoten Islands hoping to see the northern lights. It would have been exhausting if he hadn't arranged for drivers, and tour guides and bought upgraded tickets for our transportation whenever it was possible.

"If we're going to do this, we're going to do it right," he'd pledged. And he'd delivered.

I'd teased Nate about his documentation obsession as he recorded every detail before and during our trip in his book. But I was grateful for it when I organized the trip pictures into a photo book I made for him as a Christmas present. I would've had a hard time remembering the days, the locations, and the names of the people we'd met without his notes.

"Wow! This picture of you two and the northern lights is amazing," said Linda as she and Anne flipped through the photo book on Christmas morning after Nate had opened it.

"The cruise photographer took that picture. All the others in the book are ones we took. Nate's gotten quite good at holding the camera for selfies."

"I would love to see the northern lights," said Linda.

"If you want to see them in Norway, you've got an expert planner in the family." I nodded towards Nate who grinned proudly at the compliment.

"It's amazing how many places you went. Did you get any time to relax?" asked Anne.

"He scheduled that too," I said which sent Anne into fits of laughter.

"I don't want to know what else he scheduled," she said covering her ears and closing her eyes like I was going to share too much information.

"You're a bad girl," I said. "I should have told Santa to bring you nothing but a lump of coal."

"No one here deserves lumps of coal," said Nate. "Sweets and presents for my girls," he said looking quite delighted sitting by the fire with his coffee overseeing us opening our gifts.

There were lots of nice presents to open. Anne and Linda had arrived at the inn with a trunkload and Nate and I had added to the pile with presents we'd bought for the girls and the ones we'd secretly bought for each other. But the greatest gift was that Christmas morning was filled with laughter and hugs.

It was only our second Christmas as husband and wife, but you'd never know it based on how close Anne and Nate had become. The girls were enthusiastic when we'd suggested they come stay with us in Bar Harbor for Christmas. When they found out we'd have the place to ourselves through New Year's they'd asked if they could come for the whole time.

Unlike our visit with Ann, where it seemed it was a chore for her to spend time with us, Anne and Linda were determined to spend as much time as they could with us. They got out Nate's book of activity suggestions he had assembled for guests. They decided we should try to do every one of them.

"Just to make sure they're good enough for your guests," said Anne when Nate scoffed at the idea. Anne wisely recruited Nate's help planning and his resistance to the idea faded. Much to my surprise they even got Nate to go snowshoeing and skidooing. Our performance, although considerably slower than the girls, was pretty spectacular, for a couple of octogenarians.

On New Year's Eve morning, we woke up to a thick blanket of perfect packing snow. After spending the morning building four snowpeople in the front yard, we changed into the special outfits that the girls had bought for us.

"This is our idea of the perfect outfit for New Year's Eve," Linda had said handing us a large gift bag.

Inside the bag were matching flannel pyjamas. The flannel pattern was a black background with champagne bottles, popping corks and glasses. There were noisemakers, decorations, party hats and a thousand-piece puzzle in a second bag that Anne handed us once we'd had a chance to check out the pyjamas.

"We brought everything we could think of to make this an epic New Year's

Eve celebration," said Anne.

The pyjama attire was a surprise, but we'd discussed the menu in advance. Anne and Linda insisted we make all the appetizers and snacks from the family recipe book so they could practice making them with my supervision. We spent the afternoon and evening alternating between cooking, eating, making the puzzle, and playing cards. Several bottles of wine were emptied along the way.

Before midnight we turned on the TV in the kitchen to watch the ball drop in New York. Nate had his arm around me as we counted down along with the crowd on TV and then we turned to each other for our first kiss of the new year.

"I think this has been the best year of my life," said Nate holding me close and looking into my eyes.

"Not sure how you're going to top this one," I said teasing him.

"Is that a challenge?" he said with a grin.

"If you're up for it."

"Oh I'm up for it," he said, playfully pawing at my breast. "Are you?"

"Aren't they cute," said Linda.

"I hope we're still that frisky when we're their age," said Anne.

"Hey, you two, mind your own business," I said over my shoulder, lifting my arms and wrapping them around Nate's neck so I could lean in to give him another long kiss.

Nate put his hands on my hips and started to lead me in a slow dance to the strains of Auld Lang Syne coming from the TV.

"One more kiss for auld lang syne?" Nate nuzzled my cheek.

"Time long passed? You mean the last two years since our first kiss?"

"For every New Year's Eve we didn't kiss."

"Then you owe me more than 60 kisses. We could be at this all night."

"Problem or opportunity?" he replied which made me grin. "You have a beautiful smile," he said sincerely and looked at me adoringly.

"You have a knack for making me smile."

"May it always be so," he said switching our arms to a ballroom dance position and leading me in a spin between the counter and the sink.

"We have one more thing to do tonight," said Linda.

"Go to bed?" I asked.

"Not yet," said Anne going to the dining room and returning with a hat.

"Make breakfast?" asked Nate.

"Only if you're hungry," said Linda. "I couldn't. I'm full of grapes."

"I don't think it was the grapes, Lovey," said Anne nodding at the empty serving dishes and glasses that Nate had started cleaning up from the kitchen counter.

"So, what is it?" asked Nate.

"We each have to answer the first question of the New Year," said Linda.

"What's the question?" said Nate, not clueing in that the hat Anne was holding was full of questions.

"You'll have to pick one," said Anne shaking the hat. "Who wants to go first."

From the look on Nate's face, I could tell he wasn't keen on this game, and that he'd rather be getting his kitchen cleaned up, so I volunteered.

"In the next year, what do you want to do more of?" I read from the card I'd pulled from the hat. "I'm not sure I want to do more of anything. We squeezed a lot into this year."

"Maybe do more of doing nothing?" suggested Anne.

"I guess I'd like to do more travelling with Nate. He's an awesome trip planner."

"That sounds like you want Nate to do more travel planning," said Linda. "Are you OK with that Nate?"

"Anything she wants," said Nate, not looking up from rearranging the dishes Anne had put in the bottom rack of the dishwasher so they were the way he liked them.

"Me next?" asked Anne helping herself to a card when no one objected. "What's something you want to learn next year?"

"Better not be skydiving," said Linda.

"I wasn't going to say that," said Anne in a defensive tone and then in a whisper to me, "I've been told I'm forbidden from jumping out of a perfectly good plane."

"You could pick something in the area of professional development," suggested Linda.

"This isn't a performance review question. I need to think of something fun I'd like to learn," said Anne, stalling by going to the fridge and getting out the orange juice and pouring herself a glass. "Pickleball," she said finally.

"Pickleball? What the heck is pickleball?" said Nate.

"It's a cross between ping-pong and tennis. It's supposed to be fun," said Anne.

"Never heard of it," said Nate.

"Where do you play it?" I asked.

"Outside on a court. But with paddles, not rackets," said Anne.

"OK, pickleball it is then," said Linda, taking the hat away from her and taking it over to Nate for him to select a card.

"What would make this year a perfect year?" read Nate. "That's easy. Waking up beside my beautiful wife every morning."

"You're easy to please," said Anne.

"At 85, waking up every morning is already a major accomplishment," said Nate going back to his cleaning.

"You're not 85!" said Linda with eyes wide. "And we made you get on a snowmobile!"

"Don't worry. I got up the next morning," he said with his back to us, rinsing wine glasses at the sink.

"La la la la la," said Anne covering her ears. "Too much information."

"You have a dirty mind. I'm ashamed you're my daughter," I scolded.

"You always said I took after you," she fired back.

"Moving on," said Linda taking a card out for herself and reading it, "How will you make this year an adventure?"

"Skydiving would be an adventure," suggested Anne with exaggerated enthusiasm making Linda scrunch up her face and scowl at her.

"I think our other project will be our big adventure," said Linda, suddenly quite serious.

"I thought we weren't going to mention that yet," said Anne, obviously trying to squash the subject.

"Now you have to tell," I said, concerned that they were facing something difficult.

"It's still early stages," said Anne. "We don't want to jinx it."

"We're adopting a baby," blurted out Linda.

"That explains the no skydiving rule," said Nate dryly.

"That would qualify as an adventure," I said. "And you weren't going to mention it?"

"Things are still…. uncertain," said Anne. "We didn't want to get everyone's hopes up. We didn't want to get our hopes up. We've been through background checks and screening interviews and home inspections with the agency, but it was a bit of a longshot that they would match us with a birth mother."

"But I have a really good feeling about Jade," said Linda. "The birth mother who wanted to meet us," she explained ignoring Anne's glare to get her to stop talking.

"Let's just say," said Anne, "that we're going on this adventure, but we don't know how it will turn out."

"I'm sure it will all turn out the way it's supposed to," I said pulling Anne into a hug.

"I know how much you'd like to be Granny to a mini-Annie or Andy," said Anne. "I didn't want to get your hopes up… but someone couldn't keep it a secret."

"You needn't worry about me. If this is what you want, I'm a hundred percent with you. But if it doesn't work out, I'm a hundred percent with you too."

With that final bit of exciting news, we decided to call it a night.

CHAPTER 44

"They're over the moon happy, eh?" said Maddie as we hung up from our first video call with our new granddaughter.

"I think she's a very lucky baby with two wonderful parents."

"I'm just so relieved that it worked out this time."

"You can stop worrying now. I know you've been fretting ever since they told you they'd had another match."

"I won't stop worrying. Just change what I'm worrying about."

Maddie said it as if she was joking, but I knew there was a lot of truth in her words. Maddie had felt every twist and turn of the emotional rollercoaster Anne and Linda had been on over the past few months. The preparation and anticipation waiting for a birth mother to select them. Then the elation of having a baby on the way only to find out that the birth mother had changed her mind. Then the hope and fear that the second chance might also end in disappointment.

Maddie had gone down to Boston several times to be with them since we'd been back at the inn for the summer season. Initially, I'd discouraged her from going. I thought the girls wouldn't want company while they were dealing with the stress of the adoption process. But today, when Maddie suggested to Anne that she could drive down to be with her, Anne started to cry, and there was no stopping her from going to her daughter.

"Do you think you can take a couple of days so we can go meet her together?" asked Maddie in a way that I knew wasn't actually a question.

"Of course, my love," I said, knowing that was the only acceptable answer. "Next Tuesday to Thursday?"

"I was thinking tomorrow…," she said, starting to pace, as she often did when her mind was running at full tilt.

"Don't you think you should give them a few days to settle in?"

"I don't know. They might need help. Neither one of them has ever had to care for a baby."

"Had you cared for a baby when you brought Anne home?"

"I had my mother around the corner, and she was there all the time in the beginning."

"You can video chat every day. Multiple times a day. If Anne needs you, you can just go. We'll work it out."

Of course, we didn't wait until Tuesday. When Anne told Maddie that Linda's parents were away on an Alaskan cruise and not due back for a couple of weeks and that neither she nor Linda had slept at all the first two nights, we hit the road the next morning.

It wasn't just that they had a new baby in the house, they were overwhelmed by all the things they wanted to do to make everything perfect. They had decided to hold off on finishing setting up the baby's bedroom until they were certain that they were bringing one home. They couldn't bear the thought of a finished, but empty, room. They'd set up a bassinet and change table, but there was an elaborate crib that could be later converted to a bed and a dresser that needed to be assembled. They also were obsessed with childproofing their house immediately, even though it would be months before baby Ada would be mobile enough to get into trouble. While Maddie provided motherly support, taking the baby so the girls could rest and making meals and sterilizing baby bottles, I assembled furniture and baby-proofed.

As much as I hated leaving everything to Sarah on short notice, she assured me it was no problem, and she was happy to step in any time. Maddie suggested that Sarah enjoyed the independence but also the extra pay she earned when she took over when there were guests because, unlike me, the inn was her primary source of income. I'd not thought of it from Sarah's perspective. It was just one of the myriad of small ways Maddie has opened my eyes. She's intuitive about people's emotions and sees the world through the lens of her life experience, which is very different from mine. She forces me to look at things differently and she doesn't agree with me to avoid an argument. She definitely knows her own mind.

I realize how narrow I let my world become since retiring. Active and busy with the inn but, personally, very routine and confined. Maddie, sometimes quite irritatingly, disrupts my routine and questions why it has to be some way or another. When I get past being annoyed by her challenging me, I feel so much more awake and alive because she's shaken things up.

We stayed with Anne and Linda for a whole week and a half. They were grateful and assured Maddie they could manage on their own for the weekend. Barbie and Jeff would be home from vacation in a few days, so they'd be nearby to help if needed.

Maddie took a ton of pictures of baby Ada.

"I want to make them an album of pictures," she'd told me on the ride home.

"Do they need that?" I'd asked because both girls had been taking pictures constantly with their phones. Pictures of the baby asleep, the baby awake, of each other and the baby and us with the baby.

"They won't have time to sort through all their pictures and make prints… But I do," she'd explained.

Back at the inn after my first real extended baby care experience, I was dead tired. We had a guest that had just arrived, and I had a lot to catch up on having been away for 10 days in the middle of the season. I didn't really mind because it was relaxing to be back in my familiar surroundings and getting stuff done feels good.

"Wow. It's late," I said realizing the time as I checked my bedside clock to ensure the alarm was set.

Maddie rolled over and watched me as I arranged my clock, glasses, and glass of water into their proper positions on my nightstand.

"You must be tired after today," she said.

"It's the good kind of tired," I said crawling into bed beside her and snuggling close to her to get warm.

Maddie looked at me, searching my face for something.

"What are you looking at?" I asked.

"Something I never want to stop looking at," she said reaching out her hand and running her fingers over my face.

"Hey, that's my move," I said playfully swatting her hand away and reaching to touch her face instead.

"When you learn a good move, you practice it so you don't forget it."

"I should hope you'll never forget me."

"How can I forget you. You're right here."

"You know that we can't both live forever. Eventually, we're going to wear out."

"I don't want to wear out," she said with the cutest pout.

"It's inevitable my love. I feel pretty worn out today," I said moving closer and giving her neck an affectionate nuzzle. I really wanted to just hold her close and go to sleep.

"We need more than one lifetime together. This one isn't going to be enough," she said kissing my nose.

"Will you let me get some sleep next time?" I teased rubbing my nose back and forth over hers.

"Promise me you'll find me wherever we end up next."

"Promise me you won't hide from me for 60 years."

"I promise if you find me, I won't hide."

"I promise to find you even if you try to hide."

"Deal. Now you can sleep."

"I love you, Maddie."

"Love you too. Now sleep or you'll be tired tomorrow and as grumpy as a toddler."

I pulled Maddie closer and fell dead asleep.

EPILOGUE

Emily waved from the front porch as we pulled into the driveway. I could see Jake and Bob playing catch on the grassy area in front of the lighthouse. Seeing us, they stopped what they were doing and made their way over to the car.

"Grandma," shouted Ada who burst out the front door and ran towards us with Linda close behind.

"Hello, my little monkey," I said reaching down to pat her head as she tangled her arms and legs around my legs, almost knocking me over.

"Careful. You don't want to break Grandma," said Anne who'd come around from the driver's side of the car. She extracted Ada from my knees and picked her up so she could hug me properly.

"Did you bring me Man-eye-mo bars?" asked Ada.

"Nanaimo bars," I corrected, "Yes, I did."

"I was good today," said Ada.

"That's good because you know I only bring Nanaimo bars to good girls."

"I was good," said Linda, hugging me as well.

"What about good boys," asked Bob who'd got my bag from the trunk of Anne's car and was carrying it past us to the house.

"I brought enough for all the good girls and boys," I assured them.

"You didn't need to bring anything. We're just glad you're here safe and sound," said Emily as we all went into the house together.

I couldn't imagine not being at the inn for Thanksgiving. Although our exact wedding date didn't always fall on Thanksgiving Day, Nate and I had decided that's when we would celebrate it. It was a running joke that Nate got off easy because there was no way he could mess up given all the sales advertising. He had plenty of reminders that the big day was approaching.

Although we'd only celebrated one anniversary together, I know, if we'd had more, they would be much like we've celebrated it every year since; together as a family at the inn. Even Ann and Lane had joined us the first year. We'd waited until they could come to hold his celebration of life gathering. I chose Thanksgiving weekend because I was grateful for the time we had, and I know Nate would have approved.

Even though it's been five years since Nate's been gone, I still feel like he's calling me to come home when the leaves have fallen. After running the inn with

Sarah for the rest of the season when Nate had left me so abruptly, I felt torn between being here, near him, or in Toronto where I had the support of friends and relatives. Nate had set the inn up as a trust, with me the trustee. He made it clear in his will that he wanted Emily as the ultimate beneficiary. He'd included a letter with his papers that outlined that he wanted me to be able to choose if I wanted to continue living at the inn or transfer it to Emily. I was shocked and delighted when Emily and Bob had decided they would leave their jobs in Boston to become full-time innkeepers.

This year we had an extra reason to be thankful. Emily and Bob would be cutting the ribbon on the Nate Jacobs Boat House Museum. They'd renovated and expanded the lighthouse ground floor and the adjacent boat shed and relocated the majority of Nate's collection so that it could be appreciated by all. It had taken them three years, with Emily and Bob doing much of the renovation work on their own. I'd offered to contribute, to pay for some of the work out of the money that Nate left me. They refused. They reminded me that Nate had wanted to leave me something to make sure I'd never need to worry about having enough money to travel back and forth, or to have someone to help me because he wouldn't be there to take care of me.

After the ribbon-cutting, I slipped away from the reception to get some air alone. Emily and Bob had asked me to say a few words and I'd held myself together for that but now I was feeling quite emotional. It had been seeing the Madeline, that they had chosen to display with a copy of our wedding picture that brought tears to the surface. I read the description that noted that it was the last boat Nate had acquired and he'd done so alongside the love of his life who happened to have the same name. I felt a thrill that our love was immortalized but so sad that Nate wasn't here. He would have been so proud of what Emily and Bob had built.

I couldn't help talking to him as I sat on the bench by his favourite "shrubbery" with the view of the ocean where we'd spread his ashes as he'd requested. The sun was warm on my face, but I shivered at the sad memory of waking up that terrible morning. Feeling Nate's arm slump off my waist and making a small thump on the bed beside me. I'd thought to myself that he must have been really tired from our long drive and staying up late talking for him to sleep so late, only to realize he wasn't sleeping. The panic. The scream I couldn't contain.

"Until I see you again," I whispered. I know in my heart we'll meet again. We orbited each other throughout this lifetime, we were just out of time. I know we'll find each other again... Next time.

ACKNOWLEDGEMENTS

"If you were to write a novel, what would you write about?" was the question that started my five year adventure to write this book.

The first person to acknowledge is my husband Mike who not only asked the question, but was unwavering in his belief that I was capable of delivering something worth reading. He enthusiastically brainstormed when I got stuck, read every word I wrote, and critiqued, edited, and proofed multiple drafts. I'm certain that, by now, he knows Maddie and Nate's story even better than I do.

The inspiration for this novel came from Mike and I discovering, in the early days of our relationship, that we had crossed paths several times and on different continents before we met. I've often pondered how our individual decisions kept us from, and then resulted in, our eventual meeting.

In addition, a theory that's always intrigued me is the multiverse (or many worlds) concept postulated as an explanation of quantum mechanics observations. If in fact all possibilities are simultaneously occurring in mostly independent parallel universes, but we are only aware of the one we are currently observing, what would we experience if we lived one of the lives we were not observing? It's my goal to explore this idea by exploring multiple versions of Maddie and Nate's lives. The second book in this series, Next Time will observe their lives with different decisions, choices, and events.

This book would not have come to be if not for the generosity of my friends and family who have contributed each in their own way. A special thank you to Norm Stewart for sharing his experience in the corporate legal profession, Maurizio Bagnasco for being my Torinese culinary expert, Yvette Krawchuk for advising on the snowbird culture in Green Valley and to all the many others who I asked random questions about recipes, history and culture in the sixties and seventies when I was too young to have a clue about the grownup world.

A giant thank you to my beta readers Stephanie Murray-Watson, Corine Telawski, Marie Jakubowski, Valerie Rice, Julie Lindsey, and my mom, Nerina Murray. You all pointed out the errors and flaws but also provided great feedback and encouragement to help me re-write with confidence.

I'm also especially grateful to Christine Murray who guided me to learn about the craft of writing which was foreign territory for a science major like myself. Our long, mushroom-less walks in the Italian woods were fruitful in the insights you provided into story structure, character, and conflict.

And last, but certainly not least, thank you to my design team that helped me put the final package together. Thank you to Cathy DardenLentz for applying her creative vision and artistry to designing a beautiful cover and to Garry Tosti for making every page look good!

It took a village, but we did it!

Thank you everyone!

ABOUT THE AUTHOR

Ideas too big to grasp all at once are Jacqueline's favorites. She writes stories about relationships that spring from the confluence of two of her favourite big ideas: that every possible reality is simultaneously occurring but we're only experiencing the one we're observing, and, we all have a soulmate.

Jacqueline's breadth of passions results from her curiosity, fearlessness and open mind which fuel her desire to experience new things, explore new places and be constantly learning. She's a scientist, business professional, photographer, musician, and author. Jacqueline has advanced degrees in both science and business and is fluent in several languages. She gains inspiration from travel and divides her time between her homes in the USA, Italy, and Canada.

For more information about M. Jacqueline Murray, her books and to download book club discussion questions please visit her website: mjacquelinemurray.com

Manufactured by Amazon.ca
Bolton, ON

27718855R00224